these stolen lives

SHARADA KEATS

Born in Kalgoorlie in 1982, Sharada loves poetry, nature, reading, writing, electricity, hot running water, petrichor, a certain degree of cliché, and circumstances that ensure young people can enjoy basic human rights, be nurtured, and grow old happily and healthily. She feels strongly that people of all ages deserve a wider variety of stories and storytellers. Sharada grew up in Australia and Canada, with parents from Guyana and Yorkshire – influences that still shape her writing. She studied agricultural economics in university, and has spent many years working in the third sector. Sharada now lives with her partner, two young children, and ancient old cat in London, UK.

these stolen lives

SHARADA KEATS

SCHOLASTIC

Published in the UK by Scholastic, 2024
1 London Bridge, London, SE1 9BG
Scholastic Ireland, 89E Lagan Road, Dublin Industrial Estate,
Glasnevin, Dublin, D11 HP5F

ISBN 978 0702 32512 0

A CIP catalogue record for this book
is available from the British Library.

Printed and bound in Great Britain by Clays Ltd, Elcograf S.p.A.
Paper made from wood grown in sustainable forests
and other controlled sources.

1 3 5 7 9 10 8 6 4 2

www.scholastic.co.uk

With love to Edith Sucharita
and William (Bill) Keats

1

getting you out

When the night and its cold are their deepest, we go. Tonight's our only chance.

The black-iron gates of the Portcaye Glassworks bar our way, railheads stabbing at the stars. This place has owned me since before the fall of the leaf, and it's winter now, harsh as any.

I drive the Glassworks' draught kine – hulking beasts, bigger than our horses ever were – on deliveries and collections. But tonight I'm here for another reason. Kit and I are on a rescue mission.

The street lamps have burned down, leaving thick darkness, but Kit doesn't waver. He even said I should wait behind while he went after Zako on his own.

Arrogant to think he could work this without me. Zako and Kit haven't even seen each other since they met in detention, right after the Cull. I know where Venor's country estate is, where they'll be keeping Zako. I lived on the farm opposite for years, when I was first bought. Plus the Glassworks' kine trust me.

Zako and me, we're Crozoni savages. Survivors of the Cull. When the Skøl invaded six years ago, they killed nine in ten of us. Those of us who were left became *repayers*. One of the pretty Skøl words they brought with them.

"*Life Is Golden*" – that's their motto, adorning the uniforms of their law enforcement and carved into their precious Life Registry. All citizens, including the Skøl, must pay for their right to live, work hard to be a part of society. Most manage it. Some don't.

But we repayers lived life without paying – for me, my first eleven years. I owe the Skøl that debt. My life is no longer my own. I belong to the Glassworks now, just like Zako belongs to Valour Venor, the magistrate of County Portcaye Life Registry, and soon-to-be governor of the New Western Counties.

So my scruffy, curly-haired and card-mad friend, twelve-year-old Zako, who I've known since he kicked my hand through his mama's womb, tried to kill his owner last night. The price for that will be steep.

I have a key to this side gate, but before I can fumble it out, the lock yields to Kit's small slivers of metal – lock picks.

"Since when could you do that?"

"Since I was about your age. Thought I should learn."

I'm seventeen. Kit's three years older. "Why?"

"I like to be prepared."

We're at the stables now. Kit stares up at the woolly face that greets him with its big, wet eyes that stare back.

"Clomper – meet Kit."

Kit's eyes, fixed on Clomper now, are extraordinary, purple as an early orchid. I don't know if all native Makaians have eyes like his. I haven't met many. His people, the Xan, were here first, before the Crozoni – we invaded their land a hundred years ago. Now we've both been invaded.

"This creature's a ridiculous size."

I'm secretly satisfied there's another thing I can add to the short list of things Kit's afraid of: spiders, sea kraits, draught kine. His owners, the Scarlets, are tavern-keepers and don't own kine, just rent them if they need their carriage pulled.

The Skøl got rid of our horses like they got rid of most of us.

Before they came, we thought there was nothing else in the world worth knowing. To the north, only ice plains; to the west, the Crozon Isles, the islands of my forebears. Beyond them, more ocean before the Shallow Sea.

To the east of us, beyond the mountains, is a desert. We thought it endless. But there is something on the other side: Skøland. And kine, the only creatures tough enough to cross, carried its pink-skinned, pale-eyed people here.

Clomper is almost half as tall again as a horse, and

broad, with four horns tapering to dull points. Her two long ones curve back in an impressive crown. The shorter two curve down, framing the sides of her face like ancient armour, giving her a wicked look.

Kit tries to coax her out of her stall, but she's a ton and a half of having none of it.

"Let me do it. You probably smell like Caruq," I say.

"The cheek – I smell like Caruq," he grumbles, but he gives way. Caruq's the hound at the tavern house.

We've brought squares of cloth torn from old tavern aprons to cover Clomper's iron shoes. I tap her leg so she lifts it. Kit props her hoof on a thigh and bundles it, and I wrap it up like a parcel with twine.

Kit's dark hair hangs in his eyes as he works. He used to wear it past his shoulders, years ago, but I prefer it like this – fuzz-short on the sides and back, longer on top.

My Crozoni skin is deep bronze in the summer, fading in winters like this to a lighter brown that shows red in my cheeks, but Kit's skin is darker, his features sharper.

He's half smiling, probably at how daft we look. How he can smile at a time like this, I don't know.

It's a risk taking only Clomper. She'll have to carry two of us out there and three back – we hope, after a full day of work in the freezing cold. But she's well muscled, covered in locks of warm wool. She can do this.

I'm the weak link, with my old injury – the slight drag on my right side, the pain that flares without warning. Venor is responsible for that. It's a memory I keep pushed down.

Outside the Glassworks, I guide Clomper with light tugs on her rope, a few crooning words. She's not bad in the dark, probably sees better than I do what lies down the cobbled alleys that yawn into blackness.

This quarter's always quiet come nightfall. The wraps on her shoes muffle their usual iron clatter, but the noise still rings overloud in my ears. I can't hear a squeak from Kit.

I urge Clomper to a stop with my shoulder when I see movement – four men, a few corners ahead.

"Are they branders?" I whisper. Branders – firebrands, they call themselves – are the Skøl law enforcement. Technically, there's no curfew, but they wouldn't look kindly on the likes of Kit and me abroad at this hour.

"Not branders. Dockworkers," he says now, soft and calm. I find my mind drifting back to his fingers springing the lock to the Glassworks as easy as cracking an egg.

We wait in the shadows until the men have moved off.

The tension in my gut uncoils slightly when we reach the river path. No more icy cobbles, less noise, fewer houses and lights, and not a soul to be seen all the way to the Mermen Gates.

Portcaye's a walled town – walled by my great-grandparents' generation. Stone mermen, the symbol of one of the founding Crozoni families, flank the gates. They open to the north. They used to be closed at night, but not since the Skøl arrived. The Skøl don't share my people's insecurities. Why lock down when you've conquered the world entire?

The Mermen Gates' iron rails, topped with spikes, reach above Portcaye's stone walls, highest where they're designed to meet in the middle, like wings. Limestone blocks prop them wide. One of the spikes beside the easternmost merman is occupied by a shrivelled turnip fashioned as a human head. Black hollows for eyes, a wig of wavy seaweed, weathered white. A child's prank. A reminder.

The Skøl aren't stingy with the death penalty, but they usually avoid a display. There hasn't been a real criminal's head up there for years, but I imagine for the murder of Magistrate Venor they'd make an exception.

I had the news from Venor's neighbour, my old owner, Mister Heane. He came to see me with a hide-bound parcel I later found contained drawings I'd done at Heanehome, pencils they had given me and a book I'd left behind when they sold me to the Glassworks so suddenly, six months back. Mister Heane seemed to think Venor might pull through, even though Zako took a hammer to his head. I can't imagine Venor's skinny repayer, Ruzi's son, lifting a finger to anyone, let alone a weapon.

"I'm sorry… I know he was your friend," Mister Heane said, like Zako was already dead.

It'll be all over the paper tomorrow evening, but it was too late to make tonight's edition of the *Portcaye Post*.

They have him locked up at Venor's estate. They'll take him to jail in Portcaye tomorrow. Then they'll decide his sentence.

It will happen quickly.

Getting Zako out tonight is our only chance.

In the shadow of the mermen and the ghastly turnip, we unbind the cloth from Clomper's shoes. Kit boosts me like a sack of nothing on to one of the limestone blocks and scrabbles up beside me before lifting me again on to the big blanket we strapped on Clomper's back as a makeshift saddle. I grip her broad flanks with my knees.

"Sit closer and hold on to me," I tell Kit.

Tentatively, his hands find my waist. He holds on higher on the right side, my bad side, barely touching me.

Venor's estate lies to the northeast.

We make steady progress north along the deserted byway.

Clomper's hooves fall like anvil blows. I swear they never land so loudly during the day. She's not a racer, but perhaps she's got some rider's blood. She goes like the clappers. An all-purpose beast.

The cold is shocking, but at least it means no snow. I pray to Thea it holds – to Thea the Bringer, Crozoni goddess of bounty. I even whisper a plea to Macotl, the mother serpent, one of the native Makaian gods. *Hold us in your coils.* Spreading our chances. I list the names of my loved ones, all ghosts, like a litany.

There aren't any clouds yet, and the Bone Moon marking the Secondmonth, with its bright, pocked face, is over half full.

Returning to Venor's estate for the first time in two

years has dread coursing through my innards. I remind myself to look on the bright side. He might be dead.

Mora means *brave* in old Crozoni. I used to take pride in my name when I was a girl. Now I feel like a fraud.

"Good girl, Clomper, good girl," I coo to her.

"It's like I'm riding a boat," Kit shouts over the hoof-fall.

He grips too tight – the harder his legs cling, the faster Clomper goes and the more precarious we are, perched six and a half feet above the ground.

"Hang on to me, not her. She knows you're scared."

"I'm not *scared*." Kit's thighs shuffle closer, and his arms tighten around me.

He's a solid warmth at my back, smelling faintly of the sweet-onion stew he was cooking hours before – a Skøl specialty his owners keep on the menu. His chest hugs my shoulders, and when I lean back his cheek appears beside my hood, his voice reassuring in my ear.

"You're a natural at kine rustling."

I wonder what state Zako will be in.

The first time I found out Zako took a bad beating, I was fifteen. I marched on over from the Heanes' farm to Venor's property to confront him – like a complete idiot. Even then, before his promotion to ruler of the whole New West was in the offing, a Registry magistrate is not a power to be messed with.

"What kind of man hits a boy of ten? No owner would treat an animal so poorly!"

"Come with me," he ordered. Skøl's a flowing

language, but Venor hacks it up like a butcher carving up a carcass.

I went with him. Out of the heat, into his cool, dark plough shed.

A pile of bones stood on display, neatly stacked against one of the walls. Human remains. I counted four skulls, two big, two small. Probably from the Crozoni family who lived there before. Some were buried locally. My pa, Lewis Dezil; my sisters, Enca and Eben; our little brother, Char – I think they went to the big grave near Portcaye.

Venor led me to a row of cages I thought empty, until I saw the eyes, shining – huge hounds, huddled as far back as possible. Not growling, cowed.

He picked up a claw hammer from one of the benches.

"My dogs know when to bark and when to keep their snouts shut. It's a simple trick to teach." He stroked the hammer like a pet.

I stared back at him.

"Don't show your face on my land again. Don't bark, you little makkie, or your friend will live here –" he swung the hammer, gesturing to the cages – "with the other rats."

I didn't argue – but I couldn't control the look of disgust on my face before I turned to go.

Never turn your back on a Skøl with a hammer.

We're about an hour into the journey, and my hip's working up to a dull ache. We make good time to Swallow Crossing and turn east down Drumlin Road. At the big silver-barked tree marking Wending Way we head northeast, leaving the proper roads behind. Quiet silver radiance lies over the stubbled fields. Clomper's hoofbeats don't belong. Her breath comes like fog.

I remember the way. I have always been able to draw from memory, tuck images away in my mind and pull them out vivid and perfect, like a map.

Often they rise unbidden.

"This is it," I say. I rein in beside a mottle-barked tree adjacent to the track leading down to Venor's estate.

Kit slides off, then reaches up to help me down.

My legs are uncooperative and I all but fall on top of him. My cheeks flare; I can see how clumsy I must look – my crop of black curls escaping from my woollen hat, my trousers held up with a bit of rope, my great dowdy coat and my boots eternally crusted in muck. My too-wide mouth is prone to saying the wrong things, and my eyes are irredeemably Crozoni – amber as a warning.

We tether Clomper, who's sweating under her blanket. Maybe I can find her water.

Kit takes my hand and I feel a strange flutter pushing back the nervousness.

A wooden sign with the word Venorhome burned into it looms ahead.

Zako's hut is near the plough shed, back behind the hulk of the barn, well beyond the row of warm brickworkers' houses. We cling to shadows as we pass them.

It isn't really a hut as much as a small shed, flimsily

built, windowless. Easy to lock from the outside. He'll be there, I'm sure of it.

"Zako." I release Kit's hand to tap lightly on the door. Venor's workers have outdone themselves. Not just an iron padlock – four strips of board are nailed across it.

"Mora?" His muffled voice is pitched high in disbelief.

"Yeah, it's me – and Kit. We're getting you out."

2

afraid of

We've not thought to bring any heavy tools. The lock picks look laughable.

"There's bound to be something in the shed," Kit says, and heads towards it. "Though it'll be clear as day he's had help."

Reluctantly, I follow. "They won't know it was us."

My legs stop twenty paces from the door. *Come with me*, Venor said that day, and I followed him like a dog. Now I'll never walk the same.

"They'll suspect us right away – and this will add fuel to the fire," Kit says.

Guilt and panic gnaw at me, send me defensive. "We're here now. You can't back out." My voice sounds cold, brittle with tension. But I'm talking more to myself than to him.

Did you think you could pull this off? I can see our

three heads joining the turnip at the Mermen Gates – a grotesque bouquet.

"I didn't say anything about backing out."

The plough shed isn't locked.

Inside, I fumble some stubs of candles from a pocket, strike the flint to light them and pass one to him. Cages still line one wall, but they're empty – no dogs. No bones either.

Kit finds an iron bar and – I flinch – a claw hammer.

"One of these'll do. Let's go."

Back at the hut, the wood squeals under my ministrations, nails edging free. Kit springs the padlock in seconds before tackling the other side of the wood with the claw. The boards splinter loudly, and I wince, but we've got it open.

Somewhere back towards the big house, a dog barks.

I throw myself inside the hut. It's warm, and so is Zako when I hug him. He's bundled in an oversized coat.

"Are you okay? Did they hurt you?" I pull back to examine him. Dirt on his face, not bruises. He's holding in tears.

"I'm okay." It comes out a choked squeak.

In the months I've not seen him, he's grown. It's shocking how much he looks like a young Ruzi.

"Pack up all your spare clothes. Your shoes. The bedding. Anything that smells like you," Kit says. "Let's not give the hounds an easy job."

Moving swiftly, we find one of Venor's riding kine

in the nearby barn, and I throw a saddle over it. I keep forgetting to breathe, every second stretching painfully long, every sound thunderous. As Kit cracks the thin layer of ice on a trough and scoops a pail for Clomper, Zako hovers close, watching with a dazed expression. Shock, I suppose.

Then I'm leading the riding kine out of the barn, back down the track to where Clomper's tethered, waiting with the profound patience of her kind. She huffs a low grunt as I stroke the soft velvet on her cheek. Kit deposits the bucket before her, and she starts sucking great gulps.

I look to Zako and hold out my arm.

He folds into my neck and lets out a sob. "I didn't mean to hit him so hard. He went mad. He was going to kill me."

"You were defending yourself. Don't waste tears on that monster."

We get Zako on to the riding kine, then Kit and I scramble up the mottle-barked tree to mount Clomper.

When we reach the track leading to the Heanes' farm, my old abode, we haul Zako over to sit between us, his bundle of spare clothes and bedding behind me. I point the rider down the track and smack her rump. They'll find her in the morning, perhaps waste time wondering if Zako's nearby.

A fearful ringing sets up in my skull, like the bell at Ma's funeral. I hear it sometimes.

Only when a bridge over the River Rin surfaces out

of the black do I realize I've taken a wrong turn. I can't believe I've been so foolish. My memory almost never fails. Fear distracted me. Now we're pointing east instead of west. It'll cost us half an hour.

"Wait." Kit's steady voice cuts across my rising panic. "We should throw the old clothes in there."

We toss the bundle of Zako's things into the middle of the flow, watch the few items separate and billow, water-fat as drowning creatures.

This river used to mark a boundary of the Heanes' property. I used to imagine if I swam beyond it, I wouldn't be property any more.

But I'll never be free. With my low wages going on my unpaid years, plus interest, plus room and board, I'll never catch up. Never save enough to buy my freedom.

The Skøl pay their way too, of course – in monthly sums for most adults. Those who fail are rounded up quick enough. But it's their rules – their game. They get paid properly. They don't start with years of debt.

We are hurtling the right way now, west, back to Portcaye – Zako a fugitive, all of us at the mercy of Kit's owners, Mister and Missus Scarlet.

For the next two days, we'll keep Zako hidden with the Scarlets. First thing tomorrow, Kit will contact a brilliant forger they call the Artist, to order Zako fake papers. The Artist's the best in the business. Even I've heard of him.

Every county is overseen by its own Life Registry – a sacrosanct central department of the Skøl government that keeps files on every resident in its administration, monitoring who lives and who dies, who has paid and who hasn't. We'll get Zako a fake Life Record – a document registering him under a new identity, with a false record of his payments and a permit to resettle. Then we'll move him south, across the border, to start a new life in County Copper.

That's the plan. The alternative doesn't bear thinking about.

It's nearly three in the morning by the time I ease Clomper to a stop beside the Mermen Gates. We slide down to retie the cloths around her shoes.

The iron mermen sit coiled on their pillars, surveying the road, sentinel-like. Only the turnip stares up at the cloud-drowned stars.

Kit leaves with Zako, going direct to the tavern known as the Lugger. I take Clomper on the long route back to the Glassworks.

The river path is still empty, though I spot a few strangers bundled in heavy coats, hustling down a side street.

"Morning," one calls to me. An old man in a thick cloak. It's too dark to see their faces, but they're not branders. I ignore them, not trusting my voice won't betray me as Crozoni. I don't have much of an accent; I've been speaking fluent Skøl since I was thirteen. But it's not worth the risk. Let them think I'm unfriendly. They drift away.

"Mash when we're back, Clomper. Sweet, sweet." I croon and click to her, hoping she recognizes the words.

We reach the Glassworks eventually. I'm so exhausted I catch my head accidentally on Clomper's stall – but I get her in and feed her. The poor beast is so spent she barely has two mouthfuls and is sleeping before I leave.

A dim light begins to grow on the pavement a few blocks ahead. I shrink back against a wall as a pair of men swinging lanterns appear, dressed in the pressed dark-blue uniforms of the branders. They're almost always men.

I duck behind some stonework jutting from the nearest building, gloved fingers braced on the cobbles, holding my breath. They're talking in hushed tones, pink faces bent together. I pray the distance and their lantern-dazzle makes me another clump of shadows.

One raises his light and stops. "Will you look at that?" he says. "I'll be damned."

I feel ill.

The other man makes a loud growling noise, almost like a laugh. "I could go for one of those," he says.

I realize they've stopped to peer into the window of a shop further down the alley. It's a fikka house displaying glazed buns in the window.

I draw the hood further over my forehead and crawl, sticking to the shadows, round to the nearest turning.

Nearly half a year since I moved to Portcaye town and I've never been to the Lugger after hours. I enter the back way, below the big bare Makaia plane tree growing in the courtyard. The kitchen door swings open, unlocked, a good sign.

Wood polish and stale smoke, grease, ghosts of laughter. The atmosphere of the Lugger hits hard. No fires are lit, but a warmth sends tingles through my cheeks all the same. I'm always a bit jealous that this is Kit's lot – so much like a real home.

In some ways he has it better now, under the Skøl. He might not have lasted another winter if they hadn't invaded. His mother passed when he was nine – a heart complaint. His father when he was twelve. Kit left school soon after that. By the time the Skøl arrived, he was fourteen, already on the streets, odd-jobbing, thieving, drinking away any good fortune to come his way. People said he would turn out bad, and people hate to be wrong.

I didn't have much to do with Kit, even before he dropped out of school. But after the Cull, we were held in detention together, and I got to know him.

Then, when I was fifteen, I saw him again. I was in hospital after Venor's attack, and he came to see me. He heard from one of the nurses having a drink at the Lugger that I was there.

"Mora Dezil! It *is* you."

I cried. It was embarrassing.

"Did I forget my handkerchief?" He patted his coat pockets before withdrawing a ball of white fluff from one with a silly flourish. It woke up and wriggled.

"You can use this. He won't mind." It was Caruq, a tiny puppy.

I forgot to be embarrassed.

I look up now and see two dark shapes hunched over empty glasses at a table on the Lugger's mezzanine, the part that hangs out over the river, propped up on thick wooden poles. One big shape, one small. Safe. Caruq curls at their feet, a furry white mound. All hounds love Kit, but Caruq is especially devoted.

"What are you doing up here? What if someone sees you?" I ask now as I join them, anger sparking on the heels of relief. Kit knows better.

"I wanted to wait for you," Zako whispers. His long curls are greasy, plastered to his head. He needs a wash.

I slump gracelessly into the seat beside him. "Saw some branders. Had to take a longer route."

Kit's expression sharpens. "Did they see you?"

"No."

My eyes, more accustomed to the dimness now, study Zako. "Your father would say you're too low in flesh and too high in bone," I observe.

His eyes get rounder at the mention of Ruzi, but he looks away. "Your limp is worse," he fires back.

And my anger's dead before I know it. I can't stop smiling. His ragged curls, his ears that stick out, his skinny little neck that won't be stuck on an iron spike anytime soon.

Caruq's warm nose is in my hand, snuffling, defrosting my fingers.

I don't relish the journey up two flights of steep stairs to the Scarlets' private quarters, but that's where we go.

Kit taps a light tattoo on the door before he opens it himself.

Missus Scarlet's dozing in an armchair in the sitting room. She and Mister Scarlet are both in their early seventies. Their rooms are separate but adjoining – he's a snorer and she's a cougher. She isn't well, generally, and spends most of her time indoors. She looks younger asleep, her face relaxed, her icy-blue eyes lidded.

"Is that *her*?" Zako whispers.

I feel the urge to cling on to him. Bringing Zako to this Skøl woman I barely know feels like we're leaping off a cliff. Is it water at the bottom or rock?

Kit wakes her gently.

"Aha," she says, pulling black wire spectacles from her head to her eyes. "You're here. Give me one moment." She retreats to her bedroom.

I turn to Kit and hold Zako's boots up.

"Should we burn these?"

"Too smelly. I'll chuck them in the river with some stones."

Missus Scarlet comes back in, still shoving her arms into a bedcoat. She's already wearing a heavy nightgown.

"Now. They call me Missus S," she says to Zako. "What do I call you?"

"Zako."

"Very good," she says.

He blinks.

She arranges a spare blanket and pillow on the long sofa in her sitting room.

"Sleep now. We'll talk when it's light," she says, deciding for us.

Zako lies down like it's a command.

I nod at Missus S, keeping my eyes down as she retires to her room, then follow Kit out.

We go through the lounge, where Caruq's already snoring, and back up the other flight of stairs into the public rooming wing. The guest rooms of the Lugger are rarely all occupied, though it's popular enough – well situated near the Centre and the Life Registry, with river views in the fancy rooms.

Kit lets us into his room and turns the lantern low. His bed with its old, ornate frame is still unmade, the patchwork quilt bunched at its base. There's little else but a heavy wooden desk, and he hangs his jacket over the matching chair. He hasn't let go of Zako's boots, and he grabs a fresh shirt before finally looking at me. There's a distance in his gaze.

He breaks the silence. "You can sleep here. I'll be along the hall."

We decided before we left that I'd spend tonight at the Lugger instead of back at the rooms I share with Zako's father, Ruzi. Better if Ruzi can honestly say nothing about what time I got in, when they question him.

Let everyone jump to the conclusions they want about

me spending the night here. It will help with our cover story.

Not that I know about any of *that*.

I was an eleven-year-old child when the Skøl came. The years piled up like dishcloths, and I've always been *other* – savage. Even when I started to bleed, I looked like a child. Then at fifteen I was made lame, lucky not to be culled for it.

The pale eyes of Skøl men still slide over me. They think I'm dirty. My mother used to say my amber eyes were like apricots. Skøl don't see apricots when they look at me – they see wild, animal eyes.

The idea of intimate relations terrifies me.

It's a very long list, the things a coward's afraid of.

3

douse the light

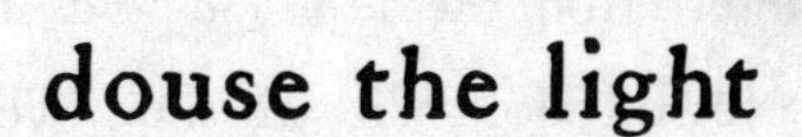

"Wait, Kit."

He stops.

"Thank you." It's clumsy and doesn't cover it. "And I know you weren't going to back out, earlier, when I said... I was just – scared."

Don't bark, you little makkie. The memory of Venor's voice fills me with thick-blooded dread.

"You told me what to do, and I did it," he says. "That's how it works, right? After all, you're a Dezil, of sorts." He cocks his head and smiles strangely.

Mora Dezil. That's my name. Dezil's a common enough Crozoni name now, but I suppose some of the branches of the Dezil family used to be well-to-do, back in the day.

"Kit, you know it's not like that – I don't see myself as ... above you." Though my parents did, before the Cull.

He sighs. "Ruzi does though, doesn't he? Man'd rather choke than give me the time of day."

And Kit just saved his son's life.

"Ruzi's not friendly with anyone. He doesn't like people." Neither do I, to be honest. I blow a curl of hair out of my eyes.

The sinews flicker in Kit's neck, then he reaches past me to grab the lantern from the desk. He holds it close to my cheek, pinched between thumb and forefinger, and splays out his other fingers to brush some hair from my forehead. "What did you do to your face?"

"What do you mean?" I swallow.

Kit's so close I can see the old scar on his cheek, behind his attempt at a beard. His long fingers trail gently over my temple. His anger seems forgotten. "A bump?"

"Oh. It's nothing. I banged it on Clomper's stall."

His eyes reflect lantern light into mine until I look away.

He turns back to the heavy wooden door, Zako's boots still swinging from his hand.

"Sleep," he says over his shoulder, pulling the door shut behind him, leaving me alone.

I look around Kit's room. I feel hopelessly out of place here, though part of me wants to belong as much as his clothes or his shoes, his papers with their Xan jottings I don't understand. To be as welcome and ordinary and commonplace as the lantern or the pillow, unremarkable as the air. Everything here is Kit's – but for the small, hide-wrapped parcel of my old drawings, paper and pencils that Mister Heane gave me when he brought me the news about Zako. The same parcel I carried directly to Kit with the news.

There are dozens of pieces of orange peel on top of it. Only hours ago, Kit and I sat there, eating oranges and planning Zako's rescue. Oranges – the madness of it. Like the madness of the whole night.

"*How'd you get these?*" I'd asked.

"*Mister S bought them. They're from Skøland, I think. Go on. Eat it.*"

"*Did you steal them from Missus S?*"

"*No.*"

We plotted our mission.

It's hours later but the orange scent lingers. I sweep the peels into the bin and douse the light.

4

till it is

Kit comes back at dawn and presses a mug of strong fikka into my hands. I breathe the steam and feel the heat soaking through.

"Thank you."

He's wearing the same clothes he was in hours before, though his feet are bare. He's washed his face. Dampness clings to his hair.

Outside in the courtyard large flakes float past. Snow covers the ground, lines the Makaia plane tree's leafless branches and frosts the cords they use to hang what washing they do here.

"It started at four," Kit offers, holding his mug in one hand and using the other to smooth his messy hair back. He looks younger than twenty.

I watch the soft flurry, the flakes colliding and clumping together before they hit the ground.

"I don't want you to feel I'm just using you," I whisper to the snow and the Makaia plane tree and the bleak grey sky. There's more I want to say, but a coward's words always stick.

Kit's frostiness from last night has thawed. He drapes an arm around my shoulders. "I should be so lucky – oh wait, I *have* been so lucky." Our cover story, our night of passion. He gives me an exaggerated wink as he releases me, draining his cup on the way to the door.

Before long, I'm ready to leave. Kit's busy in the kitchen with Gracie, one of the servants, but I don't want to sneak out. It'll be good for our alibi if Gracie thinks I've spent the whole night here. From what I gather, she's a hopeless romantic.

"I've left my drawing things in your room," I tell Kit. "I'm going to the Works – I'll get them another time." Gracie gives us both a knowing look and Kit dips his head, feigning shyness.

I feel sufficiently awkward and turn to go. Then, near the door, Kit catches me around the waist and draws me close to plant a kiss on my cheek. His beard is soft. My brain must be too, because I've forgotten how to breathe like a normal person.

Gracie says something I can't catch. Their laughter follows me into the yard.

The snow-change in the early light makes the town feel otherworldly. Skøl crunch past on their way to work, looking as dazzled as I feel. A pair of children strain to push a growing snow-boulder, something to survive the melt.

When I reach the Glassworks, Ruzi's already in the yard. It's early for him. Our shifts are longer than ever lately to keep up with the work. The Skøl have decided to appoint a Governor of the New West, and Venor's been chosen. He's being sworn in on the Sixmonth's second Endweek. If he survives, that is.

It's a new position for him and for everyone. We're expected to churn out over three thousand fancy glass panels in no time flat, to form the roof of a huge new hall being built especially for the ceremony. They've knocked down an old Crozoni place of worship in the centre of Portcaye to make space.

"There you are!" Ruzi greets me without his usual gruffness. He was worried, but he doesn't say it. "Where did you get to last night?"

"Sorry. I stayed at the Lugger with Kit."

"With Kit. Huh." His face scrunches, but before he can say more, I kick at some fresh snow.

"Didn't think so much would come down last night."

"A night for surprises," he offers.

I've lived with Ruzi since the Glassworks bought me from the Heanes. He was an old family friend.

Uncle Ruzi, we called him when we were little. He was more Ma's friend than Pa's. I'd not seen him for six years, but I spotted him that first day as soon as he trudged into the Works' yard behind the huge, creaking kine cart.

He looked so old. He's forty-seven, but the six years since the Cull have aged him. Greyer and thinner. A Cull scar on his temple like a dark-brown comet fading into his weathered skin – the sign he's been struck by a brander's gun and survived. The stamp of a hardy labourer.

"The Glassworks have you? You're staying here?" His words in Crozoni, our language, sputtered then flowed like water from a disused tap.

"They said I'm to stay with you."

"Of course. Let me finish and we'll go."

The others near the cart were eying us with open curiosity.

"Who's this, then?" one of the women asked, giving me a toothy smile.

"Cordi – this is Mora." Ruzi switched back to Skøl and introduced me to Cordi and Vertie, the other deliverers, and then to the driver. "My... Well, the daughter of an old friend."

This morning, Cordi and Vertie arrive just as we've finished hitching the pair of kine to the wagon. Still no sign of the branders.

Clomper was slower than Sugarcane – we call him Caney – to get out of her stable, but she's perky enough. I doubt anyone else will notice.

There are no deliveries for the docks. The snow's not ideal, but the Works is going through sand like nobody's business – they put it in the glass – so we go down to the shore for more. Cordi hums her favourite dockyard song about everything costing too much as she shovels. *Cost of food. Cost of rent. Cost of life.* Ruzi joins in. His singing voice is still something special. Plus, when he sings, he loosens up and forgets to be a misery guts. He knows all the Skøl worker songs in Cordi's repertoire, but he still won't sing any of the old Crozoni ones I ask for.

"No sense courting trouble," he tells me every time.

"It's not forbidden."

"Till it is."

5

right away

I half expect to see branders all day, coming to bring me in. But they don't appear. Ruzi and I finish at the same time and walk home together. The perfect white blanket of snow we woke up to is trampled to thin grey rags. Lamplighters are doing their rounds in the early dusk.

Our place is to the southwest, above a bakery at the end of Opal Alley. It's an easy fifteen minutes from the Glassworks, no distance even with my aches and pains.

"Hungry?" Ruzi sniffs as we walk past a dry-meat seller. The shrivelled flesh hangs like perverted leaves from the poles of the stall. Cubes of salted meat crushed with fat and flavoured with dried muscadine – a Skøl speciality – are displayed on a low table. It's a little joke. He knows I don't care for it, but I'm too distracted to humour him.

"Magistrate attacked! Read all about it in the *Illustrated*

Portcaye Post and Advertiser!" I can hear a barrow-seller calling.

Attacked. Not dead. My stomach churns.

Ruzi hasn't heard – he has to concentrate harder than me to understand their language.

Open wrought-iron steps lead to our door.

The space is small, but I prefer it to the lonely hut I had out on the Heanes' farm. There's a kitchen, a sitting room, a bedroom, a washroom with a small – but stained – mirror above the sink. It has running water, a flushing toilet. Things the Skøl brought when they came – lavatories inside, piped water and waste, lamps that run for hours and hours on ragleaf fuel. Impossible luxuries I sometimes feel traitorous for embracing.

When I saw it the first time, the sitting room was knee-deep in old newsprint and bits of driftwood, the kitchen empty, the corridor walls covered in black mould, the lavatory filthy.

Ruzi was ashamed of the state of the place. "I let things get on top of me," he confessed. He keeps it clean enough now.

He helped me scrub away the mould. And we got an old pallet and mattress from someone Cordi knew to transform the sitting room into another bedroom. It's bigger and brighter than Ruzi's, hardly gets damp, and has a door leading on to the kitchen with its warm stove.

Tonight someone is here, waiting for us. I can see the door slightly ajar, the wood splintered near the lock. I catch up with Ruzi on the final step.

"Who's there?" he calls out. "Mora – go back down and wait."

I ignore him, edging round. Let him think I'm brave for once. A huge ledhund, its neck fur bristling, stands by the stove, giving us a low, wet growl. A second trots out of my room.

"What is this?" I demand. "We've nothing worth stealing."

"Come," calls a husky voice from my bedroom. The nearest of the two ledhunds obeys.

"Not you, you thick beast," snarls another man, higher, angry, followed by a thump and a whine. Then both ledhunds are herding us in.

Everything's tipped over or upside down. Two firebrands in dark-blue uniforms stand in the middle of the mess. The tallest one towers a foot and a half over Ruzi. Small golden name badges adorned with one of the branders' symbols glint on their chests.

"Where have you two been, then?"

"Working." Ruzi finds his voice. "At the Glassworks. This place is Glassworks' property."

"As are you," coos the other firebrand. He's shorter than the first but still built like a brick shithouse.

"What's this about?" Ruzi demands.

"You two know a certain Zako Taler?" the shorter one sing-songs. He brandishes an old drawing of mine, of Zako's head and shoulders. "This is him, isn't it?"

He'd have found it in the room. I drew it shortly after

I arrived, on the back of some scrap paper I took from the Glassworks – so Ruzi could see how Zako looked. His son, who he hadn't seen since the Cull.

Ruzi follows the paper waving lazily in the brander's grip. I think absurdly of a hound waiting for its handler to release a biscuit. "Yes," he croaks.

"What's happened to Zako?" I ask.

"That's what we'd like to know. He's wanted in relation to a vicious attack on Magistrate Valour Venor. Seems to have absconded. Disappeared. Vanished without a trace."

I reach to grip Ruzi's arm.

"Let's go. This shithole stinks." The taller brander spits his words into Ruzi's face. "Boss wants a word with both of you."

They prod us out in front of them, hounds trailing.

It's not late. The Skøl meat-sellers and other barrow-workers – fish, baked apples, grilled yams, sugared nuts – are still out peddling their wares. Skøl of the more well-to-do variety walk arm in arm to who knows where.

The branders' station is in the same building as our old Crozoni law enforcement. It's pale brick around a gated courtyard. There's a level below ground that's all cells.

They split me from Ruzi as soon as we arrive. I follow a trainee, young and gangling with huge feet, like a kine after shearing, down a dingy corridor to a room with painted brick walls and worn wooden floors, stained with something I don't care to identify. A table stands at the centre, flanked by iron chairs. The only other thing in the room is a copy of an official head-and-shoulders portrait of their revered high governor, Clarion Lovemore. She's the head of their government – controls the Council of Magistrates back in Skøland with an iron fist.

I could draw her and her fancy gold-braid jacket in my sleep. Her big-nostrils-in-the-air face under its artful wave of pale hair is everywhere. All homes and businesses have a copy up on the wall. For all I know, it could be a law.

I don't sit down – all my senses scream to run as far from this place as I can.

It's a long time before a woman, silver hair at her temples, grey-eyed, bespectacled, three stripes on her blue sleeve for seniority, lets herself in. She's sombre and washed out, even for a Skøl, like a krait's drained her blood.

The trainee's back too, carrying a tray with a glass, a pitcher of water, a plate of thinly sliced bread with butter, and a napkin. He leaves directly, but she gestures for me to sit before seating herself opposite. She opens a folder stuffed with papers and a notebook. The golden badge on her chest shows her last name: *Hove.*

"Tell me where you were last night."

"After work?"

She nods.

"I went to the Lugger."

"The Lugger – yes. Are you in the habit of frequenting public houses? How old are you?"

"Six— Uh, seventeen."

She pours herself a glass of water and takes a sip.

I realize how thirsty I am.

"Why the Lugger?"

"My friend's a repayer there."

"A boy, yes?"

"He's twenty."

"What's his name?"

"Kalqitlan."

She sighs and shakes her head.

"Kit for short."

"And what do you call yourself?"

"Mora. Mora Dezil."

She picks up a slice of bread. "So, you and this boy..."

"I went to his room. Stayed the night."

"You had sexual relations?"

"Yes." I squirm. Let her think my reaction embarrassment.

"Your owners have no objections?"

"They don't ... they don't know." I'm quite prepared to be as dim as she expects. "Are we in trouble?"

"Are you in trouble? You tell me." A small black seed from her bread crust clings to the corner of her mouth.

"No one said it wasn't allowed."

"You were together the whole night?" She takes another slice. My stomach rumbles.

"Yes."

"When was the last time you saw Zako Taler?"

"What's happened to him?"

She drops the bread and stretches her arm out whip-fast to deliver a sharp slap to my cheek.

"I ask the questions. Get that into your thick skull."

I keep my hands folded in my lap, resisting the urge to press one to my stinging cheek. The small seed is still there.

"I haven't seen him since I was sold to the Glassworks," I offer quickly. "About half a year ago."

She holds the hand she slapped me with over the floor and pours water from the pitcher on to it, splashing our shoes. She wipes her fingers on the napkin but doesn't return to her bread.

"He's attacked his owner – almost killed him. A very important man. Why would he do such a thing?"

"He must have been defending himself."

She peers daggers over her glasses.

"Don't be insolent, girl."

I snap my mouth shut on any further protests.

"How long were you on the magistrate's estate?"

What? I freeze, then realize what she means.

"I wasn't. I lived at the neighbouring farm."

"So why did they sell you? Were you trouble?"

"No! They sold me for money. You can ask them."

A low scream, almost a groan, sounds from practically under our feet. Ghostly. Hove ignores it.

"What contact have you had with Zako Taler since your move?"

"None," I tell her.

"I hope you know better than to lie to me, girl."

"I'm not lying."

Her grey eyes slide from my face to the door.

"And if the fugitive shows up here looking for you – what will you do?"

The eerie screaming below us picks up, higher in pitch. I wince, but Hove doesn't react.

"What will you do?" she prompts.

"I don't know," I mutter.

Her gaze snaps back, eyes sharpened and shrunken by her spectacles. The hexagonal frames make me think of bees and hives.

The screaming and moaning cuts abruptly.

"Get up."

She urges me round the corner to the end of the corridor and then down a steep flight of stone stairs. We're below ground, where they keep prisoners. The corridor divides, and a sign indicates: *Forensic Science Workroom and Darkspace*. We take the other way, passing several nondescript closed doors. I guess they lead to cells. Then we pass a marked door: *Deadhouse*.

When we reach a row of barred cells, my head for direction says we're nearly below the room where Hove was questioning me. She stops in front of a cell with its door hanging open. Two big branders are inside, and beyond them a Skøl prisoner sprawled on the floor. He's shirtless, covered in bruises, breathing in painful gasps.

Something about him reminds me of the painting on

the foyer ceiling of the old Town Hall. Thea the Bringer, being punished for sharing fire with the people. A god brought low.

The man is about thirty. Pale where his skin's unbruised, paler than Hove even, tinged grey rather than pink. His eyes are closed.

"Have you heard of the famous Artist?" my interrogator asks, her glasses flashing as she turns to study my reaction. "Here he is, in all his glory."

Shit. The Artist was going to forge Zako's papers. "Never heard of him," I lie smoothly.

"Really? Most people have. There was a ten-thousand-krunan bounty on this one. He's led us a merry chase – but here he is."

"He's an artist?" I feign ignorance.

"Calls himself one. Lately he's been exploring his treason period. Making forgeries. And his phase back in Rundvaer was, well, more than a little tasteless."

I'd heard that when he lived in their capital, the Artist would paint buildings with anti-government graffiti, unflattering portraits of Clarion Lovemore with the slogan *Piss Is Golden* underneath.

One of the branders is shaking the man. His eyes drag open and catch on Hove's.

"Kept us guessing, didn't you?" Hove speaks to the Artist directly. "But rats like you can't resist sticking their ratty noses out. The magistrate will be thrilled when he hears about this. Thought you'd plot one of your little entertainments for when the high governor is sworn in, did you?"

I don't know what she means, but the Artist sputters a colourful rejoinder I've never heard before. Bloody saliva flecks his lips. His swollen eyes close again.

A shard of ice twists in my belly. So much for the forgeries we were counting on for Zako.

What the hell are we going to do now?

"What will happen to him?" I ask, to break the oppressive silence only otherwise marred by the sticky sound of the Artist's half-choked breathing. I immediately regret it. He doesn't need to overhear whatever torment they have planned.

"What happens to traitors." Hove turns around and pushes me back the way we came.

"Let's try again," she continues. "If you hear from Zako Taler, what will you do?"

"Tell you," I reply. "I'll tell you right away."

6

thank you

I wanted to be an artist when I was a schoolgirl – a real one.

Our homestead was just on the outskirts of Portcaye. I went to school in town before the Skøl came. I used to race over the cobblestones. I was fast then, and nimble. I loved to draw fast-moving things – animals, mostly. Horses and cats and bugs.

The year I was eight, Ma gave me a book of blank paper for the festival of the Cutter Moon. I filled it with birds – including a spread with a pair of vocifers I only saw once, flying off into the distance. They're the biggest birds of prey – Malan vocifers, we called them, after the mountain range. They were rare, even then.

I remember her touching one lightly with her fingertips, like it might keep flying right off the page.

It was the Tenmonth when it happened, the year I

turned eleven, the second day of the Cutter Moon festival. A time for feasting, for celebrating the bounty of the season.

I was in Mist-in-the-Valley's field with my little brother, Char, when the big men approached. We were playing marbles on a patch of weathered ground.

I could see they weren't like anyone else. Their odd hats and clothes. Their pale, stony faces. The way they walked, like they were coming to give us directions, not to ask them, even though they were the strangers.

Something was wrong. I grabbed Char's hand to pull him away. He was already five, too heavy for me to carry any distance. Still, I should have tried. He wasn't scared. He always liked people.

I felt the shock rip through him – through me, second-hand. He went floppy as we fell. The grass crushed under my knees. I forgot about the men drawing closer, desperate to wake him. I didn't even understand they'd done it.

For weeks after, I'd see him lying there, the embroidery on his collar blurred by my panicked tears. Mist-in-the-Valley's muzzle drifting over us. Father bought him for Char the year before. A little island pony. I can still see his front legs, grey and still as waymarkers, feel his hot snuffling breath in my hair and the thick weave of Char's little woollen jumper under my hands. It was deep, deep blue, flecked white and brown, and the knit went side to side over the chest and then up and down under the ribs. *I can't hear Char breathing, I can't hear, and his chest's too still.*

Later, I'd close my eyes and see Char's prone shape – a roving shadow, like the after-image that comes from looking too long at a bright light.

I could still draw, after detention, after they sold me – when I could get my hands on paper and pencils. But no one cared about my drawings. I was two arms, two legs and one head with enough of a grip on their language to follow basic, barked instructions. Long gone was any chance of growing up an artist. Growing up anything's more than most of us got.

Outside the station Ruzi's nowhere to be seen. I make my own way back to Opal Alley, but he's not at home either.

I head for the Lugger.

I've enough on me to buy the local paper. The *Portcaye Post*, they call it – it comes out every evening, Endweek included.

Zako has made the front page.

VALOUR VENOR: HAMMERED!

Magistrate Attacked Without Provocation

—

Savage Perpetrator Absconds

—

Future Governor Clings to Life:
Portcaye Holds Its Breath

There's nothing about the Artist's arrest.

I find a solitary Kit stacking pots in the Lugger's kitchen.

"You okay?" he croaks, relieved, cracking the stove door open and herding me to warm up. "Did they bring you in?"

"Me and Ruzi. Have they been here?"

"Been and gone, like we thought. Did a number on my room. The stables. Left the Scarlets alone though."

I shut my eyes, just for a moment. A respectable elderly couple – and owners at that. The authorities didn't believe for one moment the Scarlets might knowingly harbour a fugitive.

"I need to tell you something," I say. "I saw the Artist."

I tell Kit everything. His face drops, and he curses almost as colourfully as the Artist.

"I paid his agent already. Upfront. Everything. Gave him my life savings."

His life savings. What a thing to call money. My heart thuds. One beat. Two.

"Maybe he'll return it…"

But Kit's shaking his head. He makes for the door out of the kitchen to the lounge, gesturing for me to follow. He almost bumps into Renny in his distraction. She's like Gracie – works for the Scarlets. "I need five minutes," he tells her. There aren't many drinkers tonight.

Renny turns an indulgent smile my way. She thinks we're stealing an intimate moment.

Kit's room is almost worse than mine. The branders

broke his ocarina. It's in two pieces on his desk. A few of my drawings – scenes from the Heanes' farm and some rough sketches of insects and flowers – are strewn across it as well.

"They took your other drawings," Kit says, "but your paper and pencils are all there."

"Can you fix this?" I pick up the halves of his instrument.

He shakes his head. "What am I going to tell the Scarlets? I promised them he'd only be here two days."

Guilt rises again along with the panic. "What about another forger?"

"Can we pay another forger?" Kit laughs a little desperately. "It'll be all right." He's composed himself. "We'll think of something."

We. I look up at him. "Kit, I know I got you into this. I—"

He cuts me off. "Don't. I knew I wasn't signing up for a midnight kine ride. We're both in this. I'll find another forger. Tomorrow. I can take on extra work to find the fee. The Scarlets won't throw Zako out, not yet."

"I can look for more work too," I tell him, though I've no idea what.

It'll be enough. It has to be.

Back at Opal Alley, I find Ruzi sitting halfway down the iron stairs. He looks fifty years older.

"There you are." He stands when he sees me.

Inside, we pick our way through the ruined kitchen and Ruzi sets a pot to boil.

I can't leave him thinking the worst like this. "Zako's safe," I tell him.

He turns, expression blank.

"We went and got him out, me and Kit. Last night. That's why I wasn't home. He's hiding at the Lugger. They didn't find him."

Ruzi gawps like a fish as I tell him the rest. I don't dwell on the Artist. I make it sound like we have a solution.

"He's safe," Ruzi echoes, his voice thick with emotion. He's abandoned the pot of hot water. I don't fancy a fikka now either.

"You were up all night then," Ruzi rumbles.

"Yeah."

"You should sleep now." I think he wants to get to his room before the tears welling in his eyes make like Zako and escape.

In the dark hall, he pauses. "Thank you."

7

after all

Another evening, another three-subtitle headline.

CAUGHT INK-HANDED!

Foul Forger Foiled

—

Treasonous Artist to Face Justice

—

Criminal's Capture Cures Magistrate

Yesterday's edition had Venor barely clinging to life; today his recovery seems cemented.

"The bad ones live for ever. That's what my dad used to say." Kit frowns. We're in his room at the Lugger.

"Because your mum passed so young?"

He shoots me a surprised look. We don't talk about things like that. "Maybe." He pauses, then taps the article between us.

"This says they're going to announce a reward for Zako's capture by the end of the day."

I take the article from him and read. He's right.

Kit and I look at each other. His expression is grim. The Skøl do sometimes offer bounties – but for hardened criminals. Not for a child, a runaway. A boy with no previous history of violence.

It will be useless telling them Zako was acting in self-defence.

Venor won't have told the truth.

"Ruzi wants to see Zako," I say. "He hasn't seen him in six years."

"Our plan was to get Zako out fast, not host a family reunion." Kit hesitates. "Missus S is on edge. I don't think she'll like it."

Understandably, Kit's owners aren't best pleased they still have a young fugitive to harbour. "Give it a bit more time – till I find another forger and get a plan together. That would cheer her up."

Another forger. But who? The Artist wasn't the only show in town, even if he was the best. But his fellow forgers have gone to ground in the wake of his capture. The authorities will want to make an example of him. They'll have his head on a spike soon. Trade will be even scarcer.

"And if you can't find another…" My voice tapers away. What else can we do? Kit sees the question in my face.

"Mister S had an idea, actually." He sets the paper aside. "And I made some inquiries today – discreetly…"

"What was it?"

"A boy could claim he'd lost his Life Record – something beyond his control, like an accident at sea. It happens."

"And what? Pitch up somewhere with no papers, knowing no one?"

"Missus S has an old friend who moved to Vester Shells two years ago." That's the main port city on the biggest of the Crozon Isles. "She could claim to be Zako's buyer. To vouch for the details of his lost papers. She could re-register him in the Isles."

My heart drops. The Crozon Isles are two weeks' sail away. "She'd do that?"

"Missus S said she would. She says we can trust her, that she's a good woman."

"We'd never see him if he went to the islands." I'm surprised to hear such a whine in my voice.

"But he'd be safe." Kit's reprimand stings. "The issue is getting him there."

*

We need money. It all comes back to that. On Zako's third day cooped up in the Scarlets' quarters, the *Illustrated Portcaye Post and Advertiser* drops its anvil on our heads.

His picture covers half a page. Appallingly, it's my own handiwork – the one I drew for Ruzi that the branders stole from Opal Alley. The bounty is eye-watering.

₭10,000 REWARD!
WANTED: Zako Taler

ATTEMPTED MURDERER of the magistrate of County Portcaye Life Registry, and soon-to-be governor of the New Western Counties, His Eminence **Valour Venor**.
₭10,000 will be paid by the Life Registry for the apprehension of Taler.
₭5,000 will be paid by the Life Registry for any information leading to the apprehension of Taler, or for the discovery and apprehension of any accomplices proven to have participated in his disappearance.
All good citizens are urged to aid in this endeavour.

Description of ZAKO TALER:
Makaian (Island race). Repayer. Age 12 years. Height approx. 4 foot 7 inches. Weight estimated 5.5 to 6 stone. Sunken cheeks and prominent facial bones. Thick-lipped. Shoulders broad but slender in overall appearance. Naturally sullen and ill-tempered. Murderous tendencies! Approach with caution.
Voice: High, occasional stutter. Fluent in Skøl but ill-educated in accent.

Hair: Black, curling, shoulder-length and ill-kempt. No beard or moustache.
Eyes: Rust-orange, squint-shaped.
Skin: Dark complexion with darker freckles on some areas. Cull scar present (beneath clothing, exact location unknown).

To aid in the apprehension of Zako Taler, ALL REPAYERS in County Portcaye are hereby placed under curfew between the hours of **8 at night and 5 in the morning**: EFFECTIVE IMMEDIATELY. No Makaians to be seen abroad between said hours without permission from an employer, **in writing**, on pain of incarceration and/or a fine of ₭60.

I'm in the Scarlets' sitting room with Zako and Missus S. She said it was all right for me to come as I've been to the Lugger before, and it shouldn't attract attention. I'm on my best behaviour.

"It's idiocy." Missus Scarlet perches like a bird on her chair, back erect, eyes blazing blue versions of the fire before her. At least her anger's not directed at us.

"The man's a self-aggrandizer!" She's still going. "Thinks he's the biggest bean in the jar with this governorship coming. Ten thousand krunan? All this hue and cry over a child! Bump on his head's sent him stupid." She draws out the vowels in *stupid*.

Zako half smiles and then dips his chin shyly. He looks

cleaner than I've seen him in years, though his hair's still ratty.

"Ill-tempered, squint-eyed bollocks," I grumble, chasing his smile. "Murderous? Approach with caution? You're not even a teenager! They're such idiots, Zako. You don't stutter. And you've got eyes like a baby kine."

His shyness peels away. "I think my eyesight's going a bit fuzzy," he admits, narrowing his gaze.

"Oh, really?" Ruzi doesn't wear glasses, but I remember Zako's mum had them.

Missus S frowns and levers herself up from her armchair.

"Carry on," she murmurs to me. "I'm having a lie-down." The door to her room clicks closed. She's giving us some space.

Last time, I was too frightened to take in the Scarlets' rooms. Now I look around. They're clean, pleasant and spacious. Bookshelves and a corner fireplace dominate the sitting room. Two wide windows overlook the courtyard. The curtains are drawn. A washroom adjoins the sitting room, with water that can be heated in a tank by a miniature ragleaf boiler. A deep tin tub is fixed to one wall, topped with a cedarwood bench. Its window overlooks the Lugger's main entrance. The Scarlets each have a room off a short corridor from the sitting room.

Zako's been sitting cross-legged on the floor. He stands, and we share a cautious hug.

"Can't believe you drew my wanted poster so accurate, Mora," he accuses. "Thanks a lot."

"I didn't draw you for *them*!" I start to explain, before I realize he's winding me up. I'm about as wound as I can go.

He's grinning, but it looks forced.

"Are you okay?" I ask softly.

"Yeah. Ten grand." He gestures at himself dismissively.

"You're priceless," I remind him. "They'll never see it. More fool them."

But I can't ignore that such a large bounty is a shock. It's well beyond what I expected.

"Wish I felt a bit … more … like me." Zako's voice has gone small again.

I bite my lip. He does look ridiculous, wearing one of Missus Scarlet's old blouses and a pair of rather baggy women's trousers, rolled up at the cuffs.

"You look fabulous. Like a magician."

He's not convinced.

"I'll pick you up something from the ammedown market." Ruzi will have the coin. I know he keeps some in a tin. His life savings – it's barely anything. "They sell old eyeglasses too. I could try and find some for you."

"Thank you." Zako swipes a tangle of hair out of his eyes. His hair is like my own, which waves or curls or frizzes, depending on its mood. I've no patience to wrangle mine, so I mostly keep it under wraps, making my amber eyes stand out even more.

"I hate this," he tells me. Missus Venor didn't let him cut it. They had to control the smallest things.

But the Venors aren't here.

"Where does Missus S keep the scissors?"

"Look in there." Mister Scarlet surprises us, coming in from the corridor, and I realize I've let my voice reach a normal volume. He waves to the washroom. "Don't make a mess. Oh, girl…" he gestures to delay me as Zako goes in search of the scissors, "are you planning regular social calls with our most-wanted guest?"

I hang my head. "I'm sorry."

"Kit says you have a plan."

I nod eagerly. "We'll get Zako out soon. Kit told me about your friend in Vester Shells. It's a good idea." I try to sound committal. "I don't mean to disturb though," I add. "Do you want me to go?"

I hear Missus Scarlet clear her throat next door.

His face seems to soften. "No one said to go. But if someone sees you leaving, what will you say?"

"I'll say…"

"Exactly."

Zako reappears. "You can say you're doing drawings for Missus Scarlet, like you did for Missus Heane."

Mister Scarlet tilts his head at that.

"My previous owner – she asked me to draw for her. Some portraits, views of the farm, some butterflies. The kine."

"Drawings." Mister Scarlet scratches his cheek. "Like Zako in the paper? That was you?"

I nod. "She tacked some up in her kitchen."

"Well. This idea has merit. You can draw us some

luggers out fishing. We'll hang them downstairs, and you can earn some coin. Suppose you wouldn't mind that?"

I meet his eyes. "Not at all. How many do you want?"

"I think three. What is fair payment? Ten each?"

I nod again. "Missus Heane never paid me anything."

"Wait." Mister S holds up both hands. "Not like that, girl. You tell me… *Mister, I sold my last piece to a collector for fifty krunan…*" He uses a silly high voice, nothing like mine, and blocks my protests as he carries on. "And I reply… *Twenty each and not a penny more!*" His own bargaining voice is deeper. "And you say… *But I won't part with my heart's expression for less than forty!* And I say, *Thirty is my final offer.*" He claps his hands once.

"Thirty's brilliant."

"No! You say… *I am leaving. I will take my business to a serious man.*" He tosses a head of imaginary hair. "And you walk away." He mimes this, nose in the air.

Zako laughs quietly.

"And then I give in. *Wait! I will give you forty.*"

"Forty each?"

"You drive a hard bargain."

"I didn't…" I say, biting back a laugh. "But thank you, I'll do it for forty."

"I expect very beautiful boat pictures. Boats to make me cry. Do not tell Missus S what I am paying." He winks at Zako. Missus S has heard everything, no doubt, from just the next room.

Mister S takes himself off to find her and I carry another lantern after Zako into the washroom.

We share a glance in the mirror.

"He's funny," Zako whispers.

Kit never told me his owner had a sense of humour. I can't believe he's going to give me over a hundred krunan for three pictures. All he's seen of my work is Zako's wanted poster. I'd better make them good.

"We can't leave Crozoni hair in this bin," I say. I remove my hair wrap and spread it out. "I'll collect the cuttings in here and take them. How short do you want it?"

"Short."

I hack away at first, before snipping more carefully.

He relaxes as I work. Now seems as good a time as any to ask him what I've been wondering for days now.

"So, what happened with Venor...?" I meet two startled amber eyes in the mirror. "Can you remember?" I think of the shed and the dogs. "Did you annoy him? Did he lose his temper and lash out?"

Zako puffs out his cheeks. "Not really. That's the weird thing. You know, there's been lots of times he's lost his temper with me over something. But this time – it came out of nowhere. I was cleaning one of the stalls. He just went for me."

"With a hammer?"

"Yeah. He'd brought it with him. Like he'd planned it all. He ... he wanted to kill me, Mor, I know it. He wasn't even angry. He was ... *calm*."

I frown. "Did he say anything?"

"Do you remember Devotion?" I nod. Devotion Venor – the magistrate's daughter, about Zako's age. I've never met her, but she always seemed nice enough to Zako, given what her parents were like.

"He said he knew I'd been playing with Devotion in her room…" His voice hitches. "We were playing cards. Same as we would, remember?"

I nod again at him in the mirror with a small smile. Zako could beat anyone at cards.

"Go on. He didn't want you spending time with her?"

"No. He was furious." Zako frowned, remembering. "*I told you not to go near my house.*" Zako's imitation of Venor's hacking voice isn't half bad. "*How dare you sneak around…? How dare you spy on me?*" He shivers. "We were just playing. We'd done it before, and he never found out."

"Did Devotion tell on you?"

"I guess." His face seems to crumple. "It must have been her. She never came to see me … after … they locked me up. She never came. Now she…" He hiccups fat tears. "She thinks I tried to kill him."

"You don't know what she thinks," I say, but I want to say, *It doesn't matter what she thinks.*

He drags a fist under his nose, painting it with a snot trail. I can imagine how he feels.

Memory too fresh-hewn, too ugly to keep, too green to burn. A mess.

"I'm nearly done," I say. Enough for tonight.

His scar from the Cull is dead centre at the back of his neck, hovering at the top of his spine. The bones protrude. The dark circle looks bigger than mine. A scar that grew as he grew. It should have killed him, so close to his head. They must have done it at no range at all, stuck the gun on his neck like a kine in the slaughter line.

I make sure his shorter hair still hides it.

He looks older when I've finished.

"How's that?"

He raises a soft smile at his reflection in Missus Scarlet's mirror. "I look different."

"You look like Ruzi, somehow." He hasn't seen Ruzi since they were separated after detention. "You've got his eyes and chin. Only he's got long hair. It's grey."

I gather the clippings into my wrap and pocket them before giving his short hair a final swipe with one hand.

"Wait," he says, and I stop. "Do you think I can see him? Ruzi?"

I hesitate.

"Let's see," I whisper. "I'll talk to Kit, okay? We don't want to push things with the Scarlets." But I think about Mister Scarlet, teasing me, persuading me to charge more, and I think I might be able to swing it after all.

8

too savage

It's only half seven, but I need to hurry home for the new eight o'clock curfew. The door swings to behind me and I'm in another world, quiet and dark. The sign *THE LUGGER* in block letters juts out above the lintel. There's even an old Crozoni horse brass fixed at the top – so small I missed it at first. It's a Crozoni fishing boat with two four-cornered sails. Icicles grow from the eaves after all the cold nights and sunny days.

The cobbles stop at the riverbank path, near to where it passes under the Lugger's overhang. It's a muddy path, not lit well, and not well travelled after nightfall. I follow it a short distance to a narrow footbridge crossing to the Skates – the poorer district north of the river – and shake Zako's hair out beyond the stone railing. The river doesn't freeze over here, but thin ice sheets like frosted glass collect at its edges.

From the crown of the bridge, I can see the cupola on top of the old Town Hall, a silhouette against the sky. The lower floors, where they kept us after the Cull, plunge behind a disused factory block fronting the river that they're turning into fancy housing. It's their Life Registry building now, of course.

The place where the clerks make and store the paperwork to keep track of who has paid and who has fallen behind. Who gets to keep breathing and who doesn't.

Two guards are stationed at the front, night and day – two more round the back. Plus a watch inside. The paperwork is guarded jealously. It's people's lives on the line, after all, plus there's a lot of money involved when you add it all up.

I used to love that building, and they've ruined it.

The Skøl motto, *Life Is Golden*, is chiselled into the stone above the grand double doors and filled with gold paint. The Life Registry symbol bookends it – two interlocking triangles shaped like an hourglass with a diamond at the centre.

Venor's official seat, magistrate of County Portcaye Life Registry, is in there. Soon, he will be sworn in as governor of the New Western Counties, and the Portcaye Life Registry will become an even more important seat of power – a new capital of its kind.

It's a turning point for Portcaye and for Venor. I wonder whether the rest of us will notice the difference.

I stuff my empty hair wrap back in my pocket and return to the solitude of the riverside path.

Acres of starlit sky, wood smoke coiling through the air – nights like this, a girl could pretend everything isn't awful.

Then four figures, one swinging a lantern, appear round the corner ahead.

I ignore the urge to turn back. It's too late to hide my savage curls away. I keep my eyes on the mud and hug the side of the path.

"Well, look at this! Waddle, waddle!" one calls out. I realize they're boys my age or younger, maybe only sixteen, but formally dressed. I don't slow until they block my path.

"Feeling naughty? Fuck the curfew! Have a drink with us, duckie!"

"No, thank you." Polite, but firm.

"Leave it, Bunny." The tallest boy eyes me with distaste. "You're a funny-looking makkie, aren't you?" he laughs.

"I have to get back," I say, trying to wedge through them.

Fingers close around my arms. "Don't waddle off."

"Come on," the tall one drawls. "We could be warming up with an ale by now."

"My owner's expecting me."

"Show us your scar." A hand grips my waist on the bad side. "Is it here?"

"Knock it off. Someone might see," hisses the tall one.

But they ignore his protests – and mine. Three of them topple me into the frozen grass at the side of the path.

My top gives way before they succeed with the belt. I scream. I kick. My scar is plain to see, even in the starlight. Their hands are all over me, cold, clutching.

A ringing starts up in my head.

I thrash and bite down on what flesh I can reach, scrabbling and lurching from one grip to another.

"Makkie bit me," one whines in disbelief.

The tall boy laughs. "What did you expect? They're wild."

"I have a disease – a pox." I muster as much dignity as I can, pinned to the grass, and thicken my Crozoni accent to match Ruzi's. "You won't get away with this. You'll suffer my pox and my curse. It's painful."

"Rubbish," says the ringleader.

"Let me go." I try a different appeal. "If I miss curfew they might fine you too."

They look like they're wavering.

I kick with renewed effort, out of the heavy coat the Glassworks gave me, almost out of their hands – but they've somehow, unspokenly, agreed to change tack.

"In you get."

Into the River Rin, in winter, swollen with icy water – a death sentence. I hear myself screaming anew, frantic, as they manhandle me over the bank.

I clutch at mud and shrivelled grasses, but they don't stop my plunge.

The cold is so sharp it's all I can do to breathe.

The river tumbles me like a twig, its power shocking. I almost gulp it in. When I break the surface, I can hear them hooting, "Paddle, paddle, you poxy makkie!"

Their calls grow quickly faint as the current bears me away.

I kick my water-laden boots and gasp in air. Breathing's almost harder than kicking. The icy grip crushes my lungs and the world shrinks to the churning water surrounding me as I try to steer myself to the side. At least I went in without my coat. That would have sunk me for sure, strong swimmer or no. Numbing seconds later, adrift, I realize I'm not strong enough to go anywhere this river doesn't want me to go. Something inside me howls – *not now, not like Ma.*

Then my legs hit a bank of sand, shallow as anything. I dig in my boots and plunge my hands to the bottom, half dragging, half crawling my way out, smashing the glassy ice plates. Up the scree of pebbles on the shallow bank, and I'm on the path.

I want to collapse, but I know if I do, it's over.

I push on, then off at the first turning, colliding with a woman as I stagger, half drowned, mud-smeared, from the junction between two yards on to a cobbled street.

"Idiot!" she recoils. "Filth! It's gone eight! You lot are supposed to be off the streets!"

I'm glad I got her coat all muddy.

I start down the unfamiliar street. Lanterns spread circles of light over three or four barrows peddling their wares. A cobbler's sign – a big boot shape – swings in the wind. My shirt is still hanging open, my underclothes torn, my boots squelching mud and water.

"Out of the way, smut," a man sneers as he passes.

The merchants' eyes slide over me, unmoved. I speed up. It's freezing and I seem to be made of absent limbs and uncooperative stumps. I push on, half running as much as I'm able, back to a bigger street – this one I know, and it's mercifully close to Opal Alley.

The river carried me nearer to home. By the grace of Thea.

I hammer on the door until Ruzi opens it, appalled.

"What's happened?" He pulls me inside and over to the stove.

I can't talk. Ruzi stokes the stove as I collapse in front of it. He helps me pull off what's left of my wet top and sodden boots, socks and trousers – before throwing his coat over me. I peel my underclothes off underneath it while he fetches the blanket from his bed. I collapse as close to the stove as I can go without being inside it.

My teeth are chattering too much to speak. My whole body's beyond my grip, uncontrollably shivering.

"Warm up, girl, warm up." Ruzi towels my hair before asking the question he's been holding. "What happened? Is it – Zako?"

"N-no." I shake my head, for what it's worth, with the whole of me still shaking. "Zakisfine."

The heat from the stove begins to bring me back.

Ruzi fetches the blanket from my room and piles it on too.

"Did they hurt you, Mora? I mean..."

I know what he's asking.

"N-not like that. They pushedmeinthe r-r-river."

"Who?"

"Some b-b-b—"

"Tell me in a minute. Get warm. You're all right now." He pats my shoulder cautiously. "You're safe."

Something in Ruzi's plain statement undoes me. I start to sob. He produces a rag for me to blow my nose into, but it's minutes before the tears stop.

He piles more wood into the stove, starts to heat a pot of water.

"They were just boys, younger than me. Four of them." Then I realize – "My coat. I need it. My keys." My keys to the Glassworks are still in a pocket of the coat, abandoned by the river path – assuming the boys didn't throw it into the river after me out of spite. The manager, Mister Wagsen, will tear strips off me if I've lost them.

"Where did it happen?"

I tell him, through scalding sips of water. He goes to find himself another jumper.

"You can't go back now, alone," I plead. "The curfew! What if the boys are still there?"

Ruzi fetches one of the bits of driftwood from his room. "I hope they are there," he growls. "I'd love to see them." He starts pulling on his boots. "Lock the door after me."

"Ruzi, if you hurt them, you'll get in trouble."

"I won't be long," he says.

I crouch by the wood-stove in my nest of blankets and try to defrost.

Ever since what happened with Ma and that river, I've liked to imagine it as peaceful somehow. She meant to do it. It wasn't the river's fault. Now I've felt its violence. Now the mud smell is cloying – clay and weed and something foul and nameless coming off my sodden boots.

Ruzi is taking much too long.

I shrug reluctantly out of the nest of blankets and put on my spare clothes – all of them, underclothes, two jumpers, two trousers – and wrap Ruzi's coat around me again tightly. I find the old pair of boots, falling apart, that are Ruzi's spares. They're clown-sized in proportion to my feet, but my only pair are still caked in filth and drying in front of the stove.

I go out. When I reach the turning, there's Ruzi, his driftwood over one shoulder, my coat bundled under his arm. He sees me and speeds up, waving, irritated.

"Get back inside, girl, quickly. You should be in bed."

"You've been gone ages. I thought something happened."

"Found your coat, right where you said. They weren't there, more's the pity."

We head back inside. My coat's only slightly muddied. My keys are still in the breast pocket. Ruzi has something else too – a baked apple packed with sugar. It's Skøl barrow food, and a traditional treat for poorer folk.

"That'll do you good."

I've been curious to try one for months, and he knows it. It's tangy and sweet and meltingly hot. I don't care that it's burning my mouth if it chases away the last shards of ice lodged in my belly. I eat it more quickly than I've eaten anything in my life.

"I should lose my coat more often." I force out a laugh.

Ruzi gives me one of his half smiles.

"Went by the Lugger," he says. "Thought those boys might have gone there. Your friend Kit hasn't seen them."

"You talked to Kit?" This is almost as surprising as being attacked by a pack of vicious boys.

"I did. Says he'll keep an eye out for them. Four boys dressed fancy – one called Bunny?" Bunny, short for Abundance, probably. Abundantly awful.

"Keep an eye out why?"

"Well, so we find out who they are. Where they live."

"So we can do what? Tell their mothers and fathers?" I laugh, a real laugh this time. "They'd get scolded for not finishing me off properly."

His jaw clenches, then he sighs. "Well. You mustn't walk that way again."

"I won't. Doubt they will either – they were proper afraid of my poxy curse."

Ruzi brushes the wispy hair back from his forehead and smiles. "Your mother was a great one for curses."

Ruzi was someone we'd call on sometimes, before Ma died. She'd take me to his shop, where he made musical instruments. He was famous for them – the best maker in the north. His workshop smelled better than a sweet stand, or perfume or anything. Sawdust and lacquers. His craft was air and water to him. It's a waste, an artist like Ruzi doing heavy lifting for the Glassworks.

But the Skøl have their own idea of art. Their music is mostly plodding, plain and precise like the tolling of bells. They don't go in for performances in the street or in drinking establishments. Too savage.

9

dying race

There's still a patch of tenderness on the roof of my mouth from last night's baked apple. The days are getting longer, but who'd know when the sun still sets before six? I'm used to the dark settling in before I've a chance to finish with Clomper and Caney. I'm used to the street lamps. This murk never bothered me before, but those boys by the river have set something shrivelling under my ribs.

"Do you want me to wait? Could walk back together," Ruzi offers, replacing a sack of kine oats in its niche for me and holding out his ever-present paper bag of boiled sweets. He favours the buttery, minty ones.

"No, you go on. Don't worry about me." I take a sweet.

He crunches through one he started earlier and selects another, giving me a dubious look.

"Oh – I meant to tell you," I say. "Our small friend

needs glasses. Says far-off things are looking fuzzy for him. Thought you might find a cheap pair."

"Glasses," Ruzi mumbles. "Like Ibou."

"If you go now, there's time for a look in Ammedown Alley before curfew – you know, those shops in the Skates. Don't wait for me; I'll be fine."

He nods and takes his leave. I'm glad I don't have to go rifling through a bucket of old Crozoni glasses scavenged from our dead, but I'm less pleased to be alone when I click the side gate shut for the night.

I've only gone half a block before I sense a tall bulk hovering at the corner of my eye, close behind, on the left. A man. Too close. I speed up, but he matches me.

"Mor. It's me."

Kit, speaking Crozoni in a low voice.

"Did I startle you?" One of his hands wraps around my arm.

"Of course you did." My anger bubbles up above the shame. "What are you doing here?"

"Erm. Fishing?" He shows me a small crate of fresh fish. I look at him blankly, and he laughs. "I bought them just now. From the fish market."

That's nowhere near the Glassworks.

"Thought I'd go this way to see if I'd run into you. And here you are."

"How much fish does one man need?" I say, instead of acknowledging that he's come on purpose to see me.

"Renny's making fish pastries for lunch tomorrow."

We walk together. "I heard about last night," he rumbles.

"I'm all right. It's hardly the worst thing that's ever happened to me."

The silence between us stretches.

"I should've walked you home."

"It wasn't even late. You have work."

"It's this stupid bloody curfew. Makes the thugs bolder."

"Don't worry about me. We have bigger things to concern us." I shoot him a look. "Like trusting some friend of Missus Scarlet!"

It's risky. Even if this woman is trustworthy, there's a bounty on Zako's head that most Skøl would sell their grandmothers for.

"Bigger Thing's haircut looks great." Kit smiles. "And it makes him look different – older – which is helpful. Will you do mine next?"

"I thought you were growing it on purpose."

"I'm not."

"I remember when you had really long hair."

"That was years back. You didn't know me then."

"I knew of you. Mister First Place."

Everyone was talking about him the summer before I turned nine. His summer of infamy. He was still eleven.

There was an older girl in our school, Sami Cutler, fifteen or so, from good Crozoni stock. Had the blood of the mermaids in her, they liked to say – just a turn of phrase. I was a confident swimmer, but I was nothing like as good as her, and I was never into holding my breath for ages, or diving.

Sami Cutler won the oyster contest every summer. For weeks, kids would compete to swim out and prise the biggest oyster they could find off the rocks by the wreck of the *Eventide.* There was a ceremony with prizes in the old fairground for the largest shell, the most shapely shell, and finding a pearl, which hardly ever happened.

Sami Cutler took the prizes for biggest and best four years running. Until Kit beat her that summer.

Sami didn't take that well. Neither did her friends, and she had a sight more than Kit. She called him a cheater. Her friends agreed. Said the only thing he ever dived for were the wishing coins he stole from the big mermaid fountain in Fountain Square. Her friends remembered seeing him stealing those coins. They said he must have used them to buy the shell and pearl from someone.

I didn't see any of it happen. Saw Kit though. I passed him in the old fairground not long after they beat the living daylights out of him. His long hair hanging in his face couldn't hide the evidence. He's still got that scar on his cheek.

It's my only memory of him from before the Cull. *Did he steal those coins? Did he cheat?* I remember thinking. Like if he had, he'd have deserved it.

"Feels like another life," Kit sighs now.

"They were so awful to you. Over a little sea beast and its bit of shiny gunk."

"Hey!" Kit stops dramatically. "My sea beast was not *little*."

I roll my eyes.

"No one ever chucked me in a freezing river," Kit says softly.

"It's not a competition," I remind him. "Cos if it was, we know you'd just cheat. You big cheater."

He splutters. It's good to hear him laugh. "The cheek on you. I should chuck you back in there."

"Like a tiny oyster."

We sink into silence, walking past couples holding hands, couples bickering. Past a father tugging his son behind. *Do you want to be late?*

I break the silence. "Ruzi keeps asking to see Zako."

"That's another thing I meant to say – tomorrow, early afternoon, Missus S is going out. She said he could come then."

It's Endweek tomorrow. Ruzi has the day off, since the Glassworks is closed. So do I, for the most part, after I see to the kine.

"Mister S won't mind?" I probe.

"He'll be helping in the kitchen. Too emotional for him." Kit smiles. "Don't worry; it was her idea. Zako's been giving her the big eyes."

"Is that okay?"

"She likes him." He pulls a playful face at me like he has no idea why.

We're coming to the turn-off to Sinton Square, my way home. "See you tomorrow afternoon, then," I say.

"I'll walk you to your place."

"No, go on. It's quicker for you that way."

"I don't mind..."

"Honest. I'm not made of glass."

I give his arm a quick squeeze and take my leave.

People linger in Sinton Square to look at the wanted posters pasted round the plinth of the old statue there. My portrait of Zako stares from half a dozen spots. I imagine drawing him again, with short hair, with glasses, with his cheeks filled out on Lugger stew and dumplings. With rounder cheeks, I suddenly realize, he'd look a lot like me.

My eyes drift over the face of the statue. It's a Crozoni piece, like the mermen on the town's northern gates. They didn't topple them all, not in the small squares. They're a reminder. Imilia Dezil, she's called, a distant relation, *captain* and *explorer*, relic and curio of a dying race.

10

smile

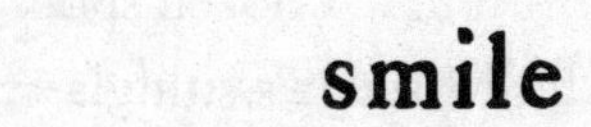

It's the Endweek. Five days since springing Zako, and his future is still a question mark. I've used any spare moments I've found to work on the fishing-boat drawings for the Scarlets – the extra money will surely help, but I want them to be good; I want them to tell their friends about me.

At least Zako gets his wish to see Ruzi. *Small victories*, I tell myself.

Ruzi's all jittery. We reach the Lugger mid-afternoon and hang our coats with Gracie's and Renny's in the kitchen. Kit ducks out of chopping onions long enough to lead us up to his room, past Mister Scarlet holding court with a few of the regulars in the bar.

They're all laughing. Mister S grips one by the hand, twists it near a lantern. Kit told me he reads palms.

"Has Mister S ever read your palm?" I ask.

Kit looks back at us. "I won't let him."

"Load of balls?" Ruzi asks.

Kit looks askance. "But what if it's true? I don't want to know what happens. Makes it real. Or it spoils the surprise."

I want to laugh. Our lives have been so full of unwelcome surprises.

We reach the right floor, and Kit pauses by a big linen closet.

"This will take you to Mister S's study – through the guest wing." He passes me a heavy iron key. "Go on round now. Mor, come see me before you go."

"I will," I nod. "Is Missus S gone?"

"Said she'd be out till sundown. Just act natural. Mora, you've already got your story about doing drawings for the Scarlets. Here." He dumps an armful of bedclothes into Ruzi's arms. "Anyone will think you're staff."

I glance at Ruzi. At least he looks all right, his checked shirt flat, tucked into neat trousers. Clean boots. He's clutching a paper bag. He shifts it to accommodate the stack of sheets. I've tidied myself up too, but all my clothes are ragged and wrinkled compared to what the Lugger staff wear.

Ruzi hesitates, for all his itching to see Zako over the last five days. He bangs Kit awkwardly on the back, twice. "Thank you," he says, frog in his throat. "Means a lot."

Zako must hear the lock turn, but he's not in the Scarlets' living room. He knows to expect us, but he also knows to hide. They've made a nook in Missus Scarlet's walk-in wardrobe, a space behind some crates that he can squeeze into.

I call *hello* and he appears on the threshold, eyes wide.

Ruzi goes still beside me.

Then he rushes forward like a wave, something big and inevitable. Like more than one man. A shoal or a flock, a murmuration of little squares on his shirt wrapping around Zako.

"My boy," he says in Crozoni, actually lifting Zako's feet off the floor.

"Papa."

The name he used six years ago, in a language he barely speaks any more, syllables awkward.

Tears ambush me. So does envy. Ruzi's crying too, but he gets it under control quickly.

"Can you even see your old man?" he teases. "Mora told us you need glasses now." He fishes two pairs he chose from the ammedown shop yesterday from his trouser pocket.

Both have roundish lenses too big for Zako's face, rimmed in copper wire. I know there can't have been many to choose from.

Zako tries them in turn and settles for the weaker pair. We crowd round the mirror above Missus S's chest of drawers. The copper frames suit him, setting off his amber eyes.

"You look like your mother." Ruzi's voice is just above a whisper. Like if he speaks too loudly, he'll break the spell.

"He looks like you too," I tell Ruzi.

"Mister S thinks I look like you," Zako tells me.

I scoff. "We all look the same to them."

Ruzi looks upset again. I offer to give the two of them some space, but he's adamant I stay.

"You have to help us eat the biscuits!" he reminds me, and Zako's dogged nods persuade me.

We crunch through the half a dozen meltingly lovely lavender shortbread biscuits Ruzi spent months of savings on from the bakery in Opal Alley.

Afterwards, Zako shows us a Skøl book Missus Scarlet's given him called *Blenny and Tornelius*. It's quite heavy going, I realize, leafing through – hard for Zako. The Venors never worked on his reading and writing, and the tale is written in a surprisingly florid style. I don't know how he's got through three chapters already.

"Missus S has been reading it to me," he confesses.

"She has?"

"Said it's that old she read it when she was a girl. And they read it to their son."

"They have a son?"

"He's grown and flown," Zako says, and I can hear Missus Scarlet's voice in his words.

"What's it about, then?" Ruzi asks.

"There's a boy called Blenny, separated from his family but on his way to meet them… Only a mighty storm wrecks the ship he's on." He lowers his voice. "Blenny alone miraculously survives, washed up on a strange shore with bits from the shipwreck. And then he finds another survivor – the ship's hound, Tornelius. But we're still at the beginning; I want to know what happens." His eyes light up as he says to Ruzi, "Could you read some?"

Ruzi casts a slightly panicked look my way. I'm sure he reads Skøl better than Zako, but he still struggles.

"Let me." I pluck the book from Zako.

"Chapter Four. In Which Blenny and Tornelius Explore Their Strange New Home…"

The sun that Blenny had considered a warm friend these fourteen years was altered in this place into a vicious, angry stranger. Here it beat upon the young fellow like a mallet. By the time he had finished dragging the heavy crates to the dubious shelter of the shaded grove, he was washed in more perspiration than seawater.

Tornelius lay panting, his tongue lolling almost to the sand…

"Makes you thirsty, doesn't it?" Ruzi interjects.

I inch through several passages – it's hot, boy and dog are running out of fresh water – but when I try to stop, Zako insists on hearing the rest of the chapter.

After a harrowing trek inland through forest replete with unnaturally aggressive spiders, peculiar foliage and so on, Blenny and Tornelius are delighted to find a small freshwater pool near a homey clearing, along with what appear to be a colony of wild chickens, very free with their eggs.

We leave them mid-afternoon, eating eggs at the close of the chapter, and Zako is satisfied.

In the real world, dusk has arrived. Time always moves quicker on an Endweek.

In the dark, Zako shows us how to spy unseen on the street below from the washroom window. We can watch the comings and goings through the front, but no one sees us through the tilted shutters.

When we spot Missus S coming back, Ruzi and I say our goodbyes and decamp. Zako's content. He almost looks like he belongs, a small shape curled in the corner of the sofa, reaching for his book.

"I'm a blessed man," Ruzi mutters as I pull the door shut behind us. "To see him again, when I never thought I… He's a lovely lad, isn't he? Ah, Mora. I feel light as a feather."

He's got tears in his eyes again. Bottled-up Ruzi, leaking two times in the same night. He collects himself. "You coming home now?"

"Kit wanted to talk," I tell him. Regardless, I think we both need space after that. Ruzi nods and heads straight home, while I stop at the bar.

I pack away a great bowl of Kit's spicy stew and nurse half an ale while he works. The Lugger's not too busy, and still he's flitting everywhere – serving food, fixing a broken game some of the young drinkers like to play in the quiet fikka lounge on the first floor, stacking away glasses, listening to one of the regulars read a letter out from his daughter back home. A young woman sits alone, eating, which is unusual.

We haven't had a chance to chat, even in quiet Crozoni.

He's wiping a puddle from the bar when the sinews in his hand stiffen. "Don't look now," he murmurs, "but brace yourself."

It's a pair of branders – the same two who took Ruzi and me to the station last week, now relaxed, off duty, but still in uniform. The taller one stops to my right, resting a heavy hand on my shoulder and leaning close. His fancy gun and his elektric prod nestle prominently in twin holsters, hilts twinkling pale gold.

"Good evening, lovers!" he says. His partner takes the stool to my left, dragging it close.

It's only seven, and they've been in another tavern already. Sweat and drink come off them like steam. Their uniforms are crumpled, their too-close noses painted with red blood vessels.

"Any news about our boy yet?" asks the shorter one on my left. "He tried to get in touch?" He lays a meaty hand on my thigh.

"We're mourning him," I say coldly. "Let us be."

They laugh, leaving their hands on me. "You're mourning him? Bit early for that, isn't it? We're still out scouring the countryside for the vicious little head-hammerer. And the town." He looks ostentatiously around the Lugger lounge and sniffs. "You makkies like this place, don't you?" Me and Kit are the only makkies in here.

"He works here." I point out the obvious, but they ignore me.

"Ten-grand boy's your friend, isn't he? Ten grand could come running into your friendly arms right here, but you're in mourning! Just imagine." The tall one shakes his head.

"I can help with your mourning," says the other. His laugh is low and dirty.

"Can I get you a drink?" Kit offers. "Or are you just here to sweet-talk us?"

"Schinns, mate – doubles. And smile," the taller one to my right answers. His partner takes his hand off my thigh and slides a crisp note on to the bar.

"Something to wet your tongue, girl?" he asks, putting his nauseating hand higher up. I struggle not to shudder.

"No, thank you," I say.

"We've been watching you and the old man. Magistrate wanted any contacts of the boy followed, and you're all he has." I flinch. I didn't see them following us. "You're all up yourself, aren't you?"

"Leave her be," Kit snaps.

The man laughs. "Oh, this one's feral. Pissing on our territory, are we?"

Kit pours schinn, the strong spirit favoured by the Skøl, into glass tumblers, his expression carefully blank.

"I'm no one's territory." I stand to push back my stool.

The taller one laughs, almost pleasantly. "You're someone's property, idiot."

Kit stops fishing through the coin box and turns to look at me. I feel a sickening lurch, like this is where it could all go bad.

The Skøl woman I noticed eating alone earlier comes to join us at the bar. "I would like a half of the red ale, please," she asks politely, though there's a bite to her tone.

Her grist-brown hair is secured in a thick plait, apart from the fringe across her prominent forehead. She's in her mid to late twenties, I guess.

"What's all the excitement?" she asks the branders, twirling a gold ring set with an amber stone around one of her pale, pinkly freckled fingers.

The taller brander eyes her up. "If you're from anywhere round here you'll have heard about it. Wild boy tried to kill his owner – the Registry magistrate, soon to be our governor. These two knew the boy. They're hiding something," he tells her.

"I see. I did hear about that. So you're asking questions in an official capacity, is that right, firebrand –" she consults the tag over his breast – "Seyll?" Her thin lips pull into a smile. "Because drinking on official business is against the branders' code, isn't it?"

"It's none of your business, missus – no offence," he shoots back.

"You're probably right," she says. "I just write about these things for the *Evening Gazette*."

That makes an impression. It's Skøland's leading newspaper, based out of Rundvaer. Its Endweek edition sells here in some of the fancy tobacconists – even if it arrives more than a month out of date. I've never bought one – too expensive – though I've leafed through the odd discarded copy. It's mostly impenetrable politics and high-society stories, but sometimes there's an interesting crime.

A journalist for the *Gazette* – she's important. Why, I wonder, is she here?

"I'm actually here to cover Magistrate Venor's appointment to governor," she goes on, like she's answering my unspoken question. She considers them. "But maybe I could add some details about the officers pursuing the investigation and their tactics." She pulls a stool close and sits down.

Kit puts a pile of coins in change on the bar in front of the shorter firebrand. He pulls the red ale.

"Ah, beautiful." The journalist sighs when he passes it over.

"On your tab?" he asks, and the journalist nods.

The firebrands drain their schinn.

"Another?" asks Kit.

"No. Let's go," one mutters, eyeing the woman uneasily.

Very faintly, she winks at me, foam from the ale still clinging to her upper lip.

"I'll forget the tab," Kit tells her when they're gone. "That one's on the house, missus. Thought they were going to kick off for a minute there."

"Please." She wipes her lips with the back of her hand.

"Anything but *missus.* You make me feel old. Felicity," she insists.

"Felicity. I remember." Kit goes to serve food.

"Felicity," she says again, holding a bony hand to me. "Felicity Greave."

"Mora Dezil." I meet her firm grip. No Skøl has ever shaken my hand. It's painful.

"Are you really writing a story?" I ask, dragging my stool back next to hers.

She takes a huge gulp of ale. Impressive. "I am. Writing about your glorious new governor-to-be."

The *Portcaye Post* has been bleating about Venor's swearing-in ceremony for months and there's still months to wait. I suppose Felicity must be writing for Rundvaer's readers.

"Clarion Lovemore's first-ever tour of the colonies," she gushes. "We're going to witness history in the making." Her grin is gleeful.

"Lovemore's coming here? To Portcaye?" *To this backwater,* I think. *The head of the beast herself.*

Felicity nods enthusiastically. "Her ship should be sailing, even now!"

Of course she loves Clarion Lovemore. The papers can't print enough about their Governor Most High. Not just her governing. Her clothes, her hair, the events she attends. Who's in favour, who's out of favour. The *Gazette* is full of her exploits.

Felicity sips the last of her ale more slowly, fixing her

blue-grey eyes on me over the rim. "Do you work in manufactory?"

I look down at my worn trousers and boots.

"How did you guess?" I smile.

"Reporter nose." She taps it, grinning.

"I'm at Green's," I tell her. "The Glassworks."

"Oh! Isn't that the place making the roof for the new Hexagon Hall?"

I nod, strangely proud.

"How wonderful."

"So, will Clarion Lovemore get here for the ceremony? Venor's signing-in at the new hall?" I ask.

"I would hope so," Felicity laughs. "She's sailing halfway round the world for it! And she's to open the big showcase too, I understand."

"Showcase?"

"The *Exhibition of the Modern Age* – haven't you heard? They'll have it up in the hall for a year, probably. Mark the momentous … turning point. Then they'll make it a boutique market full of shops for rich people." She smiles. "Didn't you know what you were working on all this time?"

I shrug. "And you're interviewing Venor?"

"As soon as he's well enough. My boss wants a personal piece, so people get a feel for him as a man –" she gestures grandly with one arm – "out here, *bringing civilization to the frontier* – his words, not mine."

"Right," I say. Her tone is dry, but I don't know how

much of that she believes. She's Skøl, after all, and they seem to think we're all savages. "I'd be interested in *your* story." The reporter's cheerful voice pulls me back to her.

"Why?"

"I'm trying to include some other voices, so it's not just Venor talking. A glassworker, a repayer coming of age in a new world, contributing to the construction of this groundbreaking building, symbol of the modern age, designed by a famous architect, site of the biggest political appointment of the century..." I've the sense she could go on for some time if she wanted to. "I'd read a story about her."

There's a beat, and her eyes meet mine. I look away.

"I don't work the glass myself. I just cart it round. I drive the kine. I'm not that interesting."

She yawns. "I disagree. Well, you know where I am if you change your mind."

Kit's back behind the bar. He takes the reporter's empty glass.

"Well, I know it's early, but I've had a long day. I'm done in," she says, standing up.

I look at the clock and realize it's half seven. Curfew is coming.

"I should have said," she adds as she turns to go. "There might be a fee."

"Goodnight," I tell her.

I slide off the stool as Kit sidles up.

"Thick and Thicker are still out front," he tells me, in Crozoni.

Through the window I can see the pair of firebrands lingering. Shadow shapes, puffs of grey smoke.

"Let's go out the back way."

I shrug into my coat and follow Kit to the kitchen.

"Can you cover for me, Gracie? I'm walking Mora home," Kit tells her.

"No problem." Gracie waves him off good-naturedly. "Don't be late back yourself."

"I've got a note," Kit reassures her. Mister S has written him a few slips granting permission to be out after curfew, in case he gets stuck.

Kit goes to find his coat while I wait for him in the courtyard.

It feels like the bottom of a huge well. The bare branches of the Makaia plane tree reach like witches' fingers to the sky, brown seed balls dangling. I look up at the Lugger's windows. The Scarlets' curtains are closed, but light seeps past the edges. Most of the guest rooms are dark, except the one where I suppose the reporter's staying. Her curtains are open, her lanterns lit.

Suddenly Kit's standing beside me, wrapped in his black wool coat. Caruq's decided to join us. His claws clack on the paving – I should ask Zako to trim them.

We take the smaller alley to avoid the firebrands, and talk in hushed Crozoni.

"What do you think of our new resident reporter, then?"

I think of the way she dispatched the branders. Her

quiet authority. I imagine what it would be like, not being scared of them. "Well … her articles are going to be awful, of course, but I quite like her."

"You don't like anyone."

"I know. I'm baffled myself."

He lowers his voice to a whisper even though we are completely alone. "Think I've found a captain who'd take Zako to Vester Shells for a fee – not an outrageous one. I've heard she runs Skøl over all the time. Mostly legitimate, but not always. I haven't told her who she's taking – just that it's a runaway."

"She might figure it out though. Can we trust her? What if she turns Zako in and collects the bounty?"

"She could, but then she'd be caught for her own sins."

"What's the fee?"

Kit sucks in a pained breath. "We don't have it. Yet. But the Scarlets have said they can scrape some cash together on the quiet to cover maybe half. They don't keep stacks at the ready, unfortunately. We'll owe them, but I'd rather that than … the alternative." He bumps my shoulder. "Plus you're making money now, aren't you?"

I'm trying. If the Scarlets like my drawings, they'll tell their friends. There might be more work. But it'll take months to save substantially.

I tell Kit, and he shrugs. "We can have enough sooner than that. I've found some extra work a few evenings."

"Doing what?"

"Er … factory work."

"At *night*? What factory?"

"Place in the Skates – needs someone for a bit of lifting and that."

He doesn't look at me, and I feel a prickle of unease. I don't entirely believe him. But how can I push him when he's doing so much for us? "I could do that interview for Felicity. She said there would be a fee."

He hesitates, then nods. "All right. But be careful. She seems all right, but she's a Skøl reporter after all. Stay on message. You know … grateful repayer, absolutely delighted to be working on Venor's vanity glasshouse hexagon and all the rest."

"Naturally."

When we get to Opal Alley, Kit takes my arm. I see what he's seen a second later.

The branders from earlier are waiting for me – Seyll and his partner – leaning a few houses down from the bakery, smoking again.

"Do you think they really suspect us?" I whisper.

"Or they're just being cautious," Kit says. "Still, I know how we can throw them off the track."

Good evening, lovers, Seyll said.

That half-smile from Kit again. "How about a goodnight kiss?"

Oh. Do I imagine he looks pleased?

We're standing in a puddle of darkness at the bottom of the stairs, but the branders are still hovering twenty feet away. I thread my hands behind Kit's back.

"Goodnight, then." My heart's going like a mallet. It must be all over my face. I can't meet his eyes.

He leans in to kiss me – a soft press of lips, a hand at my shoulder.

I freeze, my muscles all tensing at once.

He pulls away, touching his forehead to mine, and whispers, "Relax. You might enjoy it," before pulling me closer for another, deeper kiss.

His tongue touches my lips like a question, slow and warm, and I open my mouth in response. The whole sensation surprises me. I've never kissed anyone. It's like learning a dance, an easy one. His hand on my shoulder moves to my hair. His other hand hovers at my waist.

"Okay?" he whispers, drawing back. It's too dark to see his expression properly.

I raise up on my toes slightly to bring my face closer to his.

I want to repeat the experiment.

He closes the small distance between our lips again, lingering, tender. When he pulls away, his eyelids are heavy.

"Very convincing," I smile.

11

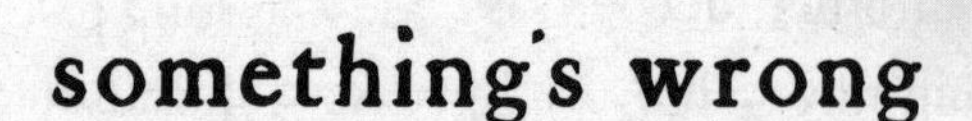

something's wrong

After work the next day, I head to the Lugger with my first fishing-boat drawing complete. Forty krunan, Mister S owes me.

If he likes it, that is. I hope it's good enough – I went for a half front, half side view. I didn't have to go down to the harbour, just closed my eyes and saw it, the ship with its two masts, its rigging and nets and chipped paint, whole and crisp in my memory.

I want to see Kit too. Of course I do. I think about him walking me home and kissing me way more than he needed to.

Gracie's serving at the bar. Mister S is up on the mezzanine, chatting and gathering empties. Gracie pours me an ale before I can ask for one.

"Where's Kit?"

"He's feeling poorly," she says. "Came down with fever

and chills sudden-like – gone to sleep it off."

I try not to look disappointed.

"Go up and see how he is," she adds.

Maybe I will, I think. My heart beats faster at the thought.

Felicity's here again. Another woman, striking – no, beautiful – sits opposite her, dressed for a fancier establishment than the Lugger. She has long pale hair, and wears a dark dress with a plunging neckline.

I carry my ale upstairs to knock at the door to Kit's room, but I hear nothing. When I try the handle it opens, but he's not in. The room looks as it always does.

He's not down the hall in the washroom. I use the slip of hard soap, the peculiar kind Kit uses, to rinse my hands. Then I go back down. Mister Scarlet's back on the ground floor. I give him my sketch, and he beams.

"This is brilliant. Look at the detail. My girl, this could be a silverprint."

A silverprint is a perfect likeness captured with a Skøl contraption using light, chemicals, fancy paper. I flush. No one has really valued my drawings apart from Kit, Ruzi and Zako – not since I was little.

"I'm relieved you like it."

"Of course. Missus S will love it. Can't wait for the next two in the series… Your money is upstairs." He glances at the customers. "I'll get it in a minute."

"No rush!" I sit back down near the end of the bar with my half-drunk ale.

"They can say it as many times as they want! They're still wrong!"

I glance round. The conversation between Felicity and her companion has heated up.

Felicity says something quietly.

"Of course Glister feels the same way!" the fancy woman continues in a high, cold voice. "A humble background is not a crime. Only the fossils believe that."

Felicity answers, too low again for me to hear, but whatever she says has the other woman standing and pushing back her chair. She looks down her nose at Felicity, who seems unfazed. Then she storms out, coat over her arm.

She must be freezing in that dress, I think.

Felicity sees me looking and inclines her head slightly. I glance away, but it's too late. She's coming over.

She half smiles as she approaches and then chooses the stool beside me, folding her fountain pen into her little red book.

"How's your story coming on?" I ask, to be polite.

"Still in the interview-and-research phase. Speaking of – can I persuade you to talk to me?"

I hesitate, but not for long.

"You mentioned a fee?"

She smiles like the cat who got the cream. "I can give you fifty krunan for an interview. And buy you dinner sometime."

I almost agree immediately – then I think of Mister S

and his bargaining tactics. "What about sixty krunan and no dinner?"

She laughs. "I'm afraid I don't set the rates. It's my paper. I could go to fifty-five and a cheap meal."

"All right." I smile. "Dinner sounds great." Can't say I didn't try.

Gracie sidles up to us across the bar, and I ask her for another small ale.

"You can show me where's good to eat in Portcaye," the journalist goes on.

"Was that woman with you earlier part of your research?"

"Oh, her? Well, yes. She doesn't need my fifty krunan though! Small change to her. Didn't you recognize her?"

I shake my head.

"Goldie Reedstone herself. Of GR Locks – biggest security business in the New West. She and her brother, Glister, run the business out of the northwest quarter."

"The Skates?" It surprises me, a rich businesswoman operating out of the poorest district. GR Locks. I'm sure I've seen that name before – yes, they advertise in the *Portcaye Post*.

"That's the one. Thought you might know them. They say she and her brother are very friendly with the lower classes in their employ. Servants, repayers..."

"Well, I don't," I admit. "Perhaps Kit does." Kit knows more people in town than I do.

She lowers her voice. "Very successful for a pair as

young as they are – no surprise though, given their origins. You know who they are."

I frown, and she continues. "Call themselves Reedstone, but their mother was a Sting. Of the Sting Elektric Company." Her eyebrows raise meaningfully.

"Oh." My blood chills. Of course I know *them*. The famous – or infamous – Sting Elektric. They made a fortune pioneering elektric lighting in Skøland before moving into weaponry: the lethal guns and cruel elektric prods used in the Cull. The kind the branders still carry to punish and kill.

"The Stings are still going at their own line of work, of course. Their latest inventions are going to be part of the Hexagon showcase as well," Felicity contends.

My stomach roils. More elektric inventions like guns and prods? Do they need more?

Gracie appears and slides over the ale I asked for. "Working again?" she asks Felicity. "How did your meeting go?"

"Not well. Goldie Reedstone didn't appreciate my questions about her controversial hiring practices." She grins. "It's all right though. You know when you're after one thing and something better comes along?" She winks at me.

I don't know anything about that. Quite the opposite.

That's when I hear a commotion in the kitchen.

Renny's voice, overloud. "What's going on?" Something's wrong.

12

no one sees me

Cold air gushes from the front as two ledhunds pour in, white tornadoes, all muscle and teeth, followed by a pair of branders.

Caruq uncurls himself and raises a lip.

My heart stutters. *Zako. Run, run, run, run.*

A third firebrand exits the kitchen and stalks past the bar.

I feel utterly rooted to the spot, my jaw clenched in terror.

This is it, I think. *They've found out Zako is here…*

The fire crackles half a room away. Everyone's gone quiet.

I can hear the paws of the strange ledhunds, thudding up to the mezzanine. I begin to unfreeze as I realize. The branders aren't headed up to Zako's hideout.

The hounds stand to attention beside a table near one of

the mezzanine windows, noses pointing to a middle-aged Skøl couple sitting thigh to thigh, nursing half-finished ales and looking terrified.

They're not here for Zako. They're here for someone else. I try to keep the relief from my face, to keep my mask of horror in place.

"Victor Gusting?" says the firebrand who came from the kitchen. He's not that loud, but the whole place has fallen so silent we could hear a mouse chewing cheese.

"Yes," says Victor Gusting.

"You have to come with us."

"Please," says the woman beside Victor Gusting. Even from here I see how pale both their faces are.

"Too long defaulted, I'm afraid, Victor. No payments since the end of last Twelvemonth. We have to take you in. You've had our notice, haven't you? You know the penalty, Mister Gusting."

"I need more time," says Victor. He's trying for stoic calm, but there's a tremor in his voice.

"Stand up, please."

Victor doesn't stand. It's like he can't.

They get his feet under him and march him down the mezzanine steps and out of the door. He barely resists. The woman follows, sobbing. The ledhunds flow behind.

There's a beat, and then the hum of voices rises again. Beside me, Felicity Greave shivers at the new blast of cold air. I see Mister S going up the proprietors' stairs. He looks worn and grey.

Gracie gives a weary sigh and Renny puts an arm around her. "Poor Victor," she whispers.

"Did you know them?" Felicity asks her softly.

Gracie looks a little teary. "Not really. They used to come in more often, last summer. Then they … stopped."

"We thought they'd moved away or … something, didn't we?" Gracie says to Renny. "I didn't realize he was a Gusting. That explains it."

"Me neither." Renny shakes her head sadly. "It's not easy for them."

Felicity nods along, but I don't follow.

"It's not easy for who?" I ask. My voice sounds too loud, shock loosening my tongue.

"His name, Gusting, it means he's a Sting Trust baby," Gracie explains. "You've not heard of it?"

I shake my head.

"It means the Sting Trust charity paid for his childhood," Renny adds in a hushed tone. "They all take the same last name, the charity babies."

"It's from Genie and Urbane Sting," Felicity jumps in. "G and U Sting – they founded the Trust. It pays for babies who would otherwise be culled – ones whose parents can't afford their life payments."

I frown. "The same Stings as in Sting Elektric that makes guns to kill people? They run a charitable trust paying for children's lives?"

"The Stings made their million in lighting, didn't they?" Renny stacks a few glasses at the bar. "And they wanted to give back to the community, so it goes. They set up the Trust back then."

"Now, of course, they make deadly weapons *and* rescue orphans. Good combination," Felicity adds drily.

"Though even the Trust has all sorts of conditions attached," Gracie continues. "They'll only pay up till age fourteen, then you're on your own..."

"But then something's better than nothing," Renny adds in her soothing voice.

Felicity sighs. "So they say. I wonder if old Genie and Urbane would do it again if they knew. It's been a bit of a failed experiment. Long and short of it is – the kids grow up and fall by the wayside, or get rounded up like Victor there. Funding them to have childhoods just delays the inevitable. People don't want to employ a Gusting."

For a moment I almost ask why, but I'm a repayer. I already know. They don't think I've earned the air I breathe either.

Thea's wounds. What a life.

"Poor Victor," Renny mutters.

"Why did they come here?" I finally ask. *Why not run? Hide? Fight?* "On his last night of freedom? He must have known..."

"I'm sure they just fancied one last drink together, reliving happier times," Felicity suggests.

Happier times. All the times with this lot are horrific. I realize I'm shaking. Why do they allow this? Why does no one scream or roar or run? How is it always so calm and bloodless? Tears and treacle when it should be fire and fury.

I drain my drink and stand.

"I should get moving." The clock above the bar shows it's only half an hour to curfew.

I want to visit Zako, but I know how unwise it would be, sneaking up there tonight, with everyone on edge and the branders just here. I'll get my money from Mister S another night.

I slip outside.

The air clears my head. The clouds are small and silver, scudding fast. It's cold, but not awfully.

I can't stop seeing them marching Victor Gusting away, hearing the woman's cool voice. *Please.*

I walk meaninglessly to block it out, circle back round the Lugger and into its courtyard. I plonk down on the round bench skirting the Makaia plane tree.

Only muffled sounds reach me here. Clouds canter through the square of sky framed by the yard walls and fractured by tree branches starting to bud. *Run, run.* I count them escaping.

I need to go, I think. *Need to make curfew.*

I close my eyes, just for a minute.

Sometime later I wake, chilled through. Gracie and Renny are locking the kitchen door behind them. The tavern noises and lights have faded.

It must be past closing time, gone eleven. I'm such an idiot. I didn't realize how sapped I was by the long days with the kine, the long evenings drawing and all the hours upon hours worrying about Zako.

I really thought that when those branders came for Victor Gusting they were here for Zako. I thought it was all over.

Gracie and Renny walk away, holding hands, talking softly. I've never held someone's hand – held hands with someone I love – not like that. They don't see me. I'm part of the bench, part of the tree.

I'm getting up, hip protesting wildly, when I hear the kitchen door behind me click open again. I stop, still as a statue, and watch.

A small wraith heads to the arched exit, swamped in a hooded coat, scuffing a too-large pair of boots. He doesn't see me in the shadows – until I hiss at him.

"Zako!"

To his credit, he doesn't make a peep, though he looks more than a little put out. His harvest-moon eyes stare, mute and questioning. I drag him over to stand by the bench in its pool of darkness.

"What are you doing?" I whisper. "Are you mad, Zako? There's branders everywhere tonight."

He looks at me angrily. "Yes," he says. "I've gone mad! Mad from being stuck inside. They gave me marbles! I'm not a baby. I'm going out for a walk."

"It's only been a week!"

He won't look at me, turning his scowl up to the stars.

"I know it's h—"

"Did you see that?" he interrupts. "A shooting star!"

His scowl dissolves, then comes back in force. "I can't see the sky from in there."

Well, you can't see the sky if you're dead either.

I take a deep breath. "Shooting stars are good luck, Zako. Make a wish."

"I wish I could do something instead of sitting around waiting."

"Venor wants you dead," I snap.

Zako shoots me a raised eyebrow. "No shit." He walks on.

I cling to his arm as we quit the relative safety of the Lugger courtyard for the alley beyond. Zako's faster than me, even in his ill-fitting boots.

"No, Zako, he *needs* you dead. He wanted you dead back on the estate." The more I think about it, the stranger that seems. Venor's always been unpleasant, but he never seemed murderous. "Why did he go for you like that? He accused you of *spying* on him, didn't he?"

"Yeah. I wasn't though! I was only playing cards with Devotion."

I'm thinking furiously now. The answer to this must lie in what happened that night. What Zako saw or heard – or what Venor *thought* he saw or heard. "No, of course not – but did you see something by accident? Hear something? "

Zako shrugs. "Me and Devotion heard him fighting with Missus Venor."

"Fighting? Did he hit her?"

"No. He shouted and threw things."

"Shouted about what?"

"Couldn't hear much." He goes silent, remembering. "She said he was *an ass*. He said she was a *frigid bitch*... What's *frigid*?"

"Cold ... cold-hearted. Anything else?"

He sighs. "I don't know, Mora. She said something like she never would have married him if she knew and he knew what she knew and ... ugh. They went round in these stupid circles."

"She wouldn't have married him if she knew what?"

Zako scowls. "What a brickhead he is, probably."

"Can't you remember anything else about their argument?" He's silent again, and I lose my temper. "Think, Zako!"

Zako pouts, frustration coming off him in waves. "I can't think with you asking me things over and over! I don't want to remember. It's awful. You know it's awful!" Then he pulls his arm out of mine and actually runs off, fast as anything even in those boots. I follow him, stuttering, out to Belor Way, but he's gone.

I can't chase him. I can't keep up.

I pushed him too far. Of course remembering that night terrifies him. But I'm desperate to *know*. Zako overheard something important – he must have – even if he didn't realize it.

I make my own careful way home, hood up, sticking to the shadows. Once I think I see branders in the distance, but no one sees me.

13

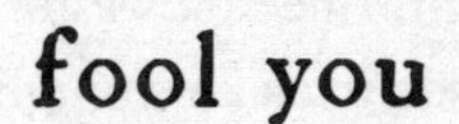

fool you

The following day we spend all afternoon packing up and delivering another large batch of coloured-glass panes to the Hexagon Hall site. They've shortened our break times so we can keep to schedule. The workers aren't best pleased – but when we return to the Works sweating and aching, Wagsen couldn't care less.

"We've said we'll deliver their bloody glass palace, and we will!" he rants. "*Green's Glassworks delivers*!" His office door slams.

It's gone six when I click the gate shut. The wind is chilly.

Felicity Greave's waiting for me. Of course. She's buying me dinner.

"So, what do repayers do of an evening?" She falls into step beside me, the latest edition of the *Portcaye Post* tucked under one sinewy arm. She looks strong, I think, for a journalist.

"Not much by the time curfew rolls around."

"But you're still free for that interview with me tonight?"

"Free?" I snort.

"Fifty-krunan fee, remember!"

"Fifty-five!" I smile.

"Crawley's, then?" It's a chip shop near the river, an easy distance from the Glassworks.

"I'm filthy though. I need a wash."

"Oh, nonsense; you're clean enough." She squints at me with a grin dimpling her cheeks. "We'll sit outside. It's not that cold today." She shifts the *Portcaye Post* to her other side and hooks an elbow through mine.

I'm not used to Skøl touching me, but I like her a little more for it – she's not disgusted by the dirt glued to my sweaty face, or the colour of my face, or the smell of kine on my ragged work clothes. How much harm can it really do?

"I saw you earlier with those draught kine," she tells me. "How can a small thing like you control such monsters?"

I'm not that small. I'm a few inches shorter than her, but built more generously. "Where did you see me? I didn't see you."

"By the Hexagon Hall site. It's coming along, isn't it? That glass roof will look beautiful."

"Suppose so," I tell her.

"Glass and metal will build the future," she enthuses. "Not this old-fashioned stone." She shoots me a sideways look. "I read it in the *Gazette*, so it must be true."

I get a piece of battered white fish and a scoop of chips, heavily salted and vinegared. She orders a vast basket of crabs, making short work of cracking their bright backs open and sucking the flesh from their claws.

"Try some!" she urges, passing me an opened body.

"Oh, that's all right. I've plenty to be getting on with." I slow down so she won't offer again. They look too pretty, soft flesh under shiny armour.

"You grew up here?" she asks.

"Nearby." I have to remind myself she's working. This isn't a social engagement. But I'm curious about her and ask a question of my own.

"What's it like where you're from?" I tilt my head at her. "Rundvaer."

"Beautiful." She sighs. "Very clean. Better than Portcaye. Rundvaer's on the coast too. The sun sets over the ocean, just like here. Have you ever seen a map of Skøland?"

"Oh, yes. Is it on the bit that hangs down?"

"The Claw." She nods, waving one of her crabs with a smile. Its orange matches the amber ring on her finger. "There's nowhere like Rundvaer. Five times the size of this place. The buildings are…" She gestures to indicate perfection. "Mansions everywhere. No glass rooftops, mind you! Still, the high governor's house would swallow the Life Registry three times over. It's got the most gorgeous plaza."

"Is it just the high governor and her family living there?"

She wiggles her head – yes and no. "Two of her close council live on the premises. They divide their time between Rundvaer and their county seats."

"So when Venor assumes the governorship of the New Western Counties…"

"Yes?"

"He'll be like a deputy to the high governor herself, right?"

"Exactly."

"Will he have to travel to Skøland?"

"Not often."

Of course not. I stuff a few chips into my mouth. That would be much too lucky.

"Is the food in Rundvaer like this?" I ask.

"Oh no. I love this, but the food back home is more sophisticated." She wipes her mouth before diving straight back to another crab. "I miss it more than anything."

"I miss our food."

"Do you?" Her voice goes soft. "What was it like?"

"Our pa made flatbreads." I stop. Why should I tell her? But the words tumble out. "He let me roll them out before he fried them, then clapped them to make them flaky… They were a bit crispy on the outside. Perfect with this baked stew our ma made – full of spices – a kind of crust round the edges. I'd come home from school and smell it halfway down the road. I don't know how she did it."

"That sounds divine."

She asks me how I came to be driving draught kine for

the Glassworks. It's true they didn't start me there. I was put to work indoors the minute I arrived, inducted into ash processing the first week.

You! Shift those crates over there! The place was full of noise. Heat like a foundry, never below sweltering. There were endless huge furnaces and heavy sacks to drag up and down levels.

I envied Ruzi's outdoor job. I saw him sometimes when I went to the yard to help bag the hauls – piles of wood ash from the houses in town, cartloads of seaweed from the bay. Sometimes limestone blocks. Often just sand.

Not two months after my move, the Works' driver left for a better job without giving notice. I went to the manager, Mister Wagsen, as soon as I heard.

"Let me drive the deliverers."

Wagsen was sceptical. "It's specialized work. You aren't strong enough."

"I've been working with kine for years. I know how to build an understanding with them. It's not about strength with a draught kine. No driver's stronger than one of them."

"And he gave you the job, just like that?" Felicity asks now.

"On a trial basis."

"You must have done well." She seems impressed.

"Well, kine are less hard work than people." Like most jokes, there's a grain of truth there.

She asks what I do on Endweeks. I tell her about taking Clomper and Caney to stretch their legs. Sometimes I visit the market for snacks or soap. More often the seafront. I don't mention my drawings. I tell her I clean the kitchen in Opal Alley – though Ruzi does most of the cleaning now, if I'm honest.

"And Ruzi looks out for you?" she asks.

"I guess." *We help each other*, I think.

When he got to see Zako the other day, that made him happy – but when I moved in, he changed his ways then too. No more papers lying around. No more mould. At first I thought it was because he was embarrassed about the state I found him living in. Now I think he was partly like that because he was depressed – too alone.

Felicity's finished her huge basket of crabs. Empty shells lie scattered like an explosion of weird crockery. Her bony fingers sweep them back into the basket.

"Shall we have a drink at the Lugger?"

"I'm tired – my monthlies. Plus I've a few errands to run before curfew," I tell her. It's mostly true.

"It's so early! I'll buy you a fizzy juice here, then – does wonders for cramps." She waves the attendant over and orders, before dropping her voice. "Listen. I know you were friends with that boy who disappeared."

"Zako?" My heart thunders, spooked. I will my clenched jaw to relax, my mouth to droop sadly for my poor lost friend.

"That's the one." She stares into the distance, forehead puckered. "Something strange about that. Everyone says the boy was meek as a lamb – but he beat the Magistrate almost to death. Anyway, it's a big story." She glances at me, searching for a reaction. I keep my expression neutral. "You know Venor too, I suppose."

"I lived on the farm next door to his country residence," I say cautiously. "I ran into Venor a few times. Zako was a sweet boy."

"Was? You think…" Her voice tails off sympathetically.

"He disappeared in a snowstorm with nowhere to go." I let my frustration over Zako's current situation bleed through, pretend I'm struggling to hold back tears.

"The magistrate seems convinced he's alive. Desperate to find him."

"I saw the bounty he's offering… Ten thousand's a lot, don't you think?" I venture. I may as well do some of my own digging. Felicity has connections – she might know something I don't.

"Well…" Felicity hums to herself. "I suppose he did attack the soon-to-be governor of the whole New West. In a few months Venor will be second only to Clarion Lovemore herself! It's a serious crime. They need to make an example of him."

"I suppose," I sigh.

"You're right though," Felicity says, twisting her ring. "It's a lot of money to find one scrap of a boy. I do wonder…"

She keeps fidgeting with her ring. The amber's a smooth oval, set in an ornate golden band. It's Xan jewellery, or it used to be. The Xan in southern Makaia were famous for trading in amber. They got it from the Badlands. Kit says they cursed the jewels destined for Crozoni buyers. I wonder if hers has a curse on it.

"How'd you come by that beautiful ring?" I ask.

Felicity looks startled. "It was a gift," she says finally, her voice unusually quiet. "From a man I was rather taken with, five years back."

"What happened?"

"He went to a better place." That's what they say when someone dies.

"I'm sorry."

I wait for her to say more.

"Ah, finally." Her eyes roll, but she forces a smile as the shopkeeper brings our juice, pink and sparkling.

Sweet bursts of rose fizz across my tongue, followed by a distinct tang – lemon. "This is lovely," I hear myself saying, though the fizz is doing strange things to my nose.

"Isn't it?"

I wipe a smudge off my glass.

"Grief never put clothes on your back," she says with a sniff.

A Skøl saying. Pretty sure we never had a Crozoni equivalent of that one.

"So – I'm interested to know... What was life like for Zako, working for the Venors?" Felicity says.

"That's hardly *Gazette* material." I frown. "No one cares how we're treated."

She considers me. "Don't they?"

"Fine," I say. "If you must know, Venor treated Zako worse than an animal. He was beaten and underfed. Will you put that in your article?"

She just asks, "Did anyone ever treat you like that?"

"Some boys almost killed me. Only days ago."

"Really? Little boys?"

"Not little – sixteen or so. There were four of them. First they tried to… Who knows what they thought they were about? Told them I was diseased, so they threw me into the river. Water was freezing. I could've died."

She looks startled. "Did no one see?"

"It was dark."

"What, after curfew?"

"Half an hour before."

"Well." She grimaces. "That's just awful. Thank goodness you didn't drown." Her expression hardens. "I could write about it, but they wouldn't print it, I'm afraid. It's not big enough. It's not that people don't care. Of course it's awful, but repayers' tales don't sell papers."

Zako's only newsworthy because he tried to kill a prominent Skøl. A Skøl trying to kill a Crozoni is totally unremarkable.

Felicity changes topic. "Your young man seems very nice." She means Kit. What can I say?

"He is very nice." My face is burning. It's not even a lie.

"Gracie told me about the pair of you. She's very invested. Says Kit's been off out a lot lately though. No time for you."

Of course Felicity thinks I should know all of Kit's secrets.

"I don't pry into his private life."

"I thought you were his private life!"

I laugh as though I don't care. "Just one slice." She gives me a sympathetic look. Maybe I even convince her.

I drain the last of my fizzy juice.

"Thank you for a delicious dinner, Felicity." I smile. "But I really should go if I'm to abide by the curfew."

"Yes, of course," she agrees. "It's getting chilly again, isn't it?"

She reaches into a pocket, and I think of my fifty-five-krunan fee. She draws out her cigarette case.

"Would you like one?"

"No, thank you. Just the fee?"

She looks momentarily puzzled. "Oh, of course." She fishes a pouch from another pocket and counts out fifty-five krunan.

I leave her sitting there, wreathed in cigarette smoke and staring at the river.

I *am* going to the Lugger, just not with Felicity, and not for a drink. Kit's in a foul mood when I find him there. He won't tell me where he was last night.

"Were you working that second job – the factory one?"

"No."

"Gracie said you had a fever."

"I wasn't that sick. I went out. Sometimes I go out.

Every night pulling pints and listening to thick pricks shooting their mouths off… I needed a break."

I can't help feeling stung, and my cheeks burn.

"Sure. Course. Not prying. Just thought maybe you had a new lead or something – you know, for Zako."

"We don't need more leads. We need money," he reminds me curtly.

For once I don't feel useless. "Well – I got fifty-five krunan out of Felicity tonight. And I finished one of the drawings for Mister S yesterday. I know it's not enough…"

Kit's mood lifts a fraction. "He showed me the drawing. One of your best. He was telling everyone in the bar about this great new artist he's discovered. We'll get it framed and up in here. I bet you'll get some commissions." He winks. "People like their hounds painted and all sorts."

While he's in a better mood, I tell him about last night, with Zako. Not his midnight wanderings – that will just make him angry, and no wonder – but my theory.

"I think Zako overheard something that afternoon, something he shouldn't have," I say. "Something Venor badly doesn't want getting out."

This gets Kit's attention. I can see his mind flitting to all sorts of dark places.

"It would explain why the bounty is so high," I go on. "Venor is terrified he's out there, knowing whatever it is he knows. Although Felicity thinks the bounty's reasonable for a soon-to-be governor."

"Well, she's from Rundvaer – they're all rich as syrup pudding over there."

I watch him. Does this mean he thinks I'm on to something?

"I'll talk to Zak later," he promises. "Will you come after work tomorrow?"

"Sure."

At least he's not avoiding me, but he doesn't mention our kiss.

But why would he? It was just for cover.

I've been a fool. I've read too much into a kiss that was all for show. *Kiss a fool if you will, but don't let a kiss fool you.*

14

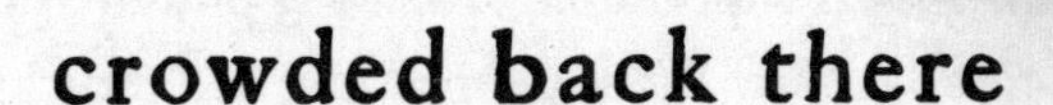

crowded back there

Felicity Greave's eating alone again when I arrive the next evening. She tears her slice of bread to bits, using them to swipe the bottom of her stew bowl clean. She waves me over enthusiastically when she spots me.

"Hmm, goodness –" she licks two fingers – "I'm going to get fat staying here!"

"Not at all!" I smile, though I think she could stand to put on some weight – she's sinewy-strong, but almost as bony as Zako.

"I talked to the magistrate today," she tells me.

"How is he feeling?" I ask, hoping for a relapse.

As though she knows what I'm thinking, she says, "Heartier than ever. Very pleased with himself too. He's bought a massive mansion in the Steeps. Calling it Lovemore, can you believe it?" She grimaces. "I went in – he's fixing it up. His wife's staying at the country estate."

"So he wants to live in town now?" On our doorsteps. Panic tightens my chest. How many months before we can spirit Zako away – and under the very nose of his pursuer?

"He says he needs to be more present at the Registry," Felicity says. "Inspire greater dedication in the staff."

"Hence buying a mansion and naming it after his boss?"

She smirks. "I suppose he didn't get picked as the first governor of the New West without a bit of bootlicking. He says the Registry needs an overhaul. There are rumours, apparently – papers and things going missing. He wants a squeaky-clean town before Lovemore gets here."

"Right," I say. "I haven't heard anything about missing papers – I thought the Registry was iron-clad – but then I wouldn't know."

"He's put in some new vault doors. Ultra secure, fireproof – all that. And have you heard about the capture of the Artist?"

I hesitate. "I did hear a rumour," I say.

"Goodness me! Venor wouldn't stop bragging. It's a feather in his cap and no denying it."

"What's he like?" I ask curiously. "To you, I mean." I know what Venor's like to those in his power.

"I'd say … a mixture of paranoid and self-assured," Felicity says. Then her expression turns grim. "Have you heard what Venor is planning for the Artist?"

"No."

She hesitates, as though she might tell me, then tosses

her plait back. "You shouldn't be hearing it from me. It'll be all the news by Skivårnat!"

"What will?"

She taps the side of her nose with one finger, then gets up.

"Look at the time. I've an appointment to keep!" She waves at me. "See you soon, Mora. It's nice to chat. I'm too used to my own company."

I'm not sure that was a chat – a one-sided one if so – but she's let slip something interesting. Our favourite magistrate has plans for the Artist, and they've shocked even Felicity.

Kit's not in the kitchen for once. I find him in his room, sprawled over the covers. My knock has woken him up. I'm suddenly worried he is poorly after all. Perhaps that's why he was in such a mood last night.

I'm at his side before I can overthink.

"Are you unwell?" His forehead's hotter than my hand, but most things are. His eyes shine with surprise in the dim light.

"Just tired." He sits up.

"Is it that extra factory work?"

"What? Oh. No. I'm fine. It's just been busy here – getting ready for the holiday."

I know the preparations for Skivårnat are intense. It's the Skøl's spring equinox festival – their main holiday. They go mad about it for a month before.

He cradles his head in his hands, fingers splayed.

I remember those fingers at my neck. Kisses melting me like the spring thaw. I'm the silly flower that popped open too early.

"I talked to Zako," he says, releasing his head and getting up to light the lantern on his desk. He splays a small pile of books across it.

I realize with a wave of excitement they're not Skøl. Most look Crozoni, though Crozoni books were burned en masse in the Cull.

I recognize a collection of recipes we had at home. Memories of it pierce me with frightening force. I can see Pa laughing, white flour on his brown hands, a cloud of it rising from a bowl. Enca and Eben clamouring to stir; *my turn, my turn now.*

Kit selects a small cloth-bound book, its script in Xan. Didn't see many of those around even before the Skøl came. I can't imagine where he found it. He flips it open to a picture that looks like a stubby, plaited whip, and taps it.

"What's that?" I ask.

"Prayer grass."

I'm none the wiser. I think of the stories about Xan witches weaving dolls from grass and casting dark magic.

"Well, we called it prayer grass," he goes on. "The Skøl use it too. They put it in schinn when it's done distilling."

"Why are we reading about it?"

"If you burn prayer grass before you sleep, breathe in the smoke and think of a time you'd like to relive, the memories come back – in your dreams." He mimes wafting smoke to his face. "That's what it says here."

"What's this book about?"

"Salar – Xan medicine. Herbal tonics, dressings to treat scars…" He turns to look at me, his pupils huge, small lanterns dancing in each.

"So burning this grass could help Zako remember what he overheard?"

"Could do. Xan medicine worked for my people for years. Can't hurt to try."

My breath trembles. Memory can be more painful than just about anything. But I know Zako will like this plan. It's better than sitting around waiting to be killed.

"How do we get hold of it?" I ask.

"I know a man who might have some," says Kit. "I'll go first thing tomorrow."

I nod. "All right. If Zako's keen, then let's do it. I'm sure he heard something important."

He flips the book closed, then gestures at the others still fanned across his desk. "You want any of these?"

"To … to read?"

"No, to stand on so you can reach high shelves." He laughs and shoots me an *of course to read* face. I feel a flicker of relief to see his warmth return.

"I can reach all the shelves already, thank you."

"Take some anyway. But don't wave them around – black market and all that."

"If they catch me, I'll say I bought them for kindling."

I flutter the thin pages of one of the novels and bring it to my nose. "I love this booky smell."

"Glue and ink and old dead trees?"

"Divine." I grin. "Thank you."

He gives me a look I can't interpret. "My pleasure."

When I get back to Opal Alley I make dinner for me and Ruzi. He's changed since Zako's escape. Before, we ate alone, mostly. Sometimes together in silence. To be honest, we still mostly stick to silence, but he's softer. Like he actually wants to sit with me in the kitchen eating charred sweet potatoes.

I show him the books I've borrowed from Kit.

"I've read this one," he splutters, surprised by the Crozoni adventure novel. "Wonder how Zako's getting on with his *Blenny and Tornado*."

"*Tornelius*. I've not had a chance to see him." I haven't told Ruzi about Zako's nighttime wandering the night before last either, or our plan to get him prayer grass.

"And how are you?" he asks his bowl of dwindling potatoes.

What does he mean, how am I? I see him every day. "I'm fine, Ruzi. You know."

He grunts and spears a charred mouthful. "Your mother was always *fine* too."

Mother... Ruzi always gets that weird, closed-off face when he mentions her. I've never asked how he and my mother became friends.

Pa used to tense up around Ruzi. He never came with

Ma and me to Ruzi's shop. But I remember the two of them at her funeral, two years before the Cull, hugging each other and crying.

At least she got a funeral.

"You and Ma..." *How can I ask?* "You were close?"

He meets my gaze, though I know he's not one for eye contact. "Once upon a time." He looks away again, shovelling the last of his potatoes down. Then he stands up from our small table, retreating. "Night, Mora," he says.

There's something I want to ask him, something half formed, but it sticks in my throat. I push my questions to the back of my mind. It's very crowded back there.

15

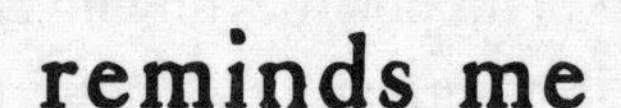

reminds me

Kit might be the bees knees at getting hold of banned books, but it's over two weeks later – the day before Skivårnat Eve – before he says he's found a peddler who'll bring him prayer grass on Skivårnat Day. Apparently it's out of season.

Zako assures me he's not going out for walks any more. I should bloody well hope not, given Venor's gone and ratcheted up the already nauseatingly large bounty – and added an open condition.

₭ 20,000 will be paid by the Life Registry for the apprehension of Taler – DEAD OR ALIVE, the new notices read.

Dead or alive.

I can only thank my lucky stars we've scraped by without any more attention on the Scarlets.

The branders still pop up, following me and Ruzi occasionally, but they're slack about it. They're starting to think that they were wrong about Zako coming to find us.

Kit and I are still saving coin. I finished the other two lugger drawings for Mister S, and he paid forty each, true to his word. He's having them framed to hang in the mezzanine. Kit's been working nights at the factory in the Skates when he can, between all the extra preparations they've had on at the Lugger with Skivårnat on its way.

"What do you do there?" I asked one evening, and he shrugged.

"Stacking, unloading. Boring."

I should have asked more, but I let it lie, ignoring the strange feeling in my gut. Skivårnat Eve falls in the third week of Thirdmonth. Ordinary years, the glassworkers have both the eve and the day off, but this year's different. The Works stays open today and only closes on Skivårnat itself. Mister Wagsen is too worried about the special glass they commissioned for the Hexagon Hall roof falling behind schedule.

I know tonight will be busy as anything at the Lugger too. They're hosting guests in every room and opening up the private meeting rooms on the first floor for the dining parties – lunch and dinner – popular on Skivårnat Eve. Skivårnat Day is busy too, but nowhere near as bad – plus I'll be off work – so I told Kit and Zako I'd see them both then. I will see the Scarlets too. They've been so kind to us, I know. And there's no way to repay them.

But when I finish work, I suddenly think of something I can do.

The Skøl exchange gifts on Skivårnat Eve. It's a bit like a harvest-time tradition we had – to give books before the Cutter Moon festival. So I stay up late working on a small sketch for them – something personal this time. I can see the subjects clearly in my mind's eye – the way they lean a little together; the small, everyday smiles – and I draw it.

I'll take it to them now. I shouldn't be out after curfew, but Ruzi's asleep, and I'm sure the branders will be too busy to worry about me tonight.

Of course I'd be wrong. I'm still a good ten minutes from the Lugger when I round a bend to see a pair of branders approaching. I duck back the way I came, but that only looks suspicious.

"Who's there?" I hear one call.

I'm in a narrow passage. I start to stumble down it.

The clomp of hard-soled boots grows louder behind me. One of their lanterns flings my shadow out miles in front and I force my pace to slow to hide the stiffness in my walk – it's too telltale.

When a large hand grabs my shoulder, I don't turn. I dodge towards his other hand and butt the lantern he's carrying with my forehead, hard.

A little too hard, perhaps. I'm seeing stars, but his lantern drops, sending glass tinkling around our feet and ragleaf fuel bursting, *whoomph*, into flames. I get slightly more than I bargained for when his trouser hem catches alight, but it certainly gives him pause. I take off as he screams obscenities, batting at his leg in a deranged dance. I can hear his partner coming up behind, actually laughing, low and mean.

I pray they're too absorbed by the accidental flames to notice the odd way I run. Until I make the corner, I'm an easy target for one of their guns – but no shot comes.

I pivot up the cross street then into another turning, lungs heaving. My left ankle's twisted, but it's a small pain.

I've lost them, but I feel foolish for risking a fine or worse – and now I've messed up my ankle and have to take the dog-leg route round to reach the Lugger.

They've closed by the time I get there. It's still Skivårnat Eve, but not for much longer. I go in through the courtyard.

"You just missed Mister S," Gracie tells me. She has her back to me in the kitchen, packing things away. I spot Renny through the doorway, wiping down the bar. "And Kit might have gone out. I'm not sure."

"I'll check his room." I can leave the drawing with him. At least it won't be a wasted trip.

Gracie turns and sees me. "Hold on! What happened there?"

My forehead has been stinging since the run-in with the brander. I reach a hand to it that comes away bloodied.

"Oh. Is it bad? I slipped on some rubbish and fell," I tell her lamely.

She passes me a polished platter and I look at my

reflection in the centre of it. There's a shallow cut on my eyebrow from head-butting the lantern. It doesn't look great. Gracie helps me clean it up, and I hide it behind my hair.

"Why don't you wait down here for Kit? You've had a shock. Have a hot drink. Sure he'll be along soon. Doing anything special for Skivårnat tomorrow?"

"I'm going to see the lights with Ruzi."

For the past four years, they've decorated the elektric lanterns all down Rafmagis Way with elaborate covers for Skivårnat, fashioned by the blowers at the Glassworks. They go up a week before the day, but are taken down promptly the next morning.

"Oh – we went last night. They're so lovely."

"I've never been – nor Ruzi."

"How is your old man?"

He's only forty-seven, I think. "Ruzi's fine."

She barely pauses for breath between questions. "What do you think of our reporter, then?" She chuckles. "Bit nosy, isn't she? Our Felicity Greave."

I bite my lip. Pots and kettles. "What's she nosing for?" I ask.

"Well, you, for starters."

"Me?"

"Asked me about you and young Kit. She's a gossip. But I suppose that's her job, isn't it?"

"What did you tell her?"

"Not much."

I suspect otherwise.

Gracie continues, "You *are* together, right? You and him?" She's looking at me anxiously.

"Sort of. Well, we were. I'll go and find him now."

"Would you like a drink?" she says. "Stay for a chat."

"No, honestly." Why is Gracie offering me drinks? "I should let you get on," I say, and duck out quickly.

"Look, he didn't think you were coming tonight," she calls after me.

The doors of the Lugger are thick, heavy hardwood, all of them, but when I reach Kit's I hear soft voices behind it.

I knock once, and a beautiful Skøl woman pulls it open. Pale waves of hair spill around her shoulders. I recognize her immediately – the woman who met with Felicity Greave here in the Lugger that day near the end of Secondmonth. The relative of the Sting Elektric family.

Goldie Reedstone.

She's wearing another low-cut dress and jewelled earrings. Kit stands by the window, his face an angry mask. Neither of them say anything, though Kit's expression shifts slowly until his head's cocked at me like a question.

"Sorry," I whisper, out of reflex more than anything. I pull the door shut again, the handle slipping easily out of Goldie's hand.

I stand on the other side a moment, feeling very young and foolish. Then I'm hurtling down the stairs.

I write a short note on the back of the drawing I did for the Scarlets – *Happy Skivårnat, thank you, Mora* – and push it under their main door. When I try to make my exit through the kitchen, Gracie catches me.

"You all right?"

"Fine," I manage breathily. "Happy Skivårnat Eve."

She pats me on the back. The first time a Skøl's ever done that.

"Men aren't worth it," she reminds me.

16

going green

Even though the Glassworks is closed for Skivårnat, I go early to see to Clomper and Caney, since they've no pasture. I walk them like I do on Endweeks, to find a patch of grass, before we head back to the Works for brushing and mucking out.

Afterwards, I make my way to the glassy sea, leaving my hair unwrapped, letting the salt wind blow it wild.

It's early afternoon before I'm back at Opal Alley. I hear low voices when I reach the kitchen.

Kit should be working, so what's he doing here, talking to Ruzi?

"Mister Scarlet's agreed to Ruzi's proposal," he tells me. I blink at him.

"Custom's always slow after Skivårnat. It could really help," Kit adds.

Ruzi looks sheepish. "Ah. I didn't mention it to Mora yet. I'd need a guitar."

"I'll find one," Kit assures him, smiling at me like nothing's changed. Maybe nothing has, for him.

"What proposal?" I ask. "What are you both talking about?"

"Ruzi thought he'd try playing music at the Lugger. Bring in some extra coin – and a good excuse to see Zako."

I look at Ruzi. "I thought you didn't want to get in trouble singing Crozoni?"

"I can keep it instrumental. Or translate the songs to Skøl."

"No…" Kit encourages him. "Sing what you like. It's not banned. I think it's a great idea."

Ruzi's expression is dreamy. "I haven't played the guitar since … well…"

"It'll come back to you," I offer primly, making my excuses and drifting to my room, pretending a social call from Kit on one of the tavern's busiest days is unremarkable. I pull the door to and perch on the bed. More talking outside. I can't hear what they're saying. Then the door bangs.

Someone has left. The coward in me hopes it was Kit, but no, he's opening my door, bold as brass. I glare at him.

"I didn't know you kept such illustrious company," I snipe, trying to raise a poised, mature expression – though it's the last thing I feel. "A Skøl heiress, no less."

"Mor." Kit releases the door, and in two strides he's leaning on the table, peering down at me. "It's not what you think."

"So you're not friendly with some rich Skøl bitch who makes elektric guns and prods, then?" I try to smile, but my mouth's too dry. My lips stick to my teeth.

"That's her uncle's business. She makes locks. And we're not friends. We have a working relationship."

"A *what* relationship?"

"There's nothing between us. You don't have to believe everything Gracie and Renny say."

He pushes off the table and comes to sit beside me, finally meeting my eye. "I met Goldie years back – and her brother, Glister. They've a place in the Skates making locks, elektric ones. The guns and prods – that isn't them."

"Sting Elektric's their family though, isn't it? They sound like a lovely bunch. Don't suppose they bankrolled their niece and nephew's business with that dirty gun money?"

He pushes his hair away angrily. "They can't help who their family is. Besides… I didn't realize at first."

The penny drops. "This is your extra factory work – in the Skates?"

Kit averts his gaze. "Yes. In a manner of speaking."

"What do you mean? What are you doing for them?" I ask.

"Off the record, petty things to make quick coin. We need it, remember?"

I stare at him. "What petty things?"

"Picking locks, mostly."

Picking locks for locksmiths? "You mean stealing?"

"Sometimes."

My eyes drift to his long fingers. Something Felicity said clatters into my mind. *They say she and her brother are very friendly with the lower classes in their employ. Servants, repayers...*

"I don't get it. I thought the Stings were richer than kings of old. What have they got you stealing?"

"It's complicated. And the less you know, the better."

I think of him and Goldie standing in his room last night, looking stressed and upset. Not like young lovers enjoying themselves.

"Just tell me. Are you in trouble?"

"It's nothing I can't handle." He examines his hands. *He's lying.*

I look at his hands too, remembering them at my waist, in my hair, hoisting me on to a kine.

"Let me help."

"No." His voice is like flint. "The less you're mixed up with them the better."

"I want to help. You're making money. Ruzi's going to be singing for the Scarlets. I've sold three drawings because Mister S feels sorry for me."

He stands to look out of the window at the grey afternoon.

"He bought them because they're good. And they love that portrait you did for them."

"I'm glad."

"They're going to put it up on the wall behind the bar. Missus S likes it more than the luggers you did."

"Really?"

"She's been trying to get Mister S to sit for a silverprint for ages – he wouldn't do it. Now she has it."

"It's not a silverprint." It was just a drawing of Mister and Missus S together.

"It's better. You really captured them… They look happy." Kit examines the knife I've left on my desk – the one I use for sharpening pencils. Then he turns to me again.

"You know those old drawings you left behind in my room – the farm scenes and that?"

He means the ones Mister Heane brought the evening he told me Zako was in trouble. The ones the branders didn't bother stealing.

"I sold them to a trader. Found out last night he fetched good money for them."

"You did what?"

He spreads his hands. "I'm sorry. I should have asked, but you're always so down on your work. It was Mister S's idea. Soon as he saw them he was sure they'd sell. It's an amazing thing that you do. Knew you could make real money from it."

It's hard to imagine Skøl buying my drawings. Scenes from an ordinary farm. A few studies of flowers and insects. Settler life in their conquered lands. Little free-living things.

"You could've told me."

"I wanted it to be a nice surprise."

More like he wasn't confident they were worth anything and didn't want to disappoint me. I watch his hands disappear into his pockets. He's using this to turn the topic away from whatever it is he's doing with that Reedstone woman – of course he is – but I can't help being distracted.

"Look, Renny's going to skin me alive if I don't get back, let alone Mister S. Come with me. Let me give you your earnings. And you can see Zako."

"Is *she* there?"

"Goldie? Course not. Mor, I told you, it's business, not pleasure." *It's trouble, is what it is*, I think. But he's already got his boots back on, and I have to rush to keep up.

We're halfway back before the sun makes a break from the lead-grey cloud, pale gold crackling through sticky spring leaves, pocking Portcaye's stonework, spilling everywhere until even the gutters stream with light. It's busier than usual, people out and about for the holiday.

Mister Scarlet isn't in the kitchen. Gracie sees Kit and me arriving together and gives us an awkward smile, but Renny pounces. "Nice of you to show up, Mister Disappearing Act!"

"Two minutes," he assures her, catching my hand to pull me after him. Renny's exasperation is lost in the general din.

In his room, Kit fishes a pouch from his desk drawer for me. "Two hundred krunan."

"Thea's wounds!" I can't believe he sold my drawings for this much.

"A dozen more sales like that, plus what I'm earning – we'll have the fee for Zako's passage in no time."

I can't stop the grin spreading across my face. "Who said Zako's getting this? I'm buying jammy biscuits tonight."

Kit doesn't laugh. "Get your biscuits." He's back by the door. Like an afterthought, he adds, "You should rent a kine with some of that. Go riding, if you want."

I told him ages ago that riding the racing kine was the only thing I missed about working on the Heanes' farm. He's remembered.

"And get some more paper. Keep drawing. Try painting. It's a seller's market." He gestures at me with a grin. "The exotic art of the Crozoni savage. Island stock. Very rare, for discerning collectors… They love all that."

I join him in the doorway. He ruffles my windswept hair with one hand.

I realize I've left my hair wrap off. I feel for it in my pocket, but it's gone.

Kit waits while I collect myself.

"I like your hair like this," he says.

"Zako says it's terrible."

"What does Zako know?"

The ground floor smells of special Skivårnat spices. I pick my way through the heave and over to the far flight of stairs, up to the proprietors' wing.

Mister Scarlet's downstairs, and Missus Scarlet's dozing in her room. I find Zako playing cards.

I tell him about Ruzi perhaps playing music here one

Endweek, and then show him my windfall from the picture sales. None of it is news to him.

"Kit tells me everything."

"Then he'll have explained the plan to you."

He grows thoughtful, pulling his glasses off to polish them on his shirt.

"I don't want to go all the way to the Crozon Isles," he confesses. "I won't see you again, or Kit. Or – or Ruzi. I'm scared."

I try to reassure him, but I'm far from reassured myself. "You'll be safe there."

We sit on the floor in front of the fireplace. He teaches me how to weave the long fur around Caruq's ruff into a kind of plaited collar. I never thought to find myself styling a dog.

"I learned it from Devotion," he says.

That's about all that family taught him. They never bothered with his reading and writing.

"Missus Scarlet's reading me *Blenny and Tornelius*," he says, like he's read my mind. His eyes are shining. "Blenny got chased by sea wolves."

"Did he? He doesn't have much luck."

"And he thought they'd eat him."

"Oh my."

"Then Tornelius pounced on the biggest one, and Blenny scared them off with fire, and the wolves showed them where to find oysters."

"Really?"

Zako nods. He's alight, drunk on the story. "Is it true pearls come from oysters?"

"It is. Maybe you'll find one in Renny's oyster stew."

He gives me a look.

"You know, Kit used to dive for oysters," I say.

"He got a huge old one once, with a pearl. Won a prize."

"Really?"

"Really," I confirm. "Maybe don't bring it up though. He's – he's funny about oysters now."

"Why?"

I think of his battered face that day. "Oh, I don't know. I think he ate a bad one."

Kit finds a free moment to join us, the *Portcaye Post*'s Skivårnat evening special edition in one hand and a small glass jar in the other.

"Prayer grass," he says, shaking it. "It holds all the answers." His peddler has come through.

"It looks like powder," said Zako.

"It's been ground up. Should still work," Kit reasons.

Zako sniffs it cautiously, then passes it to me.

It smells like almond butter.

"You can burn it tonight, Zako," I say. "Come morning, we'll know whatever it is that's hiding in this big brain –" I tug on a tuft of his hair and pretend to peer into one of his ears – "that Venor doesn't want anyone to know!"

"All right," says Zako, but he looks uneasy. I don't

suppose there can be much about that day he truly wants a vivid reminder of.

"Zako, this ear wax needs cleaning out," I scold, to distract him.

I see the paper wedged under Kit's arm then and drag it out.

HEADS OFF TO THE GOVERNORS!

Portcaye Plans the Artist's Last Performance

—

Hexagon to Host Beheading

The criminal Blithe Even Ronbor, better known by his chosen moniker, **the Artist,** has been found guilty of Treason in a special Skivårnat-morning hearing.

He has been sentenced to Beheading and Display.

Speaking at his sentencing today, County Portcaye Life Registry Magistrate Valour Venor declared that Ronbor's sentence will be suspended until the Sixmonth, whereupon it will be carried out as part of the programme of festivities to take place at the new Hexagon Hall, marking Venor's transition to Governor of the New Western Counties.

"The Artist built his career in the public eye – and so it will conclude. He will paint his last before

High Governor Lovemore at Hexagon Hall," Venor promised. "With his own blood."

Signing off on Ronbor's sentence is expected to be Venor's first official act as Governor of the New West.

The Artist remains in incarceration at Portcaye Firebrand Station…

I shiver. So this was what Felicity meant. Venor is making a statement – under his governorship, treachery will not be tolerated.

"A public beheading. Painting the nice new hall with blood. Can't wait for the rest of the *programme of festivities*," Kit snipes.

Zako flips quietly through *Blenny and Tornelius*, examining its few illustrations and purposefully ignoring the *Portcaye Post*.

I think of the coloured-glass roof panels we've been hauling across town bit by bit and feel myself going green.

17

necks bared

"Mora! Happy Skivårnat!"

Dusk has gathered, and bags hang under Felicity Greave's eyes. She stands near the trough of young plants outside the Lugger.

"Same to you."

I try not to break my stride, but her outstretched arm stops me, brandishing a small case of long, slim cigarettes to match the one she's wafting. They're a luxury – hard to get in Portcaye outside the Mermens and the Steeps, where the wealthiest Skøl live.

"No, thank you."

She snaps the case shut with a graceful click. "You're quite friendly with the owners here, aren't you?"

"They've been very kind," I confess. "They're keen on my artworks. I draw on commission."

Her face relaxes into a warm smile. "You draw?

Now that is a surprise. Though as soon as I saw you, I thought … here's a girl with hidden depths." She gestures expansively.

"I've drawn the Scarlets three luggers. And I did them a portrait."

"That portrait was by you?" Her eyes widen. "Missus Scarlet was showing it around this morning, but I was in a rush. You're very talented."

"Would you like me to draw you something?" *She's rich enough to pay*, I think.

"I'd love that, if I can think of a decent subject. I've never been one for boats. Have you eaten? I need some company for dinner." Her smile seems embarrassed. "It's Skivårnat and I've no one."

I feel a little sorry for her. I wonder how often she has to pay people fifty krunan for company. "I wish I could, but I have to meet Ruzi and be back home before curfew."

"Some other time, then." She waves me off through a plume of smoke.

Last week I persuaded Ruzi to accompany me to the Mermens tonight, to see the Skivårnat lights on Rafmagis Way. The lights are elektric because it's the fanciest shopping street in town. Silversmiths, jewellers, confectioners, haberdashers, fancy delicatessens, exotic florists.

Ruzi's never gone to see the lantern covers. He said he wasn't interested, even if his co-workers made them. But I wore him down.

One end of Rafmagis Way runs near the Steeps. Felicity said Valour Venor's new town residence is there somewhere. I'm not keen on going near his neighbourhood, but I can't let that stop me. Besides, he won't know who I am or what I've done. It's literally years since he's seen me. I'd just be another dirty makkie to him.

I have cleaned up a bit though. Ruzi too. I've wrapped my hair but left a few decorative curls out. Ruzi's blacked his boots, trimmed his beard and put on the checked shirt he wore to see Zako that first time.

The lanterns are stunning – multicoloured twirls and orbs, like great glass bouquets or tangles of tentacled underwater creatures in iron cages. They stretch off down both sides of Rafmagis Way in two glowing lines. Skøl art is usually so cold and brutal, but not these. They're spontaneous and playful, showing off the workers' skill and sense of wonder.

"Well, I never," Ruzi murmurs. "Isn't this a sight, Mora?"

The whole strip heaves with a sea of Skøl. Twice I think I see the magistrate – both false alarms.

Ruzi's eyes are glazed over like a boy's.

"Look at this one!" he blurts, and we stop to admire a violet lantern, speckled with dark bobbles. "Like a big sea urchin!"

"Same colour as Kit's eyes," I note seriously. Ruzi chuckles at me.

"Wish I could capture this," I tell him.

"You should try drawing it." We're nearing the end. It's still a good hour to curfew. "Sell it as part of the celebrations." He glances at me. "You're good, Mora."

A few people have told me that recently, but for some reason it's Ruzi's praise that warms me.

"Shall we go through again?" I suggest.

"Definitely."

Ruzi weaves through the crowd ahead of me. I pause to watch the Skøl he passes. They give him a little more space than they need to.

Then, with a jolt, I see him. One of the boys from that night on the river path, drifting my way.

He's with family this time, not friends. A much younger sister, the spit of him, trots along with a smile that splits her face in half. His mother and father follow. Just another neatly turned-out family enjoying the lively beauty of the festival.

But suddenly I'm plucked from the glow of the lanterns, thrust back into the mud and the ice water and the panic.

He has everything, this boy, and still he had to make me smaller. My lungs go wild for air as anger stifles the old fear.

"Hello, again," my voice emerges. It sounds calm.

"Hello!" The little sister turns her bright face to me. Their parents aren't looking.

What am I doing? I almost bottle it. Ruzi hasn't noticed me lagging. He's still craning his neck to look at the lights.

"We don't want anything, thanks," the boy says. His gaze slides past me.

He has no idea who I am, I realize. That's when the anger takes over.

"I didn't want anything by the river, but that didn't stop you," I spit.

"What does she mean?" the little sister asks.

"Nothing." The boy tries to push past, but I hold my ground, though he's my height or taller. He's slim, but I know exactly how strong he is. I think I've bitten his arm. Can't say that about many people.

"Not so tough without your mates, are you?"

"Leave him alone!" The girl's voice catches her mother's attention.

"What do you think you're doing?" She pulls her daughter away from me. "Don't talk to my children!"

I should stop. Confronting a boy is one thing – an adult, that's rash. But my voice is barrelling ahead of my brain now.

"Your son attacked me – a few weeks ago."

People stop and look at the lights, pretending not to look at me.

"How ridiculous," scoffs the mother, tossing an expensive-looking scarf over her shoulder and giving the waistcoated father a look.

"He and his friend, Bunny –" I'm committed now, though my heart is hammering – "and two others, four of them, attacked me on the river path. I can describe all of them. Threw me in the r-river in the middle of winter. I could've died."

"We didn't, Mother!" He looks so bemused I almost wonder if I've got the wrong boy. But no. I don't mistake faces.

"You filthy liar!" the father explodes. I think for an impossible moment he's talking to his son, but his cold eyes drill into me. "Your lot are a blight. Go drag yourself back to whatever hole you crawled out of, makkie scum, before I call the firebrands."

The whole family's gone when Ruzi reaches me. "What's going on, Mora?" He takes my elbow. I should be grateful they're walking away, but I can't seem to stop myself.

"*I'm not lying!*" I can roar as loud as any of them.

"Mora!" Ruzi shakes my arm gently until I look at him.

"He was there," I tell him, "at the river that night."

"Right!" Ruzi makes to go after them, but I catch the back of his shirt, finally calm enough to see sense. "It's no good, Ruzi. We'll only make trouble for ourselves."

He wavers.

"We don't need the attention, Ruzi," I remind him in quiet Crozoni, before he relents.

Skøl all around us are staring openly now. Pale faces, almost luminescent under the lanterns, but moon-distant and cold.

I see another repayer – a Crozoni woman, Ruzi's age, staring too. I don't know her. She says something to the fancy Skøl man beside her. He's richly dressed – wealthier than the family I just confronted. He follows her look and meets my gaze with open curiosity, but I'm not sticking around to gratify it.

The glowing lines of Rafmagis Way stretch out ahead and behind. Not for the likes of us.

"Come on, then," Ruzi says.

We take the first side street, heading down it as fast as we can go. I glance over my shoulder for one last look, and all I can see is a many-tendrilled orange lantern, the crowd gathered below it with upturned faces, lips parted and necks bared.

18

debts owed

I make for the Lugger immediately after work the next evening, rage still coursing through me. I want to know. I want to know what poor Zako saw or heard that made a grown man so set on hunting him down. What rotten secrets is our oh-so-respectable magistrate hiding? I sneak up the back way to the Scarlets' quarters. Both of them are downstairs, so Zako, Caruq and I have their rooms to ourselves.

"Well?" I say. "Did you burn the grass?"

"I'm not sure it worked," Zako begins nervously. "I told Kit everything, but it doesn't make sense."

"Can you tell me too?"

"I was there again at first, playing cards with Devotion. I dreamed the games. I'm sure I dreamed them exact. Like the real cards we played... But the argument itself was hazy..."

"Just tell me what you can," I prompt.

"We couldn't hear well. I remember Devotion looked at me when it started. She said, *Strange, they don't usually argue.* We were keeping quiet though, cos I wasn't supposed to be inside. And then what they were saying was all muffled, cos both doors were closed. They were talking quiet first off." He closes his eyes. "Then she shouted – she said he was *disgusting scum*. And he threw… I don't know. Something glass, it must have been. We heard it breaking. She said, *They'll find out! They'll send the newshounds sniffing, and when it doesn't add up, they'll send your Record to those frantic scientists, and we'll end up like the Kellins!*

"And then he said, *Don't be stupid, you frigid bitch. The Kellins were fools.*"

"Who are the Kellins?" I ask.

"I don't know. I asked Kit. He wasn't sure, but he thinks they might be some Skøl family that were in the papers last year."

"In the papers for what?"

"He didn't remember." Zako rubs his forehead.

"Okay." I chew my lip. "This is great, Zako. We can find out. Look, you didn't remember any of that before. Was there any more?"

"She said, *If I knew then, I never would have married you.* And he said, *Hindsight is golden, isn't it? If I knew what a hysterical bitch you would turn into, I never would have married you…* And she called him a *fucking ass.*" Zako grimaces. "Devotion didn't like that."

I can't help myself. "The hysterical bitch wasn't wrong."

"Yeah. I think he stormed off after that. But that's when the dream moved on… He was coming at me. And the hammer was in my hands, and I could feel it hitting his skull again. I thought I killed him."

His whole body shudders, but he rushes on.

"Then everything changed again. I went back to before – before the Cull." He sniffs. "You were there too. I didn't mean it! I'm sorry. It was nothing to do with Venor."

I touch his shoulder. "Don't be sorry. And maybe it *is* connected, in some way. Can you tell me about it?"

He looks out of the window.

"It was that last summer before… I could see it, it was so real. The last time we went to the fair in town, Mama and Papa and me. We saw you there – do you remember? You and your sisters."

The high-pitched hum that built like our excitement, the closer we got. Damp air full of powdered sugar and screaming. Happy screaming. "We were there all the time that summer," I say.

"We saw you at the Bucket Wheel. You and your sisters were coming off at the end and we were just about to go on and I was scared. Papa pointed to you and said, *Look, Mora survived. It's not scary at all.* We went on, but I was still scared. I only wanted to go on the Island after that."

"Was that the ride with swings?" I ask. That was my favourite.

"That was something else – the Whirly, maybe? No. I

mean the one with different sea animals going round to music. The middle was painted like an island, remember? There were turtles and whales…"

I remember. "Char loved that one."

"I made them let me go on it over and over." Zako takes his spectacles off to polish them, perhaps to wipe tears away. "The music came back in that dream. I knew it. But it's gone again."

Definitely tears.

"Can I tell you a secret?"

He looks up. "What?"

"I did *not* enjoy the Bucket Wheel either."

He gives me a small smile.

Of course, the Skøl didn't like any of it. A place for children to go to have fun – what use is that? They couldn't understand it if they tried. And they didn't. They tore it all down. The grounds are a fenced-off wasteland now, the fences overgrown with old blackberry canes and ivy like a prickly living boundary. It's in the Steeps, near the eastern wall.

"You're right," I admit to Zako. "Those memories don't sound related – or if they are, I don't know how. But I'm glad you got to be there again for a little while."

Downstairs, I find Kit alone, washing up.

"Go on," I whisper. "Tell me about the Kellins."

He dunks a few more plates and dries his hands. "The Kellin scandal broke last summer. Mister and Missus Kellin and their four kids – whole family was arrested and killed.

Back in Rundvaer. Mister Kellin had their Life Records forged – falsified old payments. It was to hide his gambling debts. Turned out they'd been living for years on stolen time."

I raise my eyebrows. "They forged records for the whole family? You mean they got a forger like the Artist to do it?"

Kit nods. "Probably someone on a par with the Artist. But still not good enough to fool the new detection methods."

"I didn't know there were new detection methods," I say. "Is this where the *frantic scientists* come in?"

Kit laughs. "Forensic. Forensic scientists. They examine the records using some sort of scope. Vradiant, I think. Like violet radiance?"

"I haven't heard of it."

"No. I only know about it because the Reedstones have one too." He darts a look at me – he knows I don't approve of whatever this work he's doing is. "They're using it in their security work."

"Violet radiance..." I muse, thinking of the sea-urchin lantern at Skivårnat. "Sounds pretty."

His lips quirk. "If you're not Mister Kellin."

"Or the magistrate."

He grins. "He's been up to something, hasn't he, Venor? Something not very magisterial."

"Something that Clarion Lovemore wouldn't like," I say.

"Something he was willing to kill Zako for."

"Something to threaten his future governorship, perhaps."

We look at each other.

"Do you think he falsified payments?" I whisper.

"I certainly think something in his Life Record isn't above board."

"Kit – this is big… Do you think… Could we bring him down with this?"

My heart is racing. To expose Venor – it feels impossible. And yet…

"Maybe…" I can hear Kit's hesitation, but I'm too excited to slow down.

"I could tell Felicity! She could investigate, say it's for the *Gazette*—"

"How can you tell her?" Kit interrupts, just as I see the glaring flaw myself.

I can't tell Felicity without telling her how I know.

The twinkle in Kit's eyes is gone. "Get real, Mora. Go to Felicity? She's a Skøl writing puffery about Venor for that evil paper. Her type don't stick their necks out."

I chew my lip. "An anonymous tip to the *Portcaye Post*?"

He sighs. "Saying what? Pop round the Life Registry and ask nicely for the Life Record of the magistrate? Bring along a forensic-science toolkit and you won't be disappointed?"

"So we do nothing?"

Kit sighs. "We need to be cautious with this, that's

all. It's too big." He thinks for a moment. "I'll talk to the Reedstones, see what they think."

"You can't tell them about Zako!" I hiss.

"I won't tell them about him, don't worry. I'll put out feelers, that's all. They're connected, Mora – on both sides of the law. If anyone knows about something shady in Venor's past, it'll be them."

I tell Ruzi about Zako's recollections when I get back to Opal Alley, then fill him in on what Kit remembers of the Kellin scandal – just so he's abreast of the latest, not because I think he'll have anything to add. But he's suddenly a font of knowledge.

"The Kellins. Yes – I remember. Last Eightmonth, wasn't it? Stuck with me for some reason… Got his whole family killed, he did. Gambled and lost…" Ruzi clicks his fingers. "Had some connection here, didn't he? That's why they made a big fuss in the *Post*. I'm sure it was there…"

He eyes our stack of old newspapers, piled in a basket by the stove. It's true we tend to burn the newer ones first and haven't touched the bottom in an age.

"I wonder…" Ruzi mutters.

We search the stash of kindling together, dragging out all the oldest papers we can find.

"Better than a library, my filing system." Ruzi raises his eyebrows. After an endless trawl, we turn up two articles about the Kellin family.

The Skøl do have a town library, but I'm certain I

wouldn't be welcome inside. It's more of a record-keeping place than a real lending library in the old Crozoni sense.

The first story's from last Sevenmonth. The paper's in exceedingly poor shape, stained with grease and mildewed, but just enough of it's legible. It describes how a rich resident of Rundvaer, name of Earnest Kellin, had acquired a large plot of disused land in Portcaye town, in the Steeps, with the intention of building a racetrack. The Grand Golden, it was to be called. Mister Kellin had been motivated, the article explains, by his passion for kine racing.

There were several racetracks like this in Skøland, it accounts, but this was to be a first for the New West. The whiff of Venor winning the governorship was already strong a year back, already "putting Portcaye on the map".

But Mister Kellin's dream wasn't to be.

A newer article, dated last Eightmonth, in an imported *Endweek Evening Gazette*, tells the scandal of the Kellins.

Family of SIX Culled

—

New Technique Revealed Forgery!

—

Gambling Addiction Topples Rich Family "Bankrupt for Months"

The Kellin family of Stead Green in North Rundvaer Town were culled yesterday, following their trial and conviction last week. Businessman and woman Earnest Kellin (46 years) and Galore Kellin (47 years), and their four daughters aged five, twelve, twelve and seventeen, were put to death for criminal evasion of life payments and forgery with intent to defraud the Life Registry.

The Kellin evasion and forgery was uncovered using a state-of-the-art Criminal Forensic Science technique known as "vradiance scoping", which employs a heat-free violet radiance to uncover evidence once thought to be obscured – including fingerprints and the stains of bodily fluids, as well as ink.

Speaking from Rundvaer Central Station, Senior Firebrand Inspector Shine told our reporter: "The vradiance scope is levelling the field. A favourite technique of the forgers for fifty years, one we once deemed undetectable, is now the opposite. Our message to those who think forgery is a viable option is simple: think again."

While the new technology is not yet cost-effective enough to deploy in mass screening, it is now being used in cases where questions and uncertainties arise, as in...

There are some impossible-to-read segments, soiled with splatter, but the article concludes:

… means of living several months ago owing to his weakness for gambling, and unfortunately…

… property has been confiscated and repossessed by the state in lieu of debts owed.

19

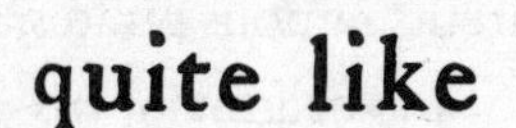

quite like

It's nearly a week after Skivårnat, and Venor's enthusiasm for Zako's blood isn't waning. I can't go two blocks without spotting one of his wanted posters. Branders follow me in the shadows. The Glassworks is still full-tilt on the endless panes for the Hexagon Hall. Elsewhere in Portcaye, cobbles are replaced, fences mended, walls whitewashed.

"He's sprucing it up before Clarion Lovemore arrives," Felicity tells me, dangling another of her slim cigarettes. "Wants to show what a good little governor he'll be."

"How's the profile coming along?" I ask her, a bit nastily. She can make all the digs she likes, but she's still puffing Venor up.

"Good, thanks," she says, and has the grace to look ashamed.

Now I'm back in my room, drawing. I have another new customer and I want to finish. The rain's making a racket, but I can still hear Ruzi snoring through the thin wall as I hunch under my blanket.

I'm in the dark – literally, because I need to refill my lantern but I don't want to quit my chair, and figuratively, because I still don't know what's so compromising about Venor's Life Record.

My mind keeps chasing the question. What is his dark secret? Were his parents famous pirates? Cannibals? Has he lied about his age or his origins or his payments?

I freeze in terror at a light knocking on my bedroom door as another snore floats through the wall. A head pokes in. It's Kit. He's let himself in.

"Saw your window light." He frowns at my feeble lantern.

I stand. "You're soaked," I say. "And it's curfew! Someone might catch you!"

Kit's hair's plastered down, his neat work shirt wet through and clinging to his body. He's clean-shaven – it suits him.

"Thought it was too warm for a coat." He ignores my mention of curfew.

I realize I'm staring.

He's carrying a cloth bag. He fishes a pouch of coin from it – half again what he gave me for the first batch of drawings.

"You've sold the second lot already?" I keep my voice low. I only gave him my latest batch of uncommissioned drawings a few days ago. Mostly easy landscapes and

Portcaye street scenes – less personal than portraits, and not too technical like boats or flowers or insects. Those consume more time.

He's dripping on the floor. I pass him my towel. It's a bit ragged around the edges, a bit off-colour. Not like the towels at the Lugger. I see it for the first time and feel ashamed. But he doesn't care. He wipes his face, his messy hair, drags it down his neck.

"I did. Went like that—" He clicks his fingers.

"Oh."

He still hovers uncomfortably near the door.

"Come in if you're here." I wave at my chair.

He hangs the towel over the back of it, stretches it out like it's nice and not frayed and faded.

"Your Reedstone friends haven't got you out stealing things in this weather?" I ask, observing, not for the first time, how the tip of a tattoo climbs out of the back of his shirt. More of it's visible now, a black smudge, darker than his dark skin under the wet fabric stretching across his shoulders.

"They're out of town," he explains. "I haven't been able to ask them about the Kellins or Venor's Record. And I'm not stealing anything tonight, don't worry."

He fetches the tin of ragleaf fuel from its corner in the kitchen and tops up my lantern. Then he takes my offered chair as I cross my legs on the bed beside him.

"What's your tattoo?" I ask.

One of his hands rubs self-consciously at the back of his neck.

"It's a vocifer."

They're raptors keen on rabbits, fish, chickens. Nowadays they're rare as hen's teeth, but I saw a pair once, when I was a child. And there was one that sometimes flew near the farm, when I worked out there. "I thought Kalqitlan meant 'bear'."

He nods. "Growling bear, or thunderstorm –" he gestures at the window – "take your pick. There's no rule about names and tattoos. That's not how it works."

"Is it on the back of your arms as well?"

"It is."

"Why did you get it?"

"My dad arranged it, just before he died. Took me to the Akani Inker."

I've never heard of the Akani Inker. I know Kit was twelve when his dad died after a long illness.

"Nena-Okuma, we called her. She was a healer. An elder of the Akani clan. Powerful. So many rituals we've lost now. Links to the old gods. They say vocifers were one of the gods' favourites."

"The Xan gods have favourites?"

"They love all the beasts that eat the other beasts. Even better if they eat people. You know – wolves and bears, sea monsters, kraits." His shoulders shudder. I know he hates kraits – they're a kind of sea snake. They smell blood in the water and drink from anything that bleeds. *Black and yellow, kill a fellow*, the old song goes.

"But vocifers don't eat people," I say.

"They say in the old days they used to snatch little babes to feed to their chicks."

"Oh, lovely."

He leans back and tilts his face up. "They dine at the gods' table. Feed on us, same as the gods," he tells the ceiling. Then, still looking at the ceiling, "You haven't been around much since Skivårnat."

A question that's not a question.

"I've been busy."

He gives me a half smile. "You've been drawing."

I heft the latest payment. "This is so much."

"You'll get more. We're still building you up. Missus S has been singing your praises to all her friends."

"I went sketching last Endweek," I say, and show him my small stack – topped with a mock wanted poster for Valour Venor. The fancy script reads:

PREFERRED DEAD TO ALIVE

FOR TREASON AGAINST HUMAN DECENCY, LIFE LARCENY AND INNUMERABLE COUNTS OF CONTEMPTIBLE SHITSACKERY

Kit lets out a stutter of surprised laughter. "Bold of you to have this lying around," he warns me.

But I don't feel cowed. Somewhere along the line, my anger's grown greater than my fear.

He leafs through my few sketches of the statue of Imilia

Dezil in Sinton Square, her stone plinth plastered with wanted posters.

I've drawn her in her high boots and wind-blown greatcoat from different angles.

"I used to fancy Captain Dezil," Kit murmurs.

"She's a statue."

"I like them hard-hearted and unattainable."

"Or shiny and silent?"

He meets my gaze like a challenge and laughs. "Maybe sometimes."

Does he always blink so slowly? I look away as his long black lashes shutter. I stand and push papers around on my makeshift desk, feeling his breath near my ribs.

"What else should I do? I was thinking animals. Missus Heane wanted me to draw kine. Or seascapes?"

"Sure. Anything you want."

A catch in his usual rasp makes me turn. He's looking at our reflections in the night-black window glass.

"Have you thought about life portraits? Bet some of them would go for that." His hands curl lightly around the arms of the chair.

Now all I want is to draw him, rain-washed, drying in my chair. Not from memory – now. Even just his hands. Before I lose my nerve, I pluck the book of white paper off the table.

"Sit back then. Turn round."

"You want to draw this?" His hands gesture to his

face. He's wearing that open expression he sometimes has. Innocent. "I look like a drowned rat."

"Don't smile."

I begin with big, loose strokes. His shirt's still clinging – there's more shoulder and chest than seems fair for a young man working in a tavern.

"Where'd you get all this muscle?"

His innocence burns away like fog. "You think the barrels carry themselves up from the cellar?"

"No way all that's just barrels."

"Breaking up brawls then. Throwing out rowdy good-for-nothings. Opening jars for Renny. It's a gruelling job."

I have seen him do all those things. And yet.

"Do you have to steal heavy things for your Reedstones? Are Goldie and Glister after cast-iron safes, perhaps?"

His expression tightens. "No. Oh, I meant to tell you … I think I've found a guitar for Ruzi."

"Ruzi will be over the moon." He will. I feel uneasy about Ruzi putting on a performance, opening himself up to a crowd of Skøl. It feels too much, somehow. It's not illegal, but it's not something we do.

"Why are you such a good drawer, then?"

"What?"

"How'd you learn?"

I pause to try and remember. I started drawing so young.

"Guess my folks always encouraged it."

"Could you draw me like this even if I wasn't here?"

I haven't tried to draw Kit from memory, but I know it'd be no challenge.

"Yes."

"What about places? Buildings? How does it work? Could you draw someplace you just walked through, or only someone or somewhere you spent time … observing?" He catches my eye.

I gather my thoughts. "I could do either if I had to." How to explain something I barely do consciously at all? Everyone thinks my memory's a blessing. It's a dagger. Sharp edges of good and bad, with a wide, flat boring in between. "Look, this might sound weird…"

"I love weird."

"There's a place in my head where all the images kind of … live. I have to reach them. It's like a cave that changes all the time, made of memories. It's got tunnels and ways into rooms and whole buildings. And I have to find the thing I want to draw. Or reach, or call – like something in between seeing and touching. It's a half-real feeling. I'm not describing it right."

"You go into your memory cave – sure."

"Close enough."

"You're weird, all right. Weirdly brilliant." His slow grin spreads.

Why am I melting like a slab of butter in a Lugger breakfast skillet?

"Can I see?" He reaches for my paper.

"Not yet. Sit still." I fill in more detail, then put down the pencil. "There."

When I pass it over the smile slips off his face.

"That was – what? Five minutes? This is … something else, Mora."

I shrug.

"Didn't get your eyes right."

"No, it's brilliant. Of course, the subject helps." He winks at me. "This'll fetch you a pretty penny." He taps the page.

"It's not for sale," I decide. "I'm keeping it."

"Are you, now?" Kit blinks. "Let me do you," he whispers, reaching for my pencil.

No one's ever wanted to draw a portrait of me before. I'm flattered.

"No peeking though."

"Where should I sit?"

"You're all right there." He tilts the book away from me so I can't see what he's doing.

"Stop moving."

"I'm not moving." I clasp my hands in my lap, worrying at a small cut on the side of my finger until fresh blood wells up.

He frowns at my hand. "Don't do that. It won't heal."

His eyes are flitting all over my face, but his pencil is still.

Then his voice is a low murmur over the sound of its scratching. "Child of conquerors. Eyes like suns. Slave of conquerors. Sunlit eyes."

"What's that?"

"Ah. Who knows. Something I read somewhere. Fowler, perhaps."

Fowler's one of the old Crozoni poets. It doesn't sound like him.

He's shading now, I think.

"How long is this going to take?"

"You can't rush genius." He looks up at me, all serious innocence again.

"Come on," I say eventually. "You've had twice as long as me."

He scratches a few final lines and hands it over. "Okay, I'm done."

My heart is beating as I take it, but then I burst out laughing. It's awful. Like a child's drawing. Deliberately bad.

"Don't laugh; that's cruel," he grumbles, but he's laughing too. "For shame. You shouldn't mock people who haven't your skill."

"I'm the one who should be offended. This is how you see me? My ears aren't cup handles."

"How I see you? Don't be stupid. You're beautiful. I just can't draw."

I feel heat creeping up my cheeks. *He thinks I'm beautiful. And stupid.* The silence between us stretches as we lean slightly too close. I notice his shirt's dry already. I find myself wondering why he came here tonight.

On the other side of the thin wall, Ruzi's faint snore

turns into a cough, breaking the spell. Then it's quiet again.

Kit passes the pencil back to me. "Could you draw the branders' station?"

"What?"

"Where they questioned you and you saw the Artist. Could you draw it – the corridors, the doors, the windows?"

I stare. "I don't know … maybe." But I can already see it, in my mind's eye. My memory cave. "Why?"

"Just curious." I close my eyes and twirl the pencil, reaching for the tendrils of memory.

I'm in the cave, and there's the thin young brander in front. Hove's glasses flashing gold. My tired feet fumbling the steep, shallow steps down. Below ground now, the lantern light harsh. *Deadhouse* in thick, formal lettering on that door. *Forensic Science Workroom and Darkspace*. The smell of urine, sweat and blood, a gaping cell door, breath rasping. That sweet, awful smell. Human decay.

I scratch a quick schematic of the route I took. The main entrance with its sombre front desk, then our way to the interrogation room, past a long, dark armoury I could see through a barred slice of unglazed window. A glimpse of rows of guns and prods, stood up on their golden ends in a long metal contraption. Sucking up power to maim with later, I suppose. I draw the stairs Hove took me down. The shut doors. The cells – one with the Artist.

I let go. Un-call, un-reach. The tendrils of memory retract. The cave rests, dormant again.

"Incredible," Kit whispers. I realize he's standing, peering over my shoulder with a frown that's at odds with his tone.

I tap my head. I'm tired now. "It's all in here."

His jaw is hard, looking down at the paper. There's a new edge to his expression I don't quite like.

20

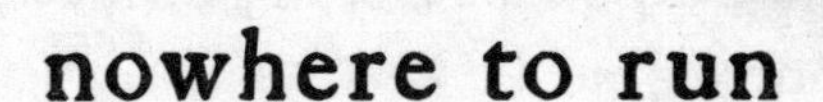

nowhere to run

"I should let you get some rest," Kit decides. I don't want him to leave but can't think of anything to say that will delay him. He lets himself out quietly.

I edge to the window and watch him from above. It's barely raining now, more mist than anything. Opal Alley's deserted.

The brief look he casts around is enough to send me ducking back. If ever a person was obviously shifty, it's Kit. An invisible fist squeezes my heart.

And, just like that, I'm not tired any more.

To hell with sleeping. I hurry down the stairs and limp off after him.

He's up to something, I know he is – something to do with the Reedstones. He walks at his normal pace – not hurrying, not dawdling. At each turning I worry I'll lose him, but I don't dare close the gap. Somehow, he's always there in the distance when I round a new corner, a solitary figure cut by moonlight.

Until he isn't. The juncture feels vaguely familiar. I stop to get my bearings, squinting at the options – dark walls, dim alleys and deserted yards.

Silence. Broken only by an irregular dripping. He could have gone any of three ways. I choose one at random, though the tired frustration creeping up my legs is starting to get the better of me.

It funnels on to the river path, further west than I thought, just upstream of Settler's Bridge. The inky river reflects a ghost bridge, rippling in a ghost sky.

I trace the ripples back to where they lap against the first stone abutment, then gaze up at the blocks of pocked grey masonry, over the parapet.

My quarry looks down at me. I didn't hear him, but he must have heard me in the end. It's too far away to see his expression in this murk, but I don't doubt it's some species of indignant glare.

I slog up the bridge to his side. Embarrassment makes me curt. "If you'd tell me about your secret Reedstone jobs, I wouldn't be trying to find out like this."

"I'm not on a job, Mor." He's not angry. If anything, his voice sounds sad. He's holding a bottle of wine. "I'm visiting the old public yard." He gestures to the opposite bank of the swollen river with his bottle, and I know why he's sad. All my self-righteous anger froths away.

This is where Kit's parents were buried. "Suppose you'd rather be alone?" I say awkwardly.

"Not if your company's going."

I grab it like the peace offering it is, walking silently beside him to the north bank.

The Skøl prefer not to be buried. They don't consider it an efficient use of land. One day they'll choke on efficiency. Mostly they burn their dead and scatter the ashes.

But my people, and Kit's – we remember our ancestors.

They've built over most of the old public graveyard and removed the few remembrance stones that were here. Only the section sloping down to the river's been left to grass – too prone to flooding. The river's high tonight. It's been high for a few weeks, tide regardless.

We stand on the terrace closest to the water without actually being submerged.

"My mum and dad used to bring an offering every year for the Odasha Sava," Kit tells me, shielding a long match from the wind as he strikes it. Odasha is a Xan celebration for giving thanks to their gods, held at least twice a year. I thought it involved honey and griddle-cakes, but perhaps that's the summer one.

Kit doesn't try to burn anything with the match, just holds it pinched between finger and thumb and shields it from the wind until it shrivels to nothing.

"Were they both buried here?"

"Near there." His chin indicates a part of the bank

closer to the bridge that's already submerged as he levers the stopper from the wine.

The public yard was only ever for poor people. Graves on this stretch weren't expected to hold their dead long from the sea.

"I'm sorry," I tell him.

He crouches to pour the dark liquid slowly into the soil. Soft words in his first language float around us, his low voice serrated.

I wish I had a candle or something to offer beside my own silent prayer.

I remember the cut on my finger. I pick surreptitiously at it until a few drops of blood drip to the ground. I don't know if Kit's gods care for blood offerings, but they say the old Crozoni gods did.

You think you have nothing to give? Think of your veins, fat with blood.

"Come on." He nudges my elbow. "You're asking for trouble, staying out like this. Let's get you back."

"You don't have to come," I say feebly, glad of his company.

I'm especially glad when we're back across the bridge and a sudden noise disturbs the night.

Wood banging. The high-pitched squeal of branders' whistles, shattering glass and the telltale elektric fizz of prods. A raid, streets away, but sound carries in the still air. We hurry into the night, until the sounds behind us fade.

My voice shakes when I say, "I wish you'd trust me

enough to tell me what work it is the Reedstones have you doing."

"Of course I trust you. If I keep things from you, it's for your own good."

"Doesn't feel like it."

He keeps my arm as we walk on. "They sometimes ask me to steal documents from certain people."

"What for?"

"They think the way to undermine the Skøl powers that be is to expose their corruption."

I blink. "Undermine the powers that be? But they're scoffing at the same trough. They're rich and elite, aren't they? Like Auntie and Uncle Oh-So-Charitable Weapons Moguls."

"The Reedstones are not the Stings," Kit says. "Course they count on that association. Goldie and Glister know they're privileged. But they're not fans of the way things are done – the Registry, repayers, all of it."

"Really?" I raise a brow. "And what are they doing about that?"

"Well, Skøland's whole identity as a nation – as a nation that eats other nations – is about how morally upright they are. How civilized. How squeaky clean. Bringing light to the darkness. The Reedstones think if they're shown to be otherwise – if their leaders are shown to be corrupt – they'll fall."

How idealistic, I think. "And have they found evidence of corruption?"

He frowns. "Small fry. They've used it to blackmail certain officials into releasing prisoners or giving less harsh sentences. Information in kind, that sort of thing. Not that they tell me everything, of course."

"So the lock-making business is just a front?"

Kit smirks. "Well, it makes the pigeons easier to pluck. GR Locks is a very popular supplier of security."

Locksmiths who sell security to the very people they're planning to spy on and steal from. I'm reluctantly impressed.

"How in the world did you meet people like the Reedstones in the first place?"

"Goldie and I chose the same place to steal from one night," he says with a grin. "She admired my work."

I don't want to be shocked, but I am. "So you were properly stealing already? Before you met them?" I say quietly. I know before the Cull he had that reputation – stealing to scrape by – but I didn't think he'd kept going, or ramped it up by the sounds of things, after the Scarlets bought him.

"I wasn't clever as you when I was your age," he says. "I used to think if I stole enough I could buy my life back. But the Reedstones have something bigger in mind. Rebellion. Fighting back. Revolution, one day."

"Is that possible?"

He plucks a big ivy leaf from the wall we're walking past and twirls it by the stem. "I don't know. But nothing in this life's ever as permanent as it feels. Change is the constant."

I sigh. Change hasn't been good to me.

"When things are this bad," Kit goes on, "big change looks better and better." I watch the leaf spinning, dark on one side, light on the other.

"And Goldie and Glister want big change?"

Kit's voice is cautious. "So they say. They have their fingers in a lot of pies. They deal in art, artefacts, antiques. Anything that brings them into contact with the great and good, so they can poke around from the inside."

"Wait. Art trade? Was it the Reedstones who sold my drawings?" My frustration flares again. If people like that say my art's worth money, does their word give it worth? These Skøl elites who've always had wealth and influence, playing at rebellion like a game. It's easy to dream of change when you've never been told no in your life.

Kit tosses the ivy leaf to the ground and gives a small nod. "As a favour to me. They didn't keep a cut. Goldie and Glister are … hard to describe. But they're not like you think."

"They're genuine rebels, then?" I ask. "Revolutionaries?" It seems so unlikely.

"Maybe one day," Kit says softly. "If it's not all a delusion."

I think of the branders' station I drew earlier … the Artist prone, flanked by his torturers. The only Skøl I've seen who fancied himself radical.

Venor will make an example of him. The Reedstones may soon change their tune.

And we're back at the bakery already. The drizzle's back too. Kit stops, and we look at each other in the glass.

My colourless reflection swims before me. Is my face shaped like Ma's? Is that why she's the one person I can't draw? She's never there in my memory cave, or if she is, she's lost in the background. A blur behind Char, or Enca, or Eben. Like the ghost of a ghost.

My amber eyes are a distraction. How did I never notice how much I look like her?

I think of that winter night, of taking Clomper from the Glassworks, riding her along the byway. Going and not coming back. More silly fantasy. You can't run away when there's nowhere to run.

21

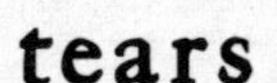

tears

"Roasted niblets, hot and fresh! Get your *Post* here! Read all the latest in the *Illustrated Portcaye Post and Advertiser*!" The barrow-seller's calls are melodious. A town noise I barely notice, like the rumbling carriage wheels or the scrapping gulls. "Warm your fingers with tonight's edition – hot off the presses…"

I don't like spending good coin on news I can have for free once it's gone stale, but I catch sight of the phrase *savage filth* on tonight's front page, and pay for fresh.

I wait until I'm in a comfy chair in the Lugger lounge to read it. Kit's given me a tower of cheese melted on toast and a bowl of greens bursting with salt and sharpness.

"Are you reading that or using it to catch crumbs?" Felicity sits beside me and helps herself to a triangle of toast.

"Spick and span's just not in my nature," I tell her, flattening out the front page so she can read with me.

PORTCAYE PREPARES

—

EVERYTHING MUST BE SPICK AND SPAN FOR THE GOVERNOR

—

NO MORE SAVAGE FILTH POLLUTING OUR STREETS!

With High Governor Lovemore scheduled to arrive on the sixth day of Sixmonth – in just nine weeks' time – Portcaye is in a race to clean up.

"It all has to go," announced Magistrate Venor at a congress yesterday. "The last remaining makkie statuary defiling our public squares and our main gates will be melted down and replaced in short order with Skøl pieces emphasising the glory of Skøland's world dominion, centring the New West settler spirit.

"Life here in Portcaye must reflect only the best of Skøland: Hard work! Enterprise! Bounty! We must be a beacon in the darkness of the New West. I have achieved much in the past six years, taming this savage land. Now is not the time to rest. We must complete the purifying purge, strip our buildings of any primitive ornamentation of Makaian origin and show our new home in its best gleaming light."

"So they're getting rid of it all," I say. "I suppose it's to be expected." Why does it feel like a warm-up for something worse? Venor talks of cleansing buildings and statues. How far is it from this to removing us?

"Venor thinks cleaning and destroying are the same thing," Felicity says. "He doesn't know what culture is."

We flip through the rest of the paper. It's mostly advertising and classifieds, but one other thing catches my eye, mentioning Sting Elektric.

STING TRUST RECIPIENT STUNG!

Nineteen-year-old Level Gusting, described by his neighbours as a "sullen and ill-tempered lout", was arrested last night on suspicion of theft. This raises more questions about the Sting Trust and the criminal tendencies of its charges…

"A Sting Trust baby." I look at Felicity. "Like Victor."

"What's that?" Felicity snags another bit of toast.

"The man they came here to arrest, remember?" I gesture to the mezzanine.

"Oh yes."

I read on as Felicity crunches toast.

When asked about the allegations against Mister Gusting, his long-time employer, Goldie Reedstone, great-granddaughter of the original founders of the

Sting Trust, said, "It's absolute rubbish. Level Gusting wouldn't steal a penny. He's been unfairly targeted because of his last name. I'm tired of the assumption that Sting Trust recipients are lazy, or criminal, or unemployable. Frankly, that assumption is lazy."

"That's why they call her eccentric." Felicity frowns at the paper.

I feel a new twinge of admiration for the Reedstones. At least Goldie's sticking her neck out for these people publicly. It can't win her any favours from her more strait-laced clientele.

"Well, I never. It says he's been released without charge – the victim retracted his accusation," Felicity reads on. "But for a more exciting story…"

She holds out the paper. The back page is dominated by an illustration of a farmer cradling his prize-winning marrow in his arms like a child.

"Now *this* is big news." She prods the farmer. "They should make that a statue."

I stifle a smile.

Felicity takes my last bit of toast with a cheeky wink and goes off to her room upstairs.

I can't help thinking something's odd about that man accusing Level Gusting and then immediately retracting his accusation. I wouldn't be surprised if the Reedstones had worked their blackmail on him.

*

Renny comes in with a tray of bowls filled with jam-and-ginger pudding, hot from the oven. Kit can't resist it either and sits with me. I hug mine a little closer when Felicity returns.

She's changed her clothes, dressed up to go out. Her lips are as red as her notebook, which she immediately pulls out of who knows where. "They raised the bounty on your friend again, did you see?"

"We saw," says Kit, through a mouthful of pudding. "More fool Venor. He thinks throwing money's the solution to everything. Won't make them find a lost boy any sooner."

"You think he did survive, then?" She looks at me, not Kit.

"I live in hope." I look away. I know my expression's turned awkward. That was something my mother used to say, *I live in hope*. She really didn't.

"Venor really wants his revenge, doesn't he?" Felicity closes her notebook again. "He's obsessed."

I stare at my bowl. "Maybe he's worried Zako knows something about him. Wants him kept quiet – permanently."

I can feel Kit's glare.

I risk a glance at Felicity, whose eyebrows shoot up behind her fringe. "That's a bold theory." She seems to consider it a moment then shakes her head. "What could someone in Zako's position know about the magistrate?"

"What about asking his family?" I say. Kit kicks me under the table, but I ignore him. "His wife and daughter? Have you met them?"

"No. I haven't been out to his country estate."

"It's not that far."

"Venor didn't seem to want me to go there," she adds slowly.

"They knew Zako too. They were probably there that very day. Might be a good angle for your article – a glimpse of the family man..."

Felicity murmurs to herself. "That's not a terrible idea." She stashes her notebook in a little leather bag. "You could be a reporter yourself one day, Mora."

She leaves. I hope I've piqued her curiosity.

"Nice work," mutters Kit. "That one's like a krait after blood."

I hope she is. I hope she sniffs out Venor's rotten secret.

A few evenings later, there's a note left at Opal Alley. *Ruzi – guitar's here! She's a beauty. Gorgeous.* Ruzi is giddy, and we go over straight away.

Kit is working in the kitchen, but he fishes a key from his pocket. "Go on up and have a look; it's on my bed," he tells Ruzi.

He's stirring something with a strong waft of garlic that spatters thick juices over the iron cooker. He looks knackered, red-eyed and lank-haired. He blows on a spoonful and holds it out to me. "Does it need more spice?"

It's smooth and full of sweet burnt pepper, with a burst of chilli.

"No. It's really good." The chilli's got a long burn. My tongue tingles.

"You look exhausted," I say. "How hard have the Reedstones got you working?"

"I'm handling it."

"Could have fooled me."

"I saw them yesterday." He clatters the pot off the heat. "And you'll be interested in this: they told me how the vradiance scope exposes forgeries."

"How?"

"Well, the forger works by removing the original ink using a special solution. It sets off a chemical reaction with the ink and then he can clean it away. He writes over it, using a perfect imitation of the original writing – good as new. Only it's not. The initial chemical reaction leaves a kind of … invisible stain. If you shine the vradiance scope over it, the old ink glows in the dark."

"So you can see what the forger changed?"

"Exactly."

"So Venor has erased and replaced something in his Life Record," I say.

Kit is silent.

"What did he change?"

"That's the question worth twenty thousand krunan, isn't it?"

If he's behind on his payments and covering it up, that would be scandal enough. But the reason would surely be all the more incriminating. Does Venor have a secret gambling problem like Mister Kellin? Or is he funding something – or someone – secret and unsavoury?

"Maybe his real name's Brickhead of Rundvaer, the Deeply Unvalorous," I offer.

"That'll be it."

Gracie and Renny come bursting into the kitchen, laughing about something, and I clomp upstairs looking for Ruzi.

I find him sitting on Kit's bed, cradling the guitar. It's one of his own making. His luthier's symbol adorns the neck. Inside, on the slightly browned label, in cursive letters it says *Ruzi Taler.* It's in good condition, with a beautiful rosette of wispy leaves.

"Thank you." His gruff voice sounds gruffer. I realize he's looking past me to Kit, standing in the doorway. "I made this one on commission for a minstrel in Wellstead. Good heavy top."

He nestles the guitar over his thigh and begins to tune by ear. Then he strums a few bars of an old Crozoni song, by a composer from one of the outer isles whose name I can never recall. I've never heard it done so slowly, but it's perfect. No dropped notes. No pauses.

Mother, you wouldn't know me. He sings only the words of the refrain, softly. The sound freezes me, not with ice, but amber, honey, time reversing. Something in my chest unfolding – a sunflower craning to follow the light, pushing its petalled head up my throat, choking me with tears.

22

my daughter

Ruzi's guitar is staying at the Lugger, too precious to haul around in the wet. Plus it's given him an excuse to visit Zako more than once in the past two weeks.

I've heard him in Opal Alley preparing for his first performance, singing snippets to himself. He's even translated one famous Crozoni piece into Skøl – I helped him.

Now the big day's here. It's late afternoon, and we're heading together to the Lugger. I've washed my curls in loads of soap and decided to wear my hair uncovered. I've even added a bit of soot to my eyelids.

Ruzi's boots bear not a speck of dust. I wanted to make them new ribbon bootlaces, like I've done for mine – I got a lovely bit of purple ribbon for a song off Cordi two days ago – but Ruzi wasn't having it.

We picked an Endweek so Ruzi could start before dark

and finish in time to make curfew. The rain's coming light for a spell, but the cobbles are still slippery as fish scales. Ruzi's trying to hide his nerves. It's not just the performance, I think, but the idea of singing Crozoni songs with a Crozoni instrument in front of an audience of Skøl. Flaunting our savage Makaian ways.

"Hope I don't put them all off Crozoni music forever," he grumbles. "Never played to a crowd that knows none of it."

"You're going to astound them. Completely. Their lives will change tonight."

Perhaps my enthusiasm's overblown. But what must it be like, living with no decent music and suddenly encountering it? Like not realizing you've been oblivious to half the world. To worlds.

Ruzi eats when he's nervous. He finished a bag of mints yesterday and he's browsing the barrows on the turning to Belor Way, looking for something sweet and fortifying, when Kit appears.

Ruzi waves us on, preferring to wait for a batch of sugared nuts.

"Your eyes look tired still." I lower my voice. "Is it mysterious jobs for the Reedstones, or Zako making you read *Blenny and Tornelius*?"

He shakes his head, but he chuckles. "Missus S can read it. She loves it." He pauses then adds, "She loves Zako. Pair of them are always cackling about something."

"Are you jealous?"

He gives me a raised brow.

"She loves you too," I point out. "No accounting for taste."

His pace slows. "She doesn't love me. She owns me."

"She both owns and loves you."

He scoffs. "Like you love a dog."

"Like a son."

"Sons aren't property." He cracks his knuckles. "I haven't been a son in eight years." He jerks his head towards Ruzi. "You're not ready to be a daughter, are you?"

I shiver. Ruzi, who cooks and cleans for me and looks out for me – and who knew my ma – is the closest thing I have to a parent.

And yet he isn't. Not by a long shot. "You're right. I'm sorry. I didn't mean they're some kind of … replacement for your mum and dad."

He swallows. "You don't stop being someone's child when they die," I say slowly. "I don't think so anyway."

"You're right," he offers softly. "I don't mean to snap. I'm just tired."

"It's okay." I badly want to hug him, but I don't quite dare. "I wish the Reedstones weren't wearing you out with their plots."

He nudges me. "Worried?"

I avert my eyes, feel my skin prickle. I do worry about Kit. But he's involved in something big, with people who seem to care more than most, who want change. If I'm honest, I'm jealous too.

"Always," I say at last. "But I want to help, too."

"Ah." His eyes clamp on mine. "There it is."

"There what is?" I feel my defences rising.

"You don't want me to stop. You just want to wade in up to your neck too."

Like he's known all along, like he knows my own mind better than I do.

"Well?" I say. "Can I help?"

"Absolutely not. You're not getting involved."

I kick a loose cobble, narrowly missing a Skøl woman, who looks scared when she sees my face. "I'm already involved!"

"I'm trying to protect you."

I shake my head. I can't have survived the Cull just to waste my life hauling glass and ash and shit around for the same people who wiped my family off the map.

I can't. There must be something more.

"You don't protect me by shutting me out," I say slowly. We've reached the Lugger courtyard, and I let my last words echo. "That just hurts me."

That just hurts me. Just hurts me. The words hang in the air. Two paces. Five. Only my footfall punctuates the silence between us. Kit's steps are quiet and graceful as ever.

"I'm sorry," he yields as we reach the door. "Don't… That's the last thing I want. Can't you see that?"

"No," I say softly, parting ways with him at the bar. Gracie's there already, but clearly worked off her feet.

I want, I realize, to be part of something. Even if it's a delusion of rebellion.

I look around. Not a bad crowd – busier than an ordinary Endweek afternoon. People have come especially to hear Ruzi. Missus Scarlet's in her comfy chair by the unlit fire. I spot a few more repayers – all Crozoni. One woman I recognize from Rafmagis Way back at Skivårnat. She's here with the same Skøl man she was with that night, sitting at a table up on the mezzanine. I do a double take when I see Cordi and Vertie from the Glassworks, with Faithie Senson and another blower called Mellow Anderbil – wedged around a table for two, here on the ground floor.

They all live in the Skates. Cordi and Vertie have youngsters to spend their Endweeks with. I doubt they've set foot in the Lugger before.

"Pull up a stool!" Vertie tells me.

I squeeze in between Cordi and a young man at the next table with a face like a pretty statue.

He smiles at me. "What's your name, beautiful?"

"No. Not 'Beautiful'."

He's nonplussed. Perhaps my joke isn't funny. I'm always falling flat.

He's not giving up though. "Sit as close as you like. I'll buy you a drink."

"That's all right; I can get my own."

"You're breaking my heart."

Cordi leans over to him. "Come off it. Faithie was

breaking your heart five minutes ago. It must be ground to powder by now. Buy me one if you want sympathy. I'm not fussy."

They grin at each other, but he shakes his head, turning back to his companions.

"No respect for his elders." Cordi nudges my arm. She's at least a decade his senior, and doesn't have Faithie's good looks.

"Thank you," I tell her. "I'll get you another."

At the bar, Kit catches my hand. "Can I have a word?" He gestures to the kitchen.

Gracie is drinking a cup of fikka and crisping sage in butter. The smell of sage and smoke always carries me back to a time I prefer not to revisit. It's not food for me – it's funerals.

"Gracie, can you get the bar a minute?" The gravel in his voice is thicker than usual.

"Course I can." She leaves the pan to one side, raises an eyebrow at me and grins as she dashes out.

"Those men at the table next to you – you know who they are?" Kit asks.

"How would I?" I'm surprised he noticed me talking to the stranger at all.

"They're branders."

"Really?"

"They're out of uniform."

"They don't have guns."

"I wouldn't be so sure."

"Where do they have them hidden? Down their trousers?"

"Please don't go looking down their trousers."

Mister Scarlet appears, blocking the wide doorway. His head's particularly shiny tonight, freshly shaven. Ruzi's behind him with the gleaming guitar.

Mister Scarlet claps his hands together. "Kalqitlan," he rumbles, with unusually accurate pronunciation. "Stop batting your eyes and get out here. We need to get the entertainment going."

"Mor –" Kit holds my wrist gently – "I'll get you a drink. Don't look so worried. But also – steer clear of those men."

Ruzi perches on a stool in a cleared space near the edge of the mezzanine, lit by a half circle of lanterns. He's still handsome, looking younger now he's shaved off his grizzled beard and slicked back his scraggly hair. He's got a strong jaw, even if his teeth are crooked, a wide-bridged nose and straight eyebrows. His hair recedes in a widow's peak, but it suits him.

As the patrons move to find seats, I finally spot Felicity Greave, sitting on a stool at the far end of the bar, chatting away with a man in a wide-brimmed hat leaning on a gold-tipped cane beside her. She doesn't see me looking.

I'm glad she came – when I invited her, she said she wouldn't know good music from bad. I told her that she'd know when she heard it.

I take my drink and head back. They've shuffled the

chairs to face Ruzi. The pretty brander slouches back, resting a hand and heavy forearm on the back of my seat. He's tall, I realize, broad and muscled – better nourished than the usual Lugger patrons. What's a brander doing flirting with the likes of me? What's he doing here at all, listening to a makkie musician? Shouldn't he be out tearing down statues and cleaning filth off the streets? An edge of fear sets in. He's here for something, and I don't like it.

The room hushes for Mister Scarlet's introduction.

"Good afternoon, my friends! Today we have a treat for you – and I'm not just talking about the sweet-onion stew … though if you haven't eaten yet, what are you waiting for?"

"The music, man!" Cordi heckles good-naturedly. Mister S laughs.

"Of course. Please raise your glasses – and your expectations. These old and precious tunes will move you. Ruzi Taler, everyone."

Ruzi nods his thanks.

"I'm starting with a famous Crozoni ballad called 'The Wreck of the *Eventide*' – that's the old shipwreck out yonder, north of the rivermouth. I'll sing it in the original Crozoni this time to spare your tears, but if you like the tune, I will translate for next time."

And he launches into it.

I sit up straighter, so my back doesn't touch the man's arm.

I can see Mister and Missus S. Zako must be alone, two flights up. How much will he hear? I wonder if he half remembers these songs, like I do, from the time before.

I drink slowly and sink into the sounds, Ruzi's baritone melding and floating with the thrum of the guitar. It's beautiful. I feel a sharp stab of pride. *Listen to this human being. This is ours. This is how we feel. Hear us.*

My heavy eyes peek at the brander beside me. *Hear us and feel ashamed of yourself, you big lump of lead.*

I look for Kit. He's watching me from across the room, watching the brander's arm on my chair. He raises a half smile when our eyes meet, before stepping aside so I can't see him through the crowd.

They're like a herd of kine when the feed's coming, murmuring gently. The men at the table beside us exchange some barb about makkie singing, but they keep it hushed.

I look at Felicity Greave, to see if she's impressed, and my blood goes cold. The man on the stool beside her has turned and removed his hat.

Valour Venor, Life Registry magistrate himself, here in the middle of Zako's sanctuary, watching Zako's father. This savage performance. This inferior culture.

Pride and fear war within me.

Venor's dressed plainly. His jacket is smart but simply tailored – no gold thread or visible insignia. It's so crowded in here he's escaped notice – so far.

The brander with his arm wandering behind me shrinks

to the smallest of my worries. I think of Zako upstairs, all alone. And here, just a few flights down, is the man who wants him dead.

I barely notice when Ruzi finishes the first piece. The clamour in my head is like the ocean. I don't remember to clap, but it seems no one else does either. It's so quiet. Oppressive. Do the Skøl not applaud? The few Crozoni repayers in the audience are silent too – taking their cues from the majority.

Is it even a good concert without the sting and elation of clapping until your hands go numb? I'm thrown back to the gathering after Ma's funeral, the prayer song for the dead, the rhythmic clapping to settle the restless spirit, sage smoke smudging the air.

I can hear Caruq whining at the tables, begging for scraps. Ruzi begins another Crozoni piece quickly. This one has less singing.

I steal a glance at Felicity and the magistrate. Felicity's attention is on Ruzi. Caruq sniffs around their ankles. I think of Venor's dogs out on the farm, so many years before – big hounds, caged and cowed. I hope Caruq doesn't get a kick for his pains. But then Venor's bending down to pat his plaited ruff, all smiles.

They still don't clap when Ruzi takes a break before the third song, but the buzz of rising voices sounds appreciative, even impressed.

Kit's holding down the heaving bar with Mister S. I catch his eye. He nods grimly. He's seen Venor too. *What in the world is he doing here?* I can feel my hands shaking.

I look back and see that Venor has gone. My heart stutters. Then I see him standing outside, talking to the pretty brander, hats together under a light mist of beading rain.

I hope Zako can't see Venor from that washroom window right now – he'd be terrified.

Leave, I urge them silently, but only the brander turns to go. Venor lights a smoke and exchanges pleasantries with some of the other surprised patrons. They're obviously star-struck to find the soon-to-be governor of the New West himself at a commoner's haunt like this.

Long minutes later, Mister S is back up on the mezzanine with Ruzi, banging an empty pot.

"Thank you all for braving the rain to be here this afternoon," his voice booms into all corners. "What a glorious – and illustrious –" he pauses to nod at Venor crossing back from the doorway to resume his seat beside Felicity – "audience we're graced with tonight!"

Venor cracks an arrogant smile into the awkward silence and waves a lazy hand, all false humility. Who does he think he's fooling?

I wonder how Mister S really feels. He must have been late to clock Venor too, or he'd have mentioned him in his introduction.

"Now," Mister S continues, "our musician has to be home before curfew. But he has a few more for us first! Are we ready?"

There's a smatter of applause now, muted but still.

"They're all yours," Mister S tells Ruzi.

Ruzi's earlier nervousness is nowhere to be seen. He looks at Venor for a beat, his expression flat. Then his animation returns, a note of defiance in his voice now.

"Thank you, Mister Scarlet. Missus Scarlet." He unfurls an arm in her direction. "Now, I've saved my two best songs – in this lovely language – for last. The first one only some of you will know. It was written by a woman from my homelands – the Crozon Isles – fifty years ago. And the second and final song will be a Skøl song. You may recognize it." He smiles. "And there's no cost to join in."

Ruzi begins the piece I helped him translate. It's an old song, famous, upbeat, a folky anthem about a washerwoman with a cruel boss.

The refrain follows her draining and hanging heavy loads. Or at least it seems so in the beginning. She's wringing, she's hoisting, they're drip-drip-dripping.

She's tired. It's been years since she felt warm and dry.

"A good one for this weather!" Cordie leans over to whisper to me.

Ruzi's in the flow, tapping one foot. His washerwoman's nearly done. Soon she'll relax in the sun. Then the twist. If you're paying attention, you realize she's not hanging the laundry. She's hanging the boss. Then she's running off.

The translation's not half bad, if I say so myself.

The crowd's paying attention. I even recognize a

startled burst of Felicity's laughter over near the bar. Venor's profile is stark in contrast, his jaw set.

I feel my shoulders hunching – curling in with the kind of fear that takes me when I see a krait, or hear angry voices in the dark.

Ruzi stands to give a shallow bow as the last notes fade. He hoists his guitar higher and settles its strap over his shoulder – preparing to play the next one on his feet – and they explode.

They can clap after all. Ruzi's beaming, all humble gratitude.

The noise is so loud I almost miss when the raid starts.

Half a dozen branders – including the one who was flirting with me half an hour ago, uniformed now, burst through the main entrance.

Seconds later, a further trio of huge branders pull open the door to the bar from the kitchen, urging Renny roughly in front of them, a pair of slavering ledhunds in train.

My heart's dropping like an anchor into a sea with no bed, dizzying.

Zako is upstairs. Both ways down – by the Scarlets' private stairway or the Lugger's public one – lead directly to the main bar.

He can't sneak out. How long can he hide behind the crates in Missus S's closet before they find him?

A too-familiar ringing fills my head. *Panic. Prepare.*

"What's the meaning of this?" I hear Mister Scarlet demanding, voice rising above the din. Lots of people are shouting now. Glasses are breaking, knocked over as people rush to exit.

The main party of branders make for the stairs leading to the Scarlets' quarters.

"That's private," Mister Scarlet booms. "Guest stairs to the other side."

The leading brander hesitates, just long enough for Kit to get from behind the bar and on to the Scarlets' stairs in front of the group of them.

"No!" Venor calls. "Search it all! The boy's here! Find him!"

Kit doesn't budge. The brander pushes him in the chest. Kit sways but holds.

This fear tastes like bile. Like a vice around my ribs. *They have prods. Guns.*

"Boss's house, his rules," I hear Kit saying, but then the bigger men smash into him like a wave. He goes down, and that sets off Caruq.

The suddenly transformed pub hound launches himself with a growl and a clumsy snap into the rear of a brander's ledhund going up the public stairwell. They're following the three branders who came through the courtyard door. But Caruq's not a fighter. He loses his grip and slides down several stairs. The invading hounds ignore him and continue up. Caruq shakes himself and bounds after them.

On the other side of the bar, the last of the branders heading up the private stairs pauses to deliver several kicks to Kit's balled-up, groaning body.

Gracie gets to them before I can, but the brander meets her appeals with such a heavy shove, her head collides with the banister. She falls into me just as I get there.

Renny leads her away. But the brander's still battering Kit. I catch at his uniformed arm, screaming for him to stop. He pauses to backhand me.

"Shut it! Or speak Skøl," he commands. "Not this *wah wah wah*."

I didn't even realize I was screaming in Crozoni.

"Mora!" Someone yanks me back before he can land a proper punch to my face. It's Felicity Greave, her Skøl vowels like liquid. "Come away – you'll get hurt too!"

At least we've created enough of a distraction for Kit to scramble to his feet. The brander swipes him aside and butts past, heading upstairs.

Kit throws a panicked glance at me before following.

I freeze, Felicity's hand still gripping my arm.

And now I'm crying. I can feel the quiet tears streaking down my cheeks. How useful.

"Find him!" Venor screeches again, quite close by. "He's here!"

Missus Scarlet has picked her way through the mêlée to Venor's elbow.

"*Who* do you think is here?" Her icy voice could slice through stone. The crowd falls silent.

Venor's not so easily cowed. He turns to meet her gaze. "The wanted boy. Zako Taler."

He pulls a folded-up wanted poster from his pocket and passes it to her. She doesn't look at it.

Ruzi reaches my side, his precious guitar still slung about his neck, his face a mirror of the horror I feel.

Felicity releases my arm.

Then an odd movement outside catches my eye: a white meteor, pelting diagonally past the mezzanine window, then the window below it.

"What in the…?" Felicity rushes to watch as the white blur hurtles into the river and thrashes briefly before separating into two discrete hounds who quickly spin from view. It must be Caruq, fighting with one of the branders' hounds.

I catch the last stragglers filtering out to Belor Way, most of the crowd now gone. No one wants to get caught up in a raid like this, though I see Cordi and Vertie defying the flow, hovering outside the door, peering in at us with concern.

Missus S is still locked in conversation with Venor, but frowning in confusion. "The runaway? Why would he be here?"

"I know he's here." Venor leans down, closer to her height. "He plaited that fur on your hound's ruff. He learned how to do that from my daughter."

Oh, Zako.

Missus Scarlet's mask of calm holds, except for a tiny wobble about her mouth.

"I see." She catches my eye over Venor's shoulder and

lifts her chin. I wipe the wetness off my face and try to keep composed. She says very slowly and clearly, "There's been some mistake. This girl here, Mora, likes to plait our hound's fur. She's friends with our repayer, Kalqitlan." She fixes her eyes back on Venor. "I saw your branders trampling all over him. He works for us. He's not to be damaged like that."

Mister S joins her, putting a bolstering arm around her back. I clock Felicity disappearing up the guest stairs – probably heading to witness the drama so she can write about it.

Missus S clears her throat and collects herself. "Magistrate Venor. Please. Mora's just there." She nods in my direction. "You can ask her yourself about the plaits."

I'm still frozen, but at least I've stopped crying. I can hear heavy footfall all over the high ceiling, but no triumphant hollering – yet.

Venor glances my way with a sneer. He doesn't even recognize me, I realize. His gaze still leaches something out of me. I feel my bones getting softer. I reach a hand to the small of my back, just to remind myself I do have a spine. I need to use it.

"Lies!" he declares. "I've had enough makkie-rat lies for a lifetime."

"M-Mister magistrate..." I step up. I'm an insignificance to this man, this man of my waking nightmares. This man who broke me two years back. I'm just another makkie, breathing his air. "I plaited the hound's fur, it's true. I learned it from Zako back when I lived on the farm…"

Venor's not listening. He gives the Scarlets a look of undisguised spite and stalks to the foot of their private stairs. "Where is he? Report!" he screams up at the branders above.

One set of footsteps starts down.

"No sign." The brander enters. "First floor and guest wing are clear, but the hound is going through again. Nothing yet in the private quarters…" He pauses as Venor's face gets noticeably redder. "But we did find some pre-Registry reading material."

"Banned books!" Venor sneers at Missus Scarlet. "Why am I not surprised?"

"A window over the river was open," the brander continues. "We lost a hound out that way, but the boy wasn't there."

"Letting in fresh air's not a crime," Mister Scarlet interjects.

"Has anyone searched the roof?" Venor hisses. "Well, go on! Move."

"Right away, magistrate." The brander rushes to comply.

I'm thinking fast. Did Zako go out there? Could he escape that way? I can see the roof in my mind's eye. I imagine the Lugger from above – how would a bird see it? What would I do in Zako's place?

If he'd jumped into the river like Caruq, we'd have spotted him. But the only other place to go from the mezzanine roof would be up, on to the roof proper. If he could climb the brickwork and the guttering. And the Lugger stands alone. No chance of jumping to the roof of another building. He'd have to climb down. Three levels. He couldn't do that.

But I suddenly realize what he could do. My heart stalls.

Everyone's ignoring me and Ruzi in the chaos. I touch his arm and gesture to the door behind the bar, into the kitchen.

It's empty. I ease the door shut. Something's burning on the range. Gracie and Renny are still in the main lounge.

"We need to lock this door," I whisper to Ruzi.

He doesn't question why. He shrugs off the guitar and examines the door handle. "It needs a key," he says.

Through the corner of my eye, through the window on to the courtyard, I see the spring-green leaves of the Makaia plane tree in the courtyard quaking. Raindrops shower down from it – as if the wind's dislodged them. But it's not the wind.

I have no idea where the keys are kept. But the door opens inward, and it's the same hard, heavy wood that everything in this place is made of. Even a brander built like a bull will be slowed down by it. I go to the pantry, which is propped open with a wooden wedge. I yank it out and take it back to the main door. Ruzi gets the idea, jams it in as far as it'll go.

I lean against the door, listening to the snatches of voices filtering through from the bar.

"… and we've cleared the rooms in the public wing."

"Keep looking! The cellar! The stables! The kitchen!" Venor's losing his certainty. "And get out there and keep an eye on the courtyard. I don't want any rats climbing down from the roof."

Ruzi braces his whole body against the door, holding the handle. His head's turned, staring out of the window.

I follow his gaze. He's there.

Zako's dropping down the lower branches of the Makaia plane tree. He's barely recognizable, wearing about as many layers of clothes as he owns. Maybe he hasn't left anything of his behind for the hounds to smell.

"Door's locked!" the brander shouts on the other side.

"You! Go round the other way!" I hear Venor order another brander, cold and methodical. Thank goodness he's the only one of them with more than two walnut halves in his skull. "And you, girl – unlock this."

"Shouldn't be locked, but let me try the key." I hear Gracie's voice. Her keys drop and chime on the flagstone floor – nerves or a deliberate fumble? I'm grateful either way.

Zako's hanging off a low branch now, dropping to the bench skirting the trunk.

Then he's off the bench. He's running to the courtyard exit.

And he's beyond it. I can't see him.

"Doesn't seem to be locked," Gracie's saying.

I go into the courtyard. The branders are on the roof,

looking down – but Zako is gone. He's got away, I think. I feel dizzy with relief.

"You!" one of them calls down. It's the handsome one who had his arm on my chair. "Seen a boy?"

"No!" I call back, too loud.

I think I see a curtain twitch in one of the guest rooms overlooking the courtyard – Felicity's. I don't have time to worry about whether or not she saw Zako.

The brander is still banging furiously on the kitchen door. The wedge drifts and it gives an inch.

Ruzi kicks the wedge away – it goes skittering out of sight under the counter – and I smile, apologetic, at the brander bursting through. "Sorry. It got stuck."

He's coiled tight and not having it. "What the fuck are you playing at?" he shouts. Gosh, his voice is loud without a door intervening.

"I'm sorry, I—"

But he's pulling something from his belt, and I hear it, the low buzz that stirs memories like wasps under my skin. I leap back on reflex, but manage to knock the cast-iron pot of burning soup from the stove – it crashes to the floor, narrowly missing my feet.

I look away, and that's when the brander sticks the prod into my neck.

Agony.

I drop to the floor, and one of my hands slides through a puddle of the burnt soup. It's hot as molten glass, but still not as painful as the elektric prod.

I can hear my protests, my voice slurred like a drunk. The brander rolls me on to my back with his foot.

Then Ruzi shouts something in his confident performer's voice.

And now the most surreal event of the evening. His beautiful guitar flashes overhead, followed by an almighty crash against the brander's skull and a heartbreaking twang.

His words filter belatedly through, echoing like the ringing in my head.

"*Stay away from my daughter.*"

23

i wasn't his

A cloud of odd events from my childhood resurfaces as I lie here on the kitchen flagstones, trying not to move. Moving hurts.

Ruzi, smiling at my mother over the counter in his workshop. A look passing between them after I told a joke. The neighbour's son going on and on about how my sisters' eyes were different to mine, until his ma told him off.

Something shifts.

Ruzi is my father.

Zako is my brother.

The commotion with Ruzi and the branders has spilled back into the lounge, and I'm alone in the kitchen.

My ears are still ringing.

Then a cool, dripping snout is exploring my burnt hand in its puddle of ruined squash soup. "Gods below," whispers a strange voice I don't recognize. Caruq's back from his adventure in the river already. I turn my head to look at him. The plaits in his ruff that caused all this trouble have unravelled. One of his ears is torn and bloody, and a foul-smelling mud's all the way up his legs to his belly, but he still looks unaccountably proud of himself. He drifts out of view again.

"Where's Kit?" I murmur as I try to sit up – and promptly pass out.

I wake the next morning, slouched under a blanket in Missus Scarlet's comfy chair in the Lugger's lounge. My hand and neck are both sore, but nothing like they were before.

Gracie and Renny appear. Apparently they manoeuvred me out of the kitchen last night and into the chair, but they couldn't carry me upstairs. They fill me in on what I missed.

Kit and Ruzi were arrested – Kit for obstructing the branders searching the Scarlets' quarters and Ruzi for smashing his guitar over the one that attacked me.

I wish he'd used a pan – the kitchen was full of them. His lovely guitar. I'm not sure he can fix it – he hasn't got the materials or the tools. *That's if he gets out*, a voice whispers in my mind.

"The branders found nothing, of course, after all that," Gracie murmurs. Her forehead and cheek beside one eye carry a huge purple bruise, big as the wing of a moon moth. "What made them think Zako was here?"

I manage a small shake of the head.

"Well," says Renny, "they turned up some old boys' clothes in a trunk in Missus S's dressing room – and some baby things too – but they were just mementoes they kept from their boy."

The Scarlets' small collection of banned books were the worst of it. Skøl aren't allowed most books that were written before their Life Registries were established. They might be fined.

"The magistrate left in a huff. He was all pretending not to care, wasn't he, but red as a new sail. We could tell he was next to bursting underneath, couldn't we?"

Renny shudders in agreement. "He was awful. Possessed. How can a man with a temper like that be made governor of the whole New West?"

"Mister and Missus S are hopping mad too, of course – with good reason! They're out for compensation."

"Compensation! Really?" I'm impressed.

"It's fair enough. Those brutes messed up everything! And Missus S says it's not right, them injuring her repayer and frightening the customers! Giving me this and all!" Gracie gestures to her bruise.

"They're paying the fine for now, to get Kit and your old friend out of jail … but they're going to see a lawyer about getting it back. I hope Caruq's okay."

They're worried Caruq drowned, but I tell them I saw him – I'm sure I did, dripping muddy river water on me while I was lying on the flagstones.

"That's strange," says Gracie. "We can't find him." *Was*

the dog I saw just a figment? It's true I was half out of my mind. Hearing things. Could've been seeing things too.

I make it to work – late, with a burnt hand and still-aching neck, but Cordi and Vertie have already made excuses for me and Ruzi to Mister Wagsen.

I pass the next two days in a strange haze, leading Clomper and Caney, leaden-footed. Then night tremors. Exhaustion. Feelings chasing around my insides that I can't pin down, like relief and despair at the same time. And something else. Something like rage.

The shock of Zako, a fraction away from being killed.

Ruzi's revelation: *Stay away from my daughter.*

The pain of the prod.

Thanks to a big chunk of the money the Scarlets were going to put towards Zako's passage and all the influence they could muster, Kit and Ruzi are released intact. Ruzi and I pretend I didn't hear his outburst and don't talk about it. I recover, slowly. But we don't know where Zako is.

We thought he might sneak back to the Lugger, or even come and find us at Opal Alley, but we've seen neither hide nor hair. I cling on to the fact that no news must be good news.

Then, two evenings after the raid, Kit comes to visit me and Ruzi.

We're at Opal Alley's kitchen table, with a pot of fikka and the latest edition of the *Portcaye Post.* Rain patters on the roof.

Kit comes in, holding a makeshift envelope addressed to him at the Lugger. There's no paper inside, but Zako has written a few sentences on the inner envelope itself – in Skøl script, Skøl language, because no one taught him to write Crozoni. Poor penmanship, peppered with errors.

Im awlrite tell pa and M downt worry
Living like Blenny and ~~Torneel~~ T off the land

I can hear his voice in my head, saying the words. Nothing's inside but a pearly flake of oyster shell.

"Living off the land?" My voice squeaks higher and I examine the envelope more critically. "No stamp." There are a few numbers in the corner where the stamp should be, hand-written, but not by Zako.

"It was posted," Kit says. "That's the post-office code in the corner there. Means it was put in a public postbox somewhere in County Portcaye – so he hasn't gone as far as County Copper. It's *receiver pays*. Post office leaves a note saying they have it, and you go to pay and collect it."

"So he's left town," Ruzi rumbles.

"He got away," I murmur. "To somewhere near the coast." I rub the oyster-shell flake between my fingers.

"He's being cautious, not telling us more, in case the branders intercept the post," Ruzi says. "He's found this paper somehow to make this envelope. It's clever."

"Exactly. He doesn't want us to worry."

"Should we go and look for him? Try to bring him

back?" I sip my cold fikka. *Where could we hide him if we found him?*

Kit throws up his hands. "He could have gone half a dozen ways – up the coast, down the coast. He could have gone inland. The shell might be there to throw off the branders. They're watching us, more than ever. He's safer alone."

"Do you really think so?"

"It's only been a couple of days. It's not winter any longer," Kit reminds us. "There's a thousand places to shelter. Caves. Abandoned farms. Missus Scarlet says their boy ran wild in the summers."

I think of Zako alone, outcast, beyond the high stone walls.

"It's not summer yet," I mumble. "I wouldn't like to be outdoors, nights like these."

Kit huffs and back-hands the latest edition of the *Portcaye Post* on the table. "Just as well you're not allowed."

NOTICE OF EXTENSION:
REPAYER CURFEW

No Makaians to be out of doors without express permission from an employer, **in writing**, on pain of incarceration and/or a fine of ₭100 between the hours of **6 at night and 5 in the morning**: EFFECTIVE IMMEDIATELY.

They've lengthened the curfew by two hours. It's not hard for Kit, who works where he sleeps and has the Scarlets to write him any number of permission notes. But for plenty of repayers, it won't be so simple. The Glassworks' manager isn't like the Scarlets. Wagsen won't give us permission. And he'll expect the same amount of work. I'll have to rush every day to get Clomper and Caney settled, and it gives me no time for anything at all after work.

Venor's punishing us.

"Vindictive brickhead," Ruzi grumbles.

"He's cracking down on banned books too," I read. All for the high governor's visit.

I turn the paper so they can read.

> The Magistrate's improvement policy comes less than two months ahead of the highly anticipated arrival of High Governor Clarion Lovemore. Lovemore, sailing on the *Herald of the New Dawn*, accompanied by the *Kineherd's Delight* and the *Vårnat Witch*, is expected to dock in Portcaye Firstday 06 of the Sixmonth, six days ahead of the New Western Governorship ceremony to be held on Endweek 12.

Kit sighs and stands. His working day's not over. Ruzi and I get up too.

"Come by tomorrow after work." Kit pauses at the door

to tell me, letting in the rain. "Don't stay cooped up here. I'll sneak you home. I've plenty saved to pay your fine if you get caught."

Plenty saved that we've been meaning to put towards Zako's safe passage. He can't hide out in the wilderness forever. I'll keep selling drawings and saving until we've raised enough. He'll need it before the winter.

I wonder if Kit will keep on working for his rebellious Reedstones. I want, now more than ever, to be part of something like that. Tonight doesn't feel like the time to bring them up though.

Ruzi twists the *Portcaye Post* into a tight wad and throws it directly in the stove, instead of on to the sagging fuel pile we rifled through together like it was a library, not long ago. *Visiting the library with my pa.*

"I'll see," is all I tell Kit. He heads down the steps.

I make for my room as Ruzi clears the cups away.

"You leaving your mucky boots in the middle of the floor there?" he asks before I reach my door. I've left them in front of the stove to dry.

"Sorry, Ruzi." I go back to move them. With Zako who knows where, alone, he's tense and irritable.

"A trouble taken now's a trouble saved later," he says.

"If you say so."

"You're just like your mother," he grumbles under his breath.

"What's that?" The words drop slow from my tensed jaw, hard as hailstones.

"Messy. Head in the clouds."

He's one to talk. *Have a look in the mirror, my friend.*

I can see the river the day she drowned herself, like someone flayed the blue sky and laid its ribbon out in the wind. Fluffy white clouds floating along, out to sea to meet their fellows at the edge of everything.

"Don't speak about her like that." My train of thought almost washes away under a wave of memories. "She was way tidier than you."

His shoulders roll higher, and I'm sure he'll ignore me. But he turns to face me, his wide mouth clamped shut, his big hands cupping the cold fikka pot. I see myself in him now, and don't know how I missed it for so long. Are all my parts made from broken people?

I suddenly notice his neat fingernails, grown long to pluck the guitar. The one he ruined over me.

His eyes meet mine and, just like that, we're not pretending any more.

"She made me promise," he says at last. "To keep it secret, no matter what. I gave her my word."

"Why?"

"Because she wanted a family and I didn't. I told her she shouldn't have you."

So few words, and I'm drowning in them. The rain's coming heavier now, rattling the windowpane.

"We were –" he clears his throat – "together, more or less, for years when we were young. Before she met Lewis. Never got to wanting the same things at the same time.

After she found out about you, Lewis was there for her. I wasn't."

"Did he know I wasn't his?"

"Oh yes. He knew. Everyone knew. She was big as a barn with you when they married. Never doubt he wanted you, my girl. He wanted her, he wanted everything..." His voice trails off.

He tilts forward like he might step closer, then flattens his palm against the nearest wall. "Everything I was too selfish to want."

His gruff voice scratches.

My heart swirls between shame, anger and grief. Did they keep me in the dark to spare me – or to spare themselves? *Both*, I think. *Both*.

"You could've said something."

"Time was never right."

His eyes are glistening now. They're so like Zako's, like my brother's, like a darker version of mine. But an angry buzzing in my ears won't fade.

"When you came here," he goes on, "I thought I could make things right between us."

I sigh. Ruzi's a musician. He sings about heroes – he'll never be one.

"Some things are too broken to be fixed," I say, and then I shut up. I think of my leg. Of Ma and Pa. Ruzi's precious guitar. I don't trust my voice not to wobble.

I was two when Ma had the twins. Real Dezil babies, with dark-brown eyes like Pa. It was four more years before they had Char. His babyhood is the one I remember. How soft he was, an animal softness. How hard he used to squeeze my face and pull my hair with his tiny hands.

Ma did love me, but not the same way as the others. I didn't quite fit. I never questioned it.

But Pa – Lewis Dezil the millwright – who we used to swing off like a tree, who used to play throw-for-crow with us and lose on purpose, who would pick up armfuls of our little shoes and stack them away – he never treated me any different.

Eleven years. He knew I wasn't his.

24

like ghosts

I have one of those dreams where my family's still alive. Pa and the three little ones, even Ma. They're all the same age they were, though I'm older. We're living together, not here in Portcaye. Not in our old house either, but another house that doesn't exist, surrounded by pinewoods.

Ença and Eben find a rotting head by the hitching post, maggots wriggling out of the eye sockets. They scream for me. *It's your brother!*

No. Char's here, I tell them. *He's here. It's not our brother.* I'm trying to shout, but I can't. I can't scream in this dream world.

I wake in a sweat, rigid-limbed, still straining to scream, the old refrain scratchy as the wool blanket – *why did I survive?*

To work meek as a kine for the people who destroyed everyone I loved?

Ruzi's an early riser, but he's still abed when I leave. It's not cold, but mist fills the streets, cloud-thick. I stop to buy a loaf of cheese bread from the bakery downstairs and head for the Mermen Gates. I'll go north to the woods. A person could build a shelter there. It's close to the sea for pickings in the rock pools. That's where I would run, if I was brave enough.

"Someone's up and about early." Round a bend in the road, I almost bump into Gracie. "This is mad, isn't it?" Her smile's dimmed behind a veil of fog. "Need a knife to cut this stuff!"

If she hadn't hailed me, I'd have gone right past her in the mist. A basket of aguatos and greens weighs down one of her arms – she's been to the costermongers near Crescent Lane.

"I'm going out for… I'm going outside the wall for a walk," I tell her lamely.

"Sure I'd rather spend a day off with my feet up," she laughs. "But each to her own." She trudges off through the whiteout with a wave.

The familiar mermen still guard the gates, though the fog's too thick to reveal more than a rough sense of them. It's only been a few weeks since the announcement of their numbered days, but I'm glad they've survived the frenzy of demolition so far. Imilia Dezil in Sinton Square hasn't been so lucky. The shrivelled turnip-head is still there too, stuck on its lonely gate spike.

I've warmed up by the time I've crossed the bridge and

the stretch of marsh into the pines. The mist still hasn't burned away. The ground is sodden and awfully muddy, even under the spreading branches.

I walk another hour as the mists dissolve. *Ancestors, guide me.* Zako said he was living like Blenny and T off the land.

They lived in a forest. This is the closest forest to Portcaye town.

I feel foolish, but that's no reason not to try. I thread my hands together in not-quite prayer. I'm his sister. Is it absurd to think intuition might lead me to him? Perhaps the ancestors sent me that dream in the pine forest.

The ordinary wild sounds seem to lull, and perhaps I'm mad as a sack of bats, but I don't feel alone.

"Zako. Zak," I call, softly at first, then loud as I can – like a deranged seagull, screaming. True seagull cries reach me only as distant echoes.

There's no answer. The chirps and whistles of the little brown forest birds grow louder when I subside.

My foot squelches into a particularly deep muddy hole tangled with roots, and I curse under my breath, trying to haul it out without losing the boot. Then someone's hand is at my elbow, steadying. It's Kit.

"What are you doing here?" I balance on his arm and try to scrape mud off my boot.

"Looking for you."

"Why?"

"Gracie said she saw you. I took the day off. You shouldn't be here alone – it's not safe."

"They've let you off for the whole day?" I realize my other boot looks just as bad and give up.

"Haven't asked in a while."

I turn to examine him. He looks fresh as a daisy. "Have you stopped working nights for the Reedstones?"

"They haven't had a job for me in a while. They thought it best to lie low while Venor's on the warpath. But they know I'm standing by. They're plotting something. Work'll pick up again."

"What are they plotting?"

"The usual, you know."

"Delusions of eccentric rebellion ... with a slice of blackmail on the side?"

Kit stops me with two hands. "You make everything sound so –" he leans closer, a smile on his lips – "delicious."

Shivers chase up my spine, not unpleasant ones. He holds my gaze like he knows what I'm feeling. Like I've made him feel the same.

No. I'm imagining again. When will I learn?

I keep walking. "I'm looking for Zako," I explain.

"So I heard – like half the forest. You'll not find him like this." His voice is gentle but firm.

"I have to try. I'm sick of doing nothing!"

He raises his hands, fingers spread to placate me.

"He might have lit a cook fire. It's not so misty now that smoke wouldn't show up. I could climb up a tree and take a look."

"Climb one of these?" Kit looks appalled.

These trees aren't welcoming like the lovely spreading Makaia plane tree in the Lugger courtyard. It's ages before we find a tall old tree with a branch low enough to reach. Kit's fingers can brush it when he jumps.

"Can you boost me?" I look at him, shrugging out of my coat and bag. "Or is all that muscle for decoration?"

"Ha," he scoffs at my challenge. "Try and keep straight." He crouches, wraps his arms around my shins and stands upright with a grunt. I wobble but hold on to his head.

"Well? Can you reach?" his words are muffled in my trousers, and I hurry to wrap my fingers around the branch and pull while he gets under me and pushes. "You're not as heavy as a full barrel, but I've never tried boosting one up a tree."

"I'm up," I tell him, breathless and scrabbling as more mud falls from my boots and narrowly misses his eyes. I can see his hands and top are covered already. "Sorry."

"Concentrate on holding on up there."

He wanders closer to the trunk as I crawl my way along and start to pull myself up the next branch. They grow closer together as I go, ladder-like, though the height's more daunting than I expected. My weak side doesn't help. I'm sweating from the effort, and I'm still only halfway up.

The top of the tree sways precariously as I climb, the grainy green lichen coating the bark crumbling under my fingers. The branches bend but don't break. A stitch gnaws dully at my side.

"Careful." Kit's deep voice filters up to me.

"I'm nearly there," I call down.

And then I am. The mist is a memory, and the sun that's all but barred by the pines is burning through towers of cloud a thousand times higher than the tree. The glassy sea winks to the west, but we're further into the forest than I thought.

My palms around the soft-needled branches are sweating despite the cold. My heart's strumming fast as anything. It's terrifying being this high. It's higher than the old Bucket Wheel used to go at the fair, and that was scary enough.

I peel my hands off one at a time to rub the sweat on my woollen trousers before turning to search for smoke. The walls of Portcaye break the middle distance to the south, cliffs rising above. The coastline is flatter to the north.

Pines stretch far inland. Crows arc and call above them, and one even swoops to perch atop a neighbouring tree. It tilts a sceptical eye at me.

"You there?" Kit again.

"I am," I call back, still catching my breath. The crow leaps off with a croak and flaps away.

"How's the view?"

It's beautiful, I think. *I wish you could see it.* "There's no smoke," I shout down. "I'll wait a bit." I peer through the branches, though I can't see him. He doesn't reply.

I stay crouched like a crow for who knows how long, the wind picking up. No smoke appears.

The crows tug at memories I haven't visited in years. I was around seven years old, and some boys at school found a crow chick, not yet fledged, feather shafts still encased in white, fallen from its nest. They thought it was a great game to take it by one of its scrawny wings and dash it to death against the tree trunk. The teacher didn't see to stop them. Then he said it mattered little – the creature was good as dead.

Ma said the teacher was a fool. *Boys will always make excuses for cruelty*, she told me, *and by the time they're men they don't need excuses at all.*

It wasn't long after that she helped me make a mobile out of thin sheets of wood scavenged from Ruzi's workshop – scraps that weren't good enough for his instruments. We cut and glued them into flat bird shapes and strung them on white threads from a cross of twigs. Pa put a hook in the ceiling over my bed, and there they danced.

My heart has stopped banging, but the memories press hard. I blow a breath in the direction of the wheeling crows and imagine them turning and diving in new directions, black shapes tethered by threads.

A slight tremor invades my hands and legs – part strain from clinging to my perch, part reaction to the memory. I've trained myself out of tears, mostly, but the body still finds ways to grieve.

I can't stay up here all day with no coat, waiting for smoke that may never come. I start down. It's harder than going up – after the climb and my heart going fit to bust from the height, my strength has burned off like the fog.

I'm more than three body lengths above the ground when a wave of light-headedness grips me.

My foot slips, my fingers clutch at nothing, then I'm falling.

I gasp, too shocked to scream, and try to grab at branches as I crash through – unsuccessfully. They catch at my face and hands. One whips like fire into my ribs as another tears my chin and snags away my hair wrap. They do nothing to slow my fall.

Then I'm crashing into Kit, legs first. He catches me awkwardly, swearing rather colourfully as I knock the breath out of him. He staggers back but somehow manages to keep his feet, steadying us against the tree trunk – one hand on my backside, another hooked under my thigh, wrapping around my waist. My chest crushes into his face as I slide to the ground, and a strange sound escapes him, almost like a growl.

"What the fuck, Mora? Would it kill you to show a bit of care?" *Is he shaking or is it me?* "Are you hurt? Are you all right?"

"I'm… I'm fine," I gasp. "I'm sorry. Did I hurt you?" My traitorous legs are still trying to give way, but it's too muddy to collapse on the ground. He braces me up against the tree.

"No." He swears some more. "You could have broken something."

I examine the grazes on my hands then look up into his eyes. "Thank the ancestors you were here, then."

My light-headedness fades, but his arms are still around me. As his hands start drawing away, my eyes flick to his lips – no distance at all, really. His expression is angry, and his eyes are a darker violet than usual. A wave of desire washes over me. My chest is still heaving from the shock. Kit's warm fingers brush the side of my neck, where a vein flutters. I feel a small pain – the branches must have scraped the skin. Then his eyes tilt to mine, and I stretch up to close the gap between us.

His lips are as soft and warm as I remember, though today there's more stubble on his chin. He deepens the kiss with a satisfied moan, his tongue parting my lips. My hands drift inside his open coat, his hard chest warm against my chilled fingers. I just want to feel him.

The bark of the tree presses firmly into my back, then Kit's touch is lighting me up. His fingers trail along one of my arms, cupping my cold cheek, warm over my ear, then burying into my hair. His teeth gently catch my lower lip, but far too soon, his mouth is gone. I whimper a faint protest before he begins kissing my grazed neck, then my collarbone. The slow caress of his lips and tongue flood my core with heat, and I can hear myself gasping.

Then his mouth is back on mine, and his hands with their clever fingers are drifting under the hem of my blouse. One slips around my back just above my waist as the other moves over the sensitive area on my ribs where the tree branch caught it, up to my breast. The calluses on his thumb draw a singing response from my skin as he strokes me.

I wrap my arms around his back, drawing him closer to feel the length of his body curving into mine. His hair smells of woodsmoke and soap – but then a different scent cuts through my pleasure like a knife.

We're still ankle-deep in mud, and it's all over his shoulders from when I climbed up earlier. The smell of mud mixed with the tang of cold sweat and the cool air on my chest pushes me back to that time by the river, fighting against too many hands clawing my blouse open – mud smeared on my skin, caked on my boots. The same foul-smelling mud sloughing off Caruq after that awful raid.

I'm shaking again now, my breath hitching. What if I try to stop Kit and he gets angry like those boys? Like that brander with his prod? My mother's warning floats front of mind again. *Boys will always make excuses for cruelty.* No, I don't want to think like that. He wouldn't.

I move my hands to his shoulders and push him away gently.

"Wait, Kit." My voice comes out small and uncertain. "I don't… I haven't…" I don't know what I want to say. The heat of him is intoxicating. My thudding heart wants all of him, here, now, knee-deep in cold mud – but my brain says I don't know what I'm doing, and I have to beware, and this isn't how friends who keep their friends behave. It has a point.

He pulls back reluctantly, biting his lip. His hands draw

away, out of my shirt. His dark pupils search mine, soft but intense.

"Sorry." He coughs once and pulls my coat off a nearby branch before helping me into it, even buttoning the first button up against my neck, precisely, hands steady, before he drops them. He won't meet my eye now, more embarrassed than I am.

"It's the mud," I stutter out, kicking it with a boot toe. "It reminds me of that night, when those boys tried to… The smell of it." I shudder involuntarily, and his arms circle me once more, drawing me to his chest in a firm but rather platonic hug that saves us from further eye contact. "Ever since … I'm scared."

"It's okay," he rumbles, his chin in my hair. "I understand."

I'm not sure I do.

"I shouldn't have done that," he says into the silence. "A moment of madness. It's not every day a girl like you falls into my arms."

I feel warm and safe. I don't want to move.

"I don't mean I'm scared of you…" I start to say. "It's not that, it's just…"

He sighs so softly I almost don't hear, pulling away, but one hand reaches down to touch my fingertips.

"Your hands are freezing," he interrupts. "What did you bring to eat?"

He's chasing the mood away. *A moment of madness* – is that really how he feels?

We break chunks off the cheese bread, greasy but filling, and sit on a fallen log sharing it in silence, the flask of water between us. I realize he came without any food or drink, and he's not best dressed for the weather, though I remember well enough he runs hot. My hands are finally warming up.

I'm worried I've gone and made everything awful by kissing him. But then, he kissed me back. And, Thea's wounds, if it wasn't good – before I went and ruined it. Goodness knows how far we might have gone if not for the mud.

It's not every day a girl like you falls into my arms.

Exactly how often do girls like me fall into your arms, then? I want to ask him. But if he wanted to talk, he'd be talking. He's clearly more experienced than me – but then, I've no experience at all. He could break my heart, and I'd be no more than a notch on his bedpost.

"We should go back," I murmur eventually. "You're right; it's pointless looking for him like this."

He turns to face me, but I stare out through the young bracken and the endless torsos of trees. "Gracie's making soup," he offers at last.

"Sounds good," I say with false cheeriness. I stand up, stoppering the flask.

It's past midday before we reach the approach to Portcaye town.

Kit's gone quiet, thinking. Suppose I have too. It's

awful, somehow, just trudging back to this godless town, back to our lives here with nothing to show.

The Mermen Gates stand out a mile now. Something's going on there. A crowd is gathered, inside and out.

"They're taking the statues down on an Endweek?" I ask.

"No rest for the wicked," Kit murmurs. "I heard they're going to melt them into blocks and call them new."

"Oh, naturally."

"Symbols of purity or strength or … who knows."

I scoff. "So imaginative."

"Not sure I'll miss the mermen either, to be honest," Kit confesses.

I will, but I don't want to admit it. "It's a miracle they lasted this long," I offer instead.

But it soon becomes clear the mermen are not the focus of today's crowd.

The ghastly turnip-head has come down. But one of the rail spikes has a new addition.

A real head. A fresh one. A Skøl – blonde and pale.

Kit's pace lurches faster. I hurry to match it, wondering if they've changed their minds about waiting until Lovemore gets here to execute the Artist. As we near I can see the head belongs to a man I don't recognize.

Spring's here and it's getting warm enough for flies. Bluebottles are already gathering at the white-and-red severing, like a mockery of a mourning ribbon.

The man's cheeks and eyes are sunken, but his curls are

remarkably kempt, wafting beyond the tip of his pointed chin.

"It's not him," I murmur, just as Kit's feet scuff loudly to a stop on the stones.

"It's him," he stutters.

"Who?"

He swears softly. "He's – he was – the Artist's agent. He's the one I paid … for the papers … Zako."

I can't speak. Kit's horrified eyes meet mine, and I feel a woozy sinking behind my breastbone.

"Did the Artist rat him out?"

"Now?" Kit's tone is uncertain. "Two moons later? Doesn't make sense."

I feel a flurry of panic. "What if he said something about you … and the papers you paid him for, for Zako … before they…"

A crow caws, harsh and rattling overhead.

Kit's eyes are still wide, but he's shaking his head.

"No." He says it like he knows for sure, like he'll make it true. "Come on." He starts walking again.

I hear buzzing. A slow, fat fly collides with my face. I rub my cheek, hard. Kit's hand is gentle between my shoulder blades. We walk through the gates and the small crowd of gawkers. Kit pulls on his jaw with his other hand.

My sinking feeling keeps on sinking.

Kraa! Kraa! The crow, fading forest-wards. I want to fly where it flies. My head is full of bird shapes, drifting like ghosts.

25

it gets rowdy

I hang about like a famished wreck in the Lugger all afternoon, downing bowl after bowl of Gracie's soup and waiting for news. Kit drinks fikka with Renny and Gracie and coos over a baby starting to totter like he hasn't a care in the world.

All the usuals are in, discussing the gruesome business at the gates. Speculation is rife as to who the man is.

He was a pirate from County Shipway with ten thousand on his head.

He was a hired assassin, plotting to shoot High Governor Lovemore at the Hexagon Hall.

He attacked the branders who came to burn his banned books.

He was a clerk, stealing from the Life Registry.

The evening's edition of the *Portcaye Post* has the story.

—

TREASON! CLERK "COLLARED"

—

ENDWEEK SHOCK AT THE GATES

—

WHY DID CLERK LOSE HIS HEAD?

A deputy clerk with nearly three years' tenure at the Portcaye Life Registry, 24-year-old Fidelity Hemman, was executed today under the Treason Act. In accordance with the Act, his head has been severed from his body and displayed in a prominent location.

Hemman was apprehended Sixday evening for the treasonous act of stealing from the Life Registry. He pleaded guilty to possession of illicit materials including Life Registry paper earmarked for Life Records, proof of payments and other official documentation – and was put to death in a private execution on Endweek morning. His head is on display at…

At least the gawpers didn't get a public beheading. But Thea's wounds. Arrested yesterday and already convicted and killed. Faster than the news could break. That's quick, even for this lot.

For stealing paper. Well, not just paper – very valuable paper, stolen for forgeries. The Life Registry uses special watermarked, part-silk-fibre paper. It's only manufactured in one factory in Skøland. Still. Stealing it can't be unheard of – there's a black market for it after all. They're making him an example. Heads haven't rolled in County Portcaye for years.

Venor's got more to prove, with his impending governorship.

> Clerk Hemman betrayed the principles we hold dear at the Life Registry. As Magistrate Venor says, "Justice must be done and be seen to be done..."

The Artist isn't mentioned in the article at all. They're keeping that one up their sleeve – a grand spectacle to impress Clarion Lovemore.

"I wonder why they didn't save Hemman for the Hexagon Hall too," says Felicity when I clock her reading over my shoulder. "You'd think two beheadings to launch the governorship would be better than one."

"Perhaps because he's small fry compared to the Artist?" I say.

"Hmm," she muses. "My guess is they killed Hemman during questioning. Interrogated him a bit too hard, and now they're making the best of things."

My soup spoon clatters to the floor. "Really?"

One day in custody and they tortured him dead.

"Will you write about it?"

She laughs again. "No. I wouldn't be allowed to write about something like that. No one would; you know that.

It's all speculation anyway, without witnesses and evidence."

"Is everything in the paper half a lie?"

Felicity dips an eyebrow and doesn't dignify that with a response.

"Did you always want to be a journalist?" I ask. Surely someone like Felicity must have been born with a plan.

"A chemist." She surprises me.

Felicity behind a counter, mixing powders and potions – I can't imagine it.

"I was too wild for that life," she confesses. "Do you know what they called me when I was a girl?"

"What?"

Her eyelashes flutter. "Ferocity."

I smile. Felicity has some sharp edges, but wild and violent? "Really? But you seem so…" *Tame*, I think. So like someone who moans at every rule before following it to the letter. "Calm," I settle for.

She laughs. "I dread to think what you were going to say."

I frown back at the paper. "If the branders killed him like you think, that's not justice. What if he was innocent? Someone *should* write about it."

Felicity only shakes her head.

"I thought the Skøl followed their own rules," I say.

"Clerks, maybe. That's how they always want it to seem. But branders, never. Venor's just another brander deep down, far as I can tell." Her shoulders droop.

It's after curfew, but hours before sundown. I've been

caught up in my reading. If I wait till it's properly dark I'll stand a better chance of avoiding notice now.

My attention is drawn to the window. A silent procession of Life Registry clerks, hooded and robed, are walking past the windows facing the river path, heading to the Mermens.

"What are they doing?" Felicity asks. The clerks don't work on Endweeks. She darts outside and speaks to one, an older man bringing up the rear, then comes back inside.

"They're off to the Mermen Gates to hold a candle-lit vigil for their executed colleague," she tells me.

"Even after the announcement of treason. That's … bold."

"Fidel was a well-liked young man," she says. "They believe he was framed and should have had a proper trial. That the branders have gone too far." She slips on her coat. "I'm going down to the gates to see this."

A sharp twinge of pain strikes my hip, and my annoyance slips out. "Why? You can't write about it."

She gives me an embarrassed frown. "I can witness it, at least," she says quietly.

I'm startled to see Gracie emerge, buttoning her own coat. "I'm going to the vigil," she says. "Those branders shouldn't get away with harassing innocent people. They're no better than thugs. The magistrate thinks he can just turn people's homes upside down at the drop of a hat looking for fugitives. Today they're killing people without a proper trial! What happens tomorrow?"

"I'm going too," says Renny, tucking a cloth over a basket of fish pastries. "The clerks will want feeding."

"It'll only be a matter of time before the branders show up with their prods," I warn them, but Gracie and Renny won't be dissuaded.

Mister S appears, wiping his hands.

"Tell them it's too dangerous," I urge him, but he shakes his head.

"For you and Kit it is. You stay back. Gracie – don't go getting another shiner. And you, my sensible one –" he grasps Renny's shoulder briefly – "watch yourself, but don't get pushed around. There's no curfew for Skøl folk, is there?" He gives Kit a sympathetic look. "No law against peaceful gathering. Hightail it if it gets rowdy."

26

worry

The Lugger feels oddly bleak without Gracie and Renny. It's still not dark. I crunch through one of the leftover pastries.

The place grows so quiet, Kit's not needed at the bar, even with Gracie and Renny out. We gather the washing they hung in the courtyard earlier. They take most of their heavy things to the laundry up the road, but they still do bits and pieces here.

Our morning in the forest feels a lifetime ago.

"Kalqitlan." I say his full name slowly, like dropping a pebble in a still pond, the syllables rippling out around us. He drops a handful of pegs into the bucket at our feet and looks at me. "Tell me what the Reedstones are plotting. No more games, please."

He shakes his head and resumes pulling dishcloths down. I wait.

"Glister Reedstone and the Artist are old friends."

I let that sink in.

But he says nothing more.

I unpeg the corner of a sheet. Snap, creak. More ripples fan out around us. The parts clunk into place.

"Oh, Mora, you're such a good drawer," I say, voice shrill. "Mora, I know, just draw me a quick plan of the branders' station. Well done, Mora." I stick the peg on his arm, hoping it pinches.

"Ow." He plucks it off.

"Admit it, they want you helping to break him out."

"I admit it."

A jailbreak. Fraught with danger.

The Reedstones want to save the Artist. Their friend. *Blithe Even Ronbor.*

I think of him in that cell, pale and bruised but still spirited. He tried to fight back. He forged people's records, bought them time – bought it at his own cost. They'll make him pay the ultimate price, Lovemore and all her cronies, because he stuck two fingers up at them and wouldn't play their game. Because Venor wants to make an example of him. To show us all that fighting back won't be tolerated.

"I want to help too," I tell Kit.

"Why?"

Because you caught me when I fell, and I'm still here. Because Venor thinks he's won. Burning books and melting statues and chopping heads off like a madman.

Because boys I've no quarrel with think they can just chuck me in the river and branders can squeeze me like a bit of meat.

Because I'm not property of the bloody Glassworks like another Clomper.

Because I want to be an artist too. And people should be able to be artists or musicians or whatever they want. People should be able to do so much more in this short, miserable life.

I didn't survive the Cull just to waste away serving these people who took everything from me. I'm tired of being their good little repayer. Yes, mister. Yes, missus. Right away.

Because I am a person. And I want to be brave, even if I'm not.

I'm not even brave enough to say a quarter of that.

"He helped people. He would've helped us. We can save him, and mess up Venor's stupid show at the Hexagon. This is about more than one man. This is about showing them – showing them all – that we count."

"You don't have to save everyone, Mor," Kit says, soft and sad and obvious.

He's right, of course. Who have I saved? I couldn't save Char, or Enca, or Eben, or Pa. I couldn't save Ma, two years before they came to smash everything to bits. Have we saved Zako? He's still holed up somewhere, with a bounty on his head.

"I want to try," I say, shaking the stiffness out of an apron.

"You both look very serious!" Felicity coos, coming in from the outside entrance to the courtyard. Her eyes are sharp. Thank goodness we've been talking in Crozoni.

She flops down on the bench wrapped around the plane

tree with her legs stretched out, crossed at the heels. "Oh, these shoes are murder."

"Have they shut it down already?" I ask.

"It was being broken up as I left. Peacefully though – at least it seemed that way." She leans forward, bending to retrieve a pair of half-buried copper-framed glasses out of the detritus – fluffy seed balls and twigs and old leaves – littering the unpaved bit of ground near the bench.

"Hello! Someone's lost their glasses," she says.

I freeze.

I recognize those glasses. Zako must have lost them when he was haring down the tree.

"Any takers?" Felicity holds them up to the light. "Oh. Filthy lenses." I leave the washing-gathering to sit next to her. The glass is smudged with rather small-looking fingerprints.

They must have bounced right under the bench to be spared a wash in the rain.

"Let me see?" I pinch them off her. "I don't recognize them. The ammedown shops have bucketfuls of these. Maybe … maybe a patron lost them here."

"Do many patrons come through here?"

She's right. Hardly any of them come this way or try to go through the kitchen. It's staff territory.

"I'll put them in the kitchen in case someone comes asking." Kit ignores her question, taking them from my hands and dropping them smoothly into a pocket.

Felicity watches his face with a strange expression

before she pushes herself up off the bench. She looks back down at me. "Is that pastry on your chin?"

"Probably."

"I hope you've left me some!"

"Help yourself." Kit gives her his most winning grin as he opens the kitchen door. "There's some on that tray." He shuts the door quietly.

"Fuck's sake," he groans, slumping on to the bench beside me.

"She won't realize." My palms are sweating.

He puffs out a quiet sigh, head tilted back to the sunset spiralling down flaking stairways of branches.

I can't think what to do next. My mind is blank. Well, I can think about what we did under another tree, a pine tree. I can think about his mouth on me. Desire descends like a swarm of bees. I swat the thought away. I have a million more important things to be thinking about.

Shadow kisses the ridges of his brows, the hinge of his jaw. He looks so careworn, dappled by light, propped against dappled bark. I've a sudden awful vision of him somewhere the light can't reach, somewhere even the night's softness never falls, a dim windowless cell, a harsh lantern without, casting the suffocating bars on to his skin. A shadow tattoo. A cage.

The Artist is in a cage like that.

Do Kit and the Reedstones have a chance of saving him? Or is he as good as dead already? Is Kit as good as dead too? Are all of us?

No. I feel a fury coiling up my spine, burning away the fog in my brain. Kit's alive – we survived. We survive.

Mister S opens the kitchen door, steps down to the courtyard with a lantern that grows the dark.

And Gracie and Renny are back, boiling over with news of the vigil.

"The branders broke it up," Renny tells us. "Magistrate's orders. Five of the clerks wouldn't budge. Branders took them away. Disobedience. Going to the drunk tank."

"Poor things," Gracie says. "Not a nice place to be sober. But they loved the pastries! Wanted more. I might have done a nice bit of business for us – said we'd bring them to the Registry in the week; the clerks will buy them at lunchtime – save them going out to get something. They only get a short break. Said they'd fetch a krunan each easily."

Mister S raises his eyebrows. "You've been busy," he says.

"They don't cost a quarter of that in the ingredients and the baking," Renny adds.

"We can make a small fortune," Gracie decides. "We can do jam ones too. And cheese with the potatoes. Bit of green onion, black ale… Can't we?" She wiggles her empty basket at Mister S. He never says no to her.

I snag a few of the last fish pastries and sneak back in the gathering dark to Opal Alley, before Ruzi starts to worry.

27

a concerned man

This is the time of year a Malan vocifer used to return to summer near the Heanes' farm. I catch myself scanning the sky, but I only see gulls, pigeons, crows and ten-a-penny sparrows. I haven't seen another vocifer in years.

As spring unfolds, the Skøl grow less hunched, trading their padded coats for lighter garments. They're frantic as ants before a storm, with their high governor on her way. They've rooted out and burned piles of forbidden books. Probably torched a fair few legal ones in their zeal. They're still knocking down the Crozoni statues that survived the first wave of destruction, replacing them with ugly cuboids carrying Skøl settler mottos.

The pair of cuboids made of melted mermen from the old Mermen Gates have a word stamped into each long face. On the left, *STRIVE. WORK. BUILD. PRIDE.* And on the right, *SWEAT. TEARS. TOIL. BLOOD.*

The cube in Sinton Square on Imilia Dezil's old plinth reads *WE. ARE. ONE. SKØLAND.* Someone's already scratched a question mark at the end of *WE*.

ARE ONE SKØLAND WE?

The five clerks the branders threw in the drunk tank are still there, over a week on. *Fidelity's Faithful Five*, the *Post* is calling them – cruelly. They're being charged with something. Venor letting everyone know free-thinking won't set you free – just the opposite. There have been no more vigils, but the town feels tense, stretched thin like a string of taffy, close to snapping.

I feel the same.

There are no more music nights. The bounty on anyone found to be aiding or abetting Zako rises. Makaians standing about in groups of *three or more* are banned on pain of imprisonment.

Strangely, my Makaian drawings sell well. High-society Skøl can't seem to get enough. I worry Venor will ban those too. "He won't," Kit assures me. "They're too popular back in Skøland. Honestly. Not just drawings – painting, sculptures, clothes, jewellery – all the … artefacts. There's a craze for collecting them, that's what the Reedstones say."

About the Reedstones' plan to free the Artist, he'll give me no detail – only that they're trying to identify a *moment of opportunity*. Meanwhile the date for Clarion Lovemore's arrival, and the Artist's execution, draws nearer.

"Your handsome young man's missing you," Cordi says one afternoon, brushing a smatter of drizzle from her shining curls. The sun's been in and out all day like the cat who can't decide, and we're in the Glassworks' courtyard loading a delivery for the docks.

"Feel like I hardly see my family these days either," she sighs.

Orders are behind again – the huge commission for the Hexagon Hall is a millstone round our necks. Wagsen's terrified about missing deadlines, so he's working everyone ragged. We start at half seven instead of eight now. Ruzi and I have permanent permission from our employer to be out after curfew. Lucky us. Glassworkers down tools with the sun these days – close to nine. By the time I'm finished and back at Opal Alley I barely have energy to sharpen a pencil before my bed's calling.

"My young man?" I repeat. I look where Cordi's nodding. Kit's coming in the side gate – that was supposed to be locked – like the manager's another Mister S who won't care if we stop in the middle of work for a chat.

I look at Ruzi, who looks at the sky. "Go in the stables. Five minutes, mind, then get him gone before Wagsen sees you slacking."

Dust glimmers in the air, and the empty stable smells pleasantly of straw. Kit fishes something from a pocket. "Sorry, I know your boss is a brickhead, but I thought you'd want to see this right away. Came this afternoon."

It's another envelope addressed to the Lugger – this time to *Mora D* at the Lugger – in Zako's messy hand.

Kit shows me the receiver-pays note.

"So they just let you collect my private correspondence!" I grumble.

"You think the fancy people collect their own post?" He raises an eyebrow. "They're not fussy at the office as long as they get paid."

Zako's used the envelope as paper again. He's included an annotated picture too. It looks like a map, but surely he can't have been so reckless.

Hello agen!!! Alls good still, hope yew all same happe as B and T on my emty iland here. See map if yew want to visit →

I feel sick. "Is he mad? What's he doing sending a map? The branders could intercept our post."

"Well, good luck to them. If they can follow that, they're all mad."

Kit's right. The map is nonsense. It appears to be pointing to an island northwest of Portcaye. There's no island there. It's labelled with transliterations of Crozoni words like "*Eventid, oystas – sorry Kit*", *wulf* and *wale* and *wirlpowl*.

"Oysters near the *Eventide*," Kit muses. "There are some old shell middens up the coast that way. Perhaps you were right to go north looking for him."

"Perhaps. Blenny and Tornelius ate oysters. Some wolves showed them."

"Course they did. He's just playing. And he says he's

happe." That's the important thing." He glances at me. "Are you *happe*?"

"Mora-of-the-Glassworks! Fancy seeing you here. How are you, my dear?"

It's the last Endweek before Fivemonth and already unseasonably warm. I'm visiting Ammedown Alley to find some new old clothes more suited to this weather, when I bump into Felicity Greave.

I'm surprised to see her at a market like this – it's surely too poor for her taste. She's full of gossip for me though.

"Our favourite magistrate's really picked his battle this time," she tells me. "Seems he thought they'd all take it lying down."

"Take what lying down?"

"The clerks. That man who had his head lopped off? Well, his colleagues pushed for an investigation and got one. It's one of the Skøl rules – they couldn't refuse. It was found to be an extrajudicial killing."

"But he did steal the paper?" I ask eagerly.

"He did. But it seems only because he was supporting his cousin's medical treatment." She frowns. "The temptation was too much, poor fellow. And now there are rumours of another clerk's vigil – maybe during working hours."

"Do you really think they will?" I ask, incredulous, and she shrugs.

"Who knew the revolution would start at the Life

Registry?" she says lightly, but I shiver. She can't know that the Reedstones really are thinking of revolution.

I wonder what those clerks would do with the information that Venor's Life Record is hiding. Something he tried to kill Zako to stop coming out.

I glance at Felicity. If I told her, would she do anything with it? *Of course she wouldn't*, I think. But still, I wonder.

I feel like one of those floating bulbs in the barometers they make at the Glassworks. Suspended. Hanging there, waiting for the pressure to change. Waiting for the Reedstones, waiting for the right moment, waiting to act, always waiting. Let Kit wait if he wants. I don't have to.

I say goodbye to Felicity – but that night, when I get home, instead of drawing, I write a quick, anonymous letter addressed to her at the Lugger – before I can change my mind.

I never write anything, so she won't recognize my writing. I send it unpaid, like Zako.

F Greave,

BE AWARE – Magistrate Venor is hiding an ALARMING SECRET. He is NOT an upright man.

He is NOT fit to govern the New West.

His Life Record contains a FRAUD that may be revealed with the forensic science of vradiance scoping.

HIS WIFE KNOWS.

Yours sincerely,
A Concerned Man

28

when you decide

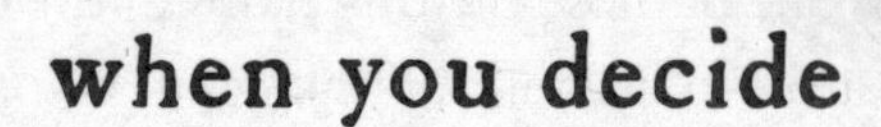

I wake early the next day, feeling lighter for having done something at least. Feeling rested, despite the early hour.

It's the first workday in ages I've woken with enough time to visit Kit before our day gets started.

The Lugger's quiet and smells of vinegar – all the windows are flung wide for a deep clean.

Gracie and Renny are already here, folding flour and fat.

"It's those clerks at the Registry," Gracie tells me. She has flour on her cheek. "They can't get enough. We're selling a basket and a half of these every midday. Need to get a bigger basket."

"Who knew reading and writing was such hungry work?" says Renny.

"And stamping things," Gracie reminds her. "And

filling up their little fountain pens. Pulling their hoods up and down."

Renny laughs, but I think of those five clerks still stuck in jail. I bet they're hungry for more than pastries.

Kit's wiping the windows, but he puts down the cloth. "Walk to the market with me, Mora," he suggests, and when Renny groans at him, he says, "What? We need a bag of grist."

It's still cool now, but I think it'll get warm as yesterday later. The sun's behind us, gently kneading our backs.

"Have you talked to Felicity lately?" Kit asks, and I flush guiltily.

"No. Why?"

"She's been digging about those bloody glasses. Said she was round the ammedown shops and someone told her a repayer bought two pairs of old glasses not that long ago."

"You think she suspects?"

"There aren't that many of us. If she's been asking, someone could have described Ruzi well enough."

My heart flips about like a fish out of water.

"He can deny it. Or say he got them for himself, then lost them."

Kit frowns. "Yeah. Anyway, you need to tell him she's sniffing. He can have his answer ready."

"I will."

"I knew we couldn't trust her," Kit mutters. He forces a smile. "Ever since she criticized my sweet-onion stew."

"Immediately suspicious."

He tickles my neck. "Everyone. Loves. My. Stew."

I remember Goldie Reedstone, the first time I saw her, sitting with Felicity. Then standing up and walking angrily away. "Do you know why Felicity interviewed Goldie Reedstone?" I ask.

"Oh yes. Goldie was furious. Seems our friend Felicity told Goldie it was an interview about GR Locks – the Reedstones are doing the security for the Hexagon."

"But it wasn't?"

"It was a lot of personal questions. About Goldie and Glister and their staff. Goldie's very private."

"What was Felicity trying to find out?"

"I don't know. But she's sharp, Mora. Like I say, we can't trust her."

I glance away. "At least she talks to me."

One of his hands grips my shoulder, forcing me to stop. I turn to face him. His violet eyes bore into me like Skivårnat lanterns.

"You want me to talk?" he murmurs. "I'm talking. You're not listening. We can't trust a person like Felicity Greave."

I can't feel anything but his hand near my neck. It pulls me back to the pine forest, after I fell, when I kissed him.

I reach to peel his hand off me, but I find now I have it, I don't want to let go. The sinews in his wrist are overlain by his thin bracelets, the beads darker than his skin, on long brown thread wrapped around his forearms many times over. He draws my hand slowly to his chest.

"Are you pushing me away or pulling me in?" His voice is still low, almost too quiet to hear in the ordinary sounds of Portcaye going to work.

I can't speak. My ears are burning.

He drops my hand. "Let me know when you decide."

29

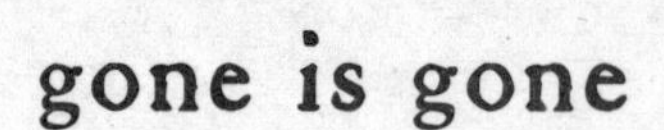

gone is gone

I keep thinking of Zako's letters. The chip of oyster shell he sent. He said he was *happe*.

I hope he is. I hope he's safe.

The Glassworks gets even busier in the warmer months, with business growing steadily every year. More ships, trade and orders to fulfil when the seas are favourable, Fivemonth to Ninemonth. I think of Clarion Lovemore, high governor, sailing towards us on clement seas.

The urgent commission for an obscene number of glass roof panes on top of the regular orders this year has pushed the pace from busy to frantic. Everything else is behind.

Our days are long, but time is short.

Clomper and Caney are more stubborn than they are in the cold, though Wagsen's sent a shearer to rid them of their wool coats.

We've crossed a milestone today though. Me and Ruzi

and Cordi and Vertie are coming back from delivering the very final batch of coloured-glass roof panes set to grace the Hexagon Hall.

Work on the Hall construction looks a little behind, but that's nothing to do with us. And the workers there still have four weeks left to get it all finished and installed.

It's near the end of the day, and two blocks from the Glassworks we hear it's in uproar. A glimpse through the gates shows at least fifty workers gathered in the yard, shouting angrily up at the wing where Wagsen's office is.

Thea's wounds. Have they actually snapped? Months of pressure. Ridiculously long days with barely a break and piddling extra coin to compensate. They've fulfilled the most urgent order. Today there should be celebrations. Never thought I'd see them like this. Skøl workers pride themselves on their grace under pressure – taking what's doled out and making no fuss. Well. This is a fuss and a half.

It's just a wall of noise. I can't hear any individual words. Clomper and Caney are spooked and refuse to enter.

"Take the kine down the road to the patch by the barrows," Ruzi says. It's one of our Endweek routines, to stretch their legs and let them graze, but I know he wants me out of the way. "I'll find you after." He plunges into the throng.

I tether the kine near the patch of grass, but I don't like to leave them hitched to the wagon. If anything scared them, they'd be off in a heartbeat, dragging the lot.

They're not flighty, but the commotion at the Works has set them on edge.

I sit in the long shadow of the empty cart, leaning against a wheel, watching workers buying provisions for the evening from the barrows opposite.

A man clatters by on a bicycle of all things. I feel the big wooden slats I'm leaning against wobble. Caney doesn't like bicycles, though thankfully they're rare.

I get up to reassure him, so I'm hidden behind the cart when Kit walks past.

He looks nothing like himself. He's wearing a boiler suit – an outfit favoured by Skøl dustmen or builders, with a flat cap low over his eyes, covering his hair. His skin's barely visible. Just his hands and a slice of face. The boiler suit even covers his neck. A toolbox swings on the hook of one finger. It's empty as a stage prop. He looks like he might be off to wrangle a generator on the blink or to fix a leaking tap. If my memory worked like most people's, perhaps I wouldn't have recognized him.

But I did. And I have to follow. I have to know where he's going, in his disguise.

"Clomper, stay," I whisper in one soft ear. "Caney, bide here a while, in the green, green grass."

It's very different, tailing Kit on a softly sunlit evening of long limber shadows, as opposed to the drizzling depths of night. At least I don't have to worry about making a noise, since there's people everywhere. Kit follows a back route – narrow alleys, sharp corners and the type of cramped, steep flights of steps I usually try to avoid.

I'm winded by the time I realize we've reached Rundvaer Square.

It was Fountain Square, before the Cull. The Skøl tore down the Crozoni fountain covered in mermaids and clam shells years ago, but that's where they're putting the new Skøl statue they want the high governor to cut the ribbon for. It's not another cuboid.

She'll be staying in the Castle Hotel, fronting Rundvaer Square. Just her and her entourage, taking over the whole huge place. It's the fanciest hotel in town, all elektric, hot water and glass and an army of gold-suited staff.

She'll be able to gaze over the biggest square in town and admire *The Spirit of the New West.* He's a naked man, made from white stone, three times man size, carrying the iron world on his shoulders. Black-iron ocean and gold-inlaid land. Their world. Skøland's dominion from sea to sea to sea.

Life Is Golden, says his plinth. They're still painting bits of it in gold.

Kit stops at a bench near the tall stone buildings on the south side of the square, directly in front of a glass-fronted shop with an awning occupying one of the ground floors. A soft, inviting light spills from its windows.

I realize the sun's calling it a day.

I should get back to Clomper and Caney. Instead, I plunge into the square, peering back to see the place Kit's stopped by is a fancy fikka house – the kind with waistcoated waiters serving jam-drenched Skølcakes on tiered plates.

Further into the square, I stop at a quiet stall as a pretext to loiter, keeping an eye on Kit's back at the bench.

A young man leaves the fikka shop – Skøl, tall and golden-haired – stopping to sit at the other end of Kit's bench.

"What can I get you?" The seller whose stall I've been pretend-perusing is a middle-aged woman, pale hair tucked under a broad-brimmed hat, face weathered almost salmon pink.

"Oh…" I focus on her wares. She is selling a kind of fruit, like oranges, if oranges had leathery green skin, and a mixture of woven baskets, tins, twine, copper wire, thread and buttons.

I touch the tips of my fingers to one of the green fruits. "What are these?"

"Oranges."

"Green oranges?"

"They're ripe." She cuts one open with a wicked-looking flick knife, leaves the halves displayed at the front of the pile and wipes her hands on her apron. They're a deep, glistening orange inside. "Sweet as nectar," she purrs, flashing a gap-toothed grin of rival sweetness. "Guess where they're from? Not Skøland. Down south. First fruiting this season. They've put in groves and groves in County Shipway. Not as fine as the ones from Skøland, but tasty. Leave them a few days; they'll be even sweeter."

Out of the corner of my eye, I see Kit getting up.

"Oh – thank you." I sound like a simpleton. "Are you here much longer?" Darkness is gathering. The lamplighters are doing their rounds.

"Here until ten."

Kit's walking off. Now his companion's getting up too.

"I'll come back," I promise, moving to follow them.

The Skøl man has something in his hand. An envelope. It catches what's left of the waning daylight as he frightens a handful of pigeons into the air.

He's in Skøl evening wear – low black shoes, pressed grey trousers and a formal jacket with gold thread.

I soon realize they aren't going far. Kit's made for the alley between the building with the fikka shop and the neighbouring one to its left. It's a dead end, filled with shadows and dust-heaps and rats.

Meanwhile, the Skøl man is heading for the steps to the same neighbouring building's rather grand-looking entrance. He skips jauntily up them as I stop halfway behind a stall selling papers and sweets to pretend an interest. The seller's occupied, talking to another customer.

I can pick out the patch of Kit-shaped shadow lurking in the alley, but I doubt anyone else could. His head's tipped back, like he's searching the narrow band of sky for a sign.

The golden-haired man knocks on the grand-looking door.

Another young man opens it after a moment to take his envelope and admit him. The door shuts.

Not ten seconds later, three more men in rich jackets

and shiny shoes are striding up the steps to gain easy admittance.

What are they up to in there? The building gives few clues. Tall columns flank the already elevated front door, to make visitors feel small. Not unusual for old Crozoni architecture. Its creamy stone face spells power and purity. I think the stonework used to carry Crozoni carvings – mermaids perhaps – but they're gone now. Patches of stone appear cleaner than others. A sign declares it the Sinskill Club, but I'm none the wiser. I edge around the stall and closer to the alley.

Kit's dim shape's not there.

Because, I realize half a second later, it's on the move, suspended between the buildings.

This is where the muscle comes from. Not carrying barrels of ale. Scaling vertical walls, empty toolbox and all. The alley is narrow. He's braced between the wall of the fikka shop building and the parallel wall on the neighbouring building. A moment later, he's reached the second level. Then he's contorting himself though what I can only assume is a window of the Sinskill Club. It's invisible from my vantage.

Thea's wounds. That was fast.

I wait, expecting at any moment screams and breaking glass, Kit launching himself back into the thin well of alley air and guns and horror.

All remains as it was.

I watch the shadows of unremarkable passers-by

sweeping the ground as they go under each iron-caged elektric lamp, lengthening and contracting like shadows thrown from a sundial, rushing through the day. Time slipping away.

A few more well-dressed men and women are admitted to the Sinskill Club.

I'm about to leave, to head back to Clomper and Caney, when a luxury carriage pulls up in front of the Club. The Life Registry's gold insignia, two triangles forming an hourglass, is emblazoned on its door.

I hunch into my shoulders as Magistrate Venor steps down. I recognize the arrogant way he carries himself. He's got his familiar gold-tipped cane as well. The door opens before he reaches the top step.

His driver pulls the carriage along and stays upright on the box, waiting.

I thread back into the square to the orange-seller. Her stall's under lamplight now, but she's still wearing her hat.

"How much for the oranges?"

"Copper each."

I hand her a five-copper piece and try to think of how best to ask. She pops it in her tin.

"What's eating you, girl?" Her tone isn't unkind. She's wrapping five green oranges in brown paper.

"Do you know that building over there?" I point to the stone steps of the Club. Another woman is heading up them. The thick grist-brown plait down her back looks uncannily like Felicity Greave's. Is it her? She's in a dress, and I never see Felicity in a dress, let alone a pale formal one. Her hair isn't so unusual for a Skøl.

"The Sinskill Club? Great and good having their fancy get-togethers. What about it?"

"Looks like the magistrate's there tonight."

"Ah. He shows up time to time if they're having one of their fundraisers. Why they have to dress up and eat five courses before they open their wallets is beyond me – but there you go." She snorts.

"A fundraiser?" I shake my head. "Raising funds for what?"

"The Sting Trust, maybe. Or another one of those." She gestures at the looming naked man with his globe. "Or for the Glass Fanny Venor's building."

"The Glass Fanny's cost enough as it is, hasn't it?" I'm going to tell Cordi the people are calling the Hexagon the Glass Fanny.

"Don't I know it!" She rearranges a few of her wares. "They could have put elektric lighting like this through the whole centre for the amount they're spending. It's the principle. They've only put it here because Lovemore's to stay at the Castle. It's for show, not to make things better for regular folk. Excuse me." She stops abruptly to help another customer with some twine. I linger, but her stall's growing busy, and she's ignoring me now.

I take my paper package and make for the bench in front of the fikka shop. It's beyond the nearest circle of lamplight, comfortingly dark.

I should get back to the kine.

Just as I stand, cradling the oranges, the young Skøl man who sat on this very bench beside Kit, the one who went inside the Club dressed to the nines, comes strolling out of the fikka shop. He's wearing Kit's boiler suit and carrying a toolbox that's clearly quite heavy. The same, only not.

He doesn't notice me staring. He must have jumped from the roof of the Club to the roof of the fikka-shop building to come down and get out unseen. I look back at the fikka-shop door, but can't see Kit. When I scan the dead-end alley, sure enough, a shadow's wedged between the walls, fair haring down.

I tread slowly to the alley mouth, but I've lost sight of him now.

He doesn't come. I inch into the gloom, willing my eyes to adjust faster.

A hot hand cups the back of my neck, steering me deeper into the alley and promptly smashing my face into the smooth stone wall. It's not so smooth as it looks from afar. My cheek and forehead feel a startling constellation of jabs. I drop the package of oranges and fight against crying out. I can't make a commotion and give Kit away.

"Pick another alley to ply your trade, girl," a man's angry voice grits in my ear. "You might see something you regret with those big eyes." It's the young Skøl man in the boiler suit. His fingers squeeze tighter into my neck, twisting my body around as I flail at him. I catch his other arm and dislodge the toolbox with a loud clatter. Something spills out. It looks like a Xan artefact. He pulls a fist back to strike me but doesn't get a chance. I hear Kit's voice and then Kit's beside me, between us.

"Hey, *no.* Stop."

I could cry from relief. I press into the possessive arm Kit wraps around my shoulders. He nudges me to face him. I am crying, actually – mostly because my face hurts from its close encounter with the wall.

Kit's wearing a dark-brown robe now, every inch a Registry clerk.

"What did you do?" he hisses at the other man. "You hurt her. F—"

"She was following us." The Skøl man crouches down to hastily shove the artefact back into the box. It's a little stone person, I see, edged in places with copper. "Why is she in a weird disguise?"

"These are my normal clothes."

"She's my friend, she's fine," snaps Kit. "Piss off. You should be halfway home by now."

"She saw me," the man says stubbornly.

"You want to lose the rest of the lamps in your garret? Touch her again."

"I didn't see anything," I whisper.

Kit and the other man ignore me, engaged in a wordless glaring match. Then the man puffs out a breath and stalks off.

We linger in the shadowy privacy of the alley. Kit

throws back his coarse brown hood to glare at me. He's very freshly shaven, his cheekbones sharp.

"Mora Dezil, what are you—"

"Was that Glister Reedstone?"

"No."

My cheek's grazed – it's stinging – but the bang wasn't that hard.

I wipe tear tracks off my face and bend to retrieve my package. "I was just buying these oranges, and I thought I saw you. He hit my face into the wall."

"I'm sorry. You're all right to get home, aren't you? You don't need me?" He flips the hood back up, then holds my elbow as we leave the mouth of the alley. "Just buying oranges my arse," he mutters.

Ruzi's standing beside Clomper and Caney in a puddle of lamplight, looking harried – then furious as he spots me.

"Hell's teeth, Mora! Where have you been?"

I've never seen him so angry. Everyone is furious with me tonight, it seems.

"Ruzi—"

"I've been going out of my mind. You left them for hours! What if something happened? If Wagsen wasn't so distracted, he would have noticed something amiss for sure. Don't you know how much trouble you could be in? Demoted, back to the floor. S-sold on – or worse."

Thea's wounds. Has he been standing here for ages worrying about me like old Father Goose?

"Ruzi. They're fine."

"The last thing we need right now is more trouble."

"What happened?"

"There was an accident." His anger deflates. "You know that young blower, Faithie Senson?"

"Yeah, of course. She's mates with Cordi – went to your music night…"

"There was an accident with the lye. Fathie's been badly burnt over half her face, her hand. They say she might lose sight on one side – that she's lucky it wasn't worse. That's why it all kicked off. Branders have shut it down now."

My hands are shaking. I brush some hair back from my face, and Ruzi must see the scrape on my cheek.

"What happened there?"

"I tripped and fell." It's a terrible excuse.

"You have to get your head out of the clouds, girl."

"I know."

"Stop looking for that bloody bird all the time. Gone is gone."

30

then nothing

The glassworkers are refusing to work in the wake of Faithie's accident. They need better conditions, they argue, or else more will happen, and worse. The factory stands locked and looming, eerily silent. I still have to feed and exercise Clomper and Caney, but no one minds me.

No work means no pay for the workers, and the only job I've got now is looking after the kine. Even Ruzi isn't expected to come in.

"This is your chance, music man. Write them a strike song," Kit ribs him. "*Making glass … is a pain in the ass…*"

Ruzi doesn't laugh. "Break'll be over before we know it. Good things don't last."

One of his favourite sayings.

I've been using the time to draw – and Ruzi's been

trying to repair his guitar. He's brought it back to Opal Alley. I hear a lot of cursing from the other room, so I'm afraid to ask how it's going.

It's warm, unseasonably so. At twilight, after the boats come in, groups of Skøl sit around driftwood bonfires. They stay out for hours. It gets dark and they're all fire-dazzled, so they don't realize Crozoni scum walks among them. The branders are busy patrolling town and burning books. They don't guard the gates, and curfew seems easier to flout outside the old walls.

Ruzi and I go one morning to the stretch of sand where they do the fires. We even light one and burn some seaweed to watch the sparks.

"Do you think you'll save the guitar?" I hazard. "Or is it dead?"

His eyes crinkle at the corners. "Let's call it a resurrection in progress."

"I'm really sorry, you know, Ruzi."

"Don't be." He catches my eye through the smoke. "I have no regrets. Enjoyed it. I'd do it again. Smash all the guitars I ever made over these brickheads."

I feed small sprigs of dry seaweed to the fire until two Skøl women – out for a morning walk – tell us off for making nasty smoke. Say we aren't allowed. They're allowed to burn books, but we aren't allowed to exist.

My anger flares, but Ruzi nods peaceably and we leave the beach to them.

"The hottest anger won't cook dinner," Ruzi reminds me. Back to platitudes.

"You have a fan," Kit tells me, matter of fact.

"What's that?"

We've been avoiding each other since I surprised him in Rundvaer Square. I must have made things awkward when I met that angry young man and his stolen artefact. Collector's item, apparently, right from under their fancy Skøl noses. I read about the theft in the *Portcaye Post*.

"Or someone heard your drawings were selling – they stole that portrait you did of the Scarlets." He gestures at the wall behind the bar where it used to hang. The one I did for them at Skivårnat. The frame's still there, but it's empty.

"Who'd do a thing like that?"

"I don't know."

"Kit, I'm sorry about the other night. I didn't mean to … bring you more trouble."

He turns back to me. "We need to talk."

My stomach flips over. I nod.

"I was thinking of taking a few hours off this afternoon – around four? Gracie says the Rainbow has a new attraction." The Rainbow is an upmarket fikka house in the Mermens.

"What've they got now?" Last time it was an elektric milk-frother.

"An ice device." He sees my confused face. "It makes ice. In this weather!"

"Why?"

"To eat. They crush it with orange syrup. Gracie won't shut up about it. Come there with me. I'll buy you one." He winks.

"Will they sell to us?" I feel suddenly shy.

"I'll wear my nice shoes." His gaze travels up and down me. "This weather suits you," he decides. Then he leaves me.

When I'm nearly home, I see Felicity downstairs, perusing the bakery window.

"Here she is! Just the girl I've been looking for. How have you been faring with this strike under way?"

"I'm all right." I frown.

She squints at me. "Are you eating enough? None of my business, I suppose." She comes closer and lowers her voice. "Listen, I think I found something out about our magistrate friend."

I freeze. "Really?"

She glances around. "I got an anonymous tip and then I did some digging and – well. I wasn't sure who to go to. Ridiculous though it may seem, I thought of you."

We look at each other. "Come on up." I gesture to our rooms over the bakery.

"No," she says quickly. I see the signs of strain then – she's pale, her hair less neat in its plait. She looks – unsually for Felicity – worried. "Do you know somewhere else? Somewhere private, where we won't be disturbed?"

"The Glassworks is empty," I suggest. "Only Clomper and Caney."

"Perfect." She forces her old smile. "Always wanted to see inside."

I lead the way.

We're crossing Sinton Square, and she pauses by the cuboid on Imilia Dezil's old plinth. *ARE ONE SKØLAND WE?*

"Isn't this charming?!" she declares, pushing the anxious tone of her voice down. She takes a deep gulp of air.

A pair of Skøl children are reading out the wanted posters still plastered about the plinth.

"Murder. Moo-tiny at sea. Petty Treason. Debbit-of-life av-avoi— … bootle-egging?" The boy laughs.

"What's pie-racky?" says the girl.

"Piracy," Felicity interrupts. "Bootlegging. Debt. Mutiny. Shouldn't you be in school, learning to read?" She seems to have collected herself again, and the children wilt timidly under her raised eyebrow.

"Truants only cheat themselves," she declares, smiling at their retreating backs. "Go to school or you'll end up on one of these posters too!"

We resume our way.

"So you're still looking after those big kine?" Putting those children in their place has anchored her. Her voice is steady now. "Isn't that breaking the strike?"

"No. I'm Glassworks property, not staff. I'm more like Clomper and Caney. I don't get to strike. Here we are."

Felicity looks behind us as I swing my keys up to the

padlock on the side gate. The yard is still deserted, and our footsteps crunch loudly in the gravel.

"I hear the strike might be over soon; is that your understanding?" she asks, peering around.

"Where'd you hear that? I heard they're planning all sorts. They're gathering with some of the Registry clerks in Rundvaer Square tomorrow."

"Really?" Her voice sounds distracted. "So, where are the famous Clomper and Caney?"

I walk over to the stable. The kine are both huffing loudly, stamping, impatient. It's not like them to be riled up – especially since I saw them this morning already.

"Don't know what's got into them," I say to Felicity over my shoulder – but she's not there.

"Felicity?" I whisper. "Where did you get to? Felicity?"

I hear a gasp from around the corner, then Clomper whickers loudly, showing her big, square teeth and banging a hoof on the door to her stall. Kine don't flash their teeth around like horses, and Clomper less than most. Weird.

"Sorry, you two. Take it easy," I coo.

Hands grab me from behind, shove something wet over my face, a strong smell of vinegar – or pickle, but sweeter. Then nothing.

31

don't i

Time drains like a maelstrom in a huge hourglass. I'm the glass, the sand, spiralling, choking, sleeping. Eventually, I wake.

I'm in a strange, cramped bed. The mat plunges and tips like a twig on the river. I reach for a steadying wall, but there's only more mat, next to me, pointing up like the world is bending. My head floats. Then it's whirling down.

I can't speak. Walls eat my words, *snap, snap.* A muted clatter.

A face swims near, brown and wavery. One of my hands is cupped in both of his.

"Stop swimming," I say.

"I'm not swimming." His growl is soft. I smell his warm smell, herbs and leaves drying in the sun. He's wrong. Everything's swimming—

I open my eyes. A familiar wispy spider hangs in its haunt in the corner. My bed at Opal Alley.

I manage to sit up, but I'm cast iron, heavy as death. A damp cloth flops off my forehead into my lap – hot as anything.

I urge my legs over the side of the bed, though they might be sacks of stones. All my muscles ache like I've been running for hours.

Grit – no, dry sand – clings to my calves and feet.

I can hear singing, the refrain from one of Ruzi's songs. *Don't leave me here. This is not my home.*

The song is inside my head.

I'm wearing a strange nightdress with long trailing sleeves that ruffle out over my knuckles. Absurd Skøl fashion. The skirt reaches halfway down my shins. I draw it up to look at my knees – both bruised, the right one torn.

I sift through fragments of memory that feel as though they've been chopped up for the pot by Renny's cleaver. Wasn't I with Felicity Greave? She had a secret to share. *I think I found something out about our magistrate friend.* Now I'm here, ragged with thirst. There's a flask I don't recognize on my table. I've half a memory of drinking from it.

Cold water, I imagine, struck with a weird terror.

My thighs are shaking. I drink from the flask. It's not water but some brew with a slightly bitter, almost mushroomy taste. I turn to take it back to bed, but my knees buckle.

I fall loudly, too spent to move. The puddle spreads across the boards, a sea edging up a wooden shore, the flask rocking like flotsam.

Light from the kitchen gushes in, and Kit's scooping me up.

"I finally get you into bed." His grin looks forced. He tucks the covers around me.

I don't know what to say. He looks so different. His hair is all shaved off. His ears stick out.

He retrieves the flask. "Did you drink any before you spilled it?"

"No. What is it?"

"Red lichen. Do you good."

"Where'd you find lichen?"

He shakes his shorn head. "I know a peddler. How're you feeling?" The tips of his fingers brush my forehead. "Do you remember what happened?"

"I saw a shearwater," I say suddenly, but that's all the memory is – a flash of a bird flying low.

"Really? Where was the shearwater?"

"I don't know." My thoughts are all gummed up. "What's wrong with me?"

"You've had a nasty fever. Gave us all a scare. We found you on the shore in the middle of the night – day before last. That's one way to get out of coming for an orange ice with me." There's an edge to his easy laugh. "You were delirious."

A day and a half. All blank.

"Do you remember what happened? Were you swimming?"

I don't remember anything. "Felicity," I mumble. "She was worried."

"You saw Felicity?"

"Think so… But was it that day? We talked to some children in the square."

"Which square?"

"I can't remember."

My memory's still in bits. Like one of the blowers fashioned my missing day from glass and then chucked it on the reject pile.

I feel like the cloth Ruzi uses to wipe our table – limp, ragged, crusty.

"It'll come," Kit murmurs. "Are you still thirsty?"

I nod.

"Hungry?"

Feel like I haven't eaten in an age.

He clatters around the kitchen and returns with a steaming cup of milky fikka, a bowl of soup – I knew I could smell something – and a wedge of thick gristbread that I recognize as the handiwork of the bakery downstairs.

He talks while I eat. "Strike's over, I'm afraid," he says. "Venor had them shut it down. Pretty brutally, by all accounts."

"What happened?"

"That gathering in the square they were planning with the clerks – you remember?"

I nod.

"All went pear-shaped."

"Where's Ruzi?" I'm suddenly afraid of why he's not here.

"He's fine. He's at work. He wasn't there."

"What did they do?"

"Well, they decided to march to the branders' station – show of solidarity with the clerks still in the drunk tank there since the vigil. They sang a song outside – that one the dockers are always singing. And the branders came out swinging. There was a fire. It got ugly."

"Do you know if Cordi and Vertie were there?"

"They're fine. Eat your food before it gets cold."

I have to focus to keep the ridiculous trailing sleeves out of the bowl. "Where's this nightdress from?"

"It's Missus Scarlet's."

"Maybe that's why I feel eighty years old."

He chuckles strangely. I realize he looks drained, his eyes almost bruised. This cropped hair's not a style I've seen on him since detention, after the Cull. The Skøl shaved us. Said our hair was dirty.

"And the strike's over?"

"Strikes are banned. Songs are banned. Marches? Banned. Standing with a frown while holding a candle outside? Banned. Blinking at Venor? Also banned. His answer to everything – ban it or burn it."

"Brickhead."

I finish eating, and he takes the bowl away. I shiver. Can't stop my drooping eyelids.

"Going … to sleep," I tell him.

"Good idea."

When I wake, the sun's lower.

Kit's leaning on the door frame as if I've dreamed him there. I'm overwhelmed with a sudden flood of feeling.

"Don't sit up," he says. I slump back down.

He flops on to the covers beside me at an angle, his head almost touching mine, his legs dangling off the side. He drums his collarbone with one thumb.

"Any more news from Zako?" I ask.

"No."

A memory snags. Someone was asking me – *What's B and T?* They were angry. Who was it? Was it real or a dream? My heart's going like a gong.

"What did you do to your hair?" I blurt out, pushing away the terror.

He swipes his hands over his face and exhales slowly before he speaks again. "You said you remembered a shearwater?"

"Oh yeah."

"Don't see them much close in."

I turn the vision of the shearwater over behind my eyes. But it's a memory of a memory now, attached to nothing more than a whiff of saltwater, a slight rocking.

His head moves until his forehead rests against mine. His eyes are closed. He lets out a long breath. I'm half asleep again when I hear the outer door creaking open. Kit rolls to his feet before Ruzi's inside.

"Thank you, son," comes Ruzi's voice from the kitchen. "How is she?"

Since when did Ruzi call him son? The shock ripples through me, but not enough to wake me fully. I hear Kit taking his leave. I roll my cheek into the pillow where his head was and sink further into sleep.

It's night when I wake next, though a dim lantern stands on the table, beside a potted geranium. That's new. Ruzi's sat with his head fallen back, mouth agape, drooling on the *Portcaye Post* spread like a bib over his chest.

I croak a greeting. "Ruzi."

He wakes with a grunt, dragging his chair closer.

"How you feeling?"

I don't feel as chilled as I did before. "Where'd the plant come from?"

"Cordi brought it for you."

"Well, that was sweet of her. I feel silly, you sitting vigil like I'm not long for this world."

Ruzi blinks. Tilts his head.

"Yesterday we thought we'd lost you," he says. "And … well…" He touches my hand gently. "Your wrists."

I pull back the trailing sleeves. My wrists are marked with bruises and scabbed-over abrasions. They hurt, I realize.

"Someone tied you."

A tremor runs down my back. "I don't remember."

"Kit says you saw a shearwater. Were you out on a boat?"

"I don't know."

"We found your keys at the Works. You dropped them outside the stables. Found you on the sand, half drowned. Cold as ice, you were."

"I can't remember," I say, panicking.

He watches me for a moment, then shakes his head. "You're all right. It'll come when it's meant to."

He sounds so sure. I want to believe him. I want to remember.

Don't I?

32

melts away

I sit bolt upright, calling, "What's happened to Felicity?"

Kit's beside my bed now. Soft morning light and street sounds filter in through my window, propped ajar.

"Kit, Felicity was going to tell me something about Venor." I can see her pinched, worried face. Hear the tremor in her voice. I remember it now, my memories slotting into order. "I took her to the stables, before I blacked out. Where is she?"

"She went missing, same day you did," Kit says. "All her luggage has been left behind."

I close my eyes, struggling to remember. I heard a gasp behind me…

"We don't even know who to tell," Kit's saying. "Did she mention any family to you?"

"No. Said she had a lover who died – gave her that ring she always had on. Didn't tell me his name."

"I don't like it," Kit grumbles.

"She came into the stables with me," I say slowly. "She had something to tell me about Venor. And that's the last thing I remember. Whoever it was who did this to me –" I hold out a wrist – "I think they attacked her too."

"I wonder what put her on Venor's scent," Kit says.

I take a deep breath and tell him about the anonymous letter I penned in haste.

"Why did you do that?" Kit blurts sharply.

"I thought it couldn't hurt! It was before you told me she was asking questions about Zako's glasses..."

"So she discovered something? Do you think Venor found out?" His tone is even again.

"She did seem frightened," I say.

"And when you went in the Works, did you lock the gate behind you?"

I close my eyes and think back. "I didn't. Someone could have followed us."

"He tried to have you killed. He can't get away with this." Kit's furious.

So am I, but Valour Venor can get away with just about anything.

Or maybe not. If Felicity uncovered his awful secret, so can we.

I close my eyes and try to reach again for the memories that won't come. Try to call, groping around the memory cave. It's never let me down – but now, for the first time, everything's topsy-turvy.

There's a door in the floor – like the one outside the Lugger for taking barrels of ale direct to the cellar. I follow the steep stairs to a cramped, echoing wooden room.

A glass of fizzy juice, the kind Felicity bought me from the chip shop, moons ago now, is on a low table, a coil of rope beside it.

Venor's here. A waking nightmare, holding something. A letter? A drawing? He's wearing the magistrate's official black hat with gold insignia. *Black and yellow, kill a fellow.* I can't look directly at him – my mind is too unsettled.

I strain to gather the threads of memory, but everything's unspooling. The cave melts away.

33

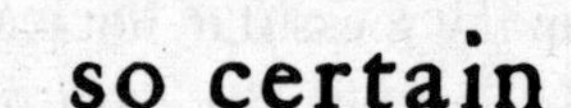

so certain

It's evening when I return from dreamland to clattering pans. Kit and Ruzi are talking in my doorway.

"Wake up, Mora. I'm making you some food," Ruzi says. Then: "She needs her rest," to Kit. He turns back to me. "Egg okay?"

"I just woke up," I groan.

"I'd love an egg," Kit says.

"Wasn't asking everyone," Ruzi grumbles, but he retreats to the kitchen.

The grin Kit was shining on Ruzi fades as he comes into my room, a box under one arm.

"He's worried about Zako," he whispers. "Told him not to fret. Zako is a bright kid."

My stomach rumbles in the silence like a creaking door. Kit hands me the box. "Got you these. See if they fit."

It's a pair of boots, soft and black with perfect treads,

painted metal round the bootlace holes and fancy plaited laces. *They're new*, I realize, astonished. *Why's he buying me boots?* They're a little higher round the ankle than my ragged old browny-grey ones. I haven't had anything new, anything this beautiful to wear since before the Cull. Didn't think I cared to. But I care about these.

"Fit like I glove," I choke out. They're a tiny bit big, but I can double up my socks. I'm not parting with them. "Thank you. Why'd you go and do this?"

"You lost your other ones."

"Did I?"

Lose your boots, girl. I hear a low whisper, something tickling my cheek. I grasp at the memory, but it dissolves like candyfloss to nothing, like all the others.

I realize I've got a hand on my cheek and I'm staring into space.

"Any progress on the memory front?" Kit asks. "Any dreams about … anything?"

It's my turn to sigh.

"None of my tricks are working."

"Shall I get some prayer grass?"

It worked for Zako.

Do I want my blank hours returned? I should, but I'm terrified. My mind flashes to Venor, full of malice – the memory of a nightmare.

"What's the matter?" Kit touches my arm.

"Nothing." My voice is overloud.

I have to move. I scramble to stand, hardly noticing

Kit's arm helping me. I look sideways at him. He smells like spices and kitchen smoke. His sleeves are bunched above his elbows, his beaded bracelets wedged high up his forearms.

"Everything all right there?" Ruzi calls from the kitchen around the sound of spitting eggs.

I glance back at Kit, biting my lip. He seems to realize his arm is still circling me and drops it.

I turn to the desk and reach out to run my fingers along the margin of an unfinished drawing. My sleeves don't cover the abrasions still clear at my wrists.

I feel shaky again.

"You're okay, Mor." Kit's voice sounds faraway.

Ruzi's here with two chipped plates, a salted fried egg and ripped-off hunk of bread on each. He sighs and disappears to the kitchen again.

My eyes float up to Kit's.

"That peddler who got the grass for Zako isn't in town any more." He runs his fingers down his jaw. My eyes are pulled to his mouth. "But I'll find some somehow."

"You don't have to."

"It's better to know. We need to."

I focus on the plate with the wobbling egg, and I shiver, though the air is warm. "Is it better?"

"If you know, you can move on." He slices his egg with a fork and eats half in one go. He sounds so certain.

34

sights higher

I recover slowly, although I'm not well enough for work. Just when I'm starting to feel desperate for a change of scene, Missus Scarlet invites me for fikka in her rooms, unexpectedly. It's strange to be here again, with Zako gone.

"I told Missus Sanders from the Rainbow about your talents," she says. "She wants to commission a portrait of her grandchild."

"Really?"

"She's very impressed. Not like her."

"Thank you."

"You gave everyone a scare, going missing like that." She coughs and folds her papery hands in her lap, before unfolding them to fidget with a cushion and then leaning forward to pick up her still-too-hot cup of fikka. "Our young man didn't take it well."

She tells me Kit was not himself the day I was unconscious.

"What happened?"

"Well, he's usually canny enough to avoid things like that. I think he was drinking, or he wouldn't have ended up there."

"But he doesn't drink. Wait, end up where?"

"He went to the workers' gathering – the march from Rundvaer Square to sing outside the branders' station. It ended up being shut down. They started a fire! People were injured – plenty." She sips fikka. "We had a job bailing Kit. They still went ahead and shaved him."

It's strange, I think, for Kit to get mixed up in that. But then I see it.

The Reedstones' *moment of opportunity.*

They must have planned to rile everyone up and, in the confusion, spring the Artist. Clearly, it didn't work.

I wonder whether that means they'll try again.

When I leave Missus S in her rooms seeking Kit, he's out running an errand with Mister S. I go back to Opal Alley and work on some sketches, then fall asleep before Ruzi's even home. It's gone ten when I next wake, actually feeling alert for the first time in days, even if I still can't remember the cause of all the exhaustion. Ruzi's asleep. I slip on my hooded top and sneak out.

It's a warm evening, the streets still rather lively. I avoid two brander patrols, including a pair who've stopped another Crozoni repayer, not far from the Lugger. I slip past on the other side of the street while she's producing a permission slip from her employer for them to inspect.

Kit's not in the kitchen. Gracie and Renny are nearly ready to leave. I'm climbing the stairs, and I can hear Mister S's voice below, telling patrons it's closing time.

Kit's stood over his desk, jotting something in Xan script in one of his notebooks. His hair's like long stubble now. His dark shirt is crisply pressed, open at the throat. The buttons look like Crozoni handiwork – pearly black shell. His trousers are dark too, with dark braces instead of a belt. Black shoes – worker's boots, not dress shoes – are beside the door, but his feet are bare.

"Mor. What's going on?" He keeps scratching with his fountain pen.

"Missus S told me about your stint at the station."

He straightens to examine me, leaving the pen on the paper. A dark blot of ink bleeds out of its nib. "Don't start."

I lower my voice to a breath. "I know what was going on. You were trying to get the Artist out, weren't you?"

"Well, if we were, we failed miserably. He's guarded and then some." He drops the pen and shuts the book.

"What happened?"

"They didn't figure out what we were there for, but I got nabbed anyway." He grimaces. "Venor's paranoid about the Artist escaping. Can't lose him before Lovemore gets to enjoy the show. And they've moved him – sent him somewhere more secure."

"Where?"

"The Life Registry."

My heart sinks. "Oh, Kit."

If they couldn't free him from the jail after months of planning, they've no chance now he's in the Life Registry, the best-secured place in County Portcaye. He'll lose his head in less than three weeks.

"I know, I know," Kit says. He gives me a sad smile. "Listen, I need to go, Mora. I have a job tonight."

"For the Reedstones?"

"Who else?" He sighs.

"Patrols are out in force tonight," I tell him. "You don't have to put yourself in so much danger for the Reedstones and their plots."

"Says the girl gadding around after curfew herself." He holds my eyes until I look away. "Mor – some risk is worth it, you know. I don't want to … get to the end of it all and think … and wonder… I don't want those regrets. You don't either. I know you. Can we stop pretending?"

"You know me," I whisper. "I want to take everything on too, Kit. Really. But if the Artist is in the Registry … it's a hopeless cause."

His fingers drum the desk. "Maybe hopeless causes are my thing."

I knew it. I knew he'd be haring along with no thought to the risk.

He gazes at me, all open and innocent. "I don't smoke, Mor. I don't drink. I barely do anything naughty. I've so few vices. Let me have my hopeless causes."

I realize all the noise from downstairs has stopped.

He stands abruptly. "I'm hungry. Let's go down." He brushes past me out of the door, leaving it open, carrying his lantern swaying down the stairs, much faster than I can comfortably go, and quiet as the dead, nonetheless.

The kitchen's dark except for the weak pool of light his lantern casts. He's already cut some bread and is biting into it. "Do you want some?"

"No thanks."

"Apple?"

"Okay."

He cuts one in two and passes half to me.

He doesn't seem himself, but I can't put my finger on it. He smiles at me in that slightly too broad way again and bites his apple, through the core. He hardly chews it, swallows.

"So they're expecting you to help break him out of that place? Sometime in the next three weeks?"

"Yes."

"And you've agreed?"

"Yes."

"No vices..." I mutter. "You're just after another dangerous thing to binge on."

His look slices right through me. "That may be true." He laughs quietly, licking apple juice off his fingers. Then he lunges at me and hugs me. He picks me up and spins me around, like some long-lost friend he hasn't seen in months. He puts me down gently.

"You smell good," he murmurs. "What is that?"

He's put me down but left his arms around me. Mine don't want to move, so I leave them around him. He tilts his face towards me. Apple and soap and his own scent fill my head.

"Nothing."

"Do you still want me to stop?" A double-edged question.

"Isn't it obvious?"

"Nothing about Mora Dezil is obvious," he murmurs.

"I want you to stop," I decide, without much commitment.

"Why?"

"Because you could get hurt." I drop my arms.

He flings his head back and laughs, almost silently, then tips forward again to look down at me. "Guess I could."

He brushes his lips against my cheekbone, my eyelashes as I close my eyes. Then he takes a small step back, drops his arms too, letting me go if I want to go. I don't move. He takes my chin between his fingers, tips my face up. I don't move. So he kisses me.

I kiss back. His fingers find the back of my neck, his thumbs hover in front of my throat, barely touching me. His tongue is a light touch against mine, his lips softly crushing. I run a hand up from his neck to the back of his head. It's as satisfying as I imagined.

He bites me gently. I bite back. He presses me backwards. I bump into the bench they use to plate the meals. He leans into me, the gentle kisses becoming more forceful, his hips pinning me against the side of the bench. Then he draws away, hoists me up with a grunt so I perch in front of him on the wooden surface. His mouth finds my throat while one hand tangles in my blouse. The other moves up my thigh.

My heart thumps like a netted bird. Like it wants more. I look at the shadow we cast in lantern light on the ceiling. One dark smudge in a dark mirror. I pull away, unwrapping my legs, sliding off the bench and out of his arms.

"What are you going out to do tonight, then?" My voice is quiet.

"Nothing."

"What do you mean?"

"I've reconsidered my plans for tonight." His voice is unravelling me.

"Where were you going?"

"Out to see an acquaintance in the Mermens."

"What acquaintance?"

"No one to be jealous of."

"I'm not jealous."

"I am. Constantly."

I can't bring myself to believe such a droll confession, so freely given.

I raise one eyebrow, but he only looks wounded.

"Mora. Do you know what *Mora* means in my language?"

"No."

"Red-back, *Mo-rah*. It's a kind of spider."

I know the one – black and bulging with an amber hourglass on its back. Poisonous. The females kill and eat the males. We used to call it a widow spider.

"That's flattering."

"Do you want truth or flattery?"

"Well, both."

He laughs low, then leans in to kiss me again, a feather touch near my eye, another on my cheek. Next my lips. He's being gentle with me, gentler than the time in the woods. Because he thinks I'll break?

I suppose getting washed up on the beach with no memory hasn't helped my cause.

I feel a falling sensation and step away. He draws back too, fluid on those long, lean legs, props himself against the counter almost warily. He hooks his hands around his braces as if he can't bear to leave them empty.

"You know I won't do anything you don't want." His rasp is soft. I know what he means. This – us … and it's true.

I feel safe with him. But he doesn't get it.

"I *don't want* you to get yourself killed for a hopeless cause you won't tell me the first thing about. I *don't want* to read how they did it in the *Post* the next day. And I didn't come here to be your evening's distraction," I add, when he doesn't answer.

His face is in shadow, but I see him flinch before his lips set in a line.

"Mora." He drags my name out like a reprimand, and still it sounds better than the way anyone else says it. "You're much more than one evening's distraction." He's inches away again. I didn't see him move. Perhaps I went to him. His hand cups the side of my face, rough thumb tracing my jaw. If he kissed me again, I'd consent to anything. As it is, I still have a measure of self-control.

I can't think with my heart pounding like this. "This is not what – this is not why I came here."

"Plans change?"

"But what are the plans? How are the Reedstones seriously planning to take on the bloody Life Registry?"

His eyes flick over my shoulder, to the door, and his mouth twists with irritation.

A pale face floats behind the glass panel like a wraith. It's Goldie Reedstone, who we were just talking about, as if we've conjured her.

She's real enough, turning the handle and letting herself in, bold as brass. How polished and poised she is. Her trousers are a fine black cotton, her blouse yellow and flowing. Her low heels click on the flagstones as her lithe form weaves round the counter towards us. I can't help thinking of a sea krait, though she smells like an orchard. Her straw-yellow hair is smoothed flat as paper, hanging almost to the small of her back. There's little contrast against her light skin.

"My, my." She kindles a thin smile for me, before extinguishing it to turn to Kit. "What an interesting conversation you two are having."

"Thought I was meeting Glister in the Mermens," Kit parries.

Goldie rolls her eyes, but I get the sense she's hiding some deeper emotion. "He can't face it," she says. "I told him to stay home."

Kit frowns.

"I'm so glad I came and caught you though." Her voice is clipped. "And got to meet your friend here. What's your name, dear?" She tilts her head at me.

I hesitate.

"Leave her out of it," Kit snaps.

"Oh, it sounds like she's already involved. And I think I know who you are. Mora Dezil, the girl who draws."

I nod.

"I've admired your work for some time." I feel a smile creeping over my lips. Then I remember the Reedstones are trouble, and flatten out my expression.

"I hear you have a knack for remembering things. Didn't realize you were quite so…" She gestures at me with one hand instead of finishing her thought.

"So what?"

"So … part of Kit's kitchen furnishings here."

"I'm not."

She smirks at Kit. "Not for want of trying, I suppose. It's fortuitous I met you tonight, Mora. I've been trying to persuade Kit to make the introduction for a while now."

Kit makes a noise of protest, but I interrupt. "Why?"

"Such a talent. A girl who can remember what she sees

exactly and replicate it perfectly on the page." She turns her dark-blue eyes back to me. They're like jewels. Hypnotic. "We need someone with your skills and creativity, Mora."

They need me. Kit's always saying I have to stay out of it – that it's too dangerous. But he'll never admit anything's too dangerous for him. Well, what's good for the gander's perfectly fine for the goose, as Ruzi would say.

"We'd have to buy you, of course." Goldie's still talking. "So your time could be your own. We can emancipate you – in all the ways that matter. Set you up wherever you want."

"What's the catch?"

"Goldie" – Kit breaks in, moving between us – "the job's getting done. We don't need Mora. I just need time to prepare. Nobody needs to buy anybody."

"I think Mora would be a tremendous asset." She smiles. "Think about it, Mora. You'd be well compensated. Kit knows where to find me when you've made up your mind."

"Go on ahead." He herds her out. "I'll meet you by the stair."

Goldie leaves, and Kit turns to me. His attention feels divided in a way it wasn't ten minutes ago.

"At least tell me what you're doing tonight," I say.

"We're getting Fidel's head down," he says softly. "His cousin wants to bury it."

Fucking hell. I puff out a breath. What a task.

"I want to help with the Registry break-in," I tell him.

"You can tell the Reedstones that. But say I don't want them to buy me." Better the demon you know, Ruzi likes to say. And I like living with Ruzi. It's the first real home I've made since the Cull.

"No, Mora," he says quickly. "I won't risk you."

"I'm not yours to risk," I remind him.

The hand that was reaching for me drops to his side. He looks at his bare feet.

I let the door bang closed behind me.

Halfway home, I realize I'm still holding most of my piece of the apple. I toss it into a gutter.

Birds will eat it. Char's little voice, out of time, washes back to me. He used to say that when he dropped food in a patch so dirty he wasn't allowed to contemplate rubbing it off and eating it anyway. *Don't worry. Birds will eat it.*

A yellow crescent moon hangs beside the bright splash of stars forming the Haymaker's Way. There are no clouds. It's the kind of sky you could fall into if you looked up long enough. I think of Fidelity Hemman's head up there on the gate, staring at the stars.

Let them do their worst. I've been down here in the mud long enough. It's time to set my sights higher.

35

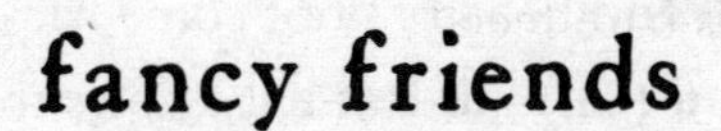

fancy friends

It's already Sixday. I wake up wondering about Zako again. Has he spent another night alone? Is he cold? Hungry? I feel well enough to work, if I'm honest, but I'm not telling Wagsen that.

Ruzi said I shouldn't rush back. They have a temporary man helping, and I need to get well. They can have me back after the Endweek.

"Last night go okay?"

I've come round from the front and managed to sneak up on Kit for once.

"It was…" He sighs and looks at me with a little shake of his head.

"Did you tell her?"

He resumes scrubbing stubborn porridge from a pan.

"Mor, you nearly died a few days ago." His tone is soft enough, but his expression's hard as slate. "Can you concentrate on surviving for five minutes?" That gravel voice. He puts the pan aside and starts wiping the stove. "I meant to tell you," he cuts in as I start sputtering a response. "I'll have to go seeking your prayer grass in the wild. It's in season now, but no one seems to have it… Not even the dried stuff."

"Oh." I deflate a little. My lost memories are still off with the fairies and Felicity's not come back. Every time I think of her, I feel afraid. But Kit knows this. He's trying to change the subject.

"And you will tell Goldie Reedstone I'm in?"

We're talking in Crozoni, but Gracie and Renny are here preparing pastries already. He tosses his cloth over one shoulder, and we sit in the courtyard.

"Do you have any idea how impossible this will be, Mora?"

"Not unless you tell me."

"All right, I will. All I have to do is crawl around on the outside of Portcaye's most impenetrable building, get a locked window open from the outside, evade four to six guards, bust open a vault, get the bloody Artist and myself back out of there without anyone noticing he's gone and without being seen or falling to my death or killing anyone."

"You draw the line at killing?"

"Course. Life is sacred."

Shame the Skøl didn't think that six years ago.

"And what are the Reedstones doing while you take all the risk?"

"They can't do it. The vault lock – it has to be me."

"Why?"

"I'm the only one who can open it."

"But isn't it a GR Locks lock? Didn't they make it in the first place?"

"They did, but they can't get round the trickiest bit."

"Can't you teach them?"

"Some things can't be taught."

I think of Ruzi and his sayings. *You can't teach an old dog new tricks.* I'm not at all sure I believe that, but Kit is adamant. I let it lie, studying my hands with their blunt, chewed nails and ever-present scrapes and callouses. "So … you need someone on the inside to open a window," I muse. "A window on the third floor."

"That's right," he says cautiously. "How did you—"

"I know the windows at the undercroft, ground and first two floors are barred. I've seen the Life Registry from the road enough times."

"It's not a memory game, Mora." Kit pulls the dishcloth angrily off his shoulder. "I can't keep you safe. I can't catch you if you fall."

"I know." I know he thinks if he fights me every step of the way I'll give up. I'll get afraid. Well, of course I'm afraid. I've a hundred fears, orbiting me like little moons, pulling the tides of me this way and that. But how big and close one of those fears has grown. Fear of sitting here, wasting away doing nothing. Its tides are going to drown me.

"Tell them I'm doing it," I say. I get up and return to

the kitchen. Kit leans back against the tree, scrunching the cloth in one hand.

I don't need his permission. And the thing is, I can already feel a plan growing.

I convince Renny she'd be doing me a favour, letting me sell pastries in her place. I tell her I'm curious to see inside the Registry, for nostalgia's sake – because it used to be an important civic building for the Crozoni. If she thinks my request strange, she doesn't say so. She must be used to looking the other way, with all of Kit's odd comings and goings. Outside the Life Registry, Gracie adjusts her dress and pinches her cheeks. "Every little helps," she quips.

"So what do we do? Wander around saying, *Come and get it*?"

"Sort of."

I peer up at the towering stone building. As well as the two guards on the door, there's a pair on part of the flat roof, idly patrolling, guns in arms.

"Is that normal?" I ask Gracie.

"Oh yes, they started having guards up there… When was it? Around when you were ill, actually. I don't know why."

It must be because they've moved the Artist here. Security's stepped up.

"So do we go selling on every floor?"

"No need. We can sell out on the first two. Third and fourth aren't worth the effort. Hardly ever open their doors. The higher-ups go out for lunch somewhere fancy like the Warbler." As if on cue, a small group of senior clerks with expensive-looking watch chains begin to make their way down the steps. Lugger fare's not for this lot.

I sling the basket rope around my neck and sway beside Gracie up the steps as the clerks sweep past us. How are they not too hot in those robes?

"First- and second-floor workers are the hungriest. It's slower on the ground, but there's a decent number of takers. Why don't you take the ground?"

"What about the undercroft?"

"We can't go in there. Whole floor's off limits – vault and Records and that. Guard on the door – if he's the skinny one with freckles – he's partial to a jam one."

The two guards out front beneath the *Life Is Golden* inscription aren't friendly. They paw through the lunches before they let us pass.

The entrance foyer is not how I remember it from my childhood. They've stripped out the mosaic tiles, the red carpets on the stairs, painted over the classic Crozoni mural across the high ceiling featuring Thea – it's all white now, white tiles, white-painted bare walls and ceiling, wooden stairs stained white. Only a few potted plants lend colour. Still, it's louder and more chaotic than I expected.

Someone stops and thrusts a handful of coins at me. "I'll take two."

Gracie and I split up.

There's plenty to see on the ground floor. The corridor

to Venor's personal office, the guards' station, the library. I've sold about two-thirds of the lunches before I make my way calmly to the third floor. I think of sneaking with Ruzi over to see Zako in the Scarlets' quarters. Of walking the streets past curfew. The trick is not to look furtive. Shoulders back, spine straight.

The first few doors I try are locked. My knocks go unanswered.

Finally, one propped ajar opens to a large room – three tall windows along the wall and four cluttered desks.

A clerk who must be boiling in his robes looks up from the only occupied desk and draws his hood back up with ink-stained fingers. He doesn't say anything, just stares. I recognize his cold blue eyes and craggy face – the clerk who stopped to talk to Felicity on the way to the vigil for Fidelity Hemman. Alone working, all his fellows gone to lunch. Perhaps clerks who partake in vigils have their breaks curtailed.

One of the sash windows is wedged open with a book. It looks out over the front, towards the river.

"Hello? I'm selling lunches. Heard some were wanted here?"

"Who told you that?" he asks, quite rudely.

"Don't know who she was."

"I don't think you're allowed here," he ventures. I realize he's a bit scared.

"Sorry. Must have got the wrong place." I turn to leave.

"I'll buy one," he says quickly, gesturing me over and fishing a few coins from a dish on his desk.

I leave the basket with him and pretend an interest in the view behind while he's choosing.

"Could you see the new statues on the gates from here?" I sidle closer to the glass.

"Not sure," he says. "What's to see anyway? They're just columns. I liked the mermen."

No key locks to the windows, but the standard brass latches. They only open from the inside. They've also got stops about half a foot up. Not wide enough for someone to fall out. Or crawl in.

He's still counting his coins. I lean against one of the stops and try to move it by hand. Not possible – it needs a wrench.

I gather my basket back up quickly and walk out. There's still one more thing I want to check before I leave.

"What took you so long?" Gracie collars me back at the Lugger. Kit materializes instantly at her side. "You've been ages."

"Sold them all, didn't I?" I fish coins from my apron pocket.

"Kit's been on at me for leaving you behind." She shoots him a wounded look.

"Sorry," Kit rumbles.

"He's such a grump today." I give him a playful prod in the chest. He scowls, then jerks his head towards the door. I collect my cloth bag from its hook and follow him through the courtyard to the stables in the alley beyond. One of the Lugger's current guests came on his kine – a roan with a pretty belled harness. Mister S usually looks after the guest kine – he misses having his own – but Kit helps occasionally.

I came prepared this morning. I pull my drawing things out of the bag and start sketching while it's all top of mind.

Kit pours oats into the trough, on to the kine's nose as it tries to snap them out of the air. I refocus on the plan of the Life Registry sprouting under my pencil.

With what I saw inside, and what I know from walking round the outside enough times, I can draw the plans with almost architectural detail – the number of windows, the location of the doors and staircases and corridors inside. I label the water closets, the entrance foyer, the library. One page of the book per floor.

Kit comes to peer over my shoulder. I hear him make a small noise of surprise and feel a surge of pride. "What are those little crosses?" he asks.

"Potted plants."

"You think we should rescue them too?"

I laugh. "Sorry. I got carried away." Only the undercroft I've drawn remains vague. I've done what I can from observing the small windows outside, but it's not much to go on.

"Third-floor window latches are standard," I tell Kit. "I'd need a tool to take the stops out, but they're simple enough ... and all the doors in that corridor have the same kind of lock – like the one on your door upstairs. They probably lock them overnight, so you'll need to teach this old dog a new trick—"

"Hang on—" Kit tries to interrupt, but I hold my pencil in front of his face.

"We can pick which window you need me to unlatch based on the outside climb. Which bits of guttering and that give you the best approach."

"Back up a second." He plucks my pencil out of my fingers. "This is useful," he gestures, grudgingly, at my beautiful schematic. "If someone can get inside in the first place."

"Oh, I know how to do *that*."

He blinks at me.

"I can go in with pastries. Go in and hide and not come out again."

"Hide where?"

"That would be telling."

He leans towards me, mouth slightly ajar with the smile swooping past his lips. Canines sharp. "You know you want to tell me." I can see him looking at my mouth.

I lean closer. "I want –" I breathe softly, so close to his lips I can feel their warmth – "to see your fancy friends."

36

i missed it

Crackling fires range every ten yards or so along the sand, rung with merry parties of Skøl, toasting their bread, dunking their dry meat in jam and sipping from stoneware. We pass about a dozen.

The last fire, the southernmost, is twenty yards from its fellows, hosting a sober party of three. Their pale faces turn to watch as Kit and I near. It's well past curfew, but we're in hooded cloaks – too hot for daytime but not out of place now, with the night breeze blowing off the water. No one has clocked us.

"Over here," the big man sitting beside Goldie greets us. I realize I've seen him before. He was with an older Crozoni woman on Rafmagis Way, out enjoying the Skivårnat lanterns. Then I saw both of them again at Ruzi's fateful music night. The Crozoni woman isn't here tonight.

He's in his mid-twenties perhaps. A little older and a lot taller than Goldie – who's not much taller than me. He reminds me of one of those enormous stone waymarks. Big and broad-chested, but slim at the waist. His hair is brown, dark by Skøl standards. He looks like a firebrand, or a sailor, or a dockworker – someone used to heavy lifting or hauling on rigging. The family similarity to Goldie is slight – their fine-boned faces, small noses and something about the eyebrows, prominent in the firelight.

"Glister Reedstone. Good to meet you at last." There's a burr to his voice that reminds me of one of the women who taught us their language, in detention, after the Cull.

The third person, sat on the other side of Goldie Reedstone, is the young Skøl man I saw with Kit in Rundvaer Square. The one who went into the Sinskill Club in evening wear and came out of the fikka shop in a boiler suit with a stolen artefact in his toolbox. The first and last time I saw him, he knocked my face into a wall.

"My name's Level," the face-smasher says when we're sitting. "But everyone calls me Lev."

A memory of what they called me at school swoops and digs its talons in. What my sisters and my brother called me. *Rourou*. No one's called me Rourou in years.

Level Gusting. I think of his brief infamy in the *Portcaye Post … promising technician or lout?* Level Gusting, who Goldie told the papers wouldn't steal a penny. I think of Felicity hunched over that paper with me and look out over the black ocean. *Where are you, Felicity?*

I've brought my sketches of the Registry layout. Goldie leans so close to the fire I worry about her loose hair whipping about in the wind.

"These are good," says Lev, startled. "Better than good. You weren't lying, Kit."

"Blithe will be in the undercroft," Goldie says. "Locked behind our own invention." She gives her brother a sympathetic look.

Glister nods at me. "Vault lock's one of ours." He looks at Kit. "Only someone with his … skills could ever get past our fail-safe."

"Yes, I wondered why only him?" I look at Kit.

He shakes his head and bats a hand playfully. "They're not as good at climbing buildings as me either." I feel he's concealing something.

"Maybe you should teach them."

"We don't have the years."

I raise an eyebrow at him.

"How many guards did you see?" Goldie asks.

"Two on the front doors. Two on the roof – Gracie said they're new. One inside, on the door to the undercroft. There's only this one way down there." I point at the symbol I've used for the stairs on my schematic of the ground floor. "Two in the guard station here. This corridor leads to Venor's office."

"There are four in that station overnight. But the guard to the undercroft is only there in the daytime – when they're open for business," Goldie says. "If our intelligence is correct, you should be able to avoid the guards entirely."

"I'd feel better about it if this one would take a gun," mutters Lev.

"I've told you, I'm not doing that," Kit says mildly. "If we can't do this without killing anyone, we're not doing it."

Life is sacred.

I'm wedged between Glister and Kit. Kit's next to Lev. They're discussing the scheduling of the outdoor guards – front and back, and now roof. "I've been keeping tabs," Lev's saying. "The plan would work on a Fourday or a Fiveday only. That's when they change the door guards in the early afternoon."

"So … if someone were to take a basket of pastries in before the switch, the later guards wouldn't be any the wiser about who'd gone in and who hadn't come out."

"Exactly."

"You could go next Fourday," Glister suggests. "Before Lovemore's ship even gets here."

"But that would only give Mora four … and a half … days to practise lock-picking for the inside door," Kit argues. "It's a skill. And she hasn't been well. She's recovering from an illness. More practice beforehand means less chance of mistakes on the day."

They look at me.

"Kit's right. We can't rush in unprepared. We should do it on Fourday after next. The ninth." It's twelve days from now. "Ruzi can tell my boss I've come down with a terrible contagious stomach flu."

"Or we can buy you," Glister says.

"No thanks," I tell him, trying not to sound short. "The Glassworks suits me fine. I don't want to be right under your noses."

He nods.

"Fourday after next is three days after Lovemore's arrival." Goldie pours ginger beer from a bottle into a little metal cup and sips it. "But that could work well for us. Branders will be thick near the centre. They'll keep their patrols tight around Rundvaer Square and the Castle Hotel. Means less interest round the Registry."

"It's only three days before the execution though. That Endweek..." Glister says. "If something goes wrong, we won't be able to try again."

"If something goes wrong, we're out of things to try," Kit says.

"I like the ninth," Lev weighs in.

They start talking about what Lev and the Reedstones will do to help. It mostly involves staging a drunken ruckus to one side of the Registry building to coincide with Kit climbing in. That way the guards at the back and on the roof will be too distracted to notice him.

Glister catches my arm.

"Tell me..." There's a rawness in his expression. "You saw Blithe." His voice cracks on the name.

"The Artist. I saw him in the jail." I nod.

"I know it was some time ago, but … did he say anything? I mean… What were they doing to him? Was he badly hurt?"

"They were questioning him. He looked rough, but he was… He was spirited. Handling himself well." Lying in a puddle of his own piss with cracked ribs and *not* crying is handling things okay in my book. "Kit says you're old friends."

"Yes. He was – is – twenty-seven. A year older than me." His smile's gone.

I was right about him. Thought Blithe was more like thirty though. Perhaps being tortured ages a person. "What was he like before he was famous?"

Glister stirs the flames. "Have you ever met someone who changed the way you look at everything?"

He doesn't wait for me to answer. His voice is still calm, his cheeks dry, but there's something pitiful in the way his hands have to busy themselves, poking at the fire, sifting shells out of the sand.

"That's Blithe. He never lets things slide. He can't pretend. He's always been better than the rest of us."

He suddenly realizes the others have stopped talking and are listening to him too.

Goldie clears her throat and flips to my schematic of the third floor, spread across her knees. "So … Mora goes in at noon. Hides in her secret nook. After closing, she goes upstairs to the third floor, unlocks the second door from this side, opens the third window from the right. Kit starts the climb at eleven. The local drinking establishments will be closing. Lev and I will stage our argument off to this side." She points at the edge of the schematic. "Kit finishes the climb, gets in through the window. Down to the undercroft. Into the vault – Kit, we will walk you through the details of the vault lock back home … tomorrow?"

"I can't tomorrow."

"Day after?"

"How about Seconday? Midday?"

She nods.

"You find Blithe, head back up. Exit through the back."

"Would be so much safer just to shoot those guards," Lev grumbles.

"We can knock them out with ether. I know how to get some," Kit insists.

"Incapacitate two guards … somehow," Goldie continues her summary. "And…"

"Leg it," Lev pipes up.

Goldie grins. "And everyone's happy. Except Venor, who's very sad," she finishes with a flourish of one hand.

"And you pay us what we agreed," Kit reminds her.

"Every last quarter krunan," she promises.

"I know the Artist is an important figure," I say cautiously, "but do you think rescuing him will really do a lot of damage to Venor?"

"What do you mean?"

"Could he … lose the high governor's support over this? Over Blithe escaping on his watch?"

The Reedstone siblings exchange a glance. "The high governor will still support him. She'll look foolish if the man she's backed for so long turns out unfit, a few days before a ceremony she's sailed five thousand miles to attend," Glister explains.

"He'll probably still be appointed governor of the New West," Goldie admits. "But his public image will be damaged. And Blithe can get back to work – to the work that put him on the wanted list in the first place... We can all keep working to undermine him. Venor will be considerably weakened."

Considerably weakened. I remember Venor's dodgy Life Record – his secret.

"The vault we're breaking into, to free Blithe," I say slowly, "that's the same vault that contains all the Registry records, isn't it?"

Glister nods. "It's the most secure vault money can buy. It holds everything of highest importance."

Venor's Record. Maybe that can weaken him fatally.

The question is – can I trust them? It isn't just me this secret endangers. There's Kit. Zako.

Goldie's watching me, but I can't read her expression.

"He will definitely look weak, then, if that vault fails." I leave it at that.

I wonder if Kit's thought of Venor's secret, just hanging there in the Registry vault, waiting to be plucked. I'm itching to ask him, but when we get up to leave, Goldie catches my arm and draws me and Kit aside.

This close to her, I can hear her complicated gold earrings tinkling in the sea breeze. Her breath smells like ginger beer, and her perfume's worn off. Perhaps she is an ordinary mortal like the rest of us.

"Just remember, if this fails..." Her eyes pierce through me. "Glister's bound to attempt something suicidally heroic at the execution. Glister will be arrested. I'll be arrested. Lev will be out of a job. Kit will be thrown under no end of suspicion. No krunan for you, for anyone. Only the man with the axe, and the man who sticks our heads on spikes."

I shrug free of her grip with a spark of irritation. She thinks she's got me sussed. Thinks I'm in this for the money, first and foremost, when I want to change things just as much as she does – more. Despite her rebel ambitions, she's still that kind of rich Skøl who's sure everyone wants what she has. A spoilt child, pretending to be tough, sending a repayer in to crack her own vault.

Kit and I nod. Goldie catches Lev's arm as she drifts away up the beach, distant and rarified again, and I shake her out of my head and turn to Kit. "Venor's Life Record," I whisper. "We should liberate it too."

Kit's smile catches the fading firelight. I realize how much I missed it.

37

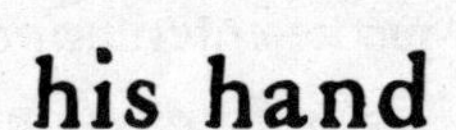

his hand

Before sunrise the next day, a pattering on the glass wakes me. I peel the drab curtains aside and peer through the murk. A soft pool of light glows from the bakery window – they always start inhumanly early. A mounted figure walks a kine into it. He waves up at me, and the kine tosses its head. Kit.

The cast-iron steps are covered in dew. I tiptoe down barefoot, hugging myself, hoping the low light hides the worst of my ragged nightgown.

"What's the matter?"

"Nothing. It's the Endweek. Come with me."

"Come with you where?"

"Get your shoes on, slug-a-bed. It'll be fun."

"What's *fun*?"

"Ha. I know you can't resist a picnic. Better than orange ice." My heart floats at the prospect of getting out, getting away for a day. "Didn't you say you like riding?" Kit pats the flank of the kine. It's a glossy black, but knobble-kneed and rather short. One of its lower horns is broken off halfway, giving it a certain jauntiness.

"I've got to walk Clomper and Caney."

"Do it when you get back. They'll keep."

"I've got to learn how to pick locks."

"That's the after-picnic entertainment."

"Where'd you find this fine figure of a fellow?"

"He's a rental, a sweetheart – don't let the look fool you. Come on. You can drive."

"I have to change."

"Go on, then. We'll wait a few minutes."

"You're such an arse."

"I know."

The kine's called Fearsome, it turns out, though he's anything but, with his short legs and his lopsided horns.

We trot out of the southern gates and pick slowly up the limestone cliffs, heading south. The Portcaye wall vanishes behind the rolling land, and I feel freer than I have in years.

"So, where are we heading exactly?" I ask.

"You know I couldn't find a soul to bring us prayer grass," he says. "So we have to go searching."

"Oh."

"This is good for us. Getting out of town for a day. You told me you missed riding."

The riding is for my benefit, then. Like the grass. I'm aware of his hands resting lightly at my waist.

"A day out. Walking out together?" I feel suddenly bold. "Are you courting me?"

"Hmm."

We crest a small hill, and I give Fearsome his head. It's exhilarating, and a little frightening, the smell of dry heather bursting under blunt hoof blows, the ocean twinkling off to one side. Kit launches loudly into a rendition of an old Crozoni romantic ballad, putting on a very bad impression of Ruzi's voice. It feels like ages since I laughed so much. The sun's well risen by the time we've run out of material, and the cliffs have disappeared under Fearsome's hooves, sloping gradually down to a beach. No one's nearby, though we see a few other riders picking their way through the hill heather in the distance. Kit slips off and reaches a hand up to me.

The sand here is coarser and more colourful than it is near Portcaye, peppered with pebbles. Pale, jagged rocks are sunken everywhere, rising out higher than my head in places.

There's a row of abandoned structures – six old seaweed-drying huts – up the far end of the beach, and a thin freshwater stream trickling out of the grasses. The beach is empty in a way it never is near Portcaye. No upturned boats, no pits of half-burnt driftwood with log seats dragged beside them, no flat slabs of stone strewn with discarded fish baskets or broken crab traps.

A cluster of wading birds with curved beaks and bright pink legs pecks along the shoreline. Beyond, a heron stands submerged to the knots of its knees. A breeze flutters its feathers and whips its black crest from side to side. I take off my hair wrap to feel the salt wind lifting my curls.

The sea stretches away, a few distant fishing boats trailed by hopeful, hungry gulls.

We sit in the grass above the sand to share the sesame bread, shoo-fly pie, plums, apples and sticky honey biscuits Kit packed. Heathers unroll to the borders of a dark forest in the distance.

"How far do we go?" I sip from a flask he's filled with fikka.

"I have all day."

"For the grass, I mean."

"There used to be some on the other side of those woods."

I look at the grass all around us. "How can you tell it apart?"

"It's shinier."

"Just shinier?"

"I'll know when I see it."

I get to the apples last. They're the tiny red apples from my childhood, with skin that stretches under the teeth before it pops, and a bit of spice to the tart flesh. They're nothing like the kind I got on the Heanes' farm, or in Portcaye's markets.

Kit brushes crumbs off his top and stands. We walk to the sea to rinse our sticky fingers.

"You've got eleven days to learn how to use these," he

says, fishing a handful of objects from a pocket. "That's ages."

There's a small lock, with a mechanism like the one on the Registry office doors, and three long, thin pieces of metal – one with a slight serration. You only need to use two.

It looks easy when he shows me, but I can't do it. The constant sigh of waves, punctured by gull song, is starting to sound pointed – weariness mixed with distant screaming.

Kit persists, guiding my hands until I manage to fool the mechanism once. Now the gulls sound like they're laughing.

"It's just practice," he assures me, slipping the lock and picks into my pocket and, despite his words, looking slightly worried.

"So … are Goldie and Lev an item?" I ask, to change the subject.

The worry lines in his face turn to amusement. "He wishes."

"They seemed quite … comfortable together."

Kit slices a look at me as we trail idly along the waterline. "So do we."

And now I don't know what to say again.

"He's worked for them since he was fourteen – five years. That's when the Sting Trust funds stop. Goldie must have been … eighteen."

"Yeah?"

"Lev's a ball of prickles, but he's that way for a reason. He doesn't feel equal to her. He's alive because of her great-granny's money – but he's been told his whole life he's less than, living on time he didn't deserve, didn't earn, by rights should be dead. You can imagine, right? Too much tension there."

I nod, but I can't help thinking they suit each other somehow. Gracie's romantic notions rubbing off on me, probably.

"And Glister and the Artist?" I probe.

"Oh yeah, definitely an item. For Goldie and Lev, this is political. For Glister, it's completely personal."

Kit stops to gather a handful of pebbles, passes me some.

"Middle of that one." I point. Throw-for-crow. It's a game we all played, before. Throwing pebbles at a rock target.

Kit's not very good at it. "Should we keep going?" I say, once I've won three times in a row.

"Probably. Cut my losses." He grins.

We start back to where we left Fearsome.

"I could almost envy Zako, days like this," I sigh. "It's so beautiful."

"Yeah. He's probably eating oysters right now with his feet up."

"Do you miss diving for oysters?"

"I … miss swimming." He says it with surprising feeling.

"But you can go swimming. Don't let the kraits put you off."

"It's not the kraits."

"Don't let the Skøl put you off either. It's not banned."

"No, it's not banned." Kit turns his faraway smile on the sea.

We walk through the heathers for a while, but still the forest recedes into the distance, so we mount up again. Soon the pines are upon us.

There's more brambly undergrowth than there was up north. The trees are a softer, more spreading variety, but their needles still throw a heady fragrance.

We go on foot again.

When we come abruptly to a clearing, I think surely I'll see a building of some sort, or a crop being raised, but there are only wildflowers bobbing their heads in welcome, grasses shedding tiny floating seeds and an invisible orchestra of grasshoppers sawing away.

"What is this place?"

Kit's wandered off and doesn't hear me.

Wild celery crushes under Fearsome's dinner-plate hoofs.

"Found it!" Kit says.

Prayer grass. Shinier than normal grass, and very long. He brings a few strands to my nose. I meet his gaze. It smells like and unlike the dry flakes he got for Zako. Stronger.

"I came to this meadow with my mother. It was a settlement, once – of her people. It was all gone by the time she was a girl."

"It was a Xan village?"

"The trees don't grow back, though they should, don't you think?"

His gaze catches on something behind me, and he strides off while I tilt my face up to feel the sun and run my fingers through some fine feathery grasses. Not prayer grass, something thinner. He clears his throat behind me, and I turn. A bright orange flower spins on its stem between his thumb and forefinger, petals flapping like wings. We used to call them river lilies, though they grow anywhere it's wet enough. He reaches to brush my curls behind an ear so he can tuck the flower there. I'm close enough to see all his eyelashes.

"Matches your eyes." His teeth catch his lower lip, and heat crawls up my neck, not from the sun.

I spin round to scan the meadow. How different to the thick shade and ankle-deep mud on our last trip out of Portcaye together. A shiver of anticipation fills me. Then I spot a flash of purple, small florets arranged in a cone – just a shade darker than his eyes. I reach for one a bee has just vacated, snap off the stem and return to Kit. He tilts his head into my touch like a cat. The flower droops from his ear, too top-heavy. I catch it and let my eyes drift across his chest. The first few buttons of his shirt are undone, so I thread the stem through the second.

He clears his throat. "No one's given me a flower before."

"Me neither," I confess, before I realize it's not strictly true. "Well. Char used to pick dandelions and daisies for everyone." I gaze sideways at the meadow again but can feel him stepping closer. The flower in his buttonhole smells of honey and herbs. His hands drift up my spine and pull me closer. I thread my hands behind his neck.

The peaceful rustle of wind in the grasses grows louder. Two deer appear, one large, one small, running at us. *What are they doing? Are they mad? Am I dreaming?*

Fearsome tears grass and chews loudly, oblivious, even to the deer who turn and spring around us at the last second. He only looks up at the sound of Kit's cursing. Then I hear them too.

Ledhunds. They burst from the bracken at the edge of the clearing in pursuit, four of them.

A hunt, I think. "We should go," Kit says, urging me back up on to Fearsome, stuffing a handful of prayer grass into a pocket of the saddle bag.

The hounds ignore us at least, bounding past with strings of slobber dangling from their jaws and burrs clinging to their undercoats. They don't look well fed. From the far edge of the clearing, I hear a voice egging them on. Then two hunters stride from the treeline.

We aren't doing anything forbidden, but we're two repayers out alone, far from town. If it was a pair of picnickers with a few hounds I would feel better. Hunters have always scared me.

"Take him and go back." Kit gives Fearsome an encouraging pat. "I'll catch you up."

"No." I haul the reins. "Get on; come with me."

The hunters have seen us. One raises a hand in greeting.

"You'll be faster alone."

"What about you? We'll look suspicious if I run off."

"We already look suspicious. I'll explain to them. You go on."

"No."

He grits his teeth, but gives up on driving me away.

We watch the hunters approach – two men, Skøl of course. One has a quiver and bow. The other carries a brander's gun slung over one shoulder. He isn't in uniform. I wonder if it's illegal.

"What's going on here?" The one with the gun points it at Kit, casually.

"We're on an errand for our owners," I tell them, keeping the quaver from my voice. Repayers aren't allowed in groups of three, but we're only two.

Kit goes for Fearsome's saddle bag, perhaps to try and show them the grass, but they don't like that.

"No! Keep your hands where we can see them," says the second one – he's holding an arrow now. They look alike, but the one with the bow is taller and wider. He has a long moustache, a scraggly beard and a brown outfit. The one with the gun's clean-shaven, wearing green.

"What errand?" he asks.

"We're collecting samples of the local plants and wildflowers. Owners are writing a book about them." My lie comes easily in this place.

"Flowers?" says the same man. *Horseshit*, says his

expression – or it would if he knew horses. The Skøl don't seem to have an equivalent evoking kine. "Hope you haven't been digging this place up. It's full of bones."

Kit stiffens.

Somewhere in the distance, their hounds howl. "Your quarry's getting away," I remind them.

"We've bagged a pretty kine though," the tall one muses. He moves closer. "And a pretty pair of makkies." He raises his chin at Kit. "What happened to your skull, boy? Get on the wrong side of the jailer's razor?" He grins at his companion before he ploughs on.

"You know what I think? You way out here, skulking like rats?" The way he draws out the word *rats* makes me think of Venor's voice the day Zako escaped off the roof. I shake my head numbly.

"It's not—" Kit starts to say something, but the man talks over him.

"You've run off. Going to meet more makkies. Three at a time's not allowed. This animal stolen?"

"He's a rental," Kit says. I can see the effort he's making to stay calm.

"Where's your papers and your permission then, troublemaker?" says the one in green. He pulls a stash of folded, grimy notices from one pocket, unfolds them. Wanted posters.

"We didn't bring any papers. We're not doing anything that needs permission," Kit tells them.

"We're not on any wanted posters," I add.

The man has both old and new copies of Zako's wanted poster. He holds up the one with the twenty-thousand bounty and the *DEAD OR ALIVE* in big letters, and narrows his eyes at me. "Looks like you."

What? "That's a twelve-year-old boy. He's nothing like me." I slide off to stand beside Kit.

"Not regular, you being here though, is it?" The one in brown stretches a long arm out to touch my hair. It's curlier than usual from the salt breeze. Kit pulls me behind him, out of reach, and steps back to put more distance between the strangers and us. "Dressed like tramps too." The man gestures at my clothes. I scowl.

"Kine's surely stolen," the first one nags.

"We should do our civic duty and take you back." The other's nodding.

"Our owners won't like that," I tell them from behind Kit.

They exchange another look. I've seen this one before. The boys on the riverbank, before they pushed me in – they looked like that.

"We've no conflict here with you," Kit growls. "Just move on, friends."

"Watch your tone, trouble," says the one with the gun.

"Your gun won't work on me," Kit tells him.

The man's pasted grin wavers. But what if they call Kit's bluff? Of course the gun can hurt us. They're designed to kill. I was knocked out for hours when they shot me in the Cull.

"This is crazy," I murmur under my breath.

The man in brown raises his bow, but Kit lunges, fast as an adder, striking the weapon aside. Then he punches the man in the face, hard. The man flies backward into the tall grasses, rolling around, groaning and holding his nose while his companion waves his gun and screams obscenities. I'm frozen. It's too fast. *Do something.* What?

I've no weapon. Then I realize what I do have. Hooves. I grab Fearsome's side horn and stick my strong leg in the stirrup to haul myself back up. I urge him towards the man in green. Not quickly enough. The man's panicking, lifting his gun, firing.

He shoots Kit in the stomach.

Time slows down, but Kit barely flinches, as if the strike is no worse than a bee sting. Perhaps the gun is faulty. Then Kit's wrenching it out of the hunter's grip and shoving it into the man's stomach. The hunter doubles over, hands at his gut. Kit slams the butt of the gun into the side of the hunter's head with a crack. He collapses on his face. Just like that.

He lies there, not moving.

Fearsome won't go forward at my urging. He's too scared. I slide off his back before he carries me further away.

The arrow that hits Kit comes out of nowhere. He slumps to his knees, crying out. The archer's nocking another arrow and I'm there, finally, diving for his legs. I hit him at the knees and we go down in a heap. The hounds bounce around us like it's all a great game. He doesn't fire – instead he tries to stab me with the arrow. He misses, just catching the fabric of one of my sleeves as I roll away. Then Kit's there, kicking him in the head.

Kit, who has an arrow sticking out of his side. *Hell's teeth.*

He whistles low to the nearest hound. Blood is dripping down his shirt, over his belt. There's so much of it.

The hounds are calming. One comes to sit in front of me and pant. One snuffles at the unconscious man with the gun.

"We have to get out of here," Kit says. "Come on."

I stare, sickened, at his bloody chest. "You can't walk around like that."

"There's no time," he says sharply. "You can take it out."

A blanket of calm settles over me. I panic in all sorts of situations, but perhaps not in a true crisis.

I pull my clean spare hair wrap from my pocket in preparation, so I can hold it to the wound in his side as soon as the arrow's out.

"You have to sit down," I tell him.

These two could wake up any minute. *We're in so much trouble.*

We have to work fast. He eases himself down on to the grass. I pull an arrow from the archer's quiver and compare it. Just touching the one in Kit's side draws a sharp gasp and wince from him. He may be right – it hasn't gone in much deeper than two lengths of the head.

"Just grab the shaft and pull straight, the same angle it went in." He grits his teeth.

"I bet you say that to all the girls."

He rolls his eyes half-heartedly, and I brace one arm against his shoulder and offer a silent prayer, more of a plea, as I wrench the arrow backwards.

The sound it makes coming out is horrific. I can hear it even through Kit's screams. More blood wells. Surely he can't lose much more than this and stay upright? I press my hair wrap over the wound to staunch the flow.

The ancestors must be smiling, because the arrow's come out whole. I was worried the head would break off.

I tear a strip off my shirtsleeve and tie it around the slow-dripping slash on his forearm, where the arrow caught before going in.

"We have to take their gun. The arrows." I can hear the pain in his voice.

I hadn't thought of disarming them. Only of running away. Perhaps I'm not so great in a crisis after all.

"Even though the gun doesn't work?" I protest.

"It does work."

Is he in shock? If the gun worked, he'd be unconscious. Still, I do what he says.

I take their flasks as well. Fearsome's run off with ours, and everything else.

I snap the bow in half for good measure. It's incredibly bendy, but I know better than most, everything breaks eventually. I shoulder the gun and quiver, complete with Kit's bloody arrow, and return to his side.

"Can you stand if I help you? We have to get you back to a doctor." I step around to his good side and haul on his arm.

He's rallying – he doesn't lean on me too heavily. We limp out of the clearing, following Fearsome's trail, deeper into the forest.

"How far do you think he's gone?"

"I don't know," admits Kit. "I'm no tracker."

"We have to leave Fearsome and go back on foot," I decide.

I'm still holding his hand. It's rough but cool. It's different to holding handles or reins. Working with kine, hauling on their ropes, I'm used to feeling not the ropes, but my own skin. The callouses like beetle backs on the tops of my palms, and my pulse thudding through them, pressing against the rope, receding.

Now I only feel his hand.

38

it's done

It's late afternoon before we reach the beach where we ate and threw stones this morning. Kit's leaning heavier on me now. I can't believe it's the same day.

"I'm going to rest," he says. "Just a minute." He sprawls in the sand behind a tower of rocks and promptly falls asleep. The purple flower I gave him is wilting in his buttonhole.

I pry my makeshift dressing off his wound. It's sodden with blood. I can't tell if it's still weeping since his shirt is dark and equally blood-soaked. I wash the dressing out in the sea and then the freshwater stream, before I fold it into a neat square and replace it over his shirt. I don't want to disturb the binding on his arm. I watch his face, listen to his breathing. I'm worried the arrow has hurt his lungs. What if he turns feverish? I lay a hand on his forehead. Normal. He doesn't wake. I finally notice there's something wet on his stomach as well, where he was shot with the brander's gun.

He moans and begins to wake when I try to peel up his shirt to look. It's sticking to the wound. So the gun did burn him. Why did he barely react?

"You could wait here while I go back for help," I tell him, lifting one of the hunters' flasks to his lips. "You need a doctor."

He drinks and fumbles for my hand. "No. You can't go back alone. It's too far. I just need a minute to rest."

I want to argue, but I also don't want to leave him alone. The clouds are mustering. Great grey curtains hang across half the horizon, and sheets of rain slant over the distant ocean.

"Let's try that hut back there," I tell him, nodding to the abandoned seaweed-drying huts. "Be shelter if it rains."

"It won't rain on our delightful day out." He grins a little deliriously, pushing to his feet.

The hut is comfortably full of drifted sand.

"You've a burn on your stomach," I tell him.

"I know. And here." He waves his good arm.

"Let me have a look."

He plucks the purple flower from its buttonhole and pockets it. Then he undoes the buttons on his shirt one-handed, and I help him peel it off. It's heavy with blood. His tattoo stretches over his shoulders and down the backs of his arms, seeming for a blink to ripple like something alive. It's a stylized vocifer with its wings spread, feathers inked in black against brown skin.

The burn on his stomach looks angry and oozing, but the one on his arm is shallow, like it only glanced the flesh. I unwrap both the bracelets he never seems to be without, so they won't drift into the burn or the cut – brown beads on brown thread, now brown with blood. He pockets them too.

The arrow's carved a deep laceration on his right arm, but the wound in his ribs is by far the worst. It's more awful than I expected, and I was braced for bad. It's bruised all around, clotted with a deep red mass and oozing yellow ichor.

"Should I clean it?" I ask. "I've no head for nursing. If you were a kine birthing a foal I might be more useful."

"Sorry to disappoint." He starts to laugh, but the pain hauls him up. "Just pour some fresh water on the burns."

Now that we've got to the burns, there's another matter I noticed when his shirt came off. He doesn't have one Cull scar – he has five.

Three on his chest, two on his lower back, below the tattoo. They're paler than his skin. Mine are darker. If he survives this, he'll have one on his abdomen and a trail on his arm as well. I pour water from one of the flasks over the burn on his stomach, and his muscles clench.

"So, the guns burn you, but the shock doesn't knock you out?"

"Yeah. Hurts like fire but doesn't lay me out like it does most people."

I've never heard of anyone being unaffected like that. The blast kills most people.

"I pretended after the third one." He finds my eyes. Then he closes his and keeps talking. "So much screaming, and I was lying there. Still have dreams about it. Still wonder if I should have tried to save someone."

I know a bit about dreams like that. "You were fourteen," I remind him.

He sighs and shifts his sliced arm experimentally, wincing.

"We all scream the same, don't we? The language everyone with ears can understand. We all hurt the same. You. Me." He pulls one of his beaded bracelets from a pocket and spins the beads in his hand. "Them."

"So why don't their guns work on you?"

"I'm protected." He takes a breath. "My mother's heart wasn't strong enough. That's what killed her. And my father had a long illness. They thought I might go the same way. But here I am. Art has power." Hair is still plastered to his forehead, but the sweat seems to have dried. "My father had a friend who was very close to the Akani Inker. Asked her to ink me. It's a ritual to court the gods' favour."

I wait for him to go on.

"I promised to honour them at a sacred site. Promised to give up something precious. And I promised to carry this image beloved by them. A vocifer."

"My people almost wiped the vocifers out."

"Yeah, and we know how much the gods love you lot

these days." His mouth twists wryly, and I feel my own lips tilt up in answer.

"What precious thing did you give up?"

"Swimming."

"Swimming?" I'm not sure what I expected him to say, but it wasn't that.

"I was twelve. Swimming was all I wanted to do. I would have given up school, but I hated it. The sacrifice had to be something that really mattered to me, or the ritual wouldn't have worked."

"So that line you gave me last summer – not swimming because you're afraid of kraits..."

"I mean, kraits are still objectively terrifying."

"What if you went swimming now you've promised not to?" I ask.

"I'd win the gods' curse instead of their favour."

"What if some boys chuck you in the river and you have to swim?"

"I don't think the gods care about the fine details."

The demons like to hide in the details, Ruzi would say.

"So how does this work, being a favourite?" I nod to his injury. "Gods don't seem so great at stopping arrows, do they?"

He huffs softly. "If only. As far as I know, the ritual made my heart stronger. That's why their guns don't work."

Their guns stop hearts. That's what they're designed to do.

"Though I don't tend to get colds and headaches, and I heal quickly when I'm hurt," he adds.

"That's magic."

"Well. They always said our faith was witchcraft."

I pour the remaining fresh water over the laceration on his arm. "I'm going to wash the blood out of this." I pick up his sodden shirt.

I refill the flask in the trickle of the stream, then take his shirt to the sea. It heaves up the beach like a sobbing creature. The wind blows a weed-and-spray smell. The quantity of blood blossoming from the dark-blue fabric surprises me. Much more than there was from the makeshift gauze I washed earlier. Red colours the shallow waves over the sand like a cloud forming and dispersing in treble time, horribly beautiful. Then a wave detaches from the others and ripples through the shallows towards me, yellow and black. Then another. I stifle a shriek and scrabble backwards up the soft sand.

Sea kraits, attracted by the blood. I see another one, sinuous, unnaturally quick. I scramble to my feet. There's four or five of them writhing around in the bloody water. I wring out Kit's shirt as I retreat along the beach, away from the huts, but the kraits don't follow me on to the sand. Perhaps they've realized the prey is gone. I've been so thick-headed. The last thing we need now is a swarm of sea kraits trying to eat us.

That's when I see the hounds.

Four again, low white clouds drifting through the

heathers, ahead of two men with pale oval faces and hair that throws the sun. They'll be on us in minutes.

I didn't even notice the sky growing dark, but the first drops are landing. It's lashing down by the time I've reached the hut.

"Mora. It's you they want."

"What do you mean?"

"Didn't you see the way they looked at you? Like they'd fit you to Zako."

"But I don't look enough like Zako," I say impatiently. "They wouldn't be able to claim the bounty."

"If your hair was cut," he says, "if you were roughed up a bit, they'd be able to claim it. If all they took in was your head."

I stare at him. He sighs like the sea.

"If we don't kill them first…" His voice trails off into the rain.

Life is sacred. That's what Kit believes. Or that's what he believed until now.

I think of the bloodied water. Turns out imminent mutilation and beheading is very focusing for the mind. "I have an idea," I say.

In a few moments, the four hungry hounds reach us in a frenzy. I shield Kit's bad side from their lean, probing snouts. Kit calms them with a few whistles and clicks. If the men were counting on them ripping into us, they'll be sorely disappointed. They settle like four skinny Caruqs in a heap on the sand, tired from the excitement.

I keep low and crawl towards a tower of rocks by the sea as Kit creeps from hut to hut until he reaches the last in the line.

I can't hear what the men are saying in frustrated tones to each other when they stop on the sand, but they seem confused to see the dogs at rest.

"Find it, Roamer?" calls the one in green. He gestures to the other man.

I can see, even from the other side of the beach, the red bruises on both of their faces. They split up and stalk the line of huts, front and back. They don't have another gun, or they'd have it out on view. Looks like they have long knives though. I should have searched them more thoroughly.

As they near the last hut in the row, I break from cover and crouch in the sand to dangle the bandage from Kit's arm in the sea. The rain is still coming down heavy, dripping off my hair and into my eyes. Lighting strikes from the mountain of clouds over the black water that minutes ago was light blue-green.

Thunder crackles immediately – the storm is on us.

I pretend I don't see the men, though it feels suicidal turning my back. I watch for kraits. Blood swirls into the shallows.

They must have started towards me, because I hear Kit make that clicking sound he does to get Caruq's attention. Then the telltale fizz of the gun.

I turn as one of the men falls, face first, into the sand.

I look back to see a terrifying knot of kraits thrashing in the shallows. I drop the cloth and stand as the second man – the one in brown – slips behind a tall rock to hide from Kit. I have to draw him out. I run towards him with both of the arrows out of my belt, then dodge and turn back. He follows me. He doesn't even see the kraits. Kit barrels from behind and shoves him hard into the water just as I crab-step clumsily aside. I didn't think Kit could move that fast *without* a hole in his side.

The man's brown coat darkens with seawater. Swirls of black and yellow latch on to him. He thrashes before growing still – paralysed by the venom, and whatever it is that keeps the blood from clotting. He can't breathe now. Two of the hounds watch, paws at the waterline. They won't brave the kraits to try and save him. Perhaps even they know it's over.

I've never seen kraits on a person. They don't tear at the skin, not like sharks would. They look graceful, anchored by their mouths, twisting languidly as they feast.

He'll be dead already, I know that.

"Don't look." Kit draws me away. His hand on my arm is icy and weak, and I notice his skin has a bluish tinge. The wound in his side's torn open again, blood running down in rivulets with the rain.

"You have to rest and get warm," I order. "Go back to that hut. Leave the rest to me."

He must be feeling awful, because he obeys. I see him to the second hut and strip the other sleeve off my blouse for him to press to his wound, though the blood's clotted again.

I return alone to the man in green, face down in the sand. No hounds nearby. The shot caught him in the side of the head. He's dead. That's a mercy. No need to finish him off. I feel strange, and then stomp on the feeling. This is no time for feelings. These are the types of bloodthirsty men just roaming the countryside, are they? The same countryside Zako's out in, living happy as Blenny and stupid Tornelius. It's too appalling.

He weighs a ton. I couldn't move a bigger man. It takes an age to drag him by his coat up towards the last hut and push and pull and wedge him inside, and then lean him slouched against a wall.

It's done.

39

you'll find out

Kit's dozing again. The hounds have gone. He grips my wrist lightly when he wakes, running a thumb along the heel of my palm. We listen to the rain easing and get ready to carry on. There's hours of light left.

I bury the arrows in the sand near the heathers. We've nowhere to hide them without Fearsome's saddlebags, and walking into town with weapons, looking like we do, would be folly.

I don't return to the body I left in the hut, but something compels me to join Kit beside the man who fed the kraits. One end of his long moustache is tangled in a strand of seaweed. He's pale as chalk and looks starved. Do the gods really love those bloodsuckers that feed on us? I think this time, at least, they must.

A strong wind is blowing the clouds away, tangling my salty hair.

We start back up into the heathers and the cliffs.

Kit's stomach growls. My hunger's gnawing too. Our food was with Fearsome.

I spot a few blueberries in the heather, but they're not ripe.

"Just think, when we get back, we can eat. Jammy, buttery biscuits. Baked apples with extra-thick brown sugar. Crispy fried fish—"

"Stop it, Thea's wounds. Just shoot me again."

"I'm trying to help."

"Ha."

When he stops to sit on a stone to rest, I wander off in search of pickings.

I spot two clusters of almost-translucent mushrooms, white with a pale-blue sheen. I know what they are, and they're not for dinner. They're not native to Makaia – they're an import from the Crozon Isles. Our pa called them Mermaid's Tears. Supposed to do awful things to your guts, make you see things, then kill you quick.

Nothing else but stones, heathers, unripe blueberries. I'm circling back to Kit at his rock when I startle a knot off her nest. She pretends an injury to draw me away, but I'd never have seen her or her four little chicks if she'd held her nerve. Their peeps are like whispers. The patterns on their tiny discarded eggs look like Xan writing.

I wish I had more to show for my troubles than empty shells.

Then I find a colony of red milk-cap mushrooms

and some wild lovage growing together in a depression. Nature's bowl. I collect them in my shirt.

Kit has slid from his perch to the ground, leaning against the rock with his eyes closed. The sight gives me an awful turn, but of course he's still breathing. Some of his normal colour's even returned.

"I've got us a feast," I say, showing him the contents of my shirt. "It was this, unripe blueberries, or a tasty but highly toxic mushroom."

"Hoo boy," he groans.

We share the strange salad. "What highly toxic thing did you find?" he asks.

"Mermaid's Tears. It's another mushroom."

"Tell me what a mushroom has to do with mermaids," he says.

"You know the Haymaker's Way – the constellation?" It's a thick cluster of stars running in a stripe across the sky.

"Hmm."

"Mermaid's Tears is an old name for it. They glow in the dark. So our pa said."

"What have the mermaids got to be so sad about?"

"Beats me."

We finish quickly, and I help Kit to his feet again.

"Did you have a nice time, then?" He gestures at the warm golden evening. "Good day out? Nice change of scene? Feel the wind in your hair?"

I snort. "It was very special."

He trudges silently for so long I assume he's done

talking. "Not sure I'd survive, courting you," he murmurs eventually.

Down below, the tide has gone way out. An expanse of flat, weed-strewn sand, razor clams, thin pools and small stones slopes half a mile before the sea, and the evening sky is monumental.

The last bright edge of sun drops away, leaving drifting nets of rippling orange. Filaments of fresh-blown glass in a purple furnace.

Kit points across the sand – three dark shapes browse the shoreline, padding south. They stop to snuffle in rock pools. A black bear and two cubs, last year's.

Night comes quickly when you're up on the treacherous cliffs without a mount, trying desperately to get your bleeding friend to a doctor.

We continue at our snail's pace, spirits flat.

"Your prayer grass is with Fearsome," Kit reminds me. My misbehaving memories. My missing friend Felicity. Our reason for going out today.

I worry at the gap in my head. It's like a stubborn splinter or a tooth that should be there and isn't. Like a scab I can't stop picking. The more I dig, the sorer everything gets.

"Don't worry about it," I tell Kit. "It wasn't meant to be."

When he begs another rest, I've lost all sense of how far we have left to go. The cluster and spray of stars says it's deep night. He sits and shuts his eyes. I sit beside him. His breathing grows gentle.

I steal away and find a place to empty my bladder. Going back I notice another clump of Mermaid's Tears. They do glow, with the blue-white memory of light.

Never touch these, Mor. My pa's voice floats up, and I can feel his hand catching my forearm, tugging me away from the danger. I wish so much that he was still here. I still need him. There's danger everywhere.

I don't mean to, but I let sleep take me, flopped over in the heathers beside Kit.

I dream of a brander hunting for Zako. She's riding a horse of all things, a big golden bay, through a field of swaying grain, heavy with seeds. The light's angled low, flooding into my eyes, thatching my eyelashes to catch rainbows and dazzling moons. Every blink brings a flash of red. A blood-drowned world. Even my uniform is golden; the badge over my chest reads Dezil. I know it's not right. I know horses are gone and branders wear blue. And I'm not a brander. I'm not a killer. *Am I?*

Kit wakes me, looking drawn. The stars have faded and spun across the universe. Gulls are already crying through the black and blue. I sit up, addled. I can't believe I slept so long without checking on him. *Aaa-aaa-aaa-aaa.* Even their racket didn't wake me.

"Look at that," he whispers.

Beyond the cliffs, the tide's back in. And three huge Skøl tall ships, one with ceremonial red sails, are bearing down on Portcaye. The *Herald of the New Dawn* and her escorts. Clarion Lovemore is early.

The creeping light from the east shows how close to town we've made it, but it's still a trek on foot.

When we find Fearsome, quite by chance, on the last of the cliffs above Portcaye, nosing the thin grasses, I could cry from relief. At least that's one less disaster to explain away. I make him kneel so Kit can mount, drag myself up behind. We reach Portcaye's southern gates as the town awakes. There's lots of hoo-ha about Clarion Lovemore's early arrival. How terribly tall the *Herald of the New Dawn* is. How golden its figurehead – a personification of Justice, apparently, with a very Lovemorish countenance.

I'm still late for work. I left Fearsome and Kit at the Lugger – the Scarlets will call a doctor – and had to go by Opal Alley to change. A shrivelled orange flower fell out of my hair when I was dressing.

I visit the Lugger after work and find Mister Scarlet in the kitchen.

"He's asleep," he says, before I can ask about Kit. "Doctor said it was a narrow miss. He's had stitches." He glances at Renny and Gracie. "You two, out."

He starts moving the pans off two stools that usually stay tucked under the counter.

"Sit," he orders. "Give me the hand you draw with."

I think of Venor's vicious smile, his human bone-stack and his hammer.

I've an impulse to refuse, but I squash it down. It's Mister S, not Venor.

I give him my hand, and he turns it gently, palm up.

"This is your life line. Twice broken – the Cull, and something else."

I think of the other times I've nearly died. Venor's hammer. The river in winter. The hunters on the beach. The incident I've forgotten that left marks on my wrists.

"Something still to come, I believe," Mister S rumbles on.

"Not sure I want my palm read," I stutter, thinking of Kit. *What if it's true?*

He traces a different line in my palm. "Your heart line curves up."

"Is that bad?"

"No. This is your head line. I thought it would be stronger, but it's not bad. It will deepen."

His hands are much bigger than mine, his wrinkled skin surprisingly soft. Mine is far coarser. I didn't think I was sweaty, but I notice my hands are clammy, where Mister Scarlet's are cool and dry.

"It's not possible to see everything that comes. All the hardships." He smiles. I watch the crinkles near his eyes, feathered like the end of my heart line. I wonder how he got them. Laughing his slow laugh, no doubt. I can't imagine him crying.

"Hardships?"

He still has my hand, and now he points again below my little finger. "See these lines. You will have children – one, two." He smiles. "Two cubs."

The bear cubs and their mother from this morning

wander through my mind. All three freer than any person. A cool shiver strokes down my spine.

Mister S lets me go and rubs his own palm, where all the lines are etched deep.

"You know, we had a son."

"I heard, but I – uh…"

"He died today – eight years now."

"I'm sorry."

He tells me their boy was almost thirty. That's why they moved – to be somewhere the memories wouldn't drown them. Missus S tells people he's estranged because it stops them asking questions. And it's easier than pretending they never had a son.

"She suffers with the grief," he tells me, swiping one big hand over his shaved head.

I think of Missus S giving Zako tooth-rotting quantities of ginger beer and reading him a storybook every night.

"Kit ending up in scrapes does her no good. She worries."

"I can't control Kit."

"You can encourage him to chart a path less reckless."

"This wasn't his fault."

Mister S grunts. "You young people rush through life like you want it to be over. Leaping after every risk you can take. It's not worth it, girl. The years go fast enough. Don't try and reach the end of yours before you must."

He produces two of the smallest oranges I've ever seen

from a pocket in his cardigan. They're slightly squashed, rather than round, but I think they're meant to be that way.

"He loved oranges. And music and animals. I think you love oranges too." For a moment I don't know who he's talking about – then I realize.

I watch the lines around his eyes. *This is his broken heart line. These are his children.*

"They're so small." I take the one he passes to me and watch him digging his thumb into the top of the other. The soft peel yields easily and comes off in thin strips, puffing a perfume that's unlike any orange I've ever smelled. The flesh inside divides almost on its own into separate half-moon segments. The strangeness of it makes my heart swell.

"I've ordered two crates for the Lugger," he tells me. "These ones are hard to get."

He stands to leave.

"Wait," I urge.

His doleful face swings my way.

"Why did you read my palm? What were you looking for?"

"The lives we give." He pauses. "The lives we take."

"We take?"

He tucks his stool away.

"What did you see?" I urge.

"More than a few stalks. Less than a sheaf."

"What does that mean?"

"I don't know, girl. Daresay you'll find out."

40

a bad omen

The prayer grass we collected and salvaged from Fearsome's saddlebags is dry already. Kit left it out in the sun.

He walked it over this morning. It's only Seconday, but he's back on his feet already. His gait's a little off. He holds himself more cautiously – his arm and ribs are still stitched and bandaged – but he wasn't lying about healing quickly.

I sniff the dry grass, sweet and almondy. I'll have to try it when I'm back from work.

"Better you're alone, no distractions." He waves to Ruzi, who's leaving already. I should go too, but Kit tarries.

"If you're having second thoughts – about the Registry," he says, "I'll find another way."

"I'm not having second thoughts. You need me." We have nine more days.

He prods his ribs gently, where the stitches are, and his eyebrows scrunch.

"You can't do everything alone, Kit. You don't have to. Just admit you need me."

"Course I need you, but … I don't want you to be hurt. I need you alive and annoying."

"You need me," I crow. "You admitted it, before witnesses."

"What witnesses?"

"Mister Spider and Missus Geranium."

Kit peers up at the corner web with a curled lip. I refused to let him clear it away when I was ill, creating something of a sore point.

"I need you –" his thumb brushes the back of my hand, and then his fingers layer through mine – "to break it off with Mister Spider."

"Never."

"I could always break the glass." He means to get into the Life Registry.

"No way they won't hear that. That's not a plan."

"*I* could hide after selling lunch."

"But they've seen me before – me and Gracie and Renny. We're women. We're not threatening."

"I'm not threatening," he grumbles. He's being contrary.

"You know they won't like a big dark-skinned man with criminal hair going in trying to sell things." He can't think it's a real option.

"I'm not big compared to most of them."

"A shifty-looking, up-to-no-good young makkie with suspiciously glinty eyes … and long lock-picking fingers."

"Sounds like you."

"They'll notice you, Kit. Someone will say something and you'll get turfed out. Or if you don't, Mister S will realize you're missing and go off to tear the place down."

"I could tell him."

"Are you crazy? He'd lock you in the cellar till you came to your senses. You can't tell the Scarlets. Or Gracie or Renny."

"I know. Have you been practising with the picks?"

"I have. I'm ready." I waggle my fingers. I'm not, but I'll get there.

"If the grass sparks anything –" he heads for the door – "come by the Lugger?"

"I will."

I haven't told him about Mister S reading my palm, but I have to get to work.

I'm leaving the Works at sundown when Mister Wagsen lumbers into the yard and calls me over. "Mora Dezil." He holds a single piece of paper, folded twice.

"Mister Wagsen. Good evening."

"I have some news. You're moving on."

"Sorry?"

"We received a good offer. Even factoring the future savings. And we need a driver who's reliable. You've had some incidents of lateness, some absenteeism."

My fingers on the brush tingle. Sugarcane bends his head until his velvety muzzle's in my hair. He nudges me with one of his front horns and blows a warm snort of hay and kine breath.

"Who's bought me?"

He unfolds the letter. "Glister Reedstone. They're lock makers. Says here he's heard you make accurate drawings and would like someone with such a skill on his staff. It's not a major relocation. The company is in the Skates."

The bloody cheek. I said I didn't want them to buy me. But of course they've done what they believe best, regardless of how I might feel about being "saved". I think of the Sting Trust.

His voice is awed as he says, "The Reedstones are well connected, you know. They're relations of the Stings – Sting Elektric. You're a lucky girl."

Lucky. Does he see the irony as he puffs up the illustrious family that invented the guns and prods used to kill and torture my people?

"I've accepted his offer of purchase. It's all arranged," he maintains, before adding with an edge of snark, "Perhaps making technical drawings will be more suited to your timekeeping. They'll be here any minute."

"But I haven't said goodbye to anyone. Nobody knows I'm going. They'll worry."

"I will inform them tomorrow." He grips my shoulder – oddly human. "How are your teeth, by the way?"

"What?"

"For your Life Record – you previously had –" he pulls

a slip of paper from his waistcoat pocket – "twenty-eight. Have you gained or lost any?"

"I don't think so." One of my wisdom teeth is coming through, not that it's any of his business.

"Here." He draws a few coins from his pocket and holds them out to me. "Send a letter to your people in the last post."

I won't have time before curfew.

"But I haven't packed my things." It's uncannily like the last time I was sold off in a hurry, with nothing but the filthy clothes on my back.

"Never mind, girl. What can you possibly have of importance? Your new workplace will provide." He escorts me to a squat carriage, crouched outside the gates like a bad omen.

41

free as the bears

The driver's kinder than Wagsen – he just shrugs a *why not* when I beg a detour to Opal Alley.

Ruzi's tinkering with his guitar, but he stops when he sees my face.

"The Skates..." Ruzi says. "You could still live here and walk over there. It's not far." I nod, but he goes on before I can say anything. "Perhaps you'll want to stay there. It might be nicer than this ratty old place."

"I want to stay here, Ruzi."

He hugs me.

"Can you go to the Lugger to tell Kit?" I ask. "I know it's past curfew, but..."

"I will if it's important."

"It is."

"Then I will."

I'm grateful he doesn't ask why. I pack a cloth bag with a

few extra clothes, paper and pencils, my nest of dry prayer grass, some matches, my practice lock picks and lock.

Anger simmers. I already agreed to help them. Do they think they're helping me? What if I like living here with Ruzi?

The carriage glides quickly over the river into the Skates. Most of the houses we pass are stuck together, one to the next. Some of them used to be large, back before the Cull, but they've almost all been partitioned up to fit more families now.

This is another reason the Reedstones are labelled eccentric. Portcaye's wealthy town-dwellers don't live in the Skates. They live in the Mermens, the Steeps, the Centre, even Riverside – the south bank. Not the north. The north is all the Skates.

The Reedstones' mansion-slash-factory is hardly humble though. Once it was a Crozoni brewery, but there's little evidence of that. It's all impeccably kept. I was expecting something large, but it's more than my imaginings.

Level Gusting opens the door.

The Sting Trust boy.

"We meet again," he says, flashing me a wicked grin. He leads me to a small annex near the entrance and gestures to a pretty-looking sofa. "Wait here."

I haven't even had a chance to wash my face or change my clothes after the workday.

The sofa's uncomfortably stuffed with stiff springs, but it's not long before Goldie Reedstone appears. Her pale hair is styled in curls today, cascading around her shoulders.

"Here you are!" She takes me and my cloth bag in with a warm smile. "Is this all your worldly goods?"

"Not quite. Nearly."

"Well, I must take you shopping when this is over. We can go to Rafmagis Way."

Where would I wear anything from Rafmagis Way?

"There must be more worthwhile things to spend your money on than that." I aim for polite, but it comes out cutting. "Anyway, I was hoping to stay in my old place."

"Wait till you see your room and then decide." She smiles again.

Gleaming wood floors, sweeping staircases, no scuffs, dents or other imperfections. Nothing's gaudy or gilded, but everything screams wealth. The house is as beautiful as its mistress.

I follow her mutely. She chatters on.

"I'm sure you have the odd question, but we'll get there."

The room she shows me to is enormous. The whole flat at Opal Alley would probably fit in here. It's lit by a ragleaf generator hidden elsewhere in the house. The sun's getting low. Elektric lamps fixed to the walls come on with the flick of a small gold lever. There's a deep bay-window seat dressed in colourful pillows to match the huge bedspread, a marble desk, a wardrobe, low tables with pieces of art displayed on them – Makaian, I think.

"Do you like it?" Goldie asks.

I can see a washroom across one side, walled off behind another dark wooden door. I plonk my bag on the bed and try not to look too stunned.

"It's very nice," I tell Goldie stiffly.

She ushers me out. "Let's sit in the drawing room."

It's a cavernous lounge with patterned rugs layered over the floor and glowing elektric lanterns on warm brick walls. Glass-paned doors on the north side stand open to a patio. The scent of jasmine growing up trellises on the outer wall competes with Goldie's nectary perfume.

"Penny for your thoughts?" she prompts softly.

"Does Kit know I'm here?" I ask.

"We'll tell him, of course," she says.

Lev brings a bowl of cherries – from their own glasshouse, ripened early, he says – and a pitcher of fresh orange juice, and sits with us.

"Why buy me?"

"It simplifies our logistics," Goldie says.

Lev eats cherries, spitting the pips into a glass.

"I already said I'd do what's needed."

"You did." Goldie holds one hand to the top of her chest. "You're wonderfully keen. And with you in our … midst, Kit will stay focused."

I think I understand. I'm a bargaining tool. They're worried that Kit might get cold feet, and if I'm under their roof, he can't. Lev's nodding, still mutely sucking cherry stones.

Goldie reaches for her untouched orange juice. "And as you know, we've had this … development. Lovemore's ship travelled faster than anyone expected. She's arrived early – very early, actually, and without fanfare. We think she wanted to observe without being obvious for a time. Everything she does is obvious though. She's settling in. She's been spotted with her entourage dining in the Mermens. And she's been shown the outside of Hexagon Hall. Venor may … panic and move forward the entertainment."

"Is that likely?"

"We can't take the risk of waiting. It simply must be this week." It's Seconday night already. She wants us to go the day after tomorrow.

"Kit was shot in the ribs two days ago," I say. "Did he tell you?"

Lev and Goldie exchange a bemused look. He didn't tell them, though he must have been here today – they were going to run through the details of the vault lock at midday.

"He's not a machine," I insist. "He needs to recover before he starts climbing up buildings for you."

Goldie tilts her head at me. Her current pair of heavy earrings, strings of pearls on gold thread this time, tinkle prettily. "Shots don't tend to bother our Kit."

"It was an arrow."

"An arrow! Whatever was he up to?"

"Nothing. We were out minding our own business – just

looking for some herbs, medicine – in the woods near town. Some hunters attacked us."

"Really?"

"Fancied fitting us to bounties."

Goldie's eyes widen. "And what happened?"

"We ran away."

"Did they chase you?"

"We had a kine. We were faster."

"Oh my goodness. Well, they should be prosecuted."

Lev shakes his head.

Surely she knows that would never happen. "We're not going to the branders. We're just glad we got away."

"Of course." She looks distracted but collects herself quickly. I chomp into a cherry.

Lev leans forward. "Kit will recover quicker than you think," he tells me. "He's reliable like that."

Goldie consults her pocket timepiece and stands abruptly.

"Lev, please show Mora around the old place. I'm afraid I have an engagement I can't cancel this evening," she tells me. "It's Thirday tomorrow – we'll run through final plans then. And we'll be ready to go on Fourday."

We'll be ready, will we? By *we* she means Kit and me. All she has to do is stand in the road nearby.

She pauses to pass me her timepiece. "Keep it. It's an old one, but it's good. You'll need it for the job."

I examine it as Lev watches her sway from the room. Old? It looks pristine – simply and practically designed.

Everything about her is clean and perfect. Her fingernails, her hair, her possessions.

Lev escorts me quickly around the house. "We'll leave the grounds for when it's light," he decides.

There are paintings, pictures and maps everywhere. Dogs pad about – huge ledhunds that remind me of Caruq, with soft white fur. "A bit of extra security," Lev claims, but they seem more like pets. One of them attaches herself to our tour.

The workshop's on the ground floor, taking up one whole wing.

"Not much to see now. They downed tools hours ago," Lev tells me, but he opens the door and flicks a row of switches up.

Such small levers to move such a quantity of light.

It's astonishing, pouring from hundreds of humming lanterns strung over the ceiling. Banks of enormous glass windows along the long north wall reflect the cavernous room back at itself. I know the effort crafting all of those must have taken.

The biggest ragleaf-fuel generator I've ever seen is bolted to the narrower far wall, purring softly, flanked by row upon row of industrial switches linked to wires that trail up through the ceiling.

"I heard the Reedstones are doing some work with vradiance?" I quiz Lev. He looks surprised I'd know a thing like that, but not upset.

"We are, yeah."

I wait for him to continue, but he says nothing.

"Look, I have to get on." His tone suggests my limping presence is an enormous personal burden, but he takes me back to my room. The ledhund shadowing us runs in when the door opens. "She likes to sleep here." Lev shrugs. "Just turf her out if you don't want her. Help yourself to food in the kitchen when you get hungry. You've free run of the house, but don't stray beyond."

I'm about as free as this hound, then. I forgot to ask her name, but find it burned into her leather collar, beneath a well-groomed mane of fur. *Lucky.*

"Are you lucky, girl?" *Good luck or bad?*

I think of Caruq, splashing into the river from on high. Did he drown? Perhaps he ran off to live in the wild, free as the bears.

42

this is a this

I fish the dry prayer grass and box of matches from my scant belongings and take them to the window seat. Kit said I should do it before I sleep. It's not late – not yet ten by Goldie's pocket timepiece – but I'm more than exhausted enough to call it a day.

I sit in the window seat, looking over the Reedstones' lantern-lit stables. A solitary plumed moth flutters just inside the glass. I twist the handle and waft it outside.

Someone knocks at the bedroom door. "Hello! Are you decent?" Glister Reedstone.

"Are you?" I retort, before I can think. I remember that's a thing they say – to ask if someone's clothed.

The door opens and Glister looms.

"Heard you'd come," he says. "Welcome. May I enter?"

"It's your house." *And I'm your property too, aren't I?*

He steps in, leaving the door open. "How are you finding it?"

What does he want me to say? "Worrisome," I snap, with more venom than I feel. "I never asked you to buy me. The opposite, in fact."

"No, I know. And I get it; you haven't much reason to trust us yet. But you'll see. We can smooth your way."

A noise from outside catches my attention. Footsteps crunching on gravel, coming up the drive to the stables.

"Mora!" Kit.

I poke my head out to see him. "Up here!"

My heart calms for the first time in two hours at the sight of him. I didn't realize how frantic it was until now. I feel like an anvil's floated off my chest. Buoyant. I never feel buoyant.

Glister sticks to my side. We meet Kit coming like a thundercloud through the same lounge I sat in earlier with Goldie and Lev.

"You don't need to pull stunts like this."

Glister, a head taller and considerably broader, claps Kit on the back and murmurs something placatory.

One of Kit's hands flutters to his injured ribs. He gives a slight wince. He can't be healing as fast as he pretends.

Glister turns to Lev, hovering in the hall. "Be a darling and fix us some fikka, will you?"

He turns back to Kit.

"Did you get everything you need?"

"I have everything. Ether, gloves, picks, waterproof

bag, black blanket… But Mora needs more prep time – for the locks."

"And Kit's not healed!" I point out.

"Hmm."

Lev appears with a fikka pot and cups. He must have had it on the go.

Glister pours.

"We're doing it this Fourday," Glister says. "So you'll need to practise, Mora."

There's no arguing with him. I've got two days instead of nine to get my lock-picking up to scratch.

I pray Kit will be healed enough. That I'll be able to pick one simple lock.

I glance sideways at Kit. He hasn't mentioned Venor's Life Record. I take my cue from him. But it's all I can think about. I'm sure once we've got it, we can bring up the use of their dark space and vradiance scope.

Goldie comes back from her appointment, and Glister tells her we're happy to pull the break-in earlier. Kit's mutinous expression says otherwise, but Goldie is delighted. She pours everyone a measure of schinn. Lev sticks his in his cold fikka. Kit doesn't drink his. Glister has two.

We leave the three of them chatting in the lounge and start up the polished stairs.

"They put you in that room over the stables?" Kit asks as we come to it. I nod, reaching for him. We lean together.

"You came right away," I murmur.

"Ruzi said you were upset." His arm cinches me closer, then relaxes.

He spots my nest of dry prayer grass on the window seat.

"You brought it," he says.

"I haven't had a chance to burn it yet." I frown. I need to uncover those missing memories, fear or no.

He leans over to touch it, so close I feel his breath on my cheek. He moves his hand to my hair, winding a curl that's escaped my hair wrap around one of his knuckles.

I turn to him and capture his other hand in both of mine. Our fingers tangle lightly as he leans to brush a kiss on my forehead.

"You should probably burn it now," he says, reluctant. "It's supposed to work better if you do it alone – without distractions, I mean. You need to concentrate. I need to talk to Lev anyway." He extracts his knuckle from my hair.

"I'd prefer a distraction," I confess.

"Hmm," he murmurs, slipping the fingers of his other hand out of mine and starting for the door. "Don't make this any harder than it already is."

"How hard is it?"

He laughs, reaching the door. "Hard enough. Good night, Mora."

"We could die in a heroic act of rebellion in two days' time," I remind him.

He pauses. "We could."

"We're still alive tonight." I pull Goldie's pocket timepiece out. "It's only just gone midnight."

"You couldn't stop yawning downstairs."

"I find planning suicidal heroism very tedious."

He mutters something I can't hear and tilts his head, appraising.

"How much time could I possibly need to burn some grass and remember a few hours of probable kidnapping and torture?"

He exhales in a rush and aims an exasperated kick at the bottom of the door. "Probably more than you have as it is. Go on…" He clears his throat. "I want to take my time with you. I want us to take our time with … this."

"Well. When you put it like that…"

"See you in the morning. I'm going to sleep here – up the hall."

I smile.

At least we're admitting this is a this.

43

blue-green nowhere

The grass burns beautifully. Tiny red embers chasing each other down dust-green lanes that shrivel to weary ash. I lie down on one side of the enormous soft bed.

It's night. I'm cold to the bone, and Kit's carrying me. He's warm as a furnace, arms, chest. He smells like black pepper. I can't move, and I can't stop moving. I'm so weary of everything spinning.

"I've got you," he's saying.

"Thank the ancestors!" Ruzi's voice. "Is she…?"

"She's alive." Kit's warmth seeps through my thin, cold blouse, through my skin.

A vision of Felicity Greave at the Lugger with one of her slim cigarettes floats up. My aching jaw won't unclench. Then I can feel the floor tilting, wooden boards of a boat under my bound hands, whispering voices. My heart falters before plunging ahead, down, down, down.

No trace of burning grass. Only wet wood, salt air and a lingering tang of wrongness in my nostrils.

A strange sensation of being out of time. *Your father's dead*. What day did he die? I couldn't recall. My face was burning, too cold or too hot. My stomach plunged, dizzying. The world pitched and yawed. I tried to open my eyes, but the light was too bright. I felt like I did after the Cull, breathless, a mouth full of cotton.

They're all dead. Father. Father's father. His mother. His babies … all three. Your aunts and uncles and cousins. Your friends. Your neighbours. Your teachers. Their mothers and fathers and families and neighbours. I remembered. *They've all been dead years.* Grief sunk its claws in.

My mouth was literally full of cotton – a gag – my hands tied with thick rope. Light stabbed in through a wrinkled round of glass. I sat up on a wave of panic, hair curling into my streaming eyes. My hair wrap was gone. I wasn't crying. It was the light, or some after-effect of whatever potion they knocked me out with.

The floor of the room, its walls and low ceiling were all wooden. Alone in a wooden box like a giant's coffin. My stomach pitched down again, then up. The coffin was floating.

I clawed the gag from my lips with fingers heavy as old wreck wood and equally uncooperative. Behind me, a door spewed light, hinges wailing like seabirds. I twisted around as a shadow bled into the white rectangle of sky, its edges barbed. The front of my brain redoubled its throbbing efforts to escape. I shut my eyes.

"She's awake," called a man I didn't recognize, wedging a massive pair of shoulders sideways into my coffin room.

"Bring her out," said another man. His voice turned my insides to water.

The big man hauled me up easily by the ropes binding my wrists, dragged me into the light. His skin was sun-gold and weather-beaten, arms thick as tree trunks. A pale beard hid half his face, but his eyes were grey, with a shape that reminded me of Mister Heane's. Kind eyes to make a kind face – but I knew well enough, looks deceive.

It was overcast, still, the veiled sun directly overhead, bisected by a square of faded red canvas. I was on a Skøl lugger, with Venor and his man-mountain.

"What is this?" I tried to say, though the words came out almost too husky to hear.

"We speak Skøl on this boat," Venor grated.

Was I speaking Crozoni? My thoughts oozed like cold treacle.

I licked my lips and tried again. "What's happening?"

"We're taking you for a boat ride."

The bearded man peered between us encouragingly.

"And a chat…" Venor went on. "You and me and the big blue sea."

That's when I saw the shearwater. They're not common close to land, outside nesting season. It sliced through the air inches above the swell. I couldn't see any land, but then I could only see what was behind Venor, not behind me. The small cabin obstructed the view. I bent forward to peer towards the front of the boat and thought at first, absurdly, that this small fishing craft of an art-starved people had a figurehead on the prow. Then I realized it was another man, his back to me, sitting cross-legged and looking out on endless ocean.

The sea's been so beautiful this season, like frosted blue-green glass. It's not been that colour for years.

"Where are we going?" I struggled to stand, then to hide my dizzy swaying, terror ringing through me like a gong. I clung to the cabin with my bound hands. Beyond it, there was land, but it was vanishingly distant, with no sign of Portcaye. No other luggers. Just a dark-green fuzz that must have been trees. Three of them to one of me, in the middle of a blue-green nowhere.

44

on the sand

"You're going to bark, you useless bitch. You're going to sing. I know you helped him escape. You were creeping around Venorhome with that savage from the tavern, weren't you? I know those witches helped you. They're helping you still, aren't they? Tell me where he is."

Witches? Venor was raving. I rubbed my wrists raw worrying at the ropes, but I held my tongue. If I didn't talk, I couldn't say something to regret. Silence buys time.

"I know you had him in that filthy pub. Riddled with makkies, isn't it? Rats to a dust-heap. Where's he got to, girl?"

He must have slapped my face a dozen times.

"I don't know."

"Useless tramp."

When the figurehead moved from the front of the boat, I started crying again.

It wasn't a man.

It was Felicity Greave.

"Just answer him so we can all go home." Her soft, reasonable voice was like oil after Venor's screeching. But shame swallowed me whole. Shame over my tears. My ignorance.

"If you've brought me here to kill me, get it over with."

"Don't be a child." She rolled her eyes and rubbed her fingers over her forehead as if I was the one giving her a headache.

"Why would you do this, Felicity?"

I think of Felicity sitting beside Venor that day Ruzi performed his music – but laughing, genuinely, at the one about the washerwoman hanging her cruel boss. Felicity mopping her stew bowl with bits of bread and bending over the *Portcaye Post* to explain something to me. Rolling her eyes at Venor with me.

"The money's good," she replied.

"Just for money?"

"Money is life."

Of course.

"Doesn't your precious *Gazette* pay you enough?"

She looked at me almost pityingly. "I don't work there, Mora. Try to keep up."

She's a bounty hunter, I realized.

"You'll *never* get the bounty on Zako," I spat, still reeling.

"You really think you're better than us, don't you?"

Her blue-grey eyes flashed with anger. "You have a lot of growing up to do."

"I don't know where Zako is, and if I did, I'd never hand him over." I stabbed my bundled hands in Venor's direction. "He's a little boy!"

"He attacked me," Venor said. "I am more than a person. I am a position. A symbol." His even voice was more chilling than his raised one – full of quiet menace.

"That's not why you're after him though, is it?" I challenged. "It's because he knows. He heard something you didn't want him to hear. He heard your wife say those things about your Life Record and the forensic science and how you're like the Kellins – frauds." Venor's face was going red. I looked to Felicity, to see if anything was landing, but I couldn't read her expression.

I kept on. "Plus she thinks you're disgusting. What did you do to make her say that? What disgusting thing would you kill a little boy over?"

Felicity's jaw loosened briefly, but she snapped her face flat. Venor's slitted eyes examined Felicity, and he started to say something. Stopped. Then he laughed, turned to me and began again. "I don't know what you're on about, thick-skull. Desperate ravings won't save you."

"Felicity, didn't you look into the note about his Life Record?" I demanded. "There's something really wrong with it! Something criminal!"

She looked at Venor, chin high. "I don't investigate magistrates! They don't break the law. They are the law."

He gave her a curt nod as the red slowly drained from his face.

She turned back to me and smoothed down her shirt. "That anonymous note – I knew it was you."

"Where is this note?" Venor snarled.

She went to retrieve a leather case from the front of the cabin. It tinkled when she opened it. Out came my anonymous letter. I caught a glimpse of the big letters at the end, HIS WIFE KNOWS, before Venor deftly twitched it out of her fingers, crumpled it and threw it overboard.

She licked her lips and came closer to me. "Missus Scarlet was so pleased with that portrait you did of them. She passed it around at breakfast that day. I noticed you'd written on the back, so I had a look again to compare the hand. Your lettering is so distinctive, and you didn't even try to disguise it! How stupid do you think I am?"

"Enough time-wasting," Venor interrupted, emphatic.

I took a breath and focused on Felicity. "You're helping a bully. He's violent. He's dangerous, Felicity. He's just a brander in a fancy coat. You said it yourself."

"I said no such thing." Felicity tossed back her plait but shot a wary look at Venor.

"He gave me this limp," I told her. "Almost killed me. And you think you can trust him? You think you're walking away with twenty thousand krunan? You think he won't—"

"I think that's more than enough on that subject,"

Felicity cut me off. She darted another look at Venor, who was watching me, eyes narrowed.

Then Felicity drew an envelope from her pocket. "The boy sent you this in the post. Receiver pays. Well, I intercepted the note and fetched it this morning..."

It was another letter from Zako – to me, this time.

"But we can't make head nor tail of his nonsense." I noticed Venor's hands were balled into fists.

"What's B and T?" Felicity demanded. "Is it a place? People? Are they helping Zako?"

I tried not to laugh. She and Venor were chasing down two fictional characters from a book one of them had fired to ashes. "I don't know."

She turned to Venor. "It's time for the serum."

Seer-em. Not a word I knew, but it had me imagining all sorts of things.

Venor's thin lips pulled into a smile. Felicity picked a small glass vial with a cork stopper from her case. It looked like the medical vials the Glassworks produce, thin, brown-tinted.

Liquid moved inside sluggishly.

"Here's what will happen," she explained. "You drink this, answer our questions, then sleep like a brick for a day and forget this whole unpleasantness. Really, we should have done it an hour ago, but I worried about the danger to your health so soon after the other drug. A sentimental mistake."

"I'm not drinking anything."

"If you're not a liar, you've nothing to fear."

"For all I know it's poison."

"Drink."

Venor drew closer. "Drink it," came his quiet, terrifying voice, "or we'll cut you open and throw you over. The kraits will find you in no time. They'll smell your stinking blood in the water."

"Go and hang," I started to say, and Felicity held the vial to my lips, tipped it into my mouth.

It tasted vile, decaying. I spat most of it out.

Felicity made a noise of irritation and produced another vial. This time, the bearded man pinched my nose and tilted my head back.

"Drink it," whispered Felicity. "Or else you'll get another dose."

I swallowed it down. Warmth settled on my chest. I felt myself smiling. The man released my nose and the sea air whistled when I inhaled. *Pheeeee!* I laughed. I couldn't stop. Then I gulped air too fast and couldn't breathe. My fingers started to tingle. I needed to breathe, but the air wasn't going in.

Blackness swallowed me.

I woke as the sun went down, confused, again with the odd sensation of jumbled time. I licked my lips – salt. They'd splashed me with seawater to revive me, but I couldn't see them. I was still on deck, head aching, my hands tied in front of me, useless as hooks on arms dead as wood.

She said I wouldn't remember, but I did.

Snatches of conversation reached me from the other side of the boat.

"It's not a precise science," Felicity said. "People react to different medicines differently."

"I'm not paying you for imprecise," Venor replied. "If she doesn't sing, you're both no use to me. People should be useful, Greave. Or they should be dead."

Felicity started towards me, and I struggled to sit up. Prickles of sensation dragged thorn-like through my limbs, and a vomit of laughter erupted from my throat, uncontrollable.

"Welcome back." Her face was inches from mine.

Behind her, I could see they'd hauled the boat around. I leaned against the cabin still, but now I faced the shore. We had returned – sort of. The Portcaye wall was a thin, dark ribbon behind the river emptying into the ocean. Vanishingly tiny, and lit only by the last reflected light draining from the clouds. Waves churned white to the north, near the sandbank over the old wreck of the *Eventide*. We were still far out. The cabin cast a weak shadow to the edge of the boat, but it was banished when Felicity lit a lantern.

Venor stepped up behind me.

"What's my name?" Felicity began. I felt utterly compelled to answer. The serum she gave me – it had me in its grip.

"Felicity Greave."

"Where do you live?"

"Opal Alley."

"Where's Zako Taler?"

"I don't know." *Truth.*

"Is he alive?"

"I hope so."

"Did you steal him from the magistrate's estate?"

I could feel the strange urge to tell her, building, relentless. *You can't steal a person. Whose estate was it? You don't know. Six years ago it was a Crozoni family farm. And before?* "No."

"Did you hide him in the Lugger?"

"No." *The Scarlets did that.*

"Did you plait that dog's fur collar?"

"I did." *He taught me how.*

"And buy those glasses from the junk shop?"

"No." *Ruzi did.*

She squints angrily. "But you must have some idea where Zako is."

"Somewhere in County Portcaye," I blurted, helpless to hold my tongue.

"How do you know?"

"The post office told Kit."

"Does Kit know where he is?"

"No."

She read from Zako's letter, still holding it so I couldn't see it myself. "*Thought you might get my clues before... Third time lucky!* What does he mean, *third time lucky*? And *clues before*?"

"He sent two other letters."

"What did the other two say?"

"Just that we shouldn't worry. Said he was living off the land. That he was happy on his island."

"What island?"

"It's a game he's playing – like he's in a story."

"Oh, she's useless," Venor spat.

Felicity looked at him, over my head, new ripples of worry wrinkling her habitual cool.

She looked back at me. "What does he mean, *B and T*?" she probed. "Who are they?"

I tried to fight the compulsion. I clamped my mouth shut on a swelling dizziness. "Blenny and Tornelius."

Felicity groaned.

"Who are they?" Venor asked.

"It's an old children's book," she told him. "Pre-Registry." She turned back to me. "What island is he on? There's no island where he's marked it on the map."

"I told you, it's just a game," I say.

Venor grunted angrily, and Felicity shot him a look that was definitely frightened.

"What's a … *wirlpowl*?" the Crozoni sounded awful in her mouth.

"He means a whirlpool," I choked out. "A twist of water, like a drain in the sea that swirls round. A maelstrom."

"Is there a maelstrom in the seas about here?"

"No. He's pretending."

She asked me about Crozoni words for *wolf*, for *oysters*, for *Eventide*, asked where they could find its wreck.

He's sent the same clues as before, I think.

"Enough!" snapped Venor. He gripped Felicity's elbow and drew her aside, behind me. "The bitch doesn't know anything. We're getting rid of her and going back."

The bearded man stepped over my legs to tug some rigging at the back of the boat.

I closed my eyes.

"Wait a minute," I heard Felicity hiss. "She won't remember a thing when the serum wears off. We can knock her out again and leave her on the sand. We agreed."

"She's outlived her usefulness," Venor said.

I opened my eyes and watched the bearded man's hard little eyes following the conversation behind me. The darkness grew thicker, but his eyes glistened like wet stones. He nodded almost imperceptibly – to Venor, I suppose – then he hooked one enormous hand under the ropes binding my wrists and practically carried me to the edge of the boat.

His other hand clasped a knife – glinting, flicked open. It looked small in his bucket-hands. But I didn't doubt it was enough to bleed me before I drowned, more than enough to lead a swarm of sea kraits to their supper. Blood like a map, running in every direction in the water. Behind us, Felicity and Venor were still arguing.

"Please," I whispered to the man, trying to find his marble eyes. I could barely see his skin behind the thick beard and shadow. But something flickered across his face. He looked back to Felicity and Venor again.

"We don't need to hurt anyone; she'll forget—"

"I pay you, woman, not the other way around," Venor said.

"Lose your boots, girl." The words whispered through his whiskers so only I could hear. "Kick them off."

I did what he said. He picked at the ropes around my wrists until they began to loosen under his thick fingers. I could feel tears spilling from my eyes again – like they did when I first saw him, looming in the light.

"Slash her and get her in the drink!" Venor's voice rose behind us. The man's knife flashed and the rope slipped off my wrists, sinking into the water.

"There's no need!" cried Felicity Greave. Too late.

"Don't fight the rip. Look for the fires." The man's voice was soft in my ear. Then he raised it and added a sinister chuckle, "Don't mind the kraits." He pushed me in.

I slid like a seal, down into the suck of cold that shrank my clothes tight against my body until they were worse than useless – deadweight.

"Get her back!" Felicity's shrieks were muffled by the water.

My trousers pulled, but I kicked through the cloying cold away from the boat and its lanterns. Their voices floated after me. I didn't try to parse meaning. I rolled to look back at the boat, picking at the soaking knot securing my belt.

Felicity's pale face squinted after me. She didn't see me. I was too far – hidden in the dark water. I peeled the trousers off and let them sink.

The big shadow of the bearded man moved slowly up the deck, adjusting the sails. Their fluttering canvas harnessed the gentle wind, *thwup*, and the lugger trotted off.

A black swell lifted me. I bobbed, going nowhere. I'd no idea of the tide schedule, but I didn't feel a pull. It could have been slack tide – when it's on the turn. Going out, or in.

I used to fancy myself a good swimmer, fancy I'd been out far. Suddenly I found myself over a mile out. I looked for stars, for the Fivemonth Moon – anything for direction. No light penetrated the cloud.

I took stock. Cold and thirsty but not hungry. Head pounding but alert. Wrists chafed but not bleeding.

I turned to the direction I remembered as the shore. Darkness. Then I saw them, tiny pinpricks flaring to my right. Not where I'd thought to find them.

The fires looked impossibly distant, but I struck out in their direction.

I tired. The fires loomed no larger. My breath grew laboured, my arms anchor-heavy. Something touched them. The same something, like slimy fins, brushed my legs. My already-bursting heart skipped faster for several beats.

It was just weed, I realized, untethered seaweed.

Was it going out? Was it being pulled with the tide away from the shore? I knew in my bones I couldn't swim against the tide. Instead of panic, I filled with anger.

These days I'm always angry, a background buzz. But this was another level – molten, crawling up my ribs. Who knew I could feel anger thick enough to chew?

I poured it into my arms, into each stroke of my legs, even the right one, so ungainly on land, but here it served. It was weaker, but I didn't feel the old ache.

More weed touched me, and I realized we were travelling together. The tide was on the flood, not the ebb, the waves carrying us to shore.

The anger went, just like that. Another feeling took over, vast and joyous.

I wasn't myself.

Feelings tossed me up and down like the waves. It was that drug that tasted like death. I was still drunk.

Joy filled me like a jug, sleepy and honeyed. *Just float on your back. The sea will carry you home.* I rolled, watching the front of my blouse billow, light and bubbly. Cold water tugged gently at my hair, pulling it into flat, weedy ribbons.

A memory swelled up like a song. It was the year after she died and a year before everyone else did. Pa took us away down the coast, a few hours' journey, and we stayed two nights in Kellerton. I was ten. Enca and Eben were eight – mine to look after that day on Kellerton sands. Father stayed with Char, building turtles and tunnels.

The sea was blue-green, the sand like powder. We met a boy with three old donkeys. Father said we could ride if we wanted, so off we went, trying to race up the dry bit of sand on these stubborn, sinking, wobbly creatures. Eben almost fell off. They were slow as anything, and so loud. Enca had a pocketful of pear drops they tried to bribe their donkeys with. The donkeys snuffled pear drops at a casual amble. I leaned round the neck of mine and coaxed it on to the harder sand near the waterline, before racing off – well, racing in a relative sense – peering back at my sisters dropping behind.

The memory swamped my spirits. I thought of the girls bent towards each other, trying to clutch hands from one donkey to the next, calling to me, breathless with giggles. Their donkeys both stopped – wouldn't budge for love or pear drops. Their high laughter was cut up and carried in pieces by the wind, cacophonous against the sound of the waves.

Then I could hear waves on a beach again. My arms and legs, even my breath shook. I swam awfully, kicking my legs like a palsied frog, pulling with reeds for arms. When I turned over to look again, the fires on the beach were nearer, but another current had me, bearing me out. A riptide. I didn't feel drugged any longer. I knew what to do. I swam along the shore, away from the fires and the pull of the rip. Then I let the waves have me. It was dark on the stretch where I landed, sand blessedly solid between my toes.

Portcaye's familiar wall loomed. My own weight hit like a hammer. Then the cold. I tried to avoid the small sunken rocks, most of them jagged, but I stumbled on one, fell and cut my knee on another. It didn't hurt at all. *The kraits would love this*, I thought, pushing my leaden body up beyond the strandline.

I looked around for Pa, like he might be waiting for us again on the sand.

45

today we fail

My memory cave is underwater. A sea vault. I can't stay too long. I'm surfacing, secrets like sediment settling in my wake. I pass old flashes of – I don't know, remembrance or fantasy? The clinging past peels away. Runs like sweat.

I toss the covers off and dash open the curtains. The sun's about to rise, making some creature – a cockerel, I realize; I haven't heard a cockerel in years – delirious with delight. His trilling sounds like a horn. Like my bewildering panic made manifest.

I stagger into the hallway.

Venor and Felicity. Working together.

Firstday before last they had me on that boat. Nine days ago. And we've heard nothing of a fugitive captured, so Venor hasn't found Zako on his impossible island up the coast near a pile of old oyster shells – not yet.

Is Felicity out there, right now, searching for Zako?

Perhaps that's why she left the Lugger in such a hurry. Is she hunting her twenty thousand krunan?

Or did she never make it back off that boat?

The cockerel is still at it outside. I have no idea where Kit went to sleep, so I walk down the passage calling his name like a second frantic bird.

He appears in rumpled vest and trousers, with an alacrity I'm coming to take for granted, though he's still half asleep.

His thin bracelets are wound round his wrists. The bandage on his right forearm has come off – I can see stitches puckering the skin. The burn on his left is bare. It looks like an ordinary burn – like he caught it on the oven.

"Forgot about that prick." He rubs bleary eyes, tilting his head to the honking noise.

"Kit…"

"Goldie thinks it's a laugh, waking the whole street up before dawn." Then he seems to realize something's off. "What?"

"I remembered," I blurt. "The grass worked. It was Venor – and Felicity. They took me on a boat. She was working for him. She was after Zako. She had a letter he sent to me…"

Thea's wounds, I suddenly think. *What if they* have *already found Zako? Are they keeping it quiet? Maybe Felicity claimed her reward and high-tailed it. Maybe the branders have been torturing Zako for days.*

"Venor would crow if he got Zako, wouldn't he? He'd

want it front page of the *Post*. Wouldn't he?" My fingers dig into Kit's arm.

"Okay. Let's not panic." Kit has to raise his voice over the cockerel. *Let's not panic. Panic. Panic.*

He leads me back to the window seat. I left the window open overnight. I take a deep breath of the cool morning air and start to fill him in properly about my boat ride.

"I knew she was bad news," he can't resist reminding me.

Felicity. *Ferocity.*

My imaginary friend. Who missed the food from her homeland and didn't rate the buttocks on the naked globe-holder in Rundvaer Square and was in love with a man who died. She slagged off Venor. We slagged him off together.

I should be angry, but I can only feel an edgeless embarrassment, laced with nausea.

Kit pushes the window wider, into the growing light of the day. "Let's focus on what we know," he says. "On the boat, he wasn't much the wiser. Zako may be … happy in the wild. If he's not, we'll know about it soon. He'll be locked up where Blithe is. And we'll be there tomorrow. They won't kill their most-wanted boy quietly – it'll be big news."

I'm back walking that underground corridor with Senior Inspector Hove, past that room with the sign on the door. *Deadhouse.*

That big news may come too late. The branders killed

Fidel Hemman before the news broke. And Venor wants to shut Zako up before he can tell anyone the dark secret he doesn't even know he's privy to. Thanks to me, Venor knows exactly how much Zako heard about his dodgy Life Record, about how he's like the Kellins, vulnerable to forensic science.

"We can search Felicity's room," says Kit. "She could have left a clue there. And for all we know, Zako could be writing us another letter right now, telling us he's *happe*. Worry won't solve anything."

I'm too scared to smile back. I just want him safe. I want him with us. Perhaps he could come here. The Reedstones could hide him, couldn't they? Put this enormous mansion to good use.

Kit puts his arms around me.

Apprehension's eating me alive on the walk to the Lugger.

"What do I tell Ruzi?"

"Nothing. Not yet. Nor the Scarlets."

"Even if Venor might be coming for them next?"

"We don't know he's got Zako. We stick to the plan until we know different. Keep it simple."

I swallow my reluctance, past the hard ball of unshed tears in my throat.

We go in through the courtyard to find Gracie rolling a round of pastry and Renny stoking up the stove. Her eyes twinkle at me in surprise. "Oh, we heard about your change of fortunes. How is it living a life of luxury?"

I hesitate. "I have a lot of space," I say at last.

"Must be a change from Ruzi's place. They wanted to buy Kit, you know – years ago. Mister and Missus S wouldn't have it."

"Why *did* they buy you?" Gracie says curiously. I mutter something about helping with their engineering schematics and drafting precise plans.

"Ohhh," Renny interrupts. "Did you hear about your friend?"

"What's that?" I ask.

"Felicity Greave—" she starts.

"If that's even her name," Gracie mutters.

"Mister S went by the station yesterday to tell them she's been missing, since she's been gone more than a week," Renny continues.

"And she didn't pay for the one before that and all," Gracie chimes in.

"No! And left all her things here. Anyway, turns out she's not a reporter for the *Evening Gazette*. You'll never guess."

I shake my head dumbly.

"She's a bounty hunter!" Renny declares. "She had to register with the branders' station when she came here."

"Really?" Kit manages convincing surprise.

"Mister S thinks she was after your young friend – Zako Taler, that they raided us over."

"Bizarre," Kit says.

"I didn't know," I stutter finally.

They tell us what Mister S learned at the station. That Felicity made tracking down fugitives to claim rewards into a career. She's older than I thought – in her mid-thirties. She used to do it in Skøland but moved to Makaia with the first wave. Once she collected four big bounties in a year.

"Well," says Gracie, "I never warmed to her."

"No," Renny agrees. "She was snobby about the clerks too."

Kit lets me in to Felicity's room while he goes to consult the Reedstones' source about prisoners at the branders' station.

It doesn't feel like a room unoccupied for a week. The bed's neatly made, nightclothes folded under the pillow. Her clothes hang in the wardrobe. A spare pair of shoes sits beneath them, sideways. A wardrobe ghost. There's a dark, hooded cloak in fine light material I've never seen before. And there's her pale dress – the one she wore to that fundraiser in Rundvaer Square. It was her, going up those steps. I don't find her little red notebook or her amber ring – she'd never be parted from those. No Zako letter.

Her leather case full of vials isn't here either. At the bottom of her small trunk, I do find a stack of wanted posters, clippings and a silverprint.

The clippings are about Zako's attack on the Magistrate. Nothing new there.

The silverprint is Felicity, looking younger, standing beside a Skøl man I don't recognize. Tall and fair, holding something aloft – a piece of wood, or a huge bone, perhaps the bone of some giant beast. I can't tell. I wonder if it's the man who gave her the ring. Perhaps he's not dead, I realize, with a new sting of embarrassment. Perhaps that was a lie too.

I'm interrupted in my musings when Kit returns. The Reedstones' source is adamant that Zako isn't in the branders' station. They have no children in custody. Certainly no savages.

"He could still be in the Registry," I say, with an odd note of hope in my voice. It's that, or he's free, or he's dead.

Kit gives me two more locks to practise with. I head back to Opal Alley with them as he settles down to scrub the soil from a sack of potatoes.

I spend the rest of the afternoon practising. It's much harder than Kit makes it look. I'm no dab hand, but I can do it – given enough time. If I can't get this right, it's all over.

Ruzi appears after work, looking unkempt. I realize his stubble's more grey than black. When did that happen? My hair's grown too, I suppose. I haven't cut it since the winter.

"He got you back!" He's surprised to see me, like he didn't really believe Kit would be able to wrest me from the clutches of my new employer-slash-owners. His smile's shaky. "You're allowed to stay here, are you?"

"They're giving me a lot of freedom. I'd still like to stay here … if that's okay?"

Are his eyes shining? "Course it's okay."

He makes us a pot of fikka and some fried eggs, goes for biscuits from downstairs to celebrate.

Lavender shortbread, like the ones we had with Zako in the Thirdmonth. "They don't do the jam ones like your mother did. Do you remember those?" He breaks off a chunk of his and crunches it. "Like little suns."

I don't. And then I do.

Circles with crinkled edges, sandwiched together, apricot jam bubbling through the hole cut in the centre of the top layer. *Apricot jam for my apricot girl.*

"Your mother was like the sun." He presses his breastbone. "A heart that just made fire. More and more. She had to let it free."

"I don't understand."

Why? I said to Pa. *I don't understand why.*

She was sad, he said. *She was angry. Feelings like demons she couldn't escape.*

Ruzi's chin dips. "It's not a thing to understand, Mor. It's just another thing that is."

I'm up before the sun next morning, sick with apprehension. My mind's worn a rut going over and over the plans we finalized with the Reedstones yesterday.

In the small mirror above the sink, I pin my curls back severely, darken my eyelids with soot, then outline my eyes with my softest charcoal pencil. I bite my bottom lip until it looks a little redder and cover my hair under a wrap like the ones the Skøl servants favour – black with a stiff front and broad ribbons tied under the chin. I bought it months back in Ammedown Alley, meaning to tear it apart and remake it when I found the time – which was never.

Now I know how a horse wearing blinkers feels, but I think I look older, and it gives me a bit of extra courage. Like a helmet.

At the Lugger, I tell Renny I'm volunteering for the lunch deliveries today.

"It's for Glister Reedstone's research on different architectural styles," I say. "He wants me to draw the foyer for him."

"You look fancy," Gracie notes. "I like the new…" She wiggles one of the ribbons under my head covering.

"Your eyes are a picture," Renny adds.

I feel shy with them both smiling at me. "Thank you."

I'm still slow with the lock picks, but it will have to serve.

Today we succeed, or today we fail.

46

a hopeful stutter

The savoury waft of pastry – molten-hot insides, rich flaky outsides – floats up from the basket.

I'm halfway up the steps when the magistrate appears, heading down, and all my calm cracks and scatters like a flock of pigeons. Of all the days. They say he's only here once a week.

I keep my head down, bobbing awkwardly, deferential, eyes on my beautiful boots. *Ancestors, don't let him realize it's me –*

His hand shoots out and grips my arm.

A ghastly smile twists his face. We stand together on the step.

"Something smells … tasty," he hisses, reaching towards the basket. I flinch. He picks up a pastry and bites through the crust. I keep my eyes averted but can feel him bending closer. He takes a deep breath. "Pretty little rat."

His hard soles click down the stairs before I can answer. *Click click click.*

I breathe shakily.

He didn't know me. Didn't associate the tidy girl with a basket with the bedraggled makkie he had thrown off the boat. He thinks I drowned. He thinks the kraits drained me.

I make it past the pawing guards in a trance, passing under the *Life Is Golden* lie. My heart's hammering, but they can't see that. They don't know my heart. They never will. It's hidden. Right now, it's murderous.

I stand in the corner of a stairwell, pretending I'm waiting for someone until I'm calm again.

I sell pastries in a fugue. When I've only three left, I find the door I need on the first floor. I came here five days ago. It was empty then, but it's safest to have the excuse of the lunches, if I need it.

It's a library now, on two floors, but I can see the old bones of it behind the books. Perhaps it wouldn't be obvious if I didn't know what it was before. The seats are gone, the balconies arranged with rows of reference books. Two staircases sweep to the ground floor, one on each side, down to where the old stalls were – now more shelves, books, journals and a few tables. Books line the rise to the old stage too, flanking a set of stairs they've installed. There are no windows anywhere – perhaps that's why they've put a library here and not more offices.

It's not empty today. A harried-looking clerk, hood

pushed back, searches for something in an ill-lit corner, pulling out and replacing thick volumes. I wait until they leave before going down.

There's a handle in what used to be one wing of the stage that opens the trap. It still works. I can crank the same shaft from inside or close it manually and throw the bolts. The trap itself is half obscured by the end of a long shelf, but there's room. I lower it only as far as I need – just as the door at the end of the stalls section swings open again on two sets of voices.

"You're sure it's not there?"

"Someone could have it."

I push the basket down and sneak to the next aisle over to place a few books in disarray on the floor.

"It's probably been put back wrong. Let's look around."

They won't see the open trap unless they come into one of the aisles it straddles, but it's not worth the risk. I squeeze in past the edge of the shelf and thud the door up with a soft bang before they reach the stage.

They'll have heard it and assumed they're not alone, but they don't call out. Library rules are the same the world over.

I don't want to tinkle the coins in my apron pocket. I can smell the pastries. I'm suddenly terrified they smell too strong, so I wrap them in the cloth lining the basket.

"Some books fell down, look. And no one's here. Must've been the ghost!"

"Oh, come off it!"

They don't mention the trap. The seams blend beautifully into the rest of the floor. Crozoni woodwork. Smooth as one of Ruzi's guitars.

They find what they came for. I hear their voices falling away.

I ease further into the trap and pat my pockets. A candle and matches, lock picks. I take off my fancy hair wrap and the apron with its front pocket full of coin from the pastry sales. Inside one of my boots is the small wrench I need to take out the stops on the window.

I don't dare to light the candle. There's nothing to do but think. I hate that.

By Goldie's pocket timepiece and the deeper silence, it's time. I eat one of the pastries before I ease out of the trap and up the stairs, exiting on the first floor to avoid the guards' station on the ground floor. Four guards will be there, swilling schinn all night if the Reedstones' intelligence is correct.

The room with the window I need is indeed locked, but it's the main type of lock I've been practising. I'm quite pleased with the full seven minutes it takes me to coax it open – even if others might have cracked it in seconds.

Six empty desks greet me. The curtains aren't drawn, and the window stops unscrew readily enough with my tool, though they've been painted over. The latch at the top isn't painted, but it's stubborn. I have to stand on a chair to get the right purchase.

The window itself is a beast. After fifteen panicked minutes of struggling with it, I finally prise it up a whole half inch. I prop it there with a book and find some lantern fuel to oil it. It's soon clear I won't raise it further without a lever.

There's nothing obvious to hand, but I've a few hours before Kit's expected, and I want to use them.

I aim to go a little off-plan.

It's not a risk I should take. It's not what I've agreed with Kit or the Reedstones. But what if the magistrate has some news or correspondence with someone – branders or bounty hunters – about Zako he's keeping in his office? Some paper trail that explains whether they found him or not. What if he has Zako's third letter?

The magistrate's office is on the ground floor. Unfortunately, the only way to reach it is past the guards' station. I can't sneak like Kit does, like a ghost – though these shoes are much lighter than my old ones.

Fortunately, they're making enough noise to wake the dead. Four voices. I could hear them from the other side of the building, and now I'm close enough to tell they're drinking and playing cards. Four guards inside, doing nothing. Two out front, two out back and two more on the roof every night. Ten men. Even the branders' station doesn't keep such a heavy night guard. It seems profligate for Skøl, but then the Registry is the thing they care about most in the world. Plus Venor's got his star entertainment for the high governor stashed in here.

I creep to the doorway of the guards' station and feel for the gravel I pocketed from one of the potted ferns earlier. I need something small to distract them. The curtains behind their table are drawn to, though a narrow gap remains between the cloth and the windowpane. I throw one of the stones, but it flies wide, bouncing off to clink on the floor. They don't even hear it through the din they're making. I aim again. This time a slightly larger rock. It hits the glass with a sharp tap and their voices fall. I flash past while they're murmuring about ghosts at the window. When one of their chairs scrapes back moments after, my heart almost stops. I race along the carpet, round the corner. A reedy squeal of hinges and a loud pouring of piss reveal the guard was only going to relieve himself.

It's darker than night outside Venor's office. I don't dare light a candle, so I rely on touch. The lock's the same type as the ones upstairs, but the sweat on my fingers slows me – I'm far too long opening it. At least his curtains are thick. I light my candle.

Tall bookshelves bracket the window, a child's skull atop one. Subtle. Two maps framed in dark wood and a vintage portrait of Clarion Lovemore – two decades old if it's a day; she has thick hair and a slim neck, accentuating her wide nostrils – adorn the wall facing his desk.

There's a family portrait on the opposite wall, in the formal Skøl style – shadowy oils, grim upholstery and daft hats. The magistrate's family. Missus Venor, a boy who must be the son at school in Skøland and tiny Devotion, a pale glow swamped in a dark dress. The magistrate must be at least a decade younger, but he still looks stern. They all do, even the baby.

Only having two children is unusual for such a wealthy couple. Perhaps she couldn't stomach having more after she found out his ugly secret.

His desk is neatly arranged, but for a gift basket sitting haphazardly on a stack of neat papers. The bottom of the basket is littered with rinds from the same type of expensive tiny orange that Mister S bought recently. There's a ribbon on the handle tied to a note – *To Magistrate Venor, with gratitude for your patriotic service.* It's from someone I've never heard of – a Mister Hayle.

A square dish of thin white pottery sits at right angles to the stack of neat papers. It holds a ring I recognize. Gold with an amber stone. I touch it with the tips of my fingers.

Life Is Golden, I think stupidly, seeing Felicity's face on that boat when she was looking at Venor, frightened. Worse thoughts crowd after it like rubbish-drunk flies. I think of that slow, fat fly colliding with my face. Disgusting. I feel like that, times a hundred. I take a deep breath and sweep the thoughts aside. Not now.

His chair is stiff leather – built for a bigger frame than mine. I turn my attention to the stack of papers under the basket with the orange peelings.

The son's called Valour Venor too, poor thing. There's a bill for his extortionate schooling – he's only one year younger than me. I feel a rare mixture of jealousy and pity.

A few thick reports comprise most of the stack. *Trends and Projections in Criminality Across the New Western Counties Under Two Scenarios* and *Labour Shortages in New Western County Shipway.*

No sign of Zako's letter. No correspondence about him.

I force my shaking hands to stack the items back neatly. There's no personal correspondence at all, actually. No missives from his wife or son or daughter. They must go to the home address. To Lovemore.

I flip open Goldie's timepiece. Kit will be on his way, and I still haven't found a lever for the window. I take one of the iron pokers from Venor's cold fireplace and creep back to the corner near the guards' station. Four voices still, absorbed in an argument about the proper way to cook Skølcakes. They're thinking about breakfast already.

It's harder to find a target to distract them from this angle. There's a wall, but it's bare. I settle on the unlit fireplace, selecting three small pieces of gravel to throw together into the iron firebed. Throw-for-crow. The soft tinkling cuts through their conversation, and I fly past the door as they start up about *bats in the chimney again*.

Upstairs, raindrops bead and weep down the glass, merging and gathering each other as they go. I thought it might drizzle, but this is a downpour. Distant thunder, lightning. Kit's climb will be wretched. I bet the guards on the roof will be sheltering under the cupola though.

*

My breath hitches. I only see him because he's told me where to look. He levers himself and his empty, rubber-lined sack to the top of the nine-foot iron fence before dropping like a stone to the Registry grounds. Surely these exertions will cost his wound. I force the window open in preparation. It squeals through the first few inches before it gives. I can hear snatches of raised voices – Goldie and Lev arguing in the street. I can't hear what they're saying, but it's growing increasingly hysterical. Rain wets the curtains, but they'll dry by morning.

Kit crouches, another shadow in the black grass.

I can see all the way to the Centre from here, see the glow over Rundvaer Square and the distant lanterns I imagine as patrolling branders. I hope they're wet and miserable. Kit crosses the grass, and I lose sight of him. Now he'll be picking his way slowly up the stretches where the guttering is best. I can't confirm without sticking my head out – too conspicuous.

I wait.

Finally his shape appears, clinging to the ledge like a bat. Then he's inside, safe. I embrace him, just as a ferocious flash and clap of thunder burst overhead.

Kit smiles like the lightning – dazzling, over in half a second.

We push on.

It's been six years since I've seen the undercroft in this building. Kit cracks the heavy-duty lock on the door leading down in a fraction of the time it took me to best the simple lock upstairs.

The Registry's main ragleaf generator squats like a dragon of old in one corner, whirring and croaking and sending vague fumes into the damp. They've installed fire-quelling bulbs in lines along every wall. I recognize the Glassworks' handiwork with a tinge of weird pride. We don't dare flick the main elektric lights on – tiny windows in the tops of the walls mean the guards outside might see – but it's clear as day the cells they detained us in after the Cull are gone.

Zako isn't here. If they have him, he'll be in the vault too.

Kit looks at the vault doors, barely a seam between them. "Showtime."

The lock is a complex system of interlinked pins, springs and rotary elements – different mechanisms requiring individual attention.

I let him concentrate.

Something grates, and he swears softly. Then a ratcheting sound.

"Rollers are stiff," he murmurs as a panel behind the keyhole cracks open like a clockwork window.

"Mor." He turns to me. "Can you stand by the side over there?"

"Why?"

"This is the less fun part." He's pulling a long glove out of one pocket, unravelling a delicate chain that dangles all the way from the glove to the floor, a bewildering fashion choice. "They've a tamper-proof fail-safe. It's attached to the main flow and its own back-up, so we can't just cut the power."

I have no idea what that's supposed to mean, but we're in a hurry and my mind's elsewhere, so I stand aside.

He twists the handle behind the panel, and I see him grit his teeth. Then lightning – in miniature. Almost like he's holding a white-and-purple stream of it, like one of the gods of old. An arc of pure elektricity that makes a noise like a huge, angry insect and a smell like burning disinfectant.

I hear thick glass cracking, exploding.

The vault doors are open an inch.

Kit's on the floor, silent and still.

I reach his side before he gasps, "Bracing," and sits up.

"Are you mad? What the hell?" Now I can smell something vinegary-sweet, something sending a spike of pure panic into the heart of me. I know that smell. It's the liquid ether that was in the glass in his pocket – that we were saving if needed to knock out the guards – now blotting the floor and Kit's clothes. Perhaps that's what's making him so woozy. That or the massive wave of power that just went through him.

"Reedstone special," he explains breathlessly. "High-security…" *Elektric locks.* "Feels like a sledgehammer, every time."

"Are you burnt?"

"Glove got most. I'll be okay." He braces his ribs as I help him to his feet. He tore his stitches climbing the building. I push at the cracked vault doors. They swing away from us, opening, scraping pre-existing grooves in the floor. I catch Kit's arm.

"You don't look good."

"Rude. Should be elektric light inside – but hang the blanket first." He props up the entryway for a second before sliding to sit on the floor just outside again.

I hang the thick black blanket he brought in his waterproof bag over the gap between the doors – to prevent the strong elektric light Glister said was inside the vault leaking out. The doors are broken now. If we close them the trick lock will trigger and they won't reopen unless someone drills through a solid inch of iron.

I duck behind the blanket with my candle and find an array of small brass levers just inside. Nothing happens when I flick one up. I try another. "Found switches here … they're not working."

I duck back out to see Kit still on the floor. He leans forward, his eyes wide. "Oh shit. Shit. Shit. Shit," he's whispering.

I hear a distant sound of footsteps on the floor above us. Voices – too far away to make out words, and some low laughter.

"The vault shock – it's tripped a fuse. The guards will come down here," Kit explains.

There's nowhere to hide.

"Then I'll un-trip the fuse."

"What?"

He can barely stand.

"Tell me how I do that. What does it look like?"

"It'll be by the generator – more than one. Cylinders on levers with wires out the ends. You can push it down or up… It should be up." He sounds hesitant.

He's trying to regain his feet. I hear a key going into the fancy lock upstairs, the door moving.

I snuff my candle so they don't see its light and creep to the generator. I couldn't move faster if I tried – the terror's like treacle.

Their voices are clear now. They're arguing over who should come down and fix it. Seems they're not supposed to patrol the undercroft at all.

I know I'm a coward. It means I'm too afraid to do brave things. It also means I'm too afraid to do stupid things likely to get me killed – like breaking into the Life Registry and trying to find a fuse in the dark before a guard arrives to shoot me in the head.

The generator's still throwing out odd moans. So are the guards upstairs.

"Go on, Creddy. I did it last time – don't be so lazy."

A murmur of agreement from the other two and grumbles from Creddy as he starts down.

Without my candle, the generator is looming and indistinct – but I can remember where the row of fuses were, before I lost the light. It's smaller than the generator

I saw in the Reedstones' mansion, but has the same fuses like levers on the channels out. I imagine them glistening in the murk as I feel along the row. Two are set to off. I flip one up. Nothing. I flip the other. Light floods down the stairs. I notice a brief, dim glow from the vault behind me – before Kit rights the switch I left on. He must have found his feet. A cheer rises from upstairs.

"Whaay! Creddy," they chorus.

"I haven't done anything," Creddy calls, letting out a loose string of curses. He's close. I can see his shadow at the bottom of the stairs. In fact, I can see his shins.

"Must've been the ghost, then – go down and check. Unless you're scared."

I stop breathing in case it stirs the shadows.

"Go down yourself," Creddy grumbles and starts back up the stairs.

Then the door shuts, blocking out the light.

My legs almost give way, but I suck in a deep breath and join Kit in the vault.

Its distant lights flicker on.

It's enormous. I was expecting capacity – but this is many times my imaginings. They've dug it out beyond the building, burrowed under the lawn.

A low groan sounds from somewhere nearby – human, not generator – and my heart sends out a hopeful stutter.

47

another busy evening

I follow the sound of the groan to our right. They've walled off a section. The door has a heavy bolt, padlocked. There's a small window high up in the door, and a flap at the bottom, also bolted. Kit stands on tiptoe to peer in the window. He looks at me and shakes his head.

"Not Zak," he says.

He's already cracked the padlock. He draws the bolts back and swings the door out.

An elektric light dangles from the middle of the ceiling – it must have come on with the others. The Artist sits, bleary-eyed, but otherwise looking remarkably well – no obvious bruises – at the edge of a low pallet. The smell of chamber pot pervades, but it's plush, for a cell. The bed clean, a jug of water. He's condemned, but they don't want him keeling over before it's time to impress Clarion Lovemore.

He startles to full wakefulness when he sees us. "What's going on?"

"Have you seen a boy?" I ask him. "Twelve years old, looks like me."

He shakes his head, confused.

"Have you?" I have to hear him say it.

"N-No," he says.

Zako's not here.

"You're going to get me killed," the Artist says. Not very grateful, all things considered.

"You do know you're to have your head cut off in front of the high governor any day now?" Kit reminds him. "Now point us to the repayer files."

Blithe glowers.

At least he hasn't wasted his few days as the Portcaye Life Registry guest of honour. He indicates the section of the vault files we need.

Kit clicks open one cabinet after another. "Getting close. Sutton, Symonds … Taler," he says softly.

Ruzi Taler, Zako Taler.

Fear clutches my throat, but I don't see any red stamp. It's safe to read. The last substantive entry is Zako's bill of sale to the Venors – six and a half years ago. His time's been paid up front to the end of this year – not unusual. If they've killed him, it's not been recorded.

He's not dead, I tell myself. *They haven't caught him.*

Kit opens more cabinets.

His Eminence Valour Venor and the whole Venor clan have files like everyone else. I don't know what I expected – a gold cabinet just for him? But no – the Skøl like to look even-handed where Life Records are concerned.

Venor's Record says he's forty-seven. Ruzi's age. He was born in County Calderok, the Scarlets' home county. He moved when he was seventeen – the paperwork's all here – to County Rundvaer, where his political career began.

The first entry in his Life Record, registering his birth, is on thick paper. Old-fashioned and coloured with the decades. The Life Registry insignia and motto's at the top, details listed in the middle, and an official stamp and signature at the bottom.

Name and Surname. Sex. Date of Birth. Place of Birth (County and Sub-County). Father's Name – *Not provided.* Mother's Name – *Serenity Venor.* Father's Profession – *Not provided.* Mother's Profession – *Mixed Labour.*

The pages that follow record his marriage, his travels, his life paid.

It's unusual for someone like Venor to have an unknown father, but that's clearly not something he's bothered to hide.

The Artist flips through the pages thoughtfully.

"You're looking for a forgery?" he says.

"We are," I tell him. "Does it all look in order to you?"

"Looks can be deceiving. The vradiance scope might reveal something," he murmurs.

"That's what we thought," I tell him eagerly.

He shuts the Record and looks at me. "But what makes you think the magistrate's had this forged?"

"I'm afraid I can't tell you. But it's a good reason. We're certain of it."

He blinks, seemingly bewildered and perhaps a little hurt.

"You can tell me," he says, affably enough.

"Maybe when we're out of here," Kit offers over his shoulder. He's breaking another lock. "Payday," he says. "Might as well take some of this lot with us, no?"

The cabinet's full of the watermarked, impossible-to-forge blank paper that Fidelity Hemman was killed over. Blithe fair salivates at the sight of it. "Gold dust," he whispers, stroking an approving hand down the stack.

"How much is one worth?" I ask.

"How many years of life can you write on it?" He grins.

Kit packs his waterproof sack with Venor's Life Record and a generous helping of the blank paper, cinching the bundle tight with a bit of rope.

It's time to go. He has to be back over the fence before the grey of pre-dawn.

I pull the open vault door shut behind us. The heavy handle twists round like it's ghost-possessed. We can hear deadbolts, four or more, sliding into place like clockwork. The trick lock.

"They won't be able to get in," Kit says. "Not without a drill anyway. It'll buy you some time."

He shoulders his bundle.

"Go on," I urge. "Don't wait for me to climb up all those stairs."

Kit touches the hand I'm trying to shoo him off with and lowers his voice. "Don't forget to put the stops back."

"I won't."

"Leave that poker somewhere else. It's not worth the risk going back to Venor's office."

"I know."

He nods at Blithe, turns to look at me again, then takes off.

I face the Artist, who's swamped in a hooded clerk's robe. The perfect disguise, and we found a stack of them in the vault. I know it's him, but the effect is still unnerving.

"You ready?"

He nods. He plans to hide in plain sight – well, in a water closet, until shortly after opening.

We're counting on the guards assuming he's just an ordinary clerk heading out on an early errand. He'll be carrying nothing if they search him, concealing no paper, wearing no bruises, raising no suspicion.

I wish I could dash out under a clerk's robe first thing too, but I have to wait for the change of the guard. The risk of someone spotting my hair or my skin or my eyes, even if I were to wear a robe, is too great.

We're cutting it fine. In an hour at most, the early workers will begin to arrive. I fold the black blanket into a neat square.

"Will you be all right?" I ask the Artist.

"Worry about yourself, young lady."

The sun's up when I reach the office upstairs. The window's almost shut. Kit must have pushed it down hanging off the outside.

I've a sudden vision of him in his black clothes, sprawled on the grass three flights below, neck broken, surrounded by fluttering white paper. Another crow, failed to fledge. I push my nose to the window and look down. The neat lawn is unmarred, glistening wetly – rain and dew – with no sign anyone's tramped through it.

I close the glass flush, lock it and screw the stops back in before wiping paint flakes and drips of rain off the sill with my sleeve. I head back down with the wrench in my pocket and Venor's iron poker cradled in the black blanket. I can leave both in my hiding space.

Round a bend in the stairwell, a man is watering a potted palm. I didn't hear him, and now I'm facing him, trying to pretend I didn't just nearly jump out of my skin. He doesn't notice. Not a clerk, a cleaner, in plain clothes. I briefly consider stoving in his head with the poker, splattering the clean, white-painted wood and pristine white walls with blood and brains. It makes me feel powerful.

Instead, I greet him brightly.

"Morning," he replies. "You new?"

"I am."

"You won't be so cheerful in a week," he predicts. I keep moving.

I'm buzzing as I throw the bolt inside the trap. Blood hums in my ears. I couldn't sleep if I wanted to, and I don't want to. What if I snored or cried out and some clerk heard me?

No – I need to think. When we have Venor's secret, will it be enough to destroy him? Enough to earn Zako a pardon? Will they believe us?

I sit in the dark under the boards, stewing.

The library's empty when I finally ease up out of the trap. So's my basket. The foyer looks no different than it did yesterday. No panic. If they've realized they can't get into the vault, they're keeping it quiet.

They don't know they've lost the bird their boss was fattening for the axe. Venor's prisoner and Venor's secret, both flown. *His secret*, I think, *whatever it is. Soon we'll know.* I can taste it already.

I skim my eyes over the few clerks loitering. No sign of any higher-ups. No Venor.

I'm crossing the foyer when I spot Gracie coming downstairs. She sees me too, does a double take. I dash her a quick smile and pick up my pace rather than waiting. She wouldn't make a scene, would she? I need to get outside before we find out.

The guards on the door give my empty basket and apron of coin a perfunctory scan. They're warning some visitors off with a tale about processing going slow today, saying clerks have been called off attending to something for Clarion Lovemore. "You're better off trying tomorrow," they say. I bet that's a line they've been told. I bet it's the vault.

Gracie catches up with me as I'm turning off the bottom of the outdoor steps.

"What's all this? *You've* got our big basket! Kit said he loaned it to friends. You weren't to be selling pastries today..." But she looks worried – on my account – and she's pitching her voice low.

"You got me." I glance at her. "Don't ask me anything, Gracie."

We walk on together in silence. Kit's at the far end of the road. I can see him hovering, like a young man at leisure, out taking the air. He's not fooling me. Still, he looks remarkably well – not at all like someone who ripped his stitches climbing fifty feet up the side of a building the night before, only to be shocked with enough force to kill a draught kine.

He takes the empty basket off me, winks at Gracie. She just gives a tired sigh and walks on alone.

"You did it!" He holds out his elbow.

"We did it." I slip my arm through it and take a deep breath. The air smells different. Fresher. "Did you take all that blank paper to the Reedstones?"

"Very nearly all of it." He grins. "Kept some for our secret stash."

"Where's that, then?"

"Let me show you."

"And Venor's Record?" I feel my free hand shaking. Nervous exhaustion.

"It's stashed too. We can take it to GR Locks and look at it under the vradiance scope."

The stash is a false compartment under one of the seats in the Scarlet Scarab – the shiny red carriage the Scarlets keep stabled in the alley behind the Lugger.

Kit takes my hand as we walk with our secret prize through the Skates to the Reedstones' building.

Goldie Reedstone's been expecting us. Her earrings are studs today. Huge blue gems to match her eyes. She leads us through to the kitchen, where Lev leans over the big wooden table, working on an elektrical diagram. He's got a huge sheet of paper I immediately covet.

"Blithe tells us you have Venor's Life Record," Goldie says, pouring lukewarm fikka into thin ceramic cups. "That wasn't part of your brief."

"We have our reasons. Can we use your vradiance scope?" I'm tired. And all out of patience.

Seems Goldie is too. She drains her fikka. "Yes, of course. Lev? Let's go."

I leave my small cup on the table and follow them to the door to the dark space. Goldie knocks sharply.

"Just a moment!" Glister calls from the other side. "Don't let the light in."

"Come in!" Blithe calls eventually. He and Glister are hovering over a metal-and-glass contraption – two long vertical tubes with a pair of glass plates and several inches of air between them, knobs and dials crusting the sides like limpets.

Glister smiles at me. "Ah. You made it out of the maw! Well done."

Goldie shuts the door behind us. There's a sweep fixed to the bottom, to prevent any light leaking in from outside.

Blithe fiddles with the vradiance scope while we stand in silence.

He eventually holds out a hand for Venor's file, which Kit passes over, opened to the first entry.

Blithe takes his time again, mounting it between the glass plates, before catching Goldie's eye. "Ready," he says.

Finally. Exhaustion and excitement play tug of war with my guts.

She nods and cuts the lights, plunging us into a darkness so thick I feel I might be floating away.

A sound like summer insects begins to build as a dim violet glow gathers around the lips of the metal tubes nearest the glass plates. It's nothing like I imagined. Not bright like the purple Skivårnat lanterns. It's a bluer violet too.

Blithe fiddles with a knob on the top of the scope until the light focuses to a triangular, violet-edged shape, dark at the centre. The beam illuminates nothing beyond its immediate target – a corner of Venor's Life Record.

A hand finds mine, anchoring and assuring. I'd recognize Kit's touch anywhere.

Blithe tilts the scope and uses a pair of dials near the base to move the glass plates with their pinched prize, crab-like, up and sideways, up and sideways. The triangle of weak violet-rimmed dark plays over the birth registration as he begins to scan from the bottom line.

Mother's Profession – Mixed Labour.
Father's Profession – Not provided.
Mother's Name – Serenity Venor.
Father's Name – Not provided.
Place of Birth – County Calderok, Sub-County North-West 2.
Date of Birth – Fourmonth 14th, Golden Era 142.
Sex – Male
Surname –

A white glow shines out of the Record. My heart soars and swoops.

I'm not the only one in the room to gasp.

Here's the lie.

The forged *Venor* appears as a dark line over a glowing white underlay the scope reveals.

He's not Valour Venor. He's Valour Gusting.

No one speaks for several heartbeats. All I can hear is the quiet scritch of Blithe moving the dials on the vradiance scope back and forth a few times. *Gusting. Gusting.*

"Well…" Blithe's the one to break our silence. "Looks like there's a stain on the magistrate's name!"

Lev stares, stunned, at the surname that matches his own.

Goldie switches the light back on and pushes the door open. Blithe powers down the scope.

My eyes blink away stars and then find Kit's.

I understand now. It falls into place so neatly. That's what Zako heard.

Venor's wife called him *Gusting scum*, not *disgusting scum*.

Venor, upright citizen, magistrate and future governor – he's like Lev. A Sting Trust child, marked by his name. But he's more than two decades older – grew up crushed under an even greater stigma. Born to a mother too irresponsible to afford his life. No father to own him. They would have said he was a feckless child, unemployable. Work-shy. Born bad. Born wrong. Useless. A drain on society. The kind of person he despises.

How he must hate himself, to come through all that and still become … Magistrate Venor. Choosing to wear his title and all its trappings like armour. Choosing a side that would purge him if it knew, then desperately *purging the town of filth* and all that nonsense. Obsessing over showing the high governor what model lives of Skøl rectitude we lead, out here in the New West.

"Let's have a drink," Goldie orders.

Blithe detaches Venor's Record from the vradiance scope and passes it to Glister. We file to the long withdrawing room, but only Lev and Blithe plonk down on the soft green sofas.

I think of Felicity on that boat – her face when I told her Venor's wife called him *disgusting*. Did she figure it out? Is that why he had her amber ring in his little trophy dish?

No one's talking. Goldie opens the decanter but can't find any glasses on her drinks stand.

Glister paces to the patio doors and opens them. He puts Venor's file down on one of the little low marble tables.

"This is it, isn't it?" I say. My voice is small in the tense room. No one answers. "We go to the high governor and her people with this – we expose Venor. Make him pay for what he's done to all of us, to Zako."

Silence. I look at Kit. Why doesn't he say something?

I plough on. "If his *name* is exposed, his *actions* will have to stop. His backers will drop him! His supporters, they'll hate him. The power he's built – he'll lose it! The power he holds over all of us, squashing all of us—"

"We can't be hasty," Goldie says. "Aside from feeding the Gusting stigma –" her eyes dart to Lev – "you got that Record illegally. Everyone will know you were in the vault. That you freed Blithe. That you know where he is."

I bite my lip. "Why don't we send it to the papers, anonymously?"

Glister sighs. "Because he'll just say it's a fake. Especially now Blithe's out. Someone frees the Artist, best forger of our time, and suddenly a document incriminating Venor turns up? It's too convenient."

I'm so frustrated I could cry. "But he won't be able to produce his real document."

"He only has to say the 'original' was stolen from the

vault in the break-in," Blithe points out. "They're right. We can't do anything with this – not yet, at least."

"I can't believe this." I hate it. The truth doesn't matter to any of these people. But I hate it even more that they're right; Venor can weather this. The futility of it chokes me.

"Perhaps we can make it work for us still," Lev offers. "Keep it to ourselves and hold it over his head. We'd have power over him. He won't want to call our bluff."

Goldie's pursed face relaxes a little. She fiddles with one of her earrings.

"Yes..." muses Glister. "Power over the governor of the whole New West."

"You – you'd let him be anointed governor?" I whisper.

My eyes meet Kit's. He shakes his head ever so slightly. The Reedstones will always be Skøl first, I realize. Brickheads playing power games while children's lives hang in the balance. I should never have entertained the hope they'd be different.

"And would this power of ours be enough to make him pardon Zako Taler?" I ask slowly, dog with a bone.

"You're thinking too small." Lev chides me like a schoolchild.

"Too small?" I murmur, anger rising, buoyed up on all their hot air. "You wouldn't have this card to play in the first place if it wasn't for Zako."

Kit walks closer to Glister. He surveys the room. A breeze through the glass patio doors stirs his shirt, and I notice a cockerel strutting past outside. It's one of their fancy breeds, shiny-winged with fluffy tufts. "We need to think of a way to protect Zako," he tells everyone, calm as ever. "You owe us."

"Naturally," Glister rumbles. "We will think on it." He glances outside and steps away from the doors.

Silence. *Is he dismissing us?*

"I'm sure it's not beyond your wit." Kit's face stays innocent, but something angry breaks through in his voice.

"We have other priorities," Glister says. "You understand us."

"Perfectly," I tell him. My anger is coldly consuming now. These brickheads aren't fit to lace Kit's boots, and they're trying to chuck us out of the back door like a pair of their hounds.

Kit and Glister both reach for Venor's Life Record at the same time. Kit gets it first, but Glister snatches it out of his fingers. "I think it's safest – for everyone – if we hang on to this." He smiles like an affable uncle.

I can't get out of here quick enough. Kit walks at my side, through the gleaming corridors, out of the front door – we leave it open, along the gravel drive. "So much for a revolution," I say.

Kit looks drained. "I know. I'm sorry."

"You're not to be sorry. They should be sorry."

"We can go to the papers like you said," Kit says. "We can go now—"

"No!" I soften my tone. "The worst part is they're right about that. It won't work. I just need… I need sleep."

I'm glad Kit doesn't argue.

I will make my own plans. I am done playing along with the Reedstones. Tonight I play for keeps.

I sleep like the dead until Ruzi wakes me after his shift.

I tell him about the Registry job. About the vradiance scope and Valour Gusting. About Felicity's ring and the boat trip with Venor and Felicity. About Zako's missing third letter.

He listens with a strangely blank expression. I wonder if that's what I look like when I'm trying to squash my feelings.

"What if the branders found him? What if they just … disappeared him?" I whisper.

And then he starts crying, red-eyed and awful. I can count on one hand the times I've seen him cry. He hugs me – he never does that either.

"Sorry," he splutters. *Sorry because he's crying on my shoulder or sorry about Zako perhaps being dead?*

I squeeze his arms and draw away, wiping my cheeks.

Ruzi's face is still crumpled, but he's in control again. He takes a deep breath.

"Zak's like you," he says. "A fighter."

"I wish I was half as brave as him," I confide in a small voice.

"You're brave, my girl. You're the bravest. Just believe it."

I tell him I'm off for a walk. That I need some time alone. I take what I need from my room. And from Sinton

Square. I pick up a pretty woven basket from one of the sellers in Rundvaer Square and head to the Lugger for the rest.

I've planned another busy evening.

48

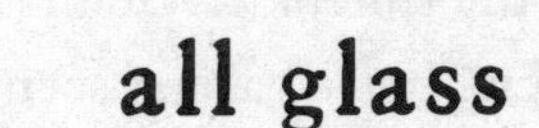

all glass

I leave the Lugger a few hours later, everything I need slung over my shoulder in a cloth bag. It's warm, but a bit blustery, and it's slow going, trudging up to the Steeps in Felicity's pale dress and low heels.

I'm dressed for the occasion. I'm even wearing some red on my lips – it was Felicity's. People are forever finding fault in my outfits, but tonight I've one that's graced a fundraiser at the Sinskill Club. I've got my ribbony hair wrap on too, Crozoni curls tucked away.

I haven't worn a dress in years. This one's not a style I admire – tight enough to pinch under the arms and too long and slender in the legs. But my normal clothes are too distinctive.

Felicity, though, was good at blending in.

Leafy trees line one side of the avenue up into the Steeps, growing older by slow degrees. I'm speeding forward in time, trudging past saplings, then mature trees, then gnarled old things. The sun's descent stains the glass of the sky and colours everything golden.

It's sunk by the time I reach Lovemore. King of the mansions on a road of big mansions. The swooping branches and silvery undersides of the leaves here reflect lantern light. Summer night's fallen.

It's after nine by the timepiece Goldie Reedstone gave me. Well after curfew, but I haven't seen any branders. I stand before the door. His servants should have left for their own homes an hour ago. He won't be entertaining guests tonight, not after the day he's no doubt had at the Registry. And he has no live-in servants – Felicity told me as much. She had no reason to lie about that.

Love … more, the plaque pleads with me. Not tonight, little sign. Tonight, I'm all hate.

The knocker's made of shiny brass, shaped like a hand hanging upside down, cut off at the wrist. It's smaller than my hand – a child's hand.

I place the main contents of my cloth bag carefully on the step and give three sharp raps with the brass appendage.

I wait an age, but he doesn't answer.

I'm about to try again when I hear a carriage beyond the gate. It's Venor's Registry carriage. Gone nine and he's only getting home now. Must have been held up on urgent Registry business – like busting through a broken vault door and finding he's lost his headline act for the Glass

Fanny and more blank paper than Fidelity Hemman might have pilfered in a year. I wonder if he checked his own file. Good thing I'm too nervous to look smug.

"No visitors!" Venor barks at me as he comes up the path. He's dressed in an elegant woollen waistcoat and grey jacket. He walks with the gold-tipped cane he's used ever since Zako hit him.

His carriage draws away down the street.

"Mister Venor." I pitch my voice to sound confident. I need to show some backbone so he'll be tempted to break it. "I have information you'll be interested in."

He laughs. "Not interested." He swipes me out of the way with his cane and puts his key in the door.

Finally he notices the basket on his step. A gift basket, full of tiny oranges.

He tucks his stick under his arm and examines the label, frowning. "Idiots have sent it twice," he mutters.

"Mister Venor, please. It's related to your earlier loss. At the vault."

"What?" he hisses. He's not distracted any more. I have his undivided attention. He holds the door and his stick in one hand and the basket of oranges in the other.

"If you've got Zako, please – I want to make a deal."

His face turns to thunder, and his choppy voice gets choppier. "You! Are you a cat or a cockroach? What does it take to end you, girl?" He's finally recognized me. "I don't trade information with makkies! I take it."

End me, is it? By the ancestors, I promise, I'll end him.

"They can't see me talking to you." I give a furtive look around. "Can I come inside for a moment? Please?"

He doesn't hesitate. My youth. My sex. My thick makkie skull. He'd never see the threat of me. He holds the door open wider, impatient.

I set my jaw. I don't even have to pretend to be frightened – I'm genuinely terrified. If he wants to beat the life out of me with his gold-tipped cane in this quiet house, no one will lift a finger to stop him.

"Come." He prods. "Don't stand there like a mullet. Move, girl."

The house smells of old stone. He leans his stick in a stand beside the front door and swaps the basket from hand to hand to take his jacket off. Then he picks the stick back up. Elektric lanterns attached to the walls glow orange.

He gestures for me to walk in front of him across a foyer of small diamond-shaped tiles. They're not Crozoni. He must have had them put in.

I go where he directs, down a long, wide corridor.

When we reach his study, he puts the basket of oranges on a desk of pale, polished wood and sits behind it. It's larger than his Registry desk. He gestures for me to take the chair opposite.

No maps. No skulls. No family portraits here. Just the familiar face of Clarion Lovemore in an ornate frame. She's on the wall behind the desk, like she's looking over his shoulder. I wonder if she's found out about Venor's broken vault and broken-out prisoner. Somehow I doubt Venor's come clean yet.

The only ornament sits atop the desk – a steel hammer in a glass box. He sees me looking at it. "Yes," he whispers. "That's the little thing that nearly killed me. Turns out I'm not so easily brought low."

Zako did tell me he used a hammer. It looks like the one that smashed my hip.

"A hammer shatters glass but forges steel." Venor's crackling voice cuts across my thoughts. "Something we say in the east. Surviving a trial can break you or make you stronger. Now tell me what you know before I call the firebrands to drag it out of you." His eyes drop to my chest.

He smirks to himself. Then he takes an orange. Not the one off the top of the pile – one below. It dislodges the top one, which rolls to the floor and stops at my feet. I stand to replace it on top of the pile.

"I know who got into your vault." I lean forward. "They've got … people backing them, important people with money. More money than you, maybe," I add stupidly.

He's still crunching pips from his first orange. "Who are they?"

I reach into my cloth bag to take out one of its remaining items. It's a wanted poster from Sinton Square, a bit weathered and ragged round the edges but perfectly legible. One of the ones from the south with bounties rivalling Zako's.

Wanted: "Pony" Dewilder. The picture shows a long-haired man who could be Crozoni or native Makaian – the hair looks more Makaian, the features more Crozoni. It's a cheap reproduction. Could even be a woman. *Wanted for Debt-of-Life Avoidance, Murder, Mutiny-at-Sea, Piracy* – the list goes on.

"This is him," I tell Venor.

Venor takes the orange at the top of the pile. My breath catches. *Yes*, I think. *Eat that one.* He holds it but doesn't peel it.

"How do you know this?"

"He came to the Lugger. Thought he could confide in me as we're both Crozoni."

He's unpeeling the orange now – in a single piece – two lobes and one long strip. He pops a few segments into his mouth.

I realize I'm staring. "He says last night he broke into the Life Registry and freed the Artist," I say quickly. "Was paid handsomely. And they took paper, lots of it, for their forgeries."

Venor's finished the orange. He starts on another, but it doesn't matter now.

It's done. He's a dead man.

"He gave me this sheet of blank paper. Says it's advance payment if I can keep him hidden. What am I supposed to do with this? I can get blank paper any day."

Venor's laugh is an ugly wheeze. "Do you know where to find him?"

"I told you. I need information first."

How long is this going to take? He doesn't look any worse for wear. Perhaps a little sweaty, but he was sweating outside, wearing that jacket he was in, and he's still in a woollen waistcoat. Perhaps it hasn't worked. I can't panic.

"I only want to know Zako's safe. So I thought to tell you."

"What makes you think I won't have your head on a spike for colluding with such criminals?"

I've started to tremble. I lock eyes with him. "Please," I whisper.

Has his pale face grown paler? I think his thin lips look less pink. He squints at me. "It remains to be seen…" he begins, in his low, threatening voice. Then he stops and stares at me.

I try not to wilt.

He stands suddenly. "Wait a moment," he says. "Greave, there's a makkie on you."

He picks up the cane he left propped against the desk and lunges at me. Everything slows down.

I push my chair clumsily back, in time to avoid him. It helps that he's equally clumsy, with a huge desk in the way. He flops across it like a seal, toppling the glass box holding his hammer. It cracks, but doesn't shatter.

Should I make a run for the door now? I thought he'd be sick and pass out, not this thrashing-around, hallucinating-Felicity nonsense.

He's picked himself up off the desk and is still holding his cane.

"Really, Greave," he says, looking annoyed. "Did that big oaf let you go?"

He straightens his waistcoat. Then he smashes his desk with the cane, once, twice – a dozen times. The remaining oranges go everywhere. Several are reduced to pulp. The basket splinters to bits. Papers scrape and flutter like huge moths taking over-ambitious flight, spiralling to the floor.

The glass box is obliterated. Shards litter the desk and spray on to the floor, on to my dress. His hands and chest are cut up, but only superficially.

I shrink towards the doorway, holding a hand in front of my face.

"Got the blighter," he says finally, holding the hammer from its claw, pinched between thumb and forefinger. "It's a heavy one."

I don't speak. I've had enough improvising.

"Greave?"

"M-Magistrate?"

"Did you let that stinking rat in here?"

Thea's wounds. I can't bear the way he says *rat*. Blood drips from a cut on his lip down the front of his waistcoat. I've a shallow cut on my chest too, I realize, from his spray of glass. My borrowed dress, such a pale, impractical colour, has grown a flowery red blot.

"No," I say.

Venor comes to stand in front of me. His fingers slip

on the hammer. It drops to the floor, forgotten. "I don't feel well."

I stifle a sob. "Why don't you rest?"

"Yes." He holds a bloody hand out. I don't want to take it. But what can I do? "Rest," he says.

I help him and his cane upstairs, flipping elektric switches. Endless stone stairs. His bedroom is on the second, not the first floor. At least he knows the way. He insists on putting on his nightgown before lying down.

"Goodnight, Greave," he says. I switch off the harsh elektric light and retreat downstairs, cutting lights as fast as I can.

I have to get out. I gulp lungfuls of ordinary summer night in his dark garden, outside the servants' entrance, shaking like the silvery leaves on his ornamental trees.

It's near eleven by the timepiece Goldie gave me. I want to run away, but I can't leave until it's over.

I had to throw Kit's favourite fountain pen away – his only one. He's going to miss it. It's sleeping in the river with the remains of the Mermaid's Tears. I washed it and washed it, but he has this way of putting pens into his mouth when he's thinking. Sometimes he licks them to get the ink to flow. I was worried some residue would linger there.

Well, it's history. He can get another.

Never touch these, Mor. Pa's voice rung like a bell in my mind when I saw the glowing mushrooms that night. Mermaid's Tears.

I pulled out a cluster of ten or so then and there, bound them in my hair wrap and pocketed them. I scrubbed my hands clean in the heathers. Then I went back to sit beside Kit and fell asleep. I didn't have a plan for them then. That took longer.

I chose one of the tiny oranges with a green star at the top – where the stem used to be. I picked the star off and made a small incision through the skin with a pin. I washed the ink out of Kit's fountain pen and filled it with the ichor I made from the Mermaid's Tears. Yes, they're still extremely poisonous even when they're drying out.

They've a faintly sweet smell, a bit musty perhaps – but not strong. I dripped some of the ichor into the orange, through Kit's fountain pen. Not too much. Enough to make the segments slightly juicier than usual. I glued the green star back down over the top with a dab of sugar. On a nice piece of card, I wrote the same message I read on the basket in Venor's office, in a similar round, cursive hand. So he'd assume an administrative error when he got it again. Then I made up the gift basket of lovely little oranges from Mister Hayle. And that one, from me.

When I fix enough fresh courage to go back inside, it's almost as cool as the garden. My boots tap too loud into the silence and the creaky walls shift and settle. A faint smell of orange zest lingers – but I might be imagining it.

First, to make sure.

I light a candle. I don't want to shine elektric lights on this. There's no give to the cold solidness of the stone stairs under my feet. It's more real than climbing wooden stairs, somehow. The stairs in my memory cave are never stone.

I climb slowly, past the first floor smothered in gloomy darkness, little hairs standing up on my arms, then up to the second. I can't hear anything, but something smells astringent, like boiling orange rinds.

The corridor is a lifeless grey. It bends sharply to the left. I go through a sitting room I didn't notice at all earlier. Well, I was distracted. His bedroom's still dark. The smell of sickness grows stronger. My dread intensifies.

The Skøl have a term – *morbid fascination*. I felt it when I saw that krait latched on to that hunter's cheek like a grotesque mock-moustache. I felt it when I positioned his friend's hand, open just so, beside the gun.

I feel it now.

This is what I wanted. This grim, swallowing silence. I can't stand anything about it, but my feet carry me closer to the bed. My arm holds the candle over him. The nightclothes he changed into are bloody from his cuts. A white shirt with long, flowing sleeves, and light cotton trousers.

He's not towering over me any longer. I can see the scar on the top of his skull – where Zako tried to stove it in. His hair only covers some of it. If only he'd spilled out like an egg then.

His eyes are closed. *Thank Thea*; I'm grateful for that.

It's clear he's not sleeping or breathing. His colour is wrong. Still, he looks peaceful. I've a strong desire to draw him.

There's a lantern on the small table at his bedside – I light it and carry it out. His washroom smells of the same sickness, with vomit in the sink. A poorly fly crawls along it, shaking its wings, drunk and clumsy.

Did Felicity outlive her usefulness? Did a big oaf kill her and take her ring as proof? Perhaps he let her go. I wash vomit and the woozy fly down the drain.

My heart won't even its fretful flopping. I will myself to walk calmly back through the sitting room, back down to his study.

I brush the glass off and sit in his chair.

In his desk drawer I find Zako's third letter.

Missin yew All. Hope alls well
Thowt yew mite get my cloos befor – Thurd tim lucky!
Shore yew can fyned me now Moral

The map is very similar to the one in his last letter. *Portcaye* at the bottom, *B and Ts place* above it to the left, a whirlpool also on the left. A wolf on the island, a whale – also on the island. A turtle near the island. A little heap labelled *oystur shells* off to the right of Portcaye with a mermaid in a square propped next to them this time. Inland oysters? Why? At the top, above the island, a circle labelled *weeul*. A sign beside the island reads *Land heer!*

Zako's clues. Maybe one day I'll understand them.

I put the letter aside and get on with my final task so I can leave Lovemore behind.

I'm shaking again – irritating given I'm trying to make a study of Venor's writing and signature. I find some letter paper and practice until I'm satisfied. *I cannot live this down. I cannot live this down. I cannot live this down.* Short and to the point.

They'll think he couldn't face the break-in to his impenetrable vault, and the loss of the Artist, just before his inauguration, with his idol, Clarion Lovemore, here to witness it all.

Should I sign it? Do people sign their suicide notes? Ma didn't leave a note, but people do.

His signature gives me more difficulty than such things usually do. *Valour Venor.* That's the monster he made himself. Who was Valour Gusting? Another boy he so desperately needed to kill. Let his secrets die with him.

When I finally produce a letter to pass muster, I carry it to the doorway of his bedroom, only to find I can't enter.

I leave it in the sitting room, on one of the empty chairs. Somewhere in the window, I can hear a fly buzzing.

A hammer shatters glass but forges steel. Venor's words drift back to me. He's glass now. He's always been glass. We're all glass.

49

coast is clear

The only part of the walk from Lovemore to Opal Alley I see is the tree-lined way. The trees all getting younger until they shrink to nothing. Going back in time, all the way, a hundred years to when the cobbles were new-laid and the steps were sharp-edged and my great-grandfathers were the powerful ones, wielding their power cruelly.

Ruzi's asleep. I want to show him Zako's letter, but it can bide.

I wake up to him tripping over Felicity's pale low-heeled shoes.

I should burn them. I burned the bloodstained dress in the stove last night – though I've never burned a rag that could be repurposed. All that fine fabric gone to smoke and ash.

Ruzi pinches his nose and then rubs the thumb and forefinger under his eyes. "It's the same," he says.

"Almost, yes."

"This one has the oysters over here though. And it says *Land heer.*"

We have both of Zako's maps side by side on the kitchen table. I told Ruzi I'd tell him later how I got hold of the newest one.

"Wheel," says Ruzi. "Whirlpool, Blenny and Tornelius on an island. Portcaye… Wait. *Land heer.*"

He looks at me. Looks back at the maps.

"We've been assuming this is all ocean. But he's telling us it's land. So the island is *on the land.*" He stops abruptly and stands.

"What? What is it?"

His eyes are wide, alight. "Mora. It's… It's the fairground. It's the … it's the bloody taffy mermaid. And the rides. The Wheel. The carousel with all the animals. Wasn't it done up like an island? He loved that one."

"*Gods alive*, Ruzi."

Of course. He gave me enough clues. Zako's voice in my head… *I only wanted to go on the Island after that … the one with different sea animals going round to music … painted like an island, remember… turtles and whales … let me go on it over and over…*

Ruzi's laughing and crying, racing to get his boots on. "How could we miss that?" he shouts.

"Shhh!" I'm crying too. "Let's go. Pretend to be calm, Ruzi." That's usually never a problem for him.

The old fairground is on the edge of the Steeps, furthest

from the Mermens and the Centre, but not that far from the street with Venor's mansion. It was going to be Mister Kellin's racecourse, before his plans went all awry.

It's a large plot of land, nestled between the yards of some of the big houses, the eastern wall and a small green they've named Settler's Park. Its gatehouse still stands on the avenue, with bricked-up doors and windows.

The rest of it's fenced off the standard Skøl way – tall wooden boards flush against each other, topped with vicious, coiling razor wire. Large sections are overgrown with vines and blackberry canes sporting hard red and green fruits. Nothing's ripe yet. What's he been eating? We're coming up to a corner near the wall and the edge of the park when a flash of grimy white slips between two offset boards. Caruq!

I can't believe a hound fits through that tiny gap he just used, let alone a human, but from the side it looks bigger. Ruzi and I both manage to follow his lead back through. I think Ruzi loses some skin in the process, but we make it in mostly one piece.

The old grounds are eerie and still, like a secret, private garden. They've knocked the Wheel over, but they've left it there, beyond the carousel, nestled in weeds. A pair of amber-glass butterflies dance above it, courting. There's a wall with a flaking mural of the *Eventide* – in full sail, decades ago – before it was wrecked. There's a pile of old oyster shells near the place where they used to judge the oyster-diving competition every year. A broken-down panel from the mermaid's taffy stand.

And there's Zako.

He's gone skinny again, compared to six weeks ago. But he's alive. Venor and all his goons couldn't find him. I brim with pride. His maps! They would never understand them. They don't know what this place was like.

Caruq looks like he's grinning. Like he's retrieved Ruzi and me as a personal gift to Zako. Ruzi and I both dive to hug him at the same time, and we end up in a huddle.

"You found me! Finally!" He's laughing.

They've been sheltering in the old gatehouse, drinking rainwater and sneaking out at night around the Steeps to the public fountains. They've found food in people's gardens and allotments, scavenged in bins, even stolen fruit from locked-up barrows, milk bottles from early deliveries and kine oats from some stables that have been keeping Caruq going.

Kit taught Zako to pick locks.

"He didn't tell us that!" I say.

"Well. He didn't want to read or play cards. I said there was nothing to do. He said he'd teach me a good skill to have. And he gave me some picks."

"When you sent us that bit of oyster shell, I was sure you were by the sea."

"It's from the pile there."

He dances about a bit, childlike in his glee.

The evening he ran, he saw Venor outside over that

pause between Ruzi's songs. He was ready to flee before the raid started.

"My clever boy." Ruzi grips Zako's rather unwashed head in his arms, laughing. "My smart boy. You fooled us all."

The only things Zako's been pining for, apart from Renny's cooking, are his glasses and that copy of *Blenny and Tornelius* – long burnt.

He doesn't know he's my brother, I think.

"Zako, would you believe … some bounty hunters tried to bag me to pass off as you," I start. "They were going to chop my hair off and chop my head off and try and sell it for your twenty-thousand reward."

His big amber eyes look horrified. This isn't going right.

"It's because we look similar, I mean…" I gulp and falter.

"She's your sister," Ruzi says, stealing my thunder. "She's my daughter." Oh, *now* he's fond of plain speaking.

I listen as they talk. Zako is confused, slightly angry, but mostly delighted. I close my eyes and rest an arm on Caruq's fluffy ruff, feel the sun on my face, feel the comfortable murmur of their low, content voices.

I wonder if Venor's been found.

Ruzi can't be too late for work. I tell Zako I'll fetch his glasses and some supplies from the Lugger and be back for lunch. We leave him and Caruq to their gatehouse and sneak out through the thin gap when the coast is clear.

50

ringing

Voices of peddlers ring from the barrows. *Three for two. Get them hot.* Gulls flash half white, half shadow, glinting against the grey.

The river looks slow as molten glass, catching watery light and flinging it everywhere.

I feel nearer to my family, closer to the sea. I know they're not where their bodies are, in that low mound outside the eastern wall.

"Did you hear?" Gracie grins.

The magistrate – he's killed himself.

A servant found him this morning.

Who will govern the New West now?

And Clarion Lovemore's come all this way. Now she has no one to anoint. They can't even behead the Artist for her – he escaped yesterday! Good for him! They kept it quiet. It wasn't in the Post, *but tonight's edition will be thick as a book.*

"How did you figure it out?" Kit's warm hand on mine as we walk to see Zako. I tell him Ruzi had a revelation while studying Zako's second letter for the hundredth time this morning.

He comes with me to bring Zako some pastries, meat and bread for Caruq, two bottles of ginger beer and the news about Venor that's ringing all over town. It hits me again. This man we were so terrified of for years, laid so ridiculously low. By us.

I'm drawing in my room at Opal Alley, when I look up and see Ruzi in the doorway.

"You want to tell me about Venor?" he offers.

"What do you mean?"

"Men like that don't deserve this life," Ruzi rumbles. He looks at me before gesturing vaguely out of the window. "You should tell someone. Tell Kit, if you won't tell me."

Tell Kit, who believes that life is sacred? Who only murdered those men to defend our lives?

"You don't have to carry everything alone. And there's no undoing the past." His voice is calm. "It only grows until it's everything."

I can't argue with that.

"I'll talk to Kit," I lie.

But I have no choice, because later, when Ruzi is out with Zako, he visits me. It's after curfew, but no one cares about that any more.

"Can we talk a minute?" Kit murmurs, perching on the bed, facing the desk.

"My hands are covered in stain."

"I don't care what your hands are covered in."

Perhaps Ruzi's been round and said something to him. Perhaps I'm the world's most transparent murderer. It's clear he knows. The truth's like a chasm cracked open between us.

"Don't you?"

"I care that you didn't tell me." His face is set and serious.

"I learned from the master." I close the jar of stain. He levers himself off the bed and stands beside me.

"If I kept you out of things it was because I didn't want you hurt. You're hurting. You have to talk to me, you have let me in, or I can't help you."

"I'm not … crying for help!" I sputter.

"He could've killed you. I wouldn't have even known where you were."

"I was careful. Look. You've been dragged into so much because of me. I didn't want you –" I take a shaky breath – "pulled into something you hate again."

He shakes his head. "Don't you know…" His eyes search mine as his voice peters out. His throat bobs. "Don't you know yet? Don't you know what I would do for you?"

His eyes are shining. His words chase each other around my blunted brain, but I still feel numb.

"I know you wanted to do things differently. Without violence."

"I want a lot of things."

I hesitate. "So do I."

"It's okay to want things."

"Is it?"

"If you have a good reason."

I snort. "Good?"

There's something heavy on my ribs. A stuck, dry grief. *A good reason?* Did I kill Venor because I love Zako? Or did I do it for me? That's not love.

I reach my other hand to Kit's chest, crossing the chasm. He's so warm. The stain on my cold fingers still isn't dry, and it smears on his shirt, ruining it.

"I'm not sorry," I blurt out.

"Good."

"Good?"

"That kind of sorry eats you up from the inside. Sorry be damned."

Be damned. The words flutter around us.

He's still holding my other hand. "Your hands are freezing again."

He cups them together in his, warmth blotting through. I think of his blood billowing out of that bandage into the shallows.

"My mother had a friend that used to say *cold hands, warm heart*, every time we met." I feel shaky and breathless. "If only she could see me now."

"You're not cold-hearted, Mor."

He kisses my cheek, the corner of my eye, and I realize my face is wet with tears. What am I even crying about? Not Valour Venor.

Devotion Venor, maybe. Wrapped in a dark dress, black shoes, navigating Lovemore's solid stone steps, its rising ghosts.

"Will you stay?" I ask Kit.

"I'm here," he says. "I'm not going anywhere."

He plucks my spare paintbrush from behind my ear and tosses it on to the desk.

There's so much I want from him. Want to say to him – want to hear him say. But not tonight. I owe him more than this emptiness I feel. And we have time, don't we?

He doesn't say anything. Just wraps his warm arms around me until I fall asleep. For the first time in weeks, I don't dream.

He's awake before me – there's a breeze blowing in the window.

"I threw your fountain pen in the river." My voice is hoarse.

He turns a serious look on me. "That's just cruel."

"Sorry."

"So you should be."

Another Endweek evening. Another summer storm on its way.

For now it's still warm and light. I've spent the day

with Zako in his fairground wilderness. He's safe, for now. He wants to stay there. He needs a proper wash, but he's otherwise perfectly fine. I'm going to the Lugger to see Kit. We're going to make plans.

And I'll spend the night. We'll take our time with each other. We'll do everything we've both wanted to for ages.

The Lugger's busy, spilling noise and drinkers into Belor Way. Music drifts like smoke over the river. Ruzi's on the mezzanine, plucking his guitar. He fixed it. He wants to perform, and Venor's not around to ban makkie music, and I can feel it in my spine, in my swaying walk, making me brave.

I step into the courtyard, where Kit and Gracie are sitting on the bench under the big Makaia plane tree, legs stretched out, drinking fikka and gossiping. A familiar shape sails across the square of sky like a sign – a vocifer.

I can't help grinning. "Gods! Look at that, Kit! Gracie, look! A vocifer!" I stumble forward, still looking up. Then I see another vocifer, slightly larger. The wind's picking up.

"Is that an eagle?" Gracie's saying.

Caruq nudging my leg draws my gaze down. Why isn't he with Zako? Then I realize it's not Caruq – it's a different hound.

Seyll, his partner and another brander enter the courtyard. My heart hardens. A second ledhund sniffs and circles.

"Mora Dezil, as was the property of GR Locks? Of Mister Glister Reedstone?"

"What's it to you?" Kit's at my shoulder, bristling. His fikka mug looks like a weapon.

I try to meet his eyes. Is it something to do with Venor?

Gracie slips inside.

"You're climbing on high in the world, Mora Dezil."

"What do you mean?"

"You've been traded. Exchanged hands. And wait till you meet your new owner." His sneer settles on me.

"Like hell," Kit growls.

"We have our orders. Come with us, please." The one I don't recognize tugs at my elbow.

"Who's bought me?"

"The high governor, idiot. Keep up." Seyll raps my head with his knuckles.

What?

"Wait." I raise my voice, digging in my heels as the brander with his hand around my elbow tugs again. "The Reedstones wouldn't sell me. They said… They didn't tell me. There's been a mistake." I can hear the whine in my voice, so I stop. I won't give them the satisfaction of begging. *So this is why they don't beg.*

"She's not going anywhere," Kit says.

Seyll's partner takes his gun from its holster, points it in Kit's face. "Try it. Come at me, boy." He's after any excuse. Kit still looks tempted. Now I see it. Now he looks like his namesake.

Gracie's back, with Mister Scarlet. He holds Kit's shoulder.

"I'm sure we can sort this out." Mister Scarlet's voice is a calm rumble.

A ferocious round of applause bursts from the floor of the tavern, loud even out here. Ruzi's finished his song. "Everyone agrees with me," jokes Mister S, deadpan.

The gusting wind hits us, even in the courtyard, and the storm breaks like someone's flipped a switch. Trundling and elektric.

Hail big as pear drops pelts the yard. The light goes grey, and my hip twinges, like an icy hand is digging into the old wound.

Seyll's partner smiles with fake sympathy. "You're a lucky girl," he shouts, over the applause, over the hammering of ice on the roof, on the leaves, bouncing like tiny rubber balls on the flagstones.

They escort me to a waiting carriage. The hail stings. I imagine the ice rattling through me. I'm an empty glass the size of a girl. I'm a cavern.

I twist my head to lock eyes with Kit. I need more time. Just a week. A day. One night. Let me say goodbye.

The carriage has bars in place of windows, and the air sings as we drive.

I can see Kit on the road behind, bisected by the bars, framed by my hands clasping them. Hail's melted on his shoulders, his face. He's shouting something, but I can't hear what it is.

The wheels clatter over the cobbles. My ears are ringing.

debts of gratitude owing...

Firstly, to the one and only Kemi Ogunsanwo, my literary agent. Thank you for seeing potential in this story and for nurturing and empowering this storyteller. To others at The Good Literary Agency (TGLA), especially Arzu Tahsin; TGLA is a rare social enterprise with equity at its heart. To the gifted Julia Sanderson, for invaluable guidance and empathy, and for making me laugh until I cried. To the wonderful Genevieve Herr (AKA Jenny Gladwell), for plot-thickening and terrible-joke-catching. To the wider Scholastic UK team, for being such strong creatives, especially to Jamie Gregory for stunning illustration and design, but equally to Wendy Shakespeare, Susila Baybars, Jo Stimfield, Kiran Khanom, Ellen Thomson, Harriet Dunlea, Olivia Towers, Sarah Dutton and Alice Pagin. To Sarah Odedina, the presenters and participants at the Writers' Weekend Workshop in 2018 in support of under-represented writers. Similarly, to the organizers, presenters and participants of BookTrust Represents in 2019. To the talented Sid Wheeler, for generous critique and general moral support; and to Vasundra Tailor and Zareena Subhani for similar bookish encouragement. Thanks to my colleagues past and present for inspiring me in small and big ways all the time. To some very dear friends and family who saw early (and awful) manifestations of this story and always responded with kindness. Huge gratitude to the ever-inventive illustrator JiaJia Hamner, to Jill Watkins, Sonia Singh and mould-breaking Melinda Janki. To Camila Zambrano Esguerra for delicious Zeticas creations and unique positive energy. An extra-special thanks to Andy, Sonia, Desmond, and Aren; and to Ma and Pa for love, support, jokes, inspirational cooking (mostly Ma's) and general nourishing of the soul.

Now to my gorgeous guys/ terribly troublesome trio. To Mark, for the inspiration, courage, critiques and caring. I would not have even wanted to do this without you. When you love anything, it inspires: a cat, a person, a place, a thing, something you do, something you raise that raises you – the bigger the love, the bigger the inspiration. So ultimately: ultimate thanks to Jonah William and Milo Jonathan.